"I DON'T WANT TO LEAVE."

He slid his hand about her waist and nuzzled her hair. Then his lips brushed her ear as he added in a husky whisper, "And I don't think you want me to leave, either."

Her body, her traitorous body trembled all over. "It—it doesn't matter what I want."

"Ah, but it matters to me."

They stared at each other in silence. His hands rested lightly on her waist. The light in his eyes promised so many things. It reminded her that he'd been the only man who'd ever aroused her desire, the only one who could transform her into a wild woman with one long kiss.

Suddenly a knock on the door made them both jump. "Madam?" called the butler, Bos, through the door. "Shall I come back in?"

"I'll make this easy for you, Catrin," Evan said in a low voice. "If you call your watchdog back in, I will leave. I swear I'll leave and never disturb you again."

His eyes burned into hers as his voice dropped even lower. "But if you send him away, be assured of this. I will make love to you. I'll lay you down on that bed there and show you all the wanting that's built in me from the day I saw you emerge from the lake. It's time to choose."

Windswept

Deborah Martin

A TOPAZ BOOK

TOPAZ
Published by the Penguin Group
Penguin Books USA Inc., 375 Hudson Street,
New York, New York 10014, U.S.A.
Penguin Books Ltd, 27 Wrights Lane,
London W8 5TZ, England
Penguin Books Australia Ltd, Ringwood,
Victoria, Australia
Penguin Books Canada Ltd, 10 Alcorn Avenue,
Toronto, Ontario, Canada M4V 3B2
Penguin Books (N.Z.) Ltd, 182–190 Wairau Road,
Auckland 10, New Zealand

Penguin Books Ltd, Registered Offices:
Harmondsworth, Middlesex, England

First published by Topaz, an imprint of Dutton Signet,
a division of Penguin Books USA Inc.

First Printing, April, 1996
10 9 8 7 6 5 4 3 2 1

Printed in the United States of America

Prologue

O London! let me turn away
From thee my saddened eyes;
With drooping soul, to grief a prey,
Long have I spent the joyless day
Beneath thy tainted skies.
—Iolo Morganwg, *Stanzas Written in London in 1773*

London, May 1802

Where was he? Catrin Price wondered. "Nine o'clock," Lord Mansfield's last letter had said. "Meet me at nine o'clock at The Green Goat in London. Go to the private supper room at the back of the inn. I shall reserve it for you."

Yet he wasn't in that private room. She was alone amidst the rich furnishings and velvet curtains, alone and distinctly uncomfortable. For the first time since she'd embarked on this scheme, she wondered how wise it was to meet a complete stranger at an inn, especially a wretched Englishman.

Perhaps that explained the foreboding that echoed in her bones, poisoning all her hopes for the evening. Ever since she'd left her lodgings to come here tonight, her throat had felt tight and dry and her heart had been racing. She'd had the uneasy sense that eyes were watching her every move. No doubt it was only her imagination. Grandmother had always accused her of being scared of her own shadow. To be sure, Grandmother wouldn't have blinked twice at the thought of being alone with any man, for she'd always been able to take care of herself.

Nonetheless . . . Catrin scanned the room, which was isolated from the rest of the inn. Had Lord Mansfield chosen this seedy inn for a reason? Had he lured her here to steal her virtue?

Don't be absurd, she told herself. *He doesn't know who you are. He doesn't know what you look like or even if you're young or old. Why would he plot against a stranger?*

Yet all her life she'd heard terrifying stories of what could happen to a woman traveling alone, especially a Welshwoman from the country. Ever since the ship from Carmarthen had docked in London yesterday and she'd touched English soil for the first time in her life, she'd been cautious. England differed vastly from Wales, and although she spoke English well, she could sense the men assessing her accent, trying to decide if she were an easy mark or no. The women, too, were hostile and suspicious, at least until she proved she could pay for the pork pies and oranges they hawked.

London oppressed her. It was too large, too crowded and noisy, and far too dirty. Where were the heather-carpeted moors and the mountains swept by bracing cold winds? Where were the arching branches of ancient oaks and the tangled bushes of wild rose? Here she was surrounded by buildings and people, hundreds of wary, snarling people. She trampled refuse beneath her feet instead of grass and tasted only misery on the wind. She felt like a scared creature caught in a pen with jailers whom she neither understood nor liked.

But after tonight, you shall be free, and you can return to Wales, she told herself. Only that thought softened the foreboding in her chest.

For the fifteenth time since she'd arrived at the inn, she slipped her hand inside her coat to finger the sheaf of pound notes, counting and recounting to be sure it was all there. It was more money than she'd ever possessed at one time in her whole life, and it angered her to give it to some Englishman who was probably rich as Croesus. She could use the money for a thousand other things—new roofs for the tenants' cottages, an addition to the servants' cramped quarters, books for the charity school. . . .

Still, this was more important. What she would gain in return for her money was well worth the expense. Freedom. Hope. And a future for her and all the people who depended on her. For those things she would pay any amount of coin.

As she started to withdraw her hand, her fingers brushed something else, a slender, leather-bound book. She drew it out and opened it. The gilt-edged pages of the diary were filled with a spidery crawl that she had come to know as well as her own handwriting. The diary had belonged to some ancestress of hers, and according to David Morys, the schoolmaster in Llanddeusant, it was over two hundred years old. Every time she saw it or felt the fragile pages, the weight of the past seemed to settle upon her like thunderclouds upon Black Mountain.

Drawing a deep breath, she turned the pages until she came to the one she wanted, then read the Welsh words:

> This is the tale of our inheritance, passed down from mother to daughter for generations. Heed its warning, all you who have the blood of Morgana in your veins.
>
> On the wedding night of Morgana's daughter, while the Saxon merchant and Gwyneth stood before the priest in the chapel of his estate at Llanddeusant, Morgana appeared in the doorway. Her eyes were glinting jewels and her hair a living flame as she cried out her daughter's name.
>
> Gwyneth was sorely tried, for she had run away with the Saxon in secret, hoping to keep her mother from learning of the wedding until it was too late.
>
> It was not to be. Morgana had seen in one of her mystical visions what was to occur on that night. Morgana was called the Priestess of the Mists because she followed the ways of the ancients, and she had come to prevent the marriage.
>
> Morgana stamped and swore. "Thou thinkst to marry this man?" she cried to her daughter. "This abomination, this Saxon of low blood? Thou couldst have any Welsh prince of my choosing if marriage is thy desire!"
>
> " 'Tis not a prince that I wish!" Gwyneth cried. "I love my merchant, and I will marry him!"
>
> "He will take thee from the old ways!" the priestess protested. "He will corrupt thy mind and body and take from thee the truths that I have shown thee!"
>
> "He will not, my mother," vowed the young girl. "I shall ever remain faithful to what thou hath taught me."
>
> "Do you promise this?" Morgana asked.
>
> "I promise," vowed her daughter.
>
> With a flourish of her hand, Morgana brought forth from the mists a bronze chalice of immense size, nearly two hands' breadth. Upon one side was a raven etched in bold detail, upon the other a warrior garbed for battle

and a fair maiden arrayed in nothing but her own hair, which twined about her body like a snake.

Morgana held the chalice before her daughter. "Thou must seal thy promise by drinking from this, daughter of my soul. Drink from it this night to show that thou art my true daughter."

The merchant begged Gwyneth not to drink, for he feared that Morgana might poison her own daughter to keep her from the marriage. But Gwyneth drank as she was bade, for she loved her mother and wished to honor her.

When every drop was drained from the cup, Morgana smiled. "Thou art my true daughter indeed. Thus I give thee this cup as a wedding gift to remind thee of thy promise. From this day forth, any woman of our lineage must drink from this cup on the night of her wedding to show that she honors the ways of her ancestors. It will give her the wisdom and beauty of the maiden and her husband the strength of the warrior, and her marriage will be blessed."

Her face grew dark as winter storms. "But be warned. If any woman of thy lineage doth not drink of the cup at her wedding, her husband shall die within three years of her wedding. Her sons shall be fruitless and her daughters as accursed as she until the day they marry and drink themselves of this cup."

The whole company gasped to hear the priestess's curse, but the daughter smiled. "It shall ever be so, my mother. The women of my line shall always honor thee and the ways of our ancestors."

Catrin closed the book, chills snaking along her spine as they always did when she read this passage. She had scoured the paragraphs hundreds of times in the last four years. She had memorized the description of the chalice and the words of the curse until they rang in her blood even when she slept.

She wanted to ignore the curse, to tell herself it was mere superstition. But after delving into her family's past, she'd been forced to recognize that the family troubles had begun only after her great-great-grandfather had sold the chalice in the seventeenth century.

To Lord Mansfield's family. At least, that was what she'd been able to determine from perusing the family records. She thought of Lord Mansfield's letters concerning the chalice he owned. His description of it perfectly matched the diary's description. After four years of searching, she felt sure she'd found the right one.

Pray heaven that it was, for without it she could never remarry and risk subjecting another man to poor Willie's fate. Without it she would have no heirs. She and her estate and all those who depended on them would have no future.

And she couldn't let that happen.

Chapter One

My heart is just as heavy.
As the horse on yonder hill;
When trying to be happy,
I can't, try as I will.
—Anonymous Welsh folk verse, "Grief"

Carmarthen, Wales, June 1802

Thomas Newcome. Born July 3, 1741. Died April 25, 1802.

Evan Newcome read the words on the gravestone twice. Nothing. He felt nothing. Shouldn't he feel some flicker of sadness, some twinge of regret? Something besides the dull thudding of hatred that had been in his chest since childhood? Something besides the fear that sometimes clutched him in the dark, the fear that cautioned, *Blood of his blood, flesh of his flesh. You are like him. You are his kind.*

He gritted his teeth, reading the words on the gravestone a third time. There was no epitaph, no words about how wonderful a father and a husband Thomas Newcome had been. Evan glanced to the older gravestone next to his father's, the one belonging to his mother, and he noted the bold carved words proclaiming her a "Beloved wife and mother."

No one who happened to look at the two graves would miss the marked contrast between the two stones. In fact, the lack of epitaph on his father's stone surprised him, not because he thought such words belonged there, but because Mary had always maintained the illusion that their father was as good a man as the next.

When his older sister had married her tailor husband and escaped their father, she'd acted as if her childhood had never been. Evan had assumed she'd forced the past from her mind. Apparently, he was wrong.

Then again, perhaps she hadn't chosen the words on the

gravestone. Perhaps his older brother, George, had done so . . . dull-witted, ham-fisted George, who wouldn't have known what to write.

It went without saying that they hadn't consulted him, especially since he'd refused to come for the funeral. Maybe they'd feared he'd have the truth carved there for all the world to see. He wouldn't have, if only to spare them the embarrassment. But of course, they couldn't have known that. They barely knew him. They'd never known him, not when he'd left Carmarthen for Eton at twelve, and not now that he was thirty-one and a respected university fellow and scholar. To Mary he was "the smart one," and to George the "nabob who thinks he's better than us." That was all.

"Evan?" came a voice behind him. "Is that you?"

He turned to find Lady Juliana Vaughan standing at the edge of the little church cemetery, and all his sober thoughts lessened. She and her husband had rescued him from his abysmal home and sent him to Eton all those years ago. Seeing her there, watching him with such concern, made gratitude well up in him all over again.

"Good day, my lady," he said softly.

She came toward him, looking as pretty as ever, her forty-odd years only enhancing her natural beauty. Glancing down at the gravestone, she tucked her hand in the crook of his elbow. "I'm sorry about your father. I know I sent my condolences in a letter, but I'm glad you're here so I can repeat them to you in person. Rhys and I want you to know you have our deepest sympathy."

He said nothing. He wanted to say he was glad the son-of-a-bitch was dead, and he hoped the bullying bastard rotted in hell. But he didn't.

At his silence Juliana gave him a searching glance. "I was surprised when you didn't come home for the funeral two months ago."

He tensed. "Were you?"

Any of his friends would have heeded the closed expression on his face that warned this wasn't a matter he wished to discuss. But not Juliana. She had begun watching out for him when he was just a boy, and even though he now towered over her by almost a foot and could lift her with one hand, she obviously still felt it within her rights to stalk in where even angels feared to tread.

"I always knew you didn't get on well with your father," she persisted, "but I thought you would come home for your sister's sake at least."

A half smile crossed his lips at the faint reproof. "Mary has her husband and George. She didn't need me there. Trust me, it would have been harder for her to endure my standing there without a trace of mourning on my face than my not attending at all. At least without me there, she could tell people I was abroad or suddenly taken ill." He paused. "What *did* she tell people?"

Juliana gave a rueful smile. "That you were suddenly taken ill."

"You see? I'm sure Mary was relieved I wasn't there."

"Well, at least you've come now," she said as she squeezed his arm.

Evan covered her hand with his own. "Actually, I didn't come to Wales because of Father, although I do plan to speak with Mary about a few matters before I leave town." He'd arrived several hours ago, but he'd put off going to his sister's. He wanted to see her and knew she'd be glad to see him, but he dreaded the awkward task of explaining why he was staying at an inn instead of with her.

The truth was, he felt ill at ease in her home. No matter how hard he tried to make her feel comfortable with him, she was always conscious of the differences between her and him, and it pained him to watch her and her husband struggle for conversation.

The alternative, staying with George, was out of the question. It was all too horribly familiar, watching George explode every time the meal was cooked wrong or one of the children crossed him. Evan hated seeing that swift fist shoot out to meet its mark on some innocent cheek. He couldn't bear watching history repeat itself, seeing his father in George.

Worse yet, it reminded him that he, too, had a violent temper, that if matters were different and he had a helpless wife and children to lash out at . . .

Blood of his blood, flesh of his flesh. You are like him.

With an unspoken curse, he shook off the bitter thought.

"I met up with that old gossip Mrs. Wynton, who told me you were here," Juliana was saying. She shot him a sideways glance. "She also said you were staying at her wretched inn. Surely you weren't planning to pass through here without even paying us a visit."

He smiled at her. "You know I'd never do that. But I left London so suddenly, I didn't have time to send a letter, and I didn't want to inconvenience you by showing up on your doorstep without warning."

"Inconvenience us? Don't be silly. You come here so seldom that it's sheer delight to have you. Do tell me you'll move your things from that inn and come stay with us at Llynwydd. I know it's two hours outside of town, but you'll be more comfortable. Besides, Rhys will be pleased to see you, as will the children." With a conspiratorial air she leaned up to add, "Mrs. Wynton keeps a sloppy house, you know."

"You don't need to convince me. I assure you I was planning to send a message to the estate about my arrival."

"Good. Now you won't have to. Rhys is over at Morgan's, but he's joining me for lunch at The Bull and Crown, and as soon as we've eaten, we can go to the inn, gather your things, and be out to Llynwydd by nightfall." She glanced down at the grave, her face darkening. "Come away from this place and join us. Will you?"

He nodded, letting her draw him out of the cemetery. It would be good to be among friends today. Perhaps it would dispel the melancholy that had settled upon him at the sight of his father's grave.

As they walked together, a companionable silence fell between them, punctuated only by the sounds of carts being driven along the streets and vendors hawking their wares. Carmarthen was a market town. For as long as he could remember, it had always been alive with activity. It reminded him of London, but he had to admit he enjoyed it more, despite the painful memories it brought to mind.

In truth, it felt good to be back in Wales. He'd forgotten how friendly the people were, how brilliant a blue the sky was, how vibrant a green the forests were that still lined the roads. The wild sweetness of his own country roused a long-buried ache in him, one he'd hidden even from himself all these years in London, the ache to be home, to be in a place where every blade of grass seemed familiar. No matter what had happened to him in his youth, Wales was home, and he was astonished at how glad he was to walk the streets of old Carmarthen once more.

All too soon, they reached the inn, a new one that had been built since he'd last lived here. Once inside, it took them only seconds to determine that Rhys was waiting for Juliana, engrossed in reading what was undoubtedly one of the radical political pamphlets he and Morgan printed with regularity.

"Good morning, darling," Juliana said. "Look whom I found wandering the streets."

As the older man glanced up, Evan grinned at the look of surprise and then pleasure that broke over the Welshman's face. It had been some time since they had spoken, so Evan was looking forward to a long conversation, especially since Rhys Vaughan was the only man likely to have the information Evan sought.

"You scoundrel!" Rhys's face was wreathed in smiles as he rose from his chair and came forward to clasp Evan's shoulders. "When did you decide to come to town? Why didn't you tell us?"

Juliana flashed Rhys a dark glance. "He was at the graveyard."

"Ah, yes," Rhys said, sobering. "I'd forgotten about your father. I'm sorry."

"Don't worry about it. And to answer your question—I decided to come only a few hours before I left, which is why I didn't tell you."

"I've ordered lunch already," Rhys said, pulling out a chair for Juliana. "You'll join us, won't you? The meal I ordered should suffice for all three of us."

Evan stepped forward to take the chair opposite the squire. "Thanks. It's been a long morning, and I'm famished."

"It's good to see you," Rhys said as Juliana sat down and smoothed her skirts, "even under the circumstances."

Evan glanced away. "As I started to tell Juliana earlier, I didn't come because of Father."

Juliana looked up. "Then why *are* you here?"

"I'm on a trek to find the Lady of the Mists."

The two of them exchanged glances, then said in unison, "The Lady of the Mists?"

"Yes. You've heard of the old lioness, haven't you? I was hoping you had."

Juliana's eyes narrowed. "The old lioness?"

"The Lady of the Mists. You know whom I mean. I heard rumors of her as a child, so you two must know of her."

"Yes, but—" Rhys began.

Juliana cut him off. "Of course we know of the *old* Lady of the Mists." She shot Rhys a meaningful glance, and the squire settled back against his seat.

Evan briefly wondered about her emphasis on the word *old,* then dismissed it. The Lady of the Mists must be at least seventy, for everyone had called her "old" when he was but a lad. "What do you know about her? I've heard the legends, of course." His voice grew sarcastic. "She rides and shoots like a man, plays the harp like a goddess, and sings like an angel. It's a wonder she bothers with us mortals at all." Years of scholarly endeavors had taught him that legend often exaggerated.

Rhys stared at Juliana, one eyebrow arched. "Yes, love, do tell Evan what we know about the Lady of the Mists."

Evan sensed some secret between them, but then the two of them were always full of secrets and had been from the day he'd first met the squire. Sometimes it amazed him that they could still be so much in love after all these years.

Just then their food came, a substantial *cawl,* a roast leg of mutton, potatoes, and cabbage . . . in short, a meal that would easily feed four normal men. Evan bit back a smile. Rhys had almost as large an appetite as Evan. He doubted there'd be much left between them.

Ever the hostess, Juliana dished the food out onto the plates. "Why are you interested in the Lady of the Mists, Evan?"

He hesitated, wondering how much he should tell them. "I don't know if you heard about the murder of my friend Justin."

"Yes, I remember reading about Lord Mansfield's death in the *Times*. We do get it out here, although quite a bit later than you do." Juliana put a plate in front of him. "The *Times* said he was robbed and killed by footpads. I'm sorry, Evan. I know he was a good friend of yours from Eton. It has been a year of losses for you, hasn't it?"

He nodded, unable to say more. Staring down into his

plate, he found he'd suddenly lost his appetite. Justin's death had cut far more deeply than his father's. Justin had been the one to help Evan weather the storms at Eton. Justin had taught him how to defend himself from all the snobbish young nobles and bullying rich merchant's sons without getting caught by the headmaster, and Justin had braved the taunts of his classmates to befriend Evan.

As they'd grown older and both had gone on to Cambridge, they'd remained friends even when Justin began to live the reckless life of a young lord. Justin had been the only one who could coax Evan from his books for a foray into London's gaming hells or a night of wenching, the only one who could make Evan forget for a little while who he was and where he'd come from. And when Evan's engagement to a wealthy merchant's daughter had ended in disaster, it had been Justin who'd forced Evan to stop brooding and start living again.

How could the mocking, carefree scoundrel be dead? It was unfathomable. Yet he was, and his senseless death left Evan with an anger that couldn't be quenched.

An anger that had brought him back home. "Justin's death is why I've come in search of the Lady of the Mists." When they both looked oddly at him, he added, "I believe she was the last person to see Justin."

He ate a bite of mutton as Rhys and Juliana exchanged glances.

Then a worried expression crossed Juliana's face. "Why do you think that?"

"Because he met with her the night he was killed."

"And you think she had something to do with it?" Juliana asked in alarm.

He considered confiding his suspicions to them, but decided not to. He wanted to know more of what had occurred the night of Justin's murder before he told anyone that he thought the Lady of the Mists had been involved. "No. But there has been little progress in finding Justin's killers. I'm hoping she saw something that will lead to their apprehension."

Juliana's face cleared. "I see. That's all right then."

"I'm so glad you approve." He couldn't keep the sarcasm out of his voice. She was behaving strangely about this.

What would she say if she knew everything? "Tell me what you know about the Lady of the Mists."

"She's a widow," Rhys said. "It's a tragic story. Her husband, Willie Price, was killed on their wedding day. Some freak accident, apparently."

Despite himself, Evan felt a twinge of sympathy for the Lady of the Mists. "That's awful."

"Yes," Juliana agreed. "But she has risen above it to make a place for herself in the world."

"We met her once, you know, when she visited Carmarthen," Rhys said. Suddenly, he grunted for no apparent reason and shot his wife a sharp glance.

Evan dipped his bread in the gravy smothering the mutton. "What was she like?"

Juliana cut Rhys off as he was about to speak. "She was as wonderful as the legends make her out to be."

"Of course, you probably already know she's the daughter of a knight and fairly well-off," Rhys said.

Evan stared at him in surprise. Somehow, he'd always thought of the old woman as having no class at all, one of those unusual creatures on the fringes of society who in past times would have been termed witches. That she was gentry gave him pause. Why would a woman of such standing seek to murder a nobleman?

"She's a bit of an odd one," Rhys added, ignoring his wife's scowl. "Despite her class, she dabbles in all sorts of peculiar things."

"You mean, aside from the harp-playing and the riding and the shooting?" Evan quipped.

There came that enigmatic smile on Rhys's face again. "Yes, aside from all that. She writes essays, you know. You might have read her work. She studies the folklore and superstitions of the Welsh. Morgan and I have offered to publish some of her essays in one of our collections." He glanced at Juliana. "You'll like her, I think. You'll like her a great deal more than you expect."

Evan tried to conceal his irritation. "Whether I like her or not is inconsequential. At the moment I'd settle for knowing her name, if she actually has such a mundane thing. I also need to know how to find her."

"Oh, that!" Juliana brightened. "That's easy enough to tell you. Her name is Catrin Price, and she lives outside of

Llanddeusant. I can tell you how to get to the village, and the villagers can direct you to her home."

Quickly, she described a route that would take him on a day-long ride to the Welsh town near Black Mountain. "Her estate is called Plas Niwl, the Mansion of Mist. It's near Llyn y Fan Fach, the lake with the legend. You know the one, don't you? About the fairy of the lake who married a mortal? Their descendants are supposed to be the great doctors of Merthyr Tydfil."

He nodded. He'd heard the tale. The merchant had fallen in love with the fairy after seeing her at the lake. She had agreed to become his wife, bringing him cattle and gold as her dowry, but she'd promised to remain his wife only until the day he'd struck her three times. After many years of marriage and three children, he'd done so, and she'd vanished, taking the cattle and gold with her.

A wise woman, he thought. Too bad Mother couldn't have vanished.

"You should see Llyn y Fan Fach while you're staying in Llanddeusant," Juliana went on. "It's beautiful, almost mystical."

A certain wistful note had entered Juliana's voice, a familiar note that made him smile. Juliana held romantic notions about places in Wales. And an estate named the Mansion of Mist near a renowned site of legend probably fired her imagination to new heights.

"I shall certainly try," he said. "But I won't have a lot of time to waste."

"Does this mean you won't be here long either?" Juliana asked.

"I'm afraid not. I can spend a couple of days here, but then I must go on to Llanddeusant." He'd need all his time for dealing with Catrin Price. He suspected that gleaning the truth from a wily old woman like her might take patience . . . and a devious mind. He must approach this cautiously to avoid spooking the woman before he got what he wanted from her.

Juliana sighed. "While you're there, stay at the Red Dragon. It's a fine inn."

Evan nodded. "Thanks."

"You *will* pass through here on your way back to the coast, however, won't you?" Juliana asked.

"Of course." Evan smiled. "And this time I'll give you fair warning."

"It doesn't matter. You know we always love to have you at Llynwydd." A sly look crossed Juliana's face. "Although I wonder if the day will ever come when I welcome you *and* a wife to our estate."

He groaned and pushed his plate away. "Don't start scolding me about finding a wife again. I've already told you—no sane woman wants a tedious scholar for a husband."

"You are *not* a tedious scholar," Juliana protested, looking to Rhys for confirmation. Her husband wisely stayed out of the discussion. "You're a strong, handsome young man. Any woman would be proud to marry you."

Evan didn't bother to disguise the bitterness that entered his voice. "Oh? I know several women who'd disagree." He drew a deep breath. "My humble bloodlines disgust noblewomen and gentry, and my education intimidates those of my class. I'm too Welsh for an Englishwoman and too English for a Welshwoman. I'm cantankerous and stubborn and lacking in the charm that sweeps women off their feet." *I'm blood of his blood, flesh of his flesh.*

He forced back that thought. "In short, I don't suit anyone at all, and it's unlikely I'd find someone to suit me. And that's the last I shall say on the subject."

"Good," Juliana retorted, "because it's all nonsense. You are considered a genius by one and all for your linguistic capabilities; your translations garner large subscriptions; and young men flock to your lectures at Cambridge. Humble bloodlines, indeed! Who cares about that? Any woman worth her salt won't. *I* didn't care a whit about Rhys's bloodlines when he came courting." When Rhys scowled, she added, "Not that his bloodlines weren't perfectly respectable, you understand. But my father was hoping to marry me to a duke, after all."

"Which would never have worked," Rhys confided to Evan. "Juliana is far too strong-minded. She would have made a duke miserable."

"Rhys Vaughan!" Juliana protested.

Rhys grinned. "But you make me perfectly happy, darling."

When Juliana gave Rhys a melting smile, Evan felt a twinge of envy, but he quickly squelched it. "In any case, while Rhys wasn't a nobleman, he was at least a squire and owned land. I'm a tenant farmer's son, without an acre to my name. No matter where I go or what I do, I am still a tenant farmer's son of modest means. No woman will forget that simply because I've achieved success in certain circles."

Juliana shook her head. "The right woman will. You just haven't found the right woman yet."

He could tell from her stubborn expression that she was determined to make him see matters her way. And at the moment he didn't feel like arguing with her. "Perhaps you're right. But until that woman comes along, I'm happy to have friends like you and Rhys." He rose from the table. "And if I am to stay with my friends tonight, I'd best return to the inn and gather my things, don't you think?"

Rhys flashed him a sympathetic smile, obviously quite aware of why Evan was hurrying off. "We'll meet you there with the carriage, as soon as we're finished here."

Evan nodded and walked out of the inn.

Juliana watched him leave, her heart tight with sympathy. She loved Evan as dearly as she loved her own children, and it tormented her to think that he might be unhappy. So much had happened to him this year. It was a great pity he had no woman to turn to in his pain.

"He'll be all right," Rhys said, leaning over and taking her hand. "Evan has survived many things, and he'll survive this."

"He needs someone, Rhys. You know he does."

"Yes, but he'll have to find her himself."

Juliana gripped Rhys's hand. "I swear I could kill the little chit who broke his heart. He was even prepared to leave the university for her, since university fellows can't marry. How dare she make Evan fall in love with her, only to end the engagement at the last minute for no apparent reason!"

"She must have had *some* reason."

"Don't defend her. I can't believe any woman would refuse Evan."

"And you're biased. Anyway, she obviously wasn't right for Evan, so aren't you glad he was saved from marrying her?"

"Yes, but now he's become a complete cynic about women. It isn't right."

"And you think that fooling him about the Lady of the Mists will help."

A startled expression crossed her face. "What do you mean?"

Rhys settled back in his chair with a grin. "You know what I mean, you little meddler. Why else wouldn't you tell him that the Lady of the Mists is not the old woman he heard about as a child, that she died two years ago and her granddaughter now holds that name? Why else wouldn't you let him know that she's a shy, bewitching miss, liable to steal his heart the second he meets her?"

Juliana didn't know if she liked Rhys's referring to any woman as "bewitching." She sniffed. "If I'd told him that, he wouldn't have gone to Llanddeusant, and you know it. Judging from his letters, he steers clear of bewitching misses these days. He shuts himself up with his books and tries to pretend he doesn't need anyone. And it's even worse now that Justin is dead. At least Justin forced him to go out in society. Justin knew, as do you, that Evan needs someone to love."

"And you think Catrin Price will fill that need?"

Juliana scowled at the obvious skepticism in Rhys's voice. "I know she will. She's perfect for him. Mrs. Price is a scholar, too. She's bright and kind and—"

"I thought you said she had turned aside every suitor who's come near her since Mr. Price's death?"

Juliana shot him a defensive glance. "She won't turn Evan aside."

Rhys laughed. "How can you be so damned sure?"

She straightened her shoulders. "A woman's intuition, that's all."

"And how can you be sure he'll like her?"

"Of course he'll like her," she flung back at him. "She's 'bewitching,' isn't she?"

At the peevish note in her voice, Rhys smiled. Then he leaned over and tipped her chin up. "Not as bewitching as you, *cariad*."

She melted at the softly spoken reassurance, welcoming the ardent kiss Rhys then placed on her lips. In truth, it was a good sign that Rhys found sweet little Mrs. Price bewitching. She only hoped Evan did, too. Because it was going to take a witch to successfully storm his walled-up heart.

Chapter Two

Dear stream! dear bank, where often I
Have sate and pleased my pensive eye,
Why, since each drop of thy quick store
Runs thither whence it flowed before,
Should poor souls fear a shade or night
Who came (sure) from a sea of light?
—Henry Vaughan, "The Waterfall"

Catrin drew a deep breath, then dove into Llyn y Fan Fach. She came up sputtering and gasping for breath, the cold lake water stippling every inch of her skin with goose bumps.

It was early afternoon and summertime, yet the water was bracingly chilly, for there'd been no sun today. Still, she didn't mind. The cold revived her aching muscles. After spending all morning with the maids making candles, she relished the chance to escape the smell of wax and to stretch her tired arms while they ate lunch.

With easy strokes she struck out across the lake, enjoying the undulations of water against her skin and the hush broken only by the faint swish of her movements. She swam enough to exercise her cramped arms, then stopped to tread water. Flinging her wet hair out of her face with one hand, she looked about her.

The mist on the lake was heavy today, so heavy she couldn't see the shale cliffs of Bannau Sir Gaer bordering part of the lake. The vaporous mass clung to the surface of the water like spiderwebs to skin, swirling and shifting from one fantastical shape into another.

Some days the mist played tricks on her, making her think she saw the Tylwyth Teg in their fairy enchantment, playing harps and dancing. Some days she even thought she glimpsed the lady of the lake herself, rising like Venus from the water. Strange how it took only a heavy mist to make one's imagination run wild.

Unfortunately, although her imagination was at its peak today, the shapes she saw were menacing and dark rather than friendly. They reminded her of her disastrous trip to London a week ago and her mad flight back to Wales.

She muttered a soft oath. Perhaps coming to the lake hadn't been such a good idea after all. With the mist so thick, being here only fed her fears and her frightening memories. She struck out for shore and headed toward where she'd left her clothes.

So caught up in her thoughts was she that she didn't notice the man standing on the shore until she rose out of the water far enough to expose herself to the waist. She stopped dead and stared at him, her mouth gaping open.

Tall and broad of shoulder, the man had one booted foot propped upon a rock and was leaning on his knee as he stared right at her, apparently as surprised to see her rise from the water as she was to see him standing there. His dark eyes widened, then moved inexorably down her face to her throat and then her breasts.

Suddenly, she remembered she was wearing only her thin chemise. With a gasp she sank to her knees, letting the water cover her to her neck as she folded her arms over her chest.

She blushed furiously even as all her earlier uneasiness came to the fore. The man was a stranger. What was he doing here? No one but she ever came here this early in the afternoon.

Panic swept her as she knelt a few feet from him, trying to decide what to do. Swim to another bank? But then she couldn't get her clothes. Besides, no matter where she swam, he could see her leave the water.

When he came away from the rock and moved forward as if to catch a closer look, her alarm at this new effrontery made her cry, "Who are you, sir, to be spying on me this way?"

He stopped short, looking almost shocked. "You're real."

When he didn't move any closer, she said, "Of course I'm real. What did you think?"

He shook his head as if to clear it. "I . . . I . . . Deuce take it. I know it probably sounds ridiculous. For a moment . . . well . . . I thought I was actually seeing the lady of Llyn y Fan Fach." A rueful grin transformed his serious expression.

"But it's clear you're flesh and blood, and not a fairy after all."

Something in the way he said it, his accented Welsh low and earthy, made her blush again.

"Normally, I know better than to put stock in such tales," he continued, "but when you rose out of the water through the mist as if by magic. . . ."

"It's all r-right," she stammered, unable to look at him.

Strangers didn't often come to this remote place. And with no one else around, there wasn't a soul to hear her cry out if the man hauled her out of the water and threw her down on the bank.

She shrank further into the water and stole a glance at him. He didn't look like the kind of man who'd do such a thing. But neither did he look like one of the naturalists who spent their holidays trekking through the wilds of Wales, with their expensive walking sticks and tour books.

She didn't quite know what to make of him. His well-built body seemed made for hefting beams, but his face was that of an ascetic, dark and stern with the knowledge of years. With a thick head of wavy chestnut hair and lovely long eyelashes, he was quite attractive, although his sober clothing marked him as someone unaware of his own attractiveness.

He'd been assessing her as she assessed him, but when she shifted her position in the water, he suddenly averted his eyes. "I should apologize for intruding upon your privacy. A friend of mine told me about this place, so I thought I'd take a look."

She wasn't sure how wise it was to converse with this studious giant, whose formal speech and bearing bespoke a learned man even while his mournful eyes hinted that not all his knowledge came from books. Still, she didn't have much choice, did she? For all practical purposes, she was trapped.

"Do you live close by?" he asked.

Alarm skittered through her. "Why do you ask?"

He seemed to understand her uneasiness, for he ventured a smile. "I'm not going to eat you, I promise. It's just that I'm looking for a place near here, and I thought you might direct me. The directions they gave me in Llanddeusant weren't very helpful."

His request was so innocuous and his voice so gentle that

she relaxed a little. "If you'll let me dress, I can show you the way. I know the roads well."

"I hate to cut short your swim," he protested.

"I don't mind."

"Then I'd appreciate your help."

When he stood there waiting, turning his hat round and round in his hand, she blurted out, "Could you turn your back, please? My clothes are on the bank."

"Yes, of course," he muttered, quickly pivoting away. "I'm sorry. I wasn't thinking."

Her eyes never leaving his back, she slid out of the water close to where her clothes lay and snatched them up. Any minute she expected him to whirl around and grab her. Fortunately, he was as courteous as he seemed, for he didn't so much as move, although she noticed that his back grew more rigid the longer he stood there.

She took off her wet shift, then donned the dry one she'd brought along. With horror, she realized that the cloth of her wet chemise was nearly transparent. What kind of woman must he think her, to be cavorting about nearly naked in the lake? But then, she hadn't expected a soul to see her or she'd never have risked it.

As the silence stretched out uncomfortably, he cleared his throat. "I do hope it's not too far to where I'm going. Everyone in town had differing opinions about the distance."

"I know what you mean," she said timidly. "They're not accustomed to strangers, and they're likely to say things like 'go past the field with the cow in it, then left at the place where the trees grow thick.' "

"Or 'left at the big rock,' " he interjected, seeming to relax. "When I asked how big the rock was, they told me, 'Oh, fairly big. You're not likely to miss it.' "

She smiled. "Did you find the big rock?" Shoving her arms through the sleeves of her wrapped gown, she fastened it in front, then bent to pick up her stockings.

"I've passed seven 'big rocks' since I left Llanddeusant, each one bigger than the last. And not a one of them near an oak with a split trunk."

An oak with a split trunk. She dropped her stockings, then caught them back up, her hands shaking. "Where is it you're going?"

"Plas Niwl. The estate of a widow named Catrin Price."

By heaven, she thought. He was looking for *her*. But why? What could he possibly want? Did it have anything to do with her disastrous trip to London?

As she drew on her stockings, her fingers numb against the silk, she tried to make her voice sound casual. "I do hope you've informed Mrs. Price of your arrival." The fact that he hadn't made his presence here all the more alarming. "She's something of a recluse. If you haven't arranged a meeting ahead of time, she might not see you."

"I've heard a great deal about the Lady of the Mists's amazing talents." His tone had taken on a steely quality utterly at odds with his earlier amiable one. "Riding, shooting, and playing the harp, among others. But I hadn't heard she was a recluse."

The very mention of the Lady of the Mists struck her with fear. Few people outside Llanddeusant called Catrin that, and she'd used the appellation only once, when writing to Lord Mansfield.

But if this man knew what she was called, why was he spouting all this about riding and shooting and such? Everyone knew Catrin only rode the gentlest pony and was terrified at the thought of shooting anything. "Who's been telling you all these stories about . . . er . . . the Lady of the Mists? Did they tell you this in town?"

She slid on her slippers, then circled to stand in front of him. He wore a shuttered expression, and the full mouth that had seemed so generous and friendly when he'd smiled at her, now looked more menacing.

He clapped his hat on his head. "I've heard such tales ever since I was a boy growing up in Carmarthen. She was spoken of with awe among the people there."

Oh, of course, Catrin thought. She should have recognized his mistake at once. He had confused her with Grandmother, who'd worn the title like a regal cloak—and who'd filled out the cloak far better than Catrin ever could.

This could be fortuitous. If he was searching for an older woman of stalwart reputation and not a shy pedant like her, then he would never guess *she* was Catrin Price. Still, he'd no doubt persist in his search until he learned the truth. Much as he intimidated her, she had best find out why he was looking for the Lady of the Mists.

"I hadn't realized our local legend's fame was so widespread," she remarked, pasting a smile on her face. "We're used to her here." She gestured to a path up the hill. "This way. I assume you have your horse up by the road?"

"Yes."

He followed her as she started up the hill. They climbed the green slope in silence, the steep ascent making it difficult to talk. When they reached the top, however, she said in what she hoped was a conversational tone, "So you've come from Carmarthen?"

"Not exactly." He brushed the dirt from his trousers, then sauntered to where his horse grazed contentedly. "I haven't lived there in twenty years. The ship from London docks in Carmarthen, however, so I stopped there to visit friends." He led his horse to the road.

She froze. London. He'd come from London. But why was he here now, asking after her? She tried to tamp down the irrational fear swelling in her chest. There was no cause for alarm yet. He could have a perfectly innocuous reason for wanting to see the Lady of the Mists.

Unfortunately, she couldn't think of one.

He waited for her at the road. "If you could show me which way—"

"Why do you wish to see Mrs. Price?" she blurted out.

Then she cursed her quick tongue, for he now regarded her with blatant interest.

"I'm afraid that's a private matter," he said.

"I see." Her throat went dry. This was not good, not good at all. What private matter would entail his appearing on the doorstep of Plas Niwl without any warning?

He continued to watch her with a steady gaze as she stood there uncertain what to do. "Do you know her well?" he asked.

She ventured a smile. "Everyone knows Catrin Price." *And I know her particularly well.*

"You said she was a recluse."

His quiet but suspicious words panicked her. "You see . . . um . . . until she grew infirm, she was quite sociable. But these days, she's too ill to venture from her bed, and probably will refuse to see you."

Forgive me, Grandmother, she thought. Grandmother had prided herself on being stout and healthy until the day she died. She was probably turning over in her grave to hear her granddaughter describe her as such a pathetic creature.

"What sort of illness does she suffer from?"

That threw her off guard. Tucking a lock of her drying hair behind her ear, she said the first thing that came to mind. "Um . . . gout." No, that wouldn't work. Gout was for old men who drank too much. Besides, it wouldn't keep her from having visitors. "And . . . and heart trouble . . . and weak lungs."

My capacity for deception is truly appalling, she thought. *But I can't help it. If he has come all the way from London to see me, it can only be for one reason, and it isn't at all wise to talk to him.*

His suspicion seemed to increase. "The poor woman is in dire straits indeed." He tightened his hands on the reins of the horse. "It's a good thing I've come when I have, before she's laid in the grave."

By heaven, she thought. *I haven't discouraged him a whit. He still intends to visit her . . . I mean, me.*

There was only one thing she could do. Devious though it was, it would have to suffice. "Let me show you the way to Plas Niwl then. It's easy enough to find, so you won't need me to take you there. I think I'll return to having my swim after all." There was another path from the lake up the hill, one that would put her at home long before he arrived, especially if he followed the directions *she* intended to give him.

He said nothing, and his silence intimidated her more than words would have. Trying not to look at him, she pointed up the road. "You travel down this road another hundred paces until you come to where the road forks. Take the left fork."

"The told me in town to take the right fork."

Her breath seemed to stick in her throat. Somehow she forced a smile to her face. "That's only if you want to go three miles out of your way. Trust me, the best way is to the left."

His gaze on her was dark and intent, making her quake inside. Gone was the amiable companion of the road, replaced by a wary Welshman who looked as if he didn't believe a word she said.

Yet she persisted in her deception. "When you come to a bridge over a spring, you're only a short way from the estate. You'll see a path beside the water. Go to the right on it, and you'll soon find yourself outside the estate walls. You can follow them around to the entrance."

That spot in the estate walls was on the far end from the manor house and the gate. If he went the way she told him, he'd arrive at Plas Niwl a good half hour after she did. That should give her enough time to warn the servants to say she was unwell.

"Can I convince you to forgo your swim to show me the way? It doesn't sound as if Plas Niwl is very far."

Did she imagine the sarcasm in his voice? "Y-you really don't need me to get there."

"But a few minutes ago, you said you would show me the way."

His suspicions had obviously been roused. She must escape him!

Suddenly, a voice hailed them from down the road. In a panic she looked up to see a man headed toward them on a bay in smart livery. She groaned. It was the pretentious Sir Reynald Jenkins, whose estate adjoined hers. He'd apparently returned from his annual sojourn to take stock of his many properties. No doubt he was coming to her with another enticement to make her sell Plas Niwl to him. No matter how many times she refused his offers, he kept coming up with new ones.

And what an awful time for him to show up! He would surely tell this stranger who she was. She must get away, before he reached them. If she left now, with any luck, her wet hair and the distance would keep Sir Reynald from recognizing her.

"I-I'm sorry," she stammered to the stranger as she edged toward the path. "I have to go."

Then she fled back the way they'd come, not even stopping when the wind gusted up briefly and took her shawl with it.

"Wait! Your shawl!" cried the stranger, but she was already at the top of the hill, moving as quickly as her skirt would allow.

Evan's eyes narrowed as the young woman vanished over the hill. If he'd been a superstitious man, he'd have thought his first assessment of her was correct, for the Lady of the Lake was said to have spoken at length with her merchant suitor the first time she'd appeared to him, only to vanish a few seconds later.

But Evan wasn't a superstitious man. He caught sight of the woman's shawl and went to pick it up, fingering the intricate lacework as he stared at the crest of the hill. This woman was certainly no spirit. Spirits didn't wear shawls.

Besides, no spirit would have made his blood race or his loins harden as they had when she'd emerged from the lake. Her wet chemise had been a second skin outlining her breasts so that even the faint rose of her nipples had shown through. It had been ungentlemanly of him to stare, but how could he not? Her breasts had been high and firm, the breasts of a woman who was obviously still young, yet mature enough to know the pleasures of the bedchamber. For an instant he'd wanted to experience those pleasures with her. Very badly.

If she had revealed any more of her thinly clad body, who knew what he'd have done? Probably acted like a Welsh raider of old, thrown her over his shoulder and carried her off. Even after it became clear she wasn't a seductive spirit at all, but a terribly timid young woman, he still found himself desiring her.

Good God, how long had it been since a woman had aroused him so thoroughly? There was nothing to compare to her in London. The mass of rich, black hair curling up around her shoulders as it dried . . . the red, red lips . . . that fair skin upon which her maidenly blushes were stamped so plainly . . . it was enough to make him curse himself for not getting her name.

And those wide, wary eyes! While she'd been in the water, they'd been blue, but once she'd left the lake and wandered near the purple heather, they'd turned almost periwinkle. The wide eyes and trembling little chin had given her the look of a startled elf. He kept seeing those eyes, which swallowed a man up when he looked into them.

The fashionable in London would consider her odd-looking, for she lacked the pleasant round features of the reigning classical beauties. Yet he found himself drawn to her, despite her other-worldly looks. He must learn more about her.

Draping the delicate little shawl over his arm, he strode back to where he'd left the horse he'd borrowed from Rhys.

The man who'd spooked his little temptress was fast approaching, so Evan waited for him, trying not to think about the woman and her mysterious behavior.

The haughty, older man reached him and halted his prancing horse. "Good day, sir," he said in an unctuous voice. A heavy smell of perfume clung to his clothing, which bordered on being dandyish. "I say, didn't I just see you in town?"

Evan forced a smile as he wound the shawl around the pommel of his saddle. "Yes. I stopped there to ask directions to Plas Niwl."

Drawing out a handkerchief, the man wiped the dust from his brow. "You're in luck then. I'm going that way myself. I'm Sir Reynald Jenkins, and my lands border that esteemed estate."

This time Evan's smile was genuine. "My name's Evan Newcome, and I'd be pleased if you'd show me the way. I was beginning to wonder if I'd find it at all." He mounted his horse.

Sir Reynald clucked his tongue and urged his horse into a walk. "Mrs. Price wasn't willing to accompany you?"

"What do you mean? I haven't met Mrs. Price." He prodded his own horse into a slow walk.

"No? Ah, then the distance must have deceived me. I could have sworn you were talking to her just now by the path to Llyn y Fan Fach."

A coldness stole over Evan. "Begging your pardon, sir, but you must be mistaken. That woman couldn't have been more than twenty years old."

The man sniffed. "I believe Mrs. Price is closer to twenty-six—black hair past her shoulders, blue eyes . . . much like the woman standing with you."

It was clear that Sir Reynald didn't think he'd been mistaken at all. The coldness spread throughout Evan's body. "I'm afraid I don't understand. I thought Mrs. Price was an elderly widow. I've heard all manner of stories about her . . . that she rides and shoots like a man, that she sings like an angel. Isn't she the one they call the Lady of the Mists?"

A smile twisted Sir Reynald's lips. "The women of Plas Niwl, including Catrin, have been called that for several generations. They've all been rather independent women. Catrin *is* a widow—tragic story that—but so was her grandmother, Bessie. In fact, it sounds as if you're looking for Bessie and not Catrin. It's Bessie whose reputation was legendary. Unfortunately, she died two years ago, so if you're looking for her, Mr. Newcome, you're out of luck."

Evan stared ahead at the road in stunned silence. No, it wasn't the grandmother he sought. After all, she'd been dead when the Lady of the Mists was in London with Justin. The Lady of the Mists he wanted must be the enchanting woman he'd met at the lake. No wonder she'd acted so strangely when he'd mentioned her grandmother's attributes. But why hadn't she set him straight? Why hadn't she revealed who she was?

Sir Reynald mopped more dirt from his forehead as he went on. "I do hope you're not one of those fools who come to Mrs. Price for knowledge of the ancients. Some claim she practices the dark arts, but the woman is no more a conjurer than that *consuriwr* in town, with his potions and his divining rod. I believe she is merely a chronicler of such practices."

Don't be too sure of that, Evan thought, remembering how she'd looked coming out of the lake, like a fairy goddess come to lure the mere mortal to his doom. He closed his fist around the lace-draped pommel, anger beating in his chest. Had she lured Justin to his doom? Is that why she'd lied about her grandmother, obviously trying to deflect him from his visit? Is that why she'd avoided his eyes during their conversation? He'd assumed she was simply shy, but now he reconsidered that assumption.

Sir Reynald shifted in his saddle. "Those essays of hers about folk legends and superstitions practically encourage the masses to continue with their absurd ideas." He wrinkled his nose with distaste, though his gaze on Evan was keen. "I cannot believe they publish such nonsense, but they tell me her essays appear in journals. Don't you think it unwise to put such fanciful ideas into print?"

"Indeed," Evan mumbled noncommittally, but his mind had taken another track. Hadn't he recently read an article about the druidic origins of harvest traditions in South Wales, referred to him by that pompous ass, Iolo Morganwg, at the Gwyneddigion? The article had been written by a C. Price. It had to be her.

Besides, Rhys had said something about her essays. Evan

straightened in his saddle. Rhys and Juliana. They'd said they'd met Catrin Price. Why hadn't they corrected him when he'd spoken of her as old?

He thought back to his conversation with the Vaughans, remembering the way Rhys had reacted when Evan had mentioned the Lady of the Mists's advanced age. Then Evan remembered Juliana singing Catrin's praises.

He groaned. This was Juliana's doing, all of it. She'd deliberately let him continue in his mistaken notions. But why? A jest? It wasn't like Juliana to play tricks on her friends, especially when the tricks had such serious consequences.

Then again, she didn't know the gravity of his visit to Catrin Price. He hadn't told Juliana or Rhys what had really happened to Justin. But perhaps he should have.

His throat tightened as he remembered the night Justin died. Evan had met up with his friend just as Justin was leaving their favorite dining establishment. Justin had explained that he was late for a meeting with a woman and had little time to talk. But he'd been eager to tell Evan what the meeting was about.

He'd had a large box with him and had drawn out an ornate and obviously very old chalice, a monstrous bronze thing with druidic symbols. He'd said it had been in the family for years, but he'd recently received a letter from a woman who wanted to buy it from him. He'd even shown Evan the letter.

Justin's excitement about the sale and about meeting the mysterious Lady of the Mists came back to Evan now. Justin had wanted the money to finance his gambling, and he'd felt that the woman's price was perfectly decent. Justin had invited Evan to go with him, but Evan had declined, since he was meeting his publisher for dinner.

But when his publisher hadn't shown up, Evan had decided to join his friend after all. Instead, he'd found Justin in an alley outside the Green Goat inn, stabbed to death.

Stricken with horror, Evan had cried for the watch, and they'd been quick to come. After hearing Evan explain why Justin had gone to the inn in the first place, they'd examined the body and discovered that the chalice and all of Justin's money were gone. That had led to the constable's decision that the murder had been a simple case of footpads trying to rob a noble, then killing the man when he wouldn't cooperate.

Evan would have agreed with them, if not for one thing. The letter written by the Lady of the Mists was also missing from Justin's body. She'd been the last person to see him, and she'd been the one most interested in the chalice. Besides, it didn't seem likely that thieves would have bothered with carrying off a box of such large size when the watch was about and they'd just murdered someone. Surely, the money Justin had been carrying would have been sufficient to make the average thief happy.

Evan had pointed all of that out to the constable. Of course, the man had scoffed at the possibility that an elderly woman would have come all the way from Wales to plot Lord Mansfield's murder. But now that Evan knew that the Lady of the Mists was a young, devious Welshwoman, he wondered if the constable might look at it differently.

The more he remembered her nervousness at hearing that he'd just come from London, the more his suspicions about her grew. When he and Sir Reynald reached the fork in the road and the man struck off in the opposite direction from the one Catrin Price had designated, Evan knew for certain she'd been trying to misdirect him.

If that didn't prove she had *something* to hide, he didn't know what did. He'd obviously alarmed her. Even though she hadn't known who he was or why he was here, she'd assumed that a stranger from London would be looking for her, and why would she assume that unless she was anticipating such a thing?

Thus he wasn't at all surprised a short while later when they arrived at Plas Niwl and a stiff-lipped elderly butler named Mr. Bos announced they couldn't see Mrs. Price because "the mistress is indisposed and unable to accept callers today."

Indisposed indeed, Evan thought as he listened to Sir Reynald express voluble concern for the lady's health. *The chit is worried. She gave me the wrong directions, then hurried back here to trump up this false tale so she wouldn't have to see me.*

Evan had to resist the urge to stalk up the stairs and ferret the lying woman out. But this situation called for more finesse. He had no proof that Mrs. Price was involved in

Justin's death or even that he had the right woman. Without the letter Justin had been carrying, Evan couldn't even prove she'd gone to meet Justin. Besides, since her real name had never been mentioned, she could easily claim that someone else pretending to be the Lady of the Mists had been there. Certainly, his instincts and his observations of her behavior couldn't be considered real proof.

No, before he could go to the authorities with his accusations again, he needed solid evidence. And to get that, he must lay her fears about him to rest. Otherwise, she'd never let him close enough to speak to her.

His eyes narrowed. Why not use Mrs. Price's interest in scholarly matters to flush her out? For once, perhaps his name and reputation could garner him more than a line of print in a dusty book.

Evan faced the servant with a smile. "I'm disappointed to hear of Mrs. Price's illness. My name is Newcome, Evan Newcome. I've come from Cambridge to research a book about . . . er . . . Welsh folklore. I thought I'd pay Mrs. Price a visit, since her essays deal with the same subject. 'Tis a pity I can't speak with her. I wish I could stay in Llanddeusant longer, but pressing matters compel me to return to London soon. You will tell her that I called, won't you? I'm staying at The Red Dragon if she should recover before I leave."

Sir Reynald was staring at him now, but all Evan cared about was making sure the servant had duly noted his name. If the woman was at all conversant in Welsh scholarship, she would recognize it. With luck, she'd be interested enough in his supposed book to seek him out. Let her come to him. It was more effective than storming her defenses and putting her on her guard.

Mr. Bos surveyed him with a sniff and repeated word for word all the information Evan had given about the purpose for his visit.

"Yes, that's right." *Rather formal chap, isn't he?* Evan thought.

"I will certainly inform madam of your visit," Mr. Bos remarked. "And of your visit as well," Mr. Bos added with a cursory glance in Sir Reynald's direction. It was clear that the pompous servant thought little of Sir Reynald.

Sir Reynald drew up his chin with a sniff and turned toward the door. "Make sure you do."

Evan started to go with him, then remembered something else. He drew out the shawl Mrs. Price had left behind at the lake and handed it to Mr. Bos. "Oh, and if you'd be so good as to give this to Mrs. Price, I'd appreciate it. It's a small gift. From one scholar to another."

Mr. Bos eyed him with suspicion, making Evan wonder if the man recognized the shawl. But the servant merely murmured, "Certainly, sir," and took the shawl with a frown that said he didn't know what to make of scholars bearing gifts.

That didn't matter. The estimable Mrs. Price would know exactly what to make of it. She would know that Evan had seen through her subterfuge. That, along with the knowledge of his substantial reputation, might prod her into seeing him, out of guilt for having lied to a man who was, after all, only a scholar come to pay her a friendly visit.

Of course, she might choose to bury her head in the sand and stay away from him. If so, he'd find another way to approach her. But one way or the other he'd have his questions answered, and he wouldn't leave Llanddeusant until he did.

Chapter Three

The saplings of the green-tipped birch
Draw my foot from bondage:
Let no boy know your secret!
—Anonymous, "Never Tell"

Catrin glanced up from her knitting to find that Bos had entered the room. He crossed to the fireplace, then began stoking up the fire with stiff little movements that betrayed the pain he must be suffering.

"Is your arthritis causing trouble again?" she asked.

He straightened, a piece of tinder in his hand. Then he lit the candlestick on the mantel. "When the air is damp, I do find it more troublesome than usual, but it is nothing for you to worry about, madam."

His haughty demeanor intimidated others, but Catrin knew the man that lay beneath the formal words. Bos had been an upper butler for the Earl of Pembroke until his arthritis had made it difficult for him to perform his duties, and the tight-fisted earl had cruelly turned him off without a pension. Shortly after her grandmother's death, when their own butler had left in search of a more grandiose position, Bos had applied for the vacant post. And Catrin had given it to him instantly, touched by the sad circumstances of his past employment.

It had proven advantageous for her as well as for him. Bos maintained the household rules and regimens that Catrin's late grandmother had established, thus relieving Catrin of the responsibility of keeping the staff in line. Thank heaven for that, since Catrin had always been dreadfully lax about discipline. She would never have kept the household in order without Bos.

It was ironic in a way, for if Bos had come to Plas Niwl a few years earlier, when Grandmother was still alive, Grandmother would have turned him away. She would have pointed out the impracticality of taking on an arthritic servant who would soon be too old for anything but a pension.

Of course, Grandmother had never needed anyone to maintain discipline for her. Grandmother had always possessed the iron will and regal bearing that made servants quake in their boots, whereas Catrin found herself bending over backward to accommodate her servants. She couldn't help it. Unlike Grandmother, widow of a viscount and a stern believer in class distinctions, Catrin couldn't bear to treat her servants as lackeys to be ordered about. Some of them had been her only companions from her childhood, and she considered them her family since she had no other family to speak of. She couldn't chastise them for petty infractions or condescend to them as if they were children.

They knew it, too. So without Bos, the household would most certainly have gone on in a lackadaisical fashion, everyone doing as they thought best. Bos, however, made sure that the servants listened to him, if not always to her. He made them all toe the line. Everything went smoothly, the work was always done, and Catrin even had time to bury herself in another tome about ancient bardic rites and customs.

"May I fetch anything for you, madam?" Bos asked when he'd finished lighting the other candles in the room. "It's growing chilly. Perhaps you would like me to fetch your shawl."

Her shawl. She dropped her knitting in her lap with a sigh. That one word reminded her of the afternoon's embarrassing events. "No, I don't want my shawl."

"As you wish."

He headed toward the door, but she called out, "I do want to talk to you, however. Sit down and stay for a bit, will you? The work can wait."

Without a flicker of expression Bos did as she asked, although the faintest "Ahhh" escaped his lips when he settled himself into the comfortable armchair by the fire.

"Tell me again what the stranger said." Resuming her knitting in an attempt at nonchalance, Catrin added, "Tell me word for word."

"The stranger?" Bos stretched his spindly legs out before the fire. "He had a name, as I recall. I believe you even said you recognized it. Mr. Evan Newcome, from Cambridge."

Yes, from Cambridge. That had been where she'd made her first error—in assuming that he was from London because he'd come on the ship from London. But he wasn't from London at all. He wasn't even really from Cambridge. "He was raised in Carmarthen, you know," she told Bos.

Bos raised one white eyebrow. "Am I to assume you came by that bit of knowledge at the same time you bestowed your shawl upon the man?"

Catrin began to knit with a vengeance. "I didn't give it to him. Not exactly. I . . . I left it behind after he saw me swimming at Llyn y Fan Fach."

"Ah, yes." Bos's stern expression radiated disapproval. He probably knew that she swam in her chemise, for Bos knew everything in the household, and Catrin had never found a way to hide her wet chemises from her maids.

Catrin's cheeks were burning now. "Although we spoke to each other at the lake, we did not . . . er . . . exchange names."

"I imagine not. Introducing oneself to a stranger when one is wearing almost no clothing can be a trifle awkward."

Bos's bland reproof brought a small smile to Catrin's lips. "Yes, a trifle. In any case, that's why I didn't know he was Evan Newcome." And not just some anonymous Evan Newcome, she thought, but *the* Evan Newcome.

She'd heard all about the great Evan Newcome through the various scholars with whom she corresponded. He was widely considered a genius. He could read, write, and speak ten different languages and had some knowledge of several others. His essays were published in prestigious journals. His books included a well-respected French grammar, translations of classical Greek and Roman texts, and an impressive theory of the development of Celtic languages.

Until today, she'd assumed he was English. "Newcome" wasn't a particularly Welsh name. But "Evan" was, and she should have known he was Welsh from the few articles he'd written on Welsh poetry—perceptive, intriguing essays that perfectly described the elusive beauty of Welsh verse.

"Am I to assume that if you'd known who your companion at the lake really was," Bos asked dryly, "you'd not have instructed me to tell him you were ill?"

An instant pang of conscience hit her. "That was awful of me, wasn't it? I do apologize for asking you to tell a lie."

"Nonsense. If you do not wish to converse with an individual, I am more than happy to speak whatever words are necessary to keep that individual away." His voice softened the merest fraction. "I am well aware that you are . . . uncomfortable with strangers."

You mean shy, she thought. *And not at all like my captivating, strong-willed grandmother.*

"That's not why I had you lie," Catrin murmured. "When I first met him, I thought—" She stopped short. She couldn't tell Bos the real reason Evan Newcome had alarmed her. She hadn't even told him why she'd gone to London, nor what had happened there during her fateful visit. If he ever found out the details, he wouldn't approve at all. "Well, it doesn't matter what I thought. I was obviously wrong. And now I shall look like a rude and ungrateful woman for avoiding him when he has honored me by reading my essays and coming to speak with me about them."

She thought it nothing short of amazing that Evan Newcome was familiar with her work. Oh, how she wished she hadn't been so hasty to assume he was here for nefarious reasons.

Bos smoothed down a single strand of white hair that had miraculously escaped his carefully oiled coiffure. "There is no shame in being circumspect, madam. If you still wish to speak to the man, then you are perfectly within your rights to do so. Merely explain to him that you were exercising caution, and I am sure he will understand why you avoided him."

She wished she shared Bos's conviction.

Bos cleared his throat. "Your little white lie becomes almost sensible under those circumstances."

"Little white lie?" she squeaked. Had Mr. Newcome told Bos how she'd led him down the primrose path by letting him go on thinking that she and her grandmother were the same person?

"That you were sick." Bos's eyes narrowed. "He should understand why you were reluctant to greet a stranger who'd caught you in such a state of undress."

"Oh, yes, *that* white lie." Unfortunately, Evan Newcome hadn't struck her as the kind of man who suffered being lied to without complaint. He'd left that shawl deliberately to show that he'd found her out. A gentleman would have waited for a private audience to return the item and accept her apologies, but she suspected that Mr. Newcome's gentlemanly qualities were the merest veneer over a character that was more forthright—and perhaps more ungoverned—than a gentleman's should be.

"What do you intend to do about the situation?" Bos asked, interrupting her thoughts.

Catrin sighed. "I suppose I shall contact Mr. Newcome at The Red Dragon and apologize for not seeing him when he came."

"Do so only if you truly desire to speak to the man. If you do not wish to converse with him, you have every right to continue pretending to be ill until he has left the shire."

Oh, how she wished she could. She usually preferred to hide at Plas Niwl, venturing out as little as necessary. Thus she avoided the speculations of people who didn't understand her quiet character and who attributed her shyness to snobbery. Not to mention the other, more vicious speculations that had arisen after Willie's death.

But despite her tendency to stay within her own little world, she had never intentionally been so rude as to ignore someone's visits to her. It was one thing to avoid a possibly painful confrontation with a man who might be a constable. It was entirely another to ignore the generous overtures of a respected scholar like Evan Newcome. She'd already insulted him by lying to him. Now she must take her medicine and apologize.

At her silence Bos added, "If you do wish to speak to him, I can send a message to The Red Dragon inviting him to call again."

She shook her head. "That won't be necessary. I'll set out for Llanddeusant in the morning and make my apologies to Mr. Newcome there."

Bos nodded, then rose from his chair. "Is there any other matter with which I might assist you, madam?"

"No. Thank you for all your insight into the situation."

Bos harrumphed. "I merely spoke aloud your own thoughts, I am sure. As always, you have an unerring instinct for the proper way to address troublesome situations."

She never knew how to take Bos's pronouncements on her character. Half the time she thought he made them tongue in cheek, the other half she thought he was being chivalrous. In either case he couldn't possibly mean them. Her "instinct" for addressing "a troublesome situation" was generally to run and hide, and she doubted Bos would consider that "proper."

"I shall leave you to your thoughts," Bos went on as he marched toward the door, his posture painfully erect. "Shall I have a tray sent up here for your dinner or will you eat with the staff as usual?"

She thought a moment. "A tray, please."

He frowned. "You are not intending to knit into the wee hours of the night again, are you, madam? Mrs. Griffiths fell into hysterics when you didn't answer her knock at your bedroom door yesterday morning. She expressed to me her concern that you had been kidnapped and sold to gypsies. It was only when I found you here—after a lengthy search of the house, I might add—that she calmed herself."

With a chuckle Catrin shook her head. "I suppose I did get carried away that night. I was afraid I wouldn't finish this blanket in time to give it to Tess as part of my wedding gift two days hence, but I think another hour or two of work will do it."

"Ah, yes, the wedding. Is it your intention to attend the joyful event?"

Bos knew, as did all the staff, that she never attended weddings, not since her own had ended in the death of her husband. Funerals, yes. Christenings, certainly. Never weddings.

Until now. "I will be attending," she said, avoiding his sudden scrutiny. "Annie would never forgive me if I didn't go to her daughter's wedding."

"I see," he murmured. When she said nothing to enlighten him further, he inclined his head and opened the door. "I shall fetch your tray, madam." Then he left.

Catrin stared down at the blanket she'd nearly finished. It was made of the finest wool from their own sheep, and in one corner she'd already embroidered the joined initials of Tess and her new husband. She fingered the letters, pleasure surging through her. For the first time in five years, looking at such a blatant symbol of a new couple's shared future didn't rouse anger or resentment or frustration in her. For the first time in five years, she felt hope.

Thanks to the chalice.

Putting down her knitting, she went to the bookshelf and pressed her hand against the right end of the second shelf down, fourth shelf from the left. The shelf rotated so that the outer shelf was now inside and the inside shelf faced out. The secret compartment had been built into the shelves before she was even born. Her grandmother had used it as a safe, and so did she. Right now it contained the most valuable items in her possession.

The diary of her ancestress. And the chalice.

She removed the chalice from the shelf, holding it in her hands as she had the night she'd bought it. It gave her the same bittersweet thrill it had then, a thrill that went straight to her heart. From the moment she'd touched it on that fateful night, she'd known it was the one she was searching for, the one that would break the curse. The markings matched the ones in the diary, and her cursory examination of it led her to believe it was at least a few hundred years old. It was the right one. She just knew it.

She stared at the bronze etchings . . . the maiden with her cloud of hair wrapping her body, the stalwart warrior, and the raven, whose dark eyes seemed to glitter at her. A series of symbols ringed the edge of the chalice, probably some druidic code. She knew of such cabalistic codes, but didn't know how to interpret them. Lord Mansfield hadn't been able to enlighten her on the subject either.

Lord Mansfield. Clutching the chalice to her chest, she sank onto a nearby chair. Poor Lord Mansfield.

She could still remember the morning after she'd bought the chalice from him. She'd been breakfasting in a little English inn and reading the *Times* when to her shock she'd discovered that thieves had apparently robbed and murdered him just outside the inn where she'd met with him.

Thinking about it now, she shuddered. No wonder she'd felt uneasy that night, so uneasy that she'd gone out the back way of the inn. She had even changed her lodgings that very night and had decided to hurry back to Wales by coach in the morning instead of waiting two days for the ship she'd booked passage on to set sail. For once in her life, acting on her fears had been the right thing to do. She'd probably sensed the thieves watching the inn. Perhaps if she hadn't left through the back door, they'd have attacked her instead of Lord Mansfield.

A lump formed in her throat. She should have told the authorities that she'd been with Lord Mansfield right before he died, but the thought of enduring all those Englishmen's questions had terrified her. It had already taken every ounce of her meager courage to brave London for the chalice. Besides, what could she have said? She'd seen nothing. She couldn't point them to the murderers.

And if she'd gone to them, they might have misconstrued her presence there that night, especially if they'd learned how she'd used her appellation, the Lady of the Mists, to lure Lord Mansfield to meet her.

Now she wished she hadn't done that. But at the time she'd seen no other way to coax him to a meeting. He hadn't been the first member of the family whom she'd approached about the chalice. She'd written his mother about buying it, and Lady Mansfield had absolutely refused to sell, so Catrin had decided to tempt the son into selling it. She hadn't given him her right name for fear he'd mention it to his mother. As a result of her deception, he'd met her in a public place instead of at his home. And he'd been murdered.

No, the authorities wouldn't look kindly on all her devious manipulations, especially if they learned that Lady Mansfield had been against the sale. What's more, they probably would take the chalice away from her. And for what? She couldn't tell them anything that would help.

At a sound in the hall, she shoved the chalice back into the compartment and closed the little shelf. Her heart racing, she listened as footsteps passed the door to the study without pausing. Then she let out her held breath. Thank heaven it was only a maid lighting the sconces.

As the pounding of her heart lessened, she walked back to the chaise longue. This fear of being found out was absurd. One day, she'd have to reveal she had the chalice, if only to whomever she married. After all, the whole point of acquiring it had been to make sure that she had someone to share Plas Niwl with. She needed a husband and children so that upon her death, the estate wouldn't fall to Sir Huw, her father-in-law, or his designated heir, either of whom would probably raise the rents and put tenant farmers out of their homes, all in the name of progress.

Thoughts of her blustering father-in-law automatically led to thoughts of his dear son Willie, whose character had been as different from his father's as hers had been from her grandmother's. She and Willie had gravitated toward each other because he was a gentle soul like her. He'd liked books and privacy and the simple comforts of good conversation. He'd spent all his life in the shadow of an aggressive, voluble father, so he'd understood her withdrawal.

Indeed, they'd met when his father and her grandmother had been engaged in a dispute over whom the landowners planned to support in the election for M.P. of the borough. While the two older people had thrown blistering pronouncements at each other, Willie and Catrin had discovered a mutual interest in Welsh *englyn* and had retired to a quiet corner to recite their favorite verses to each other. From there, their friendship had grown into a sweet understanding.

The lack of strong feeling in their friendship hadn't particularly bothered her. She'd relished Willie's companionship and had looked forward to living with a man who'd share her concerns and her affections, who'd allow her to run Plas Niwl once her grandmother was dead, and who'd give her children to pass the estate on to.

When Willie had died and she'd found the diary and thus learned about the curse, her future had looked bleak indeed. There was to be no companion for life, no children. And life at Plas Niwl would end with her death.

Then she'd located the chalice. Now she had a chance to live again. Thank heaven, for the need to find a companion was becoming more intense every day, and not just because of the practical considerations. To her utter mortification she had discovered that she had urges . . . strange, wild urges that came upon her late at night when she was alone in the massive state bed. Unfamiliar urges.

Although she and Willie had shared a few kisses before their marriage, they'd never gone further. Yet she knew what went on in the bedroom, and she found herself thinking about it more every day. It astonished her that such violent longings could overwhelm her. Could she really be thinking about men in *that* way?

Yes, she could. Most definitely.

She knew that widows sometimes took lovers. Widows were allowed such privileges, even widows who'd never shared a bed with a man. But she couldn't imagine doing something so brazen, suffering more of the townspeople's whispers and rumors about her.

Besides, she wanted more than a lover. She wanted a man who would be hers forever, who would look at her with longing in his eyes and mean it as more than simple lust.

Unbidden, an image entered her mind . . . of a tall man standing on the banks of Llyn y Fan Fach. Once again, she felt his gaze move down over her, growing in heat as it touched first her throat, then her shoulders, then her breasts—

Stop it! she told herself as the blood rushed to her face.

How could she even think of Evan Newcome that way? He was a renowned scholar. He probably had a wife tucked away at Cambridge. And if not, he still wouldn't look twice at a timid Welshwoman from the country when scores of English noblewomen probably offered him their patronage every day.

Then a smile tipped up her lips. He *had* looked twice when she'd emerged from the lake, hadn't he? He'd looked twice . . . and thrice and many more times. It had been unnerving the way he'd stared, as no man ever before had stared at her, as if he wanted to eat her up.

The very thought of it made her breath quicken. Would he stare at her like that tomorrow? By heaven, she hoped not. If he did, she'd never be able to stammer out her apology. If he did, she'd make a fool of herself again.

Only this time, she'd never recover from the embarrassment.

Chapter Four

Let not a man who's been born
Know any place your purpose:
That's the way a fool is known,
He reveals what he's thinking.
—David Llwyd, "The Fox's Counsel"

Having eaten a large and satisfying breakfast, Evan leaned back in his chair and surveyed the common room of The Red Dragon. What a rarity it was to sit and leisurely eat breakfast without having to rush off to a lecture or a meeting. The day stretched ahead of him, and it was all his.

As he sniffed the air redolent with the scent of wild roses and gazed out the window at the sun burning off the mist, he was glad he'd come. He'd missed Wales. If he could, he'd live here now.

For a fleeting moment, he thought of the dream of his early manhood—to be a gentleman farmer . . . have a place of his own and spend his days tending a little plot of land in Wales and his nights poring over his books before sharing a bed with a loving wife.

A bitter sigh escaped his lips. He'd quickly learned that such a life was not open to him. He had no land, and his income wasn't sufficient to allow him to purchase it, if any could be had. The only way he could make a decent living was through the universities, and there were none in Wales. As for the loving wife . . . his experience with his former fiancée, Henrietta, and his observation of his brother's stormy marriage had taught him he wasn't meant to marry. Not ever. No matter how much he might want it, marriage and a life as a gentleman farmer in Wales were not for him.

In any case, he could still enjoy this visit to Llanddeusant, couldn't he? After all, it was a lovely little town set in the foothills of Black Mountain, a perfect place to get one's mind off one's troubles.

What's more, the Lady of the Mists had proven to be an

intriguing puzzle. She was unlike any woman of her class that he'd ever met, even Juliana. He found himself anticipating his next encounter with her. He told himself it was only because her suspicious behavior made it almost certain she knew something about Justin's murder. But he knew that wasn't the only reason he couldn't wait to see her again.

The innkeeper's wife, Mrs. Llewelyn, came to clear the plates from his table. She was a congenial woman who enjoyed having guests at her little inn. When he'd told her he was a scholar from Cambridge, she'd turned her motherly instincts to making him feel welcome.

"Will that be all for you, Mr. Newcome?" she asked now, holding the plates in one hand while with the other, she used her long apron to wipe her round, red face.

"Yes. The meal was excellent."

She beamed. "It's a pleasure having you here, sir. It's not often we have guests as distinguished as yourself. I do hope you're planning to stay a bit."

"I'm not sure how long I'll be here." He gave her the same tale he'd given Mrs. Price's servant. "I'm doing research into the local legends. When I've gathered what I need, I'll return to Cambridge, but that may take a few days."

"Legends? Like the story of Llyn y Fan Fach and such?"

At her mention of Llyn y Fan Fach, an idea occurred to him. "Yes. Say, I wonder if you could tell me more about that tale?"

She broke into a smile. "Of course. Let me put this away, and I'll be back for a chat."

Five minutes later, she had seated herself across the table from him, a cup of steaming tea in her hand. "Well then, Mr. Newcome, I'm all yours. You wanted to know about Llyn y Fan Fach?"

"Yes. I was there yesterday, and I'm curious to know the whole story, since I have only a vague memory of it."

She gestured to his empty hands. "Don't you want to fetch a notebook or some such, so you can write it all down?"

A notebook. Deuce take it. He had none.

He flashed Mrs. Llewelyn a reproachful smile. "Surely you don't think my memory is as bad as all that, do you?"

He tapped his forehead. "I have the memory of an elephant. I never forget an interesting story."

She laughed. "Ah, you're a true Welshman then, lad. Well, let me see. . . ."

With that the woman launched into a lengthy tale about the lady of the lake and her merchant husband. Evan listened with half an ear. His question had merely been a ruse to get her talking. He waited until she began telling him that some travelers still saw the lady of the lake, then turned the subject to what really interested him.

"It's odd you should mention seeing ghosts at the lake. Yesterday I met a woman there. Catrin Price was her name. When she came out of the lake, she gave me quite a start. I thought *she* was the lady of the lake at first."

"Did you now?" A knowing smile played over Mrs. Llewelyn's mouth. She lifted her cup to her lips, eyeing him over the edge of the chipped china. She took a long sip, then set the cup down gingerly.

"She certainly roused my curiosity," he prodded.

She arched one graying eyebrow. "I'll bet that's not all she roused."

He stared at her. Surely she didn't mean what he thought she meant.

"Come now, Mr. Newcome," she said, "I know Catrin's appeal. Half the lads in Llanddeusant sneak out to the lake to watch her swim when she thinks she's all alone."

An irrational anger gripped him at the thought of a herd of randy boys seeing what he'd seen yesterday. "Perhaps someone should tell her."

"Oh, no, if she knew they were watching, she'd be mortified. She's painfully shy. Once she learned of it, she'd never go near the lake again, and I'd hate to deprive her of one of her few pleasures."

Painfully shy? he thought. *Mrs. Price?* Now that he thought about it, perhaps shyness explained her nervousness at the lake. But why would a shy woman have approached Justin so boldly about buying the chalice? Could Evan possibly have the wrong woman?

"So you saw Catrin swimming in the lake, did you?" Mrs. Llewelyn added, a sly look on her face.

He stiffened. He couldn't believe he was having this conversation with an innkeeper's wife. He'd forgotten how frank the Welsh were, compared to the English. "Yes, but *I* wasn't spying on her. I merely happened along and saw her—"

"Naked as my nail."

"In her chemise," he said, correcting her.

"Which was next to nothing." She wagged one finger at him. "You saw her in her chemise, and you got ideas in your head." He opened his mouth to retort, but she cut him off. "I know what goes on in a man's head—and his body—when he sees a fetching girl. And now you want to know all about her, don't you?"

Evan was thoroughly nonplussed. Yes, he found the young woman attractive. And yes, he had indeed felt a strong bolt of lust for her until he'd discovered who she was. But it didn't mean his interest in her was prurient.

On the other hand, it might be better to let Mrs. Llewelyn think it was. Then she might tell him more. He forced a smile to his face. "You've found me out. I did find the woman intriguing."

"Intriguing, eh? A good word for Catrin." A sudden scowl darkened her sunny features. "Some people aren't so kind. They call her peculiar."

"Peculiar? Why? Because she swims near naked in the lake?"

Mrs. Llewelyn hunched over the table and lowered her voice. "There's people in this town who don't understand anything out of the ordinary. A woman like that, living alone, buried in her books and rarely venturing out to speak to anyone . . . they think that's odd."

"But you don't."

She shook her head. "Catrin Price has had enough tragedy in her life to destroy a lesser woman. I'd think something amiss if she *weren't* odd."

"What kind of tragedy?" he asked, thinking of what Juliana and Rhys had said about Willie Price's death.

"Her husband died in an accident on her wedding day. He was but a young lad. And her parents died young, too, before she was three, which is why her maternal grandmother raised her. A lot of tragedies, that."

"Yes." It was a lot of tragedies, wasn't it?

"Let me give you a piece of advice, Mr. Newcome," Mrs. Llewelyn said, leaning forward. "There are some in this town who spout a lot of nonsense about Catrin. But don't believe them. She's not a witch or a seeress. And she's not casting secret spells up there at Plas Niwl."

He couldn't hide his amusement. "They say she's a witch? Really?"

She scowled at him. "'Tis not so strange as you think. I know you university chaps are too clever to believe in such things, but it's different around here. A few people in Llanddeusant are still suspicious of a young woman living alone, no matter what her station. They look at the tragedies in her life, then cast about for someone to blame. They hear of Catrin ordering books from London on druids and such, they look at Willie's and her parents' freakish deaths, and they leap to conclusions."

"That's absurd. They shouldn't blame her for things beyond her control."

"I agree. But people will talk and most of it nonsense, about how she's casting spells, how she married Willie for his wealth." She gave a harsh laugh. "'Tis indeed absurd. Catrin has never shown concern for wealth. But the truth don't affect folks when they've got a maggot in their heads about something. And it don't help that her father-in-law encourages the stories, the old bastard. He blames her for his son's death, he does. But the tale-telling isn't all his fault. People will talk when they don't understand a person. And they don't understand Catrin and her quiet ways . . . or her interests."

An instant surge of sympathy welled up in him. He knew what it was like to be different from the others in the community. "So she's an outcast here."

"Oh, no. Only a few speak badly of her." A faint sarcasm entered her voice. "And even those are careful not to say things to her face, for they know it's her patronage that keeps the charity school going, her land that keeps the tenant farmers round about here well fed, and her generosity that maintains our little chapel."

He thought of how Mrs. Price had at first offered to give him directions. Until she'd figured out where he was going, she'd been more than helpful. That was the act of a generous woman, wasn't it?

A wry smile creased his lips. He was already making excuses for the woman, based only on the tales of an innkeeper's wife. "Why are you telling me all this?" he asked suspiciously.

"Because I want you to know Catrin's true character before you hear a lot of nonsense from one of those superstitious fools. If you're . . . er . . . interested in our Catrin, you should know the truth of things."

Evan fought down a pang of guilt. Mrs. Llewelyn obviously cared about Mrs. Price, and he was misleading her about his interest in the woman. But he couldn't tell her the truth. She'd go straight to Mrs. Price with it. Besides, he still had to discover whether Mrs. Price had been to London recently and if she'd bought a chalice there.

Suddenly, an image of the chalice flashed into his head. The chalice had looked druidic. And Mrs. Price's article had concerned the druids.

"Tell me something, Mrs. Llewelyn," he said, trying to keep his voice even and nonchalant. "You said Mrs. Price had an interest in druids. It so happens that I do as well. I'm planning a whole chapter on them. Do you think she could tell me about them?"

"I imagine she could." Mrs. Llewelyn smiled at him, apparently pleased that her stories about her friend hadn't put him off. "Catrin knows a great deal about everything. Her grandmother made sure she had the best tutors. She's a smart one, she is."

He'd have thought she was talking about her own child from the way she spoke of Mrs. Price, pride evident in her voice.

"Do you think she'd have any druidic artifacts? Daggers or . . . perhaps chalices used in rituals? I'd like to put sketches of that sort of thing in my book." *This fictitious book is growing to phenomenal proportions, isn't it?* he thought.

She screwed up her face as she considered the question. "I don't think so. She's never spoken of any such thing."

He tried another tack. "I suppose antiquities of that nature are difficult to come by, even out here. I've seen such items only in a few shops in London. She'd probably have to go there for them, and I don't suppose she goes to London much."

He waited with indrawn breath for Mrs. Llewelyn to take the bait.

Fortunately, she did. "She's been to London only once that I recall, and that was recent. Came back a week ago, she did."

Ah, so now he needn't wonder if he had the right woman. Catrin Price had to be the one who'd met with Justin in London.

"But she didn't tell me about buying anything," Mrs. Llewelyn went on, "although I heard she sold a painting to Sir Reynald for a hundred pounds directly before she left. A hundred pounds! Can you imagine? For a painting! But then, she's an heiress. I suppose she has a hundred paintings worth that much and more."

"No doubt," Evan said dryly, unable to miss Mrs. Llewelyn's blatant attempt to demonstrate Mrs. Price's eligibility. Mrs. Llewelyn had probably assessed his financial worth at once and decided that an heiress would tempt him.

Suddenly, a pretty young woman rushed down the stairs, her face distraught. "There you are, Mama. You must come set these sleeves. I can't make them work at all! It'll never be finished before tomorrow!"

"I'm coming, I'm coming," Mrs. Llewelyn said. She rose from the table with a helpless shrug. "My daughter's getting married tomorrow, and she's in a state. You must excuse me a moment. If you'll wait, we can continue our chat about local legends when I'm done."

From the way she said "local legends" with a meaningful wink, he knew she was hinting that she'd seen through his subterfuge and had known precisely whom he'd been interested in discussing and why. Well, he would let her continue in her misconception as long as it suited his purpose.

As Mrs. Llewelyn trotted off up the stairs, he leaned back and mused on what he'd learned. Catrin Price had been to London. Mrs. Llewelyn seemed to think she'd returned empty-handed. That may or may not have been the case—the chalice, though large, was still something she could pack in her bag if she wanted.

Nonetheless, the bit about the hundred pounds intrigued him. It was exactly half the amount she'd offered in the letter to Justin. What about the other half? Had she been unable to come up with it and thus decided to have the chalice stolen from Justin? But then, why sell a painting to raise any funds at all for the purchase? Why make such a sacrifice if she was planning to have hirelings steal the chalice?

For the first time since he'd set off from London with the desire for truth burning in his chest, he stopped to reconsider his suspicions. Until now, he'd postulated that Mrs. Price might have lured Justin to the inn with the aim of stealing the chalice.

Now he wasn't so sure. The shy woman Mrs. Llewelyn described wasn't the type to engineer such a scheme. Certainly he couldn't imagine the daughter of a knight being mixed up in a murder. The rumors of the villagers he dismissed entirely as mere gossip. Although he still didn't know how her husband had died, everyone said it was an accident, and he didn't believe in spells and such. As for her interest in druidic objects, obviously she *had* wanted the chalice. But was that suspicious, especially in a woman who studied such things? Of course not.

Still, why hadn't she written to Justin in a forthright manner, stating her real name? Why hadn't she met him at his home, for God's sake? And what about the missing letter? All of that was very suspicious.

The sound of someone entering the inn jerked him from his thoughts. He glanced up to find the very object of his ruminations hesitating on the threshold. She briefly squinted as her eyes adjusted to the change in light. Then she scanned the room, twisting a handkerchief in her hands as her gaze flicked over every table before coming to rest on his.

An instant flush stained her cheeks, making his pulse quicken. She looked nothing like she had yesterday. She was dressed fashionably in a morning gown and spencer, the very picture of a woman paying a formal call. It made him instantly aware of the difference in their stations. He could wear clothing of good quality and display the manners of a gentleman, yet inside he was no better than the lowliest farmer on her estate.

Certainly, his body's response to her wasn't gentlemanly in the least. He felt as profoundly affected now as he had seeing her in her wet chemise, for with the swell of her breasts and her slender throat rising from amidst a froth of lace and painted muslin, she resembled nothing so much as a delicious confection. And like the coarse creature he was, he wanted to devour her.

He shook his head to clear it. What was he thinking? No matter what her station or enticing looks, no matter what Mrs. Llewelyn said about her kindness to the village, she had acted suspiciously in London. She was a privileged woman who'd thought nothing of lying to him yesterday.

Remembering how she'd evaded him brought all his suspicions back full force. He rose and gave her a sketchy bow. "Good morning. You seem fully recovered from your 'illness.' "

The stain on her cheeks deepened to a rosy color as she dropped her gaze from his. "I-I suppose I deserve that. I behaved very badly yesterday."

"Yes, you did."

Her chin quivered as she screwed the handkerchief up into a ball in her hands. "I've come to apologize."

"I see. I trust you received your shawl?"

Her voice was the merest whisper. "Yes." She gestured to the chair Mrs. Llewelyn had recently vacated. "May I join you?"

"Certainly, Mrs. Price." He remained standing until she was seated, then settled back into his chair. "I *do* have the name right, don't I?"

That seemed to rouse her from her embarrassment. "Don't you think you've rubbed it in quite enough?"

"Oh, I don't know. You haven't apologized yet."

Her tone turned desperate. "But you haven't given me the chance!"

"True. Then again, I don't have to, do I? I'm the one who was misled and then turned away on your whim. I don't have to talk to you at all."

She sucked in a heavy breath, the faint tightening of her lips showing her distress. "Why are you making this so difficult for me?"

He leaned back in his chair, wondering the same thing. The truth was, flustering her gave him a petty satisfaction. Besides, flustered women often said things they didn't mean to. "I'm afraid I become cantankerous when I'm lied to."

"Will explaining why I lied make you less cantankerous?" she asked in a small voice.

"Perhaps."

"Very well. You see . . . I . . . I'm . . . well, I'm shy. I know it probably sounds silly, but when I heard you were heading toward Plas Niwl, I . . . I panicked and said a lot of nonsense to put you off because I never quite know what to do with strangers."

He could tell from the way her eyes wouldn't meet his that at least part of what she was saying was a lie. She might be shy, but that was *not* why she'd tried to avoid him. Or at least, it wasn't the only reason. He lowered his voice to a silken murmur. "Shy? I wouldn't have guessed it from the way you came up out of the lake wearing nothing but your chemise."

Never had he seen a woman grow so red. "B-but that's just it," she stammered. "After you'd seen me like that . . . I knew I could never face you again."

"So what are you doing here now?"

She met his gaze, looking miserably humiliated. "I realized later how badly I'd behaved, and I wanted to rectify my error."

"That's a bold-faced lie. You wouldn't be here at all if I hadn't left your shawl at Plas Niwl to show that I knew who you were."

And if I hadn't left my name, he thought with a little stab of anger.

She stood abruptly, her chin trembling. "I am so . . . so very sorry. Obviously, I underestimated how much I offended you yesterday. It's clear that no apology can excuse my abominable actions. So if you'll excuse me—"

When she turned away from the table, he jumped to his feet. "Wait!"

She halted, her back to him.

He forced a conciliatory note into his voice. He would get nowhere with the woman if he drove her away. "Please, Mrs. Price. Sit down. I promise I'm finished being a beast about yesterday."

Still she hesitated. "You have every right to be a beast. It wasn't hospitable of me to take advantage of your misconception about Grandmother and me. I should have set you straight from the beginning."

"Enough, please. You've made your apology, and I accept it. All right?"

When she turned to look at him, her eyes misty with tears, he felt a stab of guilt. Softening his voice even more, he asked, "Won't you join me for tea?"

She hesitated a moment, then pulled out the chair and sat down, folding her hands primly on the table.

"I'll fetch Mrs. Llewelyn and order us a pot," he murmured.

"That's not necessary. I just breakfasted. I don't need anything."

He shrugged and took his seat. When she stared down at her hands, obviously uncertain how to go on, he said, "I hope you're not going to be shy again. After all, we have much to talk about. You write essays on Welsh folklore, and I'm researching a book on the subject. We have a great deal in common, don't we?"

For the first time since she'd entered The Red Dragon, she smiled, a soft, uncertain smile that crushed every one of his male defenses to dust. "I'm afraid we really don't. I've only begun to scratch the surface of Welsh literature and the oral tradition, whereas you have mastered it."

The hint of awe that had crept into her voice struck him with surprise. "So you did recognize my name."

"Instantly." She ducked her head. "I've read many of your essays and three of your books. I even own a copy of *The Development of Celtic Languages*."

Despite himself, he smiled. "I'm flattered."

"Oh, no, 'tis I who am flattered, nay, astonished that you even know my name." She flashed him a shy glance. "When Bos said you'd read my essays, I could hardly believe it."

Her essays. Deuce take it. He'd only read one of them.

His smile grew forced. "Actually, I have a confession to make. I'm not as familiar with your essays as I implied."

Instantly, that wariness she'd shown at the lake entered her expression. "But you told Bos—"

"I wanted to see you."

"Why?" Her voice was the barest whisper.

"You'll laugh when I tell you."

She remained silent.

"I came to Wales to research my book on folklore, of course. But as I told you before, I stopped in Carmarthen to visit my friends, the Vaughans, and they told me this intriguing tale—"

"The Vaughans?" Her face lost some of its wariness. "You know Lady Juliana?"

"Yes. She and her husband have been friends of mine for

years." He couldn't bring himself to tell this well-dressed knight's daughter the whole truth—that his father had been one of Rhys's tenant farmers, that if it weren't for the generosity of the Vaughans, he'd be no better than a farm laborer right now.

A genuine smile lit up her features. "The Vaughans are wonderful people, aren't they?"

"Yes." Then he added in a dry tone, "Of course, they were the ones who misled me about you in the first place."

"Oh?"

"We began talking about legends of the region, and Lady Juliana mentioned the Lady of the Mists. I'd heard of the Lady of the Mists all my life, so I made some comment about the old woman. Juliana got this peculiar look on her face and began going on and on about your advanced age. I should have guessed then that she was jesting with me, but I didn't. And she never set me straight."

"That's awful! Why on earth would she do such a thing?"

He shook his head. "There's no telling with Lady Juliana. In any case, she told me about your writing, and I remembered that I'd read an essay of yours. She also suggested I see the lake. So I thought, why not take a jaunt up to Llanddeusant and see this old woman for myself? Maybe I'll put her in my book about Welsh legends. Then when Sir Reynald told me *you* were the Lady of the Mists—"

"You became angry at me for having let you continue in your misconception," she said, lowering her gaze from his.

"Not entirely. I also became interested. You're an intriguing woman, Mrs. Price."

She lifted her head, and her eyes met his. Something passed between them . . . a frisson of awareness that shook him clear to his bones. Despite himself, he wondered what those eyes would look like glazed with passion . . . how that luscious mouth would feel under his—

With an inward oath he beat down his lascivious urges. He wasn't here to seduce the woman. He was here to find out what happened the night of Justin's murder.

"So you didn't really want my help with your book," she said, disappointment evident in her voice.

"Not at first. But last night I thought about it and realized it would be a good idea. You know the area. You know the superstitions and local tales. Perhaps you wouldn't mind showing me around and helping me collect information." *Yes*, he thought, pleased at his own brilliance. *What a perfect excuse for getting to know Mrs. Price and finding out all her secrets.*

She bit her lip. "Oh, I don't know. I'm not nearly the scholar that you are. I might not be able to—"

"Catrin!" exclaimed a voice behind Evan.

Both he and Mrs. Price stood as they saw Mrs. Llewelyn hurrying down the stairs.

Mrs. Price instantly broke into a smile. "Good day, Annie. It is so good to see you. How are things with you?"

"Fine, fine." Mrs. Llewelyn hurried to Mrs. Price's side, and the two women kissed cheeks. Then Mrs. Llewelyn held Mrs. Price out at arms' length. "You're looking well." She cast Evan a sideways glance. "She's looking well, isn't she, Mr. Newcome?"

"Quite well," he said, relishing the blush that briefly touched Mrs. Price's cheeks. "Quite well indeed."

"You *are* coming to the wedding tomorrow, aren't you, dear?" Mrs. Llewelyn asked Mrs. Price. "I know you generally avoid weddings, but Tess will be so disappointed if you don't come."

"Of course I'll be there. I wouldn't miss Tess's wedding."

"Good, good." Mrs. Llewelyn turned to Evan. "And you should come, too, Mr. Newcome." As he stood there, uncertain how to respond, Mrs. Llewelyn continued, "A wedding is the perfect place for you to hear about our local legends, you know. The whole town will be there, and we'll have a lot of storytellers among our guests." Mrs. Llewelyn cast Mrs. Price a sidelong glance. "I'm sure Mrs. Price would enjoy having you accompany her."

Mrs. Price colored. "Oh, I doubt Mr. Newcome would want to—"

"I'd be honored to accompany Mrs. Price to your daughter's wedding," Evan said, wondering if Mrs. Price realized that her friend was playing matchmaker.

"That's set then," Mrs. Llewelyn smiled, then gave Evan a surreptitious wink. "I'd best get back to Tess before she has another fit of the nerves. We must continue our conversation later, Mr. Newcome."

"Whenever you can," he murmured as she hurried toward the stairs.

But she stopped abruptly on the first step and turned around with a frown. "By the way, Catrin, David Morys may be here any moment. He promised to stop by this morning and show me the verse he's planning to recite for the wedding."

Instantly, a change came over Mrs. Price. Her face turned ashen. "Thank you for warning me, Annie." Though her voice was steady and calm, he could tell from the way she resumed twisting her well-wrung handkerchief that she was agitated.

"I thought you'd want to know," Mrs. Llewelyn said before hurrying up the stairs.

"Who's David Morys?" Evan asked when Mrs. Price continued to stand there, looking uncertain.

"The schoolmaster." She cast a nervous glance at the entrance to the inn, then turned toward the door. "I'm sorry, Mr. Newcome, but I must go."

"He must be a dreadful man to make you run off so quickly," Evan remarked as he followed behind her.

She stopped short and faced him with a forced smile. "He's not dreadful. Not exactly." She sucked in a heavy breath. "But if you'd be so good as not to tell him I was here, I'd appreciate it."

This grew more and more curious. "May I know why?"

Averting her gaze, she murmured, "It's a personal matter. You do understand."

Though he wanted to ask more, he didn't. This wasn't the time to alarm her with prying. Instead, he asked, "But you will let me accompany you to the wedding tomorrow, won't you?"

She swallowed. "Only if you want to. I wouldn't want to impose—"

"I'd be the one imposing on you. Please, do go with me."

A brief smile touched her lips. "If you wish, Mr. Newcome."

"Evan," he corrected.

"I-I beg your pardon?"

"Call me Evan. If we're to work together, there's no point in standing on formalities."

She looked a bit startled. "To work together?"

"Yes. You said you'd help me with my book." She'd never actually said she would, but he didn't intend to give her any chance to refuse.

After a slight hesitation, she nodded. "I'll do what I can, if that's what you really want."

"I do."

"Then good day, Mr. Newcome."

"Evan," he repeated.

"Oh, yes. Evan. And you must call me Catrin."

"Good day, Catrin," he said, but before she could get away, he caught her gloved hand and lifted it to his lips. Her fingers seemed small-boned and fragile within the white leather of her gloves, yet there was surprising strength in the fingers that curled around his. He brushed a kiss across the leather and wished that gloves were not all the fashion, for he wanted to press his lips to her bare skin. He wanted to very much.

When he released her hand, she stood there, the color rising in her cheeks. Then she mumbled, "Good day, Mr. . . . er . . . Evan," and left.

He went to the window and stared after her, wondering at the perverse impulse that had made him kiss her hand. No matter how much he told himself that she was not as innocent and sweet as she seemed to be—and as Mrs. Llewelyn obviously believed her to be—he couldn't help his absurd attraction to her. It had been a long time since such intense sexual hunger had run rampant through his body.

The whole time she'd been talking, he'd been wondering what it would be like to cover her mouth with his, to plunge his tongue between those wine red lips. How would she react? Would she slap him and tell him he was being too forward, as Henrietta had done the first time he'd kissed her? Or would she blush prettily and return his kiss?

Much as he wanted to find out, he mustn't try it. Despite her excuses for her behavior yesterday and despite the fact that she obviously *was* shy, she still hadn't sufficiently explained why she'd lied to him, then hurried to town to apologize afterward. And why would a "painfully shy" woman, as Mrs. Llewelyn had termed her, travel to London and meet with a strange man in a strange inn to acquire a chalice that hadn't seemed worth the two hundred pounds she'd offered for it? It didn't make sense at all.

The woman was hiding something, and he intended to find out what it was. And he mustn't let his attraction to her stand in the way.

Chapter Five

It's no secret except it be between two.
—Welsh proverb

Catrin's hand tingled as she left the inn. Beneath the too thin leather of her gloves, her hand tingled madly, and all because Evan Newcome had kissed it.

With a furtive glance about her, she flexed her fingers. At least they still worked. By heaven, if this was what happened after one brief encounter, how would she survive spending half the day with him tomorrow? What could Annie possibly have been thinking to suggest it?

But she knew what Annie had been thinking. Annie had been scheming to find Catrin a husband again. This time, Catrin wasn't entirely averse to the scheme, though she recognized it as futile. Mr. Newcome . . . Evan . . . couldn't possibly be interested in a quiet sparrow from the country, not when he was a great scholar and a distinguished gentleman.

He was a gentleman, wasn't he? He certainly dressed the part, and his position at Cambridge bespoke someone who had money and connections. Perhaps he was the second son of some noble. Yet she'd never heard of a nobleman in Carmarthen with a son named Evan. In any case, he must be of sufficient station to allow him the privilege of attending renowned universities. Though she might be of equal station, she certainly couldn't compare to the sophisticated, daring women with whom he probably socialized in Cambridge and London. No, Annie would have to look closer to hand for a husband for Catrin.

At least Annie wasn't trying to match her up with David. Silently, Catrin thanked Annie for her timely warning. Annie knew Catrin had been avoiding David. Annie wasn't overly fond of the handsome young schoolmaster, even though her daughter liked him well enough to have him recite verse for the wedding.

Annie no doubt sensed what Catrin had known for a long time, that despite David's poetic fervor and dashing air, he was cold as stone inside. There was something calculating about David that had made her shy from him the first time she'd met him. Over the past four years her impression of him hadn't altered a bit.

She couldn't go on avoiding him like this, however. One day she must deal with his interest in renewing his courtship of her. Unfortunately, when she rounded the corner by the inn and caught sight of him a mere ten feet away from her, she realized that the time had come, and much too soon. She barely suppressed a groan before he spotted her.

Instantly, his scowl changed to a reproachful smile as he hastened to her side. "I heard you'd returned. You've been back from London a week, haven't you?"

She ignored his implication that she should have come to see him sooner. "Yes, but you know how it is after one has been away, even for only a short time. All the servants are in a dither about this or that and there's a great deal to do."

"I wouldn't know." His scowl returned. "I don't have servants."

She bit her tongue to keep from commenting on David's obvious resentment of her moderate holdings. David was the second son of a squire in Merthyr Tydfil. He'd had the choice of becoming a merchant, a cleric, or a teacher. His dislike of "the vagaries of trade" and his hatred of the church had necessitated his becoming a teacher. He'd served as such in Merthyr Tydfil for a few years before he'd left there abruptly to come to Llanddeusant to be headmaster of the small school.

Although he wasn't brilliant and hadn't been as successful in his studies at Oxford as he'd hoped, his chosen profession nonetheless suited him. His position as headmaster afforded him a high status in the small community and provided him with a decent, though not extravagant living. It also enabled him to move among the gentry of the area and indulge his interest in Welsh poetry and antiquities.

Yet he seemed continually to feel it wasn't enough. Catrin

wondered, and not for the first time, if his sole reason for courting her was to acquire her estate through marriage.

Now he took her arm in a possessive gesture that she found disturbing. "In any case, I'm glad I've finally met up with you. We need to talk."

"I'd like to, David, but I really must get home. Mrs. Griffiths is waiting for me to go over the household accounts with her so she can send someone to the market and—"

"I've been waiting for you for four years, Catrin. Can't you spare me a moment?"

She sighed. He was right. She'd let this go on long enough, even if she'd done so unwittingly. "All right, then. Will you walk with me back to Plas Niwl?"

He nodded. Drawing her hand into the crook of his elbow, he fell into an easy pace up the road.

They drew stares as they passed two young women. David always drew the stares of Llanddeusant's women, both young and old, especially when he was with her. She was so . . . so unremarkable, while David was every woman's dream, with his sculpted features and the dramatic shock of dark hair he allowed to fall casually over his forehead. He had an orator's voice and read verse often at weddings and funerals. Most of the women thought him a gallant and poetic figure, the brooding artist, and he cultivated that image.

Today, however, he didn't seem to notice the women watching him, for his eyes were fixed on Catrin. The weight of his gaze and his silence worried her immensely. She hoped she'd guessed wrong about what he wanted to discuss.

She hadn't, however. He only waited until they were on the outskirts of Llanddeusant before he asked, "Did you get the chalice?"

Oh, what should she say? If she told him she'd acquired it at last, he'd renew his suit with a vengeance, and then she'd have to tell him she truly had no desire to marry him. Wouldn't a gentle lie be kinder than the harsh truth? If he thought she wouldn't marry him because of the curse, he might be able to stomach her refusal.

You lied to him before, remember? That's the coward's way out, her conscience told her.

Nonetheless, she was a coward, especially when it came to David. "I'm afraid I was unsuccessful."

His jaw tensed and he clenched his fists. "That wretched Englishman, Lord Mansfield, refused to sell it to you after all?"

His reaction made her glad she'd lied. How much more angry would he have been if she'd told him the truth? "He was willing to sell it, but it wasn't the right chalice. And you know it has to be the right one to break the curse."

He nodded and fell into a brooding silence that made her wish she'd never told him about the curse in the first place. David was the only person she'd ever told. But she hadn't meant to.

The first time he'd proposed to her, four years ago, she'd responded to his proposal with the same answer she'd given every other suitor—"Thank you for your offer, but I have no desire to remarry."

Unfortunately, David hadn't accepted her blanket statement, preferring to believe she was refusing him because of his lowly station. When he'd gone on and on about how he could understand why a mere schoolmaster wouldn't be a suitable spouse for a woman of her wealth and position, her soft heart had prompted her to soothe his wounded pride. She'd shown him the diary and told him about the curse and how she couldn't marry because of it.

He had seemed to accept that explanation, although he had insisted on taking the diary away for a few days to determine if it was authentic. She'd let him do that, because she'd wanted to know the same thing. And when he'd returned to pronounce mournfully that it was indeed more than two hundred years old, he had agreed that she dared not marry.

Four years had passed, during which time they'd been cordial to one another and lived their separate lives with equanimity. She'd assumed the subject of marriage was dead, especially since he actively courted other young women in the village.

Nonetheless, he'd never married any of them, which should have told her something. If she'd heeded that warning, she'd never have made the mistake of telling him that she'd located the chalice. But she'd wanted his opinion about whether he thought, from Lord Mansfield's description, that it could be genuine, since he knew a great deal about antiquities.

To her distress, the moment she'd told him of the chalice, he'd pointed out that if she regained it, they could marry. She'd been astonished to learn that he'd never relinquished his plan to marry her, that the other women he'd dallied with in the village had been nothing more than that—dalliances.

So now she found herself in the same position she'd been in four years ago. And once again, she couldn't bring herself to wound his pride. It was the only thing that kept her from blurting out the truth.

"Are you going to search elsewhere?" he clipped out.

She swallowed. "I have nowhere else to search. I think you should just accept that you and I were never destined to marry, David."

He stopped short, taking her by the shoulders. "You're wrong. I know you're wrong. Perhaps I could search for you. If you'd let me peruse the diary again and look at the family records—"

"No!" She forced her voice to be more even. "Listen to me. If I'd had any idea these past few years that you were still hoping for marriage between us, I would have quashed the idea at once. I knew there was only a slim possibility of locating the right chalice."

She sucked in a deep breath. This was so difficult. She hated confrontations, especially when they resulted in hurt feelings. But if she didn't discourage him now, she'd never persuade him to look elsewhere. "Now that I know you've persisted in these foolish hopes, I must insist that you stop. It's no use, David. I know you don't want to marry me badly enough to sign your own death warrant, and it's unfair of me to keep you waiting."

At her mention of the curse, he swallowed hard, his Adam's apple bobbing up and down. "What if I said I didn't believe in your blasted curse? What if I said I'd marry you in spite of it and take my chances?"

"Four generations of dead husbands," Catrin reminded him, feeling like an absolute wretch. "Can you really ignore that?"

He blanched, obviously affected by her words. One thing she knew for certain about David was that he had a superstitious bent. It went along with his love of poetry and antiquities. He didn't quite live in the real world, so it was easy for him to believe the world wasn't quite real.

Suddenly, his eyes darkened to chips of ebony. He clasped her about the waist and drew her near. "We don't have to marry." He bent his head until his mouth hovered inches from hers. "You're a widow. You have a right to your pleasures."

Her eyes went wide. Was he implying what she thought he was implying? By heaven, did he truly believe she'd do such a scandalous thing? After a lifetime of celibacy, was she to relinquish her virginity to the first man who touched her?

Now embarrassed that she'd encouraged him at all, she stammered, "I-I can't believe you'd suggest such a thing. . . . I'm not the kind of woman to . . . Please, just forget about me."

"I can't," he said brokenly. "I think of you all the time, Catrin. I think of your lovely, sky blue eyes and your raven hair. I think of the way your smile brightens a room and your lilting voice turns prose into sheer poetry."

His romantic language irritated her, and she couldn't help wondering how many other women he'd used such words with.

His voice dropped to a husky murmur. "I think of you all alone at Plas Niwl, and I can't stand it. I want to take care of you, to look after you."

And my holdings, she thought cynically. Now feeling much less remorse than before, she reminded him of the curse. "I don't want you to die. And I can't carry on a furtive liaison with you. Everyone in town already gossips about me. I refuse to add to their tales."

When she lifted her gaze to his, she flinched from the anger flickering in his eyes, but went on nonetheless. "Find someone else, David. And until you do, I think it best we keep our distance from each other."

"Oh, you do, do you?" His tone had turned ugly, and with a swiftness that surprised her, he clasped her about the waist and brought his mouth down on hers.

Shock held her speechless and motionless. David had never kissed her before. His first proposal had been very formal, made after only a month's acquaintance, and his second had so flustered her that she'd made some excuse for fleeing his presence and had avoided him ever since.

But now he was kissing her with alarming fervor. She turned her head, muttering, "No, David. Please don't—" but he merely clasped her chin and twisted it back, bringing his mouth more firmly down on hers.

Panic assailed her. She pressed against his chest, but he tightened his other hand on her waist, forcing her flush against him, making her all too aware of his arousal.

He thrust his tongue against her clenched teeth, and when she refused to open them, he tightened his fingers on her jaw, forcing her mouth open so he could push his tongue inside.

The very touch of his wet tongue inside her mouth made her gag. When he dropped his hand to clamp her against him, she succeeded in tearing her mouth away, but he merely began to kiss and suck her neck as he enfolded her so close that her arms were pinned between his.

She struggled, frightened by the surprising strength in his body. Oh, why had she let him walk so far with her? Why hadn't she discouraged him more ruthlessly?

When he slid his hand down to cup her rear, she kicked out at him, wincing when her walking shoes proved no match for his heavy boots. Still, she bucked against him in a panic, bringing her knee up in what she feared was a futile attempt to thrust him away.

Without warning, he cried out and fell back from her, bending over double. She didn't know what she'd done, but she didn't stay to find out. Lifting her skirts, she turned and ran down the road toward Plas Niwl as he released a string of foul curses behind her.

She was nearly out of hearing when she heard him call out, "I shan't relent, Catrin! Somehow I'll find a way around that curse of yours, and then you'll marry me! Whether you admit it or not, you and I were meant for each other!"

She covered her ears with her hands as she ran faster, praying that he didn't come after her. And all she could think was thank heaven she hadn't told him the truth about the chalice. Thank heaven.

The man sat inside the deserted cottage on an ancient wooden stool, scowling as he watched the path that led from the overgrown woods. A shiver racked him, and he cursed the damp chill of late evening. He should have built a fire, but he had not wanted anyone to notice smoke coming from the chimney.

Instead, he withdrew a flask of port and uncorked it, then took a swallow before replacing the cork. The sweet burn of port warmed him faintly, but certainly not enough.

If that fool David Morys does not have news for me today, the man told himself, *he shall be in trouble. Catrin Price has been back in Llanddeusant for several days now. He ought to know something.*

He had just begun to consider leaving when he saw the familiar lanky form emerge from the trees. He waited until the knock came at the door, then barked, "Come in!"

As soon as Morys had entered the sadly dilapidated room, the man turned toward him with his hands folded together. "So, Morys, you have come at last. You are late."

Morys avoided his gaze. "Yes, I know."

"I should not have had to summon you," the man said menacingly. "But I have been coming here every morning, looking for your message, and there has been nothing. It was risky sending a note to you at school, but you left me little choice."

"I-I was going to leave a message for you tonight. I swear it. You summoned me before I had the chance."

"Does that mean you have finally talked to the chit?"

There were faint lines about Morys's mouth, attesting to his distress at Catrin Price's obvious reluctance to see him. "Yes, I caught up to her today."

"What did she tell you about the chalice?" asked the man.

Morys hesitated, thrusting back his wayward shock of hair with the dramatic gesture the women of Llanddeusant found so enticing.

It did not entice the man he had come to meet, however. "Well?" the man asked with a sneer. He thought Morys a ridiculous character, a posturing fool. But Morys had his uses. "Does she have it?"

Morys shook his head.

"What do you mean?" the man prompted. "Of course she has it. That is what she went to London for, is it not?"

"She says Lord Mansfield's chalice wasn't the right one, so she didn't purchase it. She says she's given up the search."

The man frowned. "Perhaps she is lying to avoid refusing your offer of marriage. The chit is certainly the type to do something like that. She is woefully tenderhearted."

With a haughty lift of his chin Morys faced down his interrogator. "Have you known any woman to refuse me what I wanted . . . ever? Do you think it likely that a woman of Catrin's age, with an uncertain reputation and no prospects for a husband, would turn down an offer from me if she didn't have to?"

"A woman of Catrin's age? You mean, an attractive, wealthy widow who must beware fortune hunters at every turn? I think it is possible."

Despite her meek demeanor, Catrin was no fool, and could be suspicious at times. That was how she had evaded him in London. Somehow she had sensed him watching her. With a canny nature worthy of that grandmother of hers, she had fooled him by leaving the inn another way and changing her lodgings that very night. She had even eluded him on the ship. He had heard later that she had taken the coach instead. Now she was back in her stronghold, with servants everywhere, making it impossible for him to discover where she had hidden the chalice.

He noted the red flush that crept up Morys's neck to darken his cheeks. "It's not Catrin's money I'm interested in," Morys said sullenly.

"Oh? Are you telling me you would detest being a gentleman farmer, lording it over a substantial estate?" The man gave a harsh laugh. "If so, then you lie."

"You *would* look at it that way. You don't have an ounce of passion in your veins, old man, do you? That's why Father and his friends always called you Blackheart, because there's nothing beneath your ribs but a piece of hard coal."

The man smiled to hear his old nickname, which not by chance sounded a great deal like blackguard. "You are right about my heart, but your father called me Blackheart for another reason, because I would not forgive the debts he owed me. Or should I say, the debts he still owes me, for you know as well as I do that you would not have that position at the school if it were not for me."

Morys glanced away. "That's not true."

The man chuckled. "What? Do you think they would have hired you here if I had not taken care of the mess you got into at your previous position, when that . . . er . . . passion you regard so highly prompted you to impregnate a student?"

A stony silence was his answer.

"As I recall, you did not valiantly offer to make the girl your wife. In fact, I believe you were more than pleased when I arranged to have her blamed for some petty crime and then transported to Australia before she could betray you. So do not talk to me about black hearts," the man growled as he rose from the stool. "Yours is not exactly pristine, is it?"

"That's all behind me," Morys protested. "You may not believe this, but my desire to marry Catrin is pure. I love her. She's the only woman in this accursed town who has any appreciation for the fine arts."

"And the finer things in life, eh? She is also the only woman who *has* the finer things in life. And you covet them so badly you cannot even separate true feeling from greed."

"Think what you will." Morys tossed his head. "But I want Catrin—and everything that goes with her. I want her and I will have her."

"How? Without the chalice in her possession, she will never accept your suit."

Morys scowled and turned to pace the study. "Surely there's a way to counteract that blasted curse! If I could only get a peek at that diary again, perhaps I could find out where that chalice is and get it myself."

"You think so? I do not. Remember, I saw the diary, too, when she first told you of the curse and you offered to have the diary authenticated. *I* am the one who said it was genuine."

"I wish I'd never shown it to you," Morys muttered. "If I'd known you'd take such an interest in it, I'd never have involved you."

"I know. But you *have* involved me now. And I can help you. I can get Catrin for you, if you get me that chalice."

"What is your interest in the blasted thing anyway? Is it to keep her from remarrying? Because if it is, I won't let you have it. I *will* marry Catrin."

The man chuckled. "There are other ways to have a woman than marriage. If it is true you only want her for 'love' or rather, lust, then that is easy enough to arrange. Find the chalice, and I shall make certain you get what you want from Catrin . . . as well as the fortune you crave."

Morys seemed surprised by his offer. "Very well. I'll hold

you to that. But how can I get the chalice when she doesn't have it?"

"Stay close to the chit. Follow her moves for me. No matter what she said, she will not stop looking for that chalice. I am sure of it. A woman like her wants a husband, and without the chalice she cannot have one. She'll keep searching. And when she finds it, I want you to know about it."

Staring down at his dusty boots, Morys shifted from foot to foot. "It won't be easy to stay close to her. She says she can't bear to be around me, knowing how I feel, and that my pursuit of her is hopeless." He stiffened. "But that won't last. She'll come around. I know she will. I kissed her today, and she didn't resist until I went too far. She has some feeling for me. I'm sure of it."

The man rolled his eyes. Despite what Morys seemed to believe, it was clear Catrin Price didn't share Morys's passionate feelings, or she would have at least offered to make Morys her lover. Perhaps the girl had indeed lied to Morys about her acquisition of the chalice.

In any case, Morys would clearly not relinquish his pursuit of her, which was all to the good. There was plenty of time to wait until Morys uncovered more useful evidence—or until Catrin Price herself revealed whether she'd gained the chalice.

He could wait . . . for a time. But if Morys wasn't successful soon, then other tactics would have to be put into place. Because one way or another, he fully intended to have that chalice.

"I'd best go back now," Morys said. "It's getting dark, and since you won't let me carry a light when I come up here, that path is dangerous to tread at night."

"Listen to me, Morys," the man said as Morys turned toward the door. "I want to be kept better apprised of what occurs between you and Catrin from now on. I want regular reports. Leave them here for me."

Morys gave a weary sigh. "I don't understand all this subterfuge. Why can't I just go out to your estate and—"

"No!" the man exploded. "There must be no connection between you and me! I explained that to you when you first came to this town! I do not want to lose everything I have worked for if your past ever emerges and my part in covering it up is found out."

Half turning toward him, Morys shot him a shrewd glance. "No, I don't suppose that would do, would it, Blackheart?"

The man's eyes narrowed. "Do not use that threatening tone with me, Morys. The only way I would be found out is if you were found out. Then you would lose your comfortable position and any chance at snagging Catrin Price for a wife. So you will keep these meetings secret and do as you are told. I don't think your father will put up with any other mistakes on your part."

Morys's expression changed. For a moment the glint in his eyes was full of a surprising wrath. Then he smoothed his features into his usual haughty expression. "Whatever you say, sir."

That is much better, my boy, the man thought as he watched Morys stalk from the cottage. *Do not even consider taking me on. You wouldn't win. No one ever does.*

Chapter Six

Oversleep, wild feasting and excess of mead,
And unrestrained passion given its head—
Sweet things—but bitter in the Day of Dread.
—Anonymous, "On Christians, Mercy Will Fall"

As the wedding bells chimed at the ceremony's end and the couple rushed down the aisle with faces aglow, Catrin fought down a flood of memories. Five years ago, she, too, had left the chapel smiling, her husband on her arm as the bells pealed with wild joy. Little had she dreamed then that the bells weren't tolling her happy future but her husband's tragic death.

Though her grief had subsided to a dull ache over the years, today's celebration roused it again. It didn't help that Sir Huw Price, her late husband's father, was here, too. As usual, he ignored her, but she was all too aware of his presence in the small chapel, of the silent condemnation he emanated toward her.

He'd always blamed her for Willie's death. He'd been against the marriage from the beginning, for he'd hoped to find his only son a better match. When Willie had died so heedlessly, the light of Sir Huw's life had gone out. So he'd turned his anger and grief toward the only person he could blame. Her.

She even understood his irrational desire to blame her, especially since she already felt it was her fault because of the curse. But that didn't make his hatred any easier to stomach, especially on an occasion like this when she could have used his sympathy and support.

You mustn't dwell on it, she told herself as she rose from her seat. *There's nothing you can do about Sir Huw. Nor Willie's death either. It's time to put the past behind you and start anew.*

Evan, who'd sat beside her throughout the ceremony, now

stood and took her arm to lead her down the aisle behind everyone else, who hurried to follow the bride and groom out of the chapel. She flashed him a grateful smile, then turned to find David sitting in a pew at the back of the church, watching as she and Evan moved along. She felt his eyes on her, saw him scowl at the sight of her companion. Thrusting her chin out, she ignored him, even when he rose and stood with his eyes boring into her as she and Evan passed his row.

Put the past behind you and start anew, she reminded herself.

She wouldn't think about facing David later at the wedding feast or enduring her former father-in-law's dislike. Today she would enjoy herself, no matter what obstacles they put in her path. She would forget the past. She would eat and drink and dance—with Evan.

A blush stole over her face as she glanced up at the stalwart Welshman. He'd been attentive through every aspect of the wedding, murmuring a question or two when some tradition emerged with which he wasn't familiar. There'd been something so intimate about having him whisper in her ear, feeling his breath brush her hair.

It was insanity for her to think of him in this way. His presence here really had nothing to do with her, as he'd so matter-of-factly pointed out yesterday. Yet she couldn't help being attracted to him. Even David's assault yesterday hadn't dimmed the attraction, for she sensed that Evan was as different from David as Wales was from England. She couldn't believe Evan would ever treat her with David's callous disregard.

Evan seemed to sense her gaze on him, for he turned his head to smile down at her. "Did you enjoy the wedding? Sometimes you didn't look as if you did."

She managed a smile as they emerged from the church. "It was very lovely. I only hope you didn't find it too dull."

"Not at all. It's been some time since I've attended a wedding in Wales. I'd forgotten how colorful they are. English weddings are rather boring by contrast."

English weddings. Why, she still didn't even know if he was married, did she? Yet how could she ask without making him wonder at the question? She thought a moment, then said, "Do you go to many weddings?"

He released her arm and glanced around him as most of the people attending the wedding set off down the road toward The Red Dragon, where Tess's parents were hosting the wedding feast. "Not too many. Most of my friends are bachelors. University fellows aren't allowed to marry."

So he wasn't married. Then again, he was saying he couldn't marry. "Never?" she asked, trying to ignore her ridiculous dismay.

His voice was nonchalant. "Never. When a fellow decides to marry, he usually leaves the university to engage in some other sort of work. As you might imagine, we lose fellows to marriage all the time."

He sounded so casual about it that she wondered if he'd ever considered marrying. She started to ask him, but noticed that his gaze was now fixed on David, who stood a short way off.

"Tell me something," Evan said as he nodded to David, who ignored the friendly gesture. "Who is that man who's been glowering at me for the past hour?"

With a groan she tugged Evan's elbow until he fell into step with her behind the others who headed toward The Red Dragon. "That's David Morys."

Evan glanced down at her, one eyebrow raised as he settled her hand more firmly in the crook of his elbow. "So that's the man you were avoiding yesterday. After you left the inn, Mrs. Llewelyn told me he's something of a scholar. She even thought I might find him helpful in my research. She was planning to introduce us when he came, but he was late arriving, and I wanted to walk about the village, so I missed him. Is he as knowledgeable as she said?"

"Very knowledgeable," she said flatly, "although he knows more about poetry and Welsh antiquities than local superstitions."

Evan cast her a searching glance. "That doesn't explain why he's been scowling at me for the last hour as if I were the devil incarnate."

She sighed, unable to meet his eyes. "It's not you he's scowling at. It's me."

"I beg to differ. Although I'll admit he watches you almost constantly, it isn't with anger. He scowls only when he looks at me."

Evan Newcome was certainly perceptive, wasn't he? she

thought. Obviously, he would persist in this vein until she answered his question. "If you must know, I suppose he is . . . er . . . perturbed to see me with another man, no matter how innocuous the circumstance."

"Ah. He's a suitor of yours, I take it?"

"Yes, but I don't want to marry him. Unfortunately, he won't take no for an answer. That's why I've been avoiding him."

Evan's probing gaze was on her again, but she refused to meet it. A plague on David! Must he act as if she were his personal property and scowl at any man with whom she saw fit to keep company?

"Why don't you wish to marry Mr. Morys?" Evan asked. "He looks like a handsome enough chap, and if he's as learned as Mrs. Llewelyn claims, you ought to get along with him very well."

She stiffened. Oh, how to explain this embarrassing situation? It wouldn't be right to bias Evan against David, since David might indeed help him with his book. She said the only thing she could think of. "We aren't suited to be husband and wife. That's all."

"I see." Evan's voice had grown inexplicably hard. "I don't suppose a schoolmaster *is* an appropriate husband for a woman of your station."

Her gaze flew to his as first shock, then outrage, swelled in her chest. "No, that's not it at all. David's position has nothing to do with my refusal to marry him. If I loved him, I wouldn't care what his station in life was."

Evan searched her face a moment, then gave the faintest smile. "Then you're different from most women." He lowered his voice. "And I well understand why Morys pursues you."

Under his steady gaze Catrin colored, then glanced away. By heaven, he was as smooth-tongued as David. So why did his words have an entirely different effect on her? Why was it all he had to do was glance at her to make her heart's pace quicken?—and make her act like a complete fool?

A voice behind them fortunately saved her from further embarrassing herself. "Good morning, Mr. Newcome, Mrs. Price. Lovely wedding, wasn't it?"

They turned to find Sir Reynald strolling toward them. He

raised one eyebrow as he caught sight of their linked arms. "I see you two have finally met."

Belatedly, she remembered that Sir Reynald had been a witness to her shameful behavior two days ago. She ducked her head as she heard Mr. Newcome say, "Yes, Mrs. Price seems fully recovered from her illness. And by the way, Sir Reynald, you *were* mistaken about who that was on the path to Llyn y Fan Fach. As it turned out, it was only someone who resembled Mrs. Price."

Catrin lifted her face to Evan in pleased surprise. He gave her the faintest smile, and her heart lurched. How considerate of him to protect her from embarrassment.

Even if Sir Reynald *did* look skeptical.

"Quite a resemblance," the middle-aged knight murmured, but seemed content to say no more on the subject, so the three of them walked on together.

"I say, Mr. Newcome," Sir Reynald remarked conversationally when the silence grew long. "How do you find our quaint country weddings? Not quite like the ones in England, eh?"

"No. And not like other Welsh weddings I've seen either. I noticed that the bride and groom rode in a carriage both to and from the church. Don't they have horse-weddings around here? When I was growing up in Carmarthenshire, anyone who could afford it raced to the wedding on horseback, with the groom and his men pursuing the bride and her guardian. Sometimes they raced to the feast, too. As I recall, it made for an animated procession."

Bad memories flooded Catrin at once, reminding her that the past was not so dead to her as she might wish.

Sir Reynald cast her a glance before he said dismissively, "Oh, horse-weddings are much too dangerous. We do not have them in these parts."

"They don't seem so dangerous to me," Evan persisted. "It would be a shame to put an end to the colorful practice on the slim chance that someone might get hurt. Besides, young men need an outlet for their energies."

An outlet for their energies? she thought, the casual words tearing into her.

But Evan seemed oblivious to the tension building in her. "I can't imagine Mrs. Llewelyn worrying about such danger.

I must ask her why her daughter chose not to have a horse-wedding."

When she bit back a sob, Sir Reynald shot her a glance, then said quietly, "Tess Llewelyn chose not to have a horse-wedding because Mrs. Price's husband was killed after his wedding to Mrs. Price. During the mad dash from the church to Plas Niwl, where the wedding feast was to occur, his horse stepped into a hole and sent him flying into a rock. He hit his head and died shortly afterward." Sir Reynald ran his hand over his thinning hair. "Ever since that happened, couples here are reluctant to follow the tradition."

Catrin couldn't look at Evan, but heard the shock in his voice when he murmured, "Good God. And here I am talking about—I'm terribly sorry, Catrin. I wouldn't have mentioned it if . . . I mean, I had heard that your husband died in an accident, but I didn't know—"

"It's all right," she murmured, staring straight ahead at the road. "You couldn't have known."

Sir Reynald seemed perturbed by the entire exchange and murmured something about finding a friend of his before wandering away.

Evan covered her hand. "No wonder you were so quiet and solemn during the ceremony. It must have brought back terrible memories. I *am* sorry."

She squeezed his hand, grateful that he understood. "It's all right. I . . . I have learned to deal with the memories."

But that wasn't entirely true. At night sometimes, she couldn't sleep for seeing the relentless images of that horrible day. . . . Willie galloping at breakneck speed behind her . . . his face flushing as he struggled to gain on the horse ridden by her and the old friend of the family playing the role of guardian for her . . . the wind whipping her hair into her face as she leaned back to shout encouragement at Willie and laugh at his harried expression.

Many were the nights she replayed the awful scene in her mind . . . the horse going down . . . Willie hurtling headfirst against a rock . . . the sickening crack of his head as he'd hit. She'd screamed and grabbed the reins from her guardian, fighting to turn the horse around. But they'd returned to where the horse lay with its leg broken to find Willie lying motionless, blood streaming from his wound. She'd known then that he would die. She'd known it instantly, although it had taken him two days to slip from unconsciousness into eternal sleep.

She shivered now at the memory . . . and the cold guilt rushing into her heart. Poor Willie had never stood a chance. The curse had seen to that. Still, how could she have known? She hadn't even discovered the diary until a year after his death.

"How long has it been?" Evan asked, his voice gentle.

Catrin started. She'd been so lost in the past, she'd forgotten he was even there. "Five years," she managed to say. She couldn't look at him. She knew she'd see pity in his eyes. Although pity was better than the reproach she received from those villagers who thought she had somehow cast a spell on Willie that caused his death, it wasn't much better.

Fortunately, they'd finally reached the inn, giving her an excuse to change the subject. "Here we are," she said brightly. "I do hope you're prepared to eat a lot. Mrs. Llewelyn prides herself on her cookery and has probably been baking and roasting and boiling all manner of delicious things for the past two days."

She could feel him watching her with concern, but he merely said, "Probably," as he let her lead him to the entrance of the inn.

To her relief, he made no more mention of Willie's death as they waited to go through the formality of greeting the bride and groom at the door. And once they were inside, milling around with the other guests, she relaxed, grateful to drop the subject of her late husband.

A fiddler was already tuning up his red fiddle, while two harpists set up their harps. The tables that normally crowded the ground floor of the inn had been pushed against the walls to make a space for dancing, but were heavily laden with roast beef and goose, mutton, turnips, cabbage, and potatoes. True to form, Mrs. Llewelyn was dashing about, directing servants to add more food to the already groaning tables. And in one corner, as customary at Welsh weddings, the groom's father was recording each gift, mostly money or livestock, in a ledger that would be used to repay the gift obligation when it was the giver's turn to marry.

Catrin breathed in the warm air with a faint smile. At least the feast wouldn't bring back awful memories. Thanks to the accident, she and Willie had never made it to their wedding feast, so she had no memories of it, good or bad.

"Would you like something to drink?" Evan asked. "It appears that Mr. Llewelyn has already opened the taps."

Glancing over to where Mr. Llewelyn, a wiry, quiet man, was filling mugs of ale, she nodded. "That sounds wonderful. I'm parched."

The next half hour there was little conversation between them. In truth, Catrin was still a bit intimidated by Evan, and Evan seemed reluctant to speak himself. But there was no real need for them to talk, since everyone else was chattering as they wolfed down the food they'd waited through the long ceremony to eat. Some of the guests discussed the ceremony, recounting tales of their own weddings. Others teased the bride and groom mercilessly. All of them included Catrin and Evan in the merriment, which touched her to the core and reminded her that there were many in this town who ignored the vicious rumors about her and regarded her as a valued citizen.

Trying not to look as out-of-place as she always felt, Catrin sat primly on a chair near the center of the room while Evan stood at her side, balancing a plate full of food. She picked at her mutton and potatoes, too self-conscious to do more than that, but she noticed that Evan ate with lusty enjoyment, not at all as she'd imagined a scholar eating. No doubt it took a great deal of food to keep a man of his large build going, she told herself. Even scholars had to eat.

Still, it wasn't only his eating that marked him as different from the usual pedant. There was something about the way he responded to the bantering of the locals and the ease with which he ate standing up that made her think he seemed oddly at home with her fellow villagers. He had none of the fastidiousness she'd have expected. He didn't wrinkle his nose at the strong ale or complain about having to stand. Indeed, if it hadn't been for his fine clothing and the glint of intelligence in his dark eyes, she might have thought him just another laborer enjoying the festivities.

She remained silent while the men talked about farming and husbandry, but as usual she paid attention to what they said, for she often gleaned much helpful advice from listening to simple farmers. That was one advantage to her shyness. She'd discovered that one learned a great deal more when one wasn't talking.

Suddenly, she felt Evan's eyes on her. "Tell me about your estate," Evan said. "I thought I spotted sheep pastures on my way to Plas Niwl yesterday. You raise sheep?"

"Mrs. Price has some of the finest sheep this side of Black Mountain," one of the laborers put in as he wiped his mouth on the back of his sleeve. As if he, too, realized that Catrin hadn't been participating in the conversation, he turned to her and asked, "And how did you fare with the shearing this year?"

Evan's interested gaze unnerved her so much that she answered haltingly at first. But Evan joined the others in prodding her to talk, and before she knew it, she was talking with earnest animation about the shearing and wool prices and the feeding and care of sheep. Evan asked particularly knowledgeable questions, and she soon forgot he was a man she regarded with awe, a scholar of amazing reputation and enviable status among literary circles. Instead, he became just another honest, hard-working man . . . more like the farmers crowding into the room than like David, who stood at the far end, holding court with a bevy of females and looking down his nose at their uneducated male companions.

After she'd been talking a while with the farmers, one of them said, "Why, Mrs. Price, you know as much about the sheep as your old grandmother. 'Tis no wonder ye've been gathering a fine price for your wool these past two years."

The compliment meant far more to her than anything David had ever said about her hair and eyes and such. And when she heard Evan murmur his agreement that she was indeed knowledgeable, her face flushed with pleasure.

By the time the fiddler struck up a tune and the harpists fell in with his song in preparation for the dancing, Catrin had to forcibly remind herself that Evan Newcome wasn't another country Welshman, ready to dance a lively jig. No doubt he was accustomed to more sophisticated forms of entertainment.

She flashed him an apologetic smile. "It looks as if the dancing is about to begin, but I'm afraid there won't be a single minuet played here. Our dancing is rather untutored. I hope you don't mind."

He smiled as he set his plate aside and held out his hand.

"Not at all. I know a jig or two from my days in Carmarthen. I'm a bit rusty, of course, but I shall try not to tramp on anyone's feet."

Trying to hide her pleasure that he would be so willing to fit in, she stood and let him lead her into the crowd of would-be dancers.

Except for the dances she held at the end of the harvest for her tenants, she seldom had the opportunity to dance, and now she realized how much she'd missed it, especially when Evan proved to be far from rusty. Although she had to show him the steps for some of the dances, he quickly caught on to them. Before long, he was falling into step with everyone else, obviously enjoying himself as he linked arms in one dance and kicked up his heels in another.

After three dances she was aglow. For the first time in years, she felt part of the community, and the smiles of Evan and the farmers helped her ignore the scowls of David Morys and Sir Huw. Even when she had to stop for a moment to catch her breath, Catrin's spirits remained high.

Until Sir Huw appeared at her side, his perpetual frown beetling his aging skin. He clapped a hand on her shoulder, then bent down to mutter, "Why, if it isn't Mrs. Price, the merry widow."

Despite the stench of liquor on his breath that told her he was drunk, she tried not to panic. Her father-in-law had always intimidated her, but today of all days, it was worse, for she desperately wanted to avoid arguing with him in front of half the town. "G-good day, Sir Huw," she stammered. "I hope you're enjoying the feast."

"Not nearly as much as you seem to be," he said with a sneer, leaning heavily on her shoulder. "No one'd ever guess you buried a husband not too long ago."

Her hands began to tremble. "Five years ago," she reminded him. "It's been five years."

"I guess five years seems like a long time to be without a husband, eh, Catrin? But it's an even longer time to be without a son." His voice rose a fraction. "I suppose you think it's time for you to look elsewhere. I see you've already picked out a new man? Does he know what danger he's in? Does he know that keeping company with you can be dangerous to a man's health?"

Startled, she stared up at the glowering man. "What do

you mean?" He couldn't know about the curse. She had certainly never told him. Of course, David might have revealed it out of spite after what had happened yesterday.

"Come now, I'm not a fool." His voice rose more, and she winced when the people nearest them turned to listen. "I can see the pattern even if no one else can—your great-grandfather, your grandfather, your father." His black eyes smoldered. "And my Willie. All dead within a short time after marrying a Lady of the Mists. Think you I can't tell what all of you were after?"

"And what is that?" Anger was rapidly replacing her embarrassment.

"Filthy lucre. Each time the ladies marry, they gain wealth, and each time their husbands die, they have the freedom to spend it as they wish. You wanted my estate, didn't you? You married my Willie to gain his wealth. Then you killed him for it. And when I die, you'll have my estate, won't you? It was all his, and it will be yours. He made sure of that."

It would be hers. That much was true. Willie had been careful to have a new will drawn up before their wedding, but she'd never cared what he might leave her. "You know I don't want his money nor your estate," she protested with an edge of desperation to her voice. "I haven't asked you for a penny since he died, have I?"

He clasped her shoulders and leaned so close, his foul breath nearly stifled her. "Nay. You've been biding your time until *I* die. I'll be the next to have an accident, won't I? The next to fall off a horse and break my neck. You'll see to it."

Tears welled in her eyes, especially when she noticed the people around her drinking up the entire conversation. It was so unfair! At least Evan was too far away to hear Sir Huw's drunken accusations. "Even if I wished it—and I don't—I could no more cause your death than I could make the sun rise! I have no such power!"

She tried to wrench away from him, but he wouldn't release her. His face was contorted with an anger partly born of liquor and partly of a grief held too long in check. "When I took a wife after Willie's mother died three years ago, I thought I could sire another heir, but my wife is barren." He shook her roughly. The music had stopped, and now everyone could hear his loud, angry words. "Barren, do you hear? And who is making her barren? Who is keeping her from giving me another son if not you, with your druid spells and enchantments?"

"It isn't my fault," she whispered. "It isn't my fault."

Annie pushed her way through the crowd. "Here now, Sir Huw, what's this all about? Leave the girl alone. We're celebrating a wedding here, and I'd thank you not to spoil it by manhandling women and spouting nonsense."

She tried to draw him away from Catrin, but he shoved Annie aside with one hand, his other hand still gripping Catrin's shoulder as he snarled, "I'm not the one spoiling it, and it isn't nonsense. This . . . this evil woman shouldn't even be here. She's poison to all men, like her mother and her grandmother and her great-grandmother before her. She doesn't belong at a celebration like this."

He thrust Catrin against a wall. From the wild light in his eyes, she feared he might strike her. She'd already closed her eyes and held up her arm instinctively when suddenly his hand left her shoulder.

She opened her eyes to find that Evan had jerked Sir Huw around to face him. Evan's eyes glittered dangerously as he drew himself up to his full height. "Mrs. Llewelyn asked you to leave Mrs. Price alone. I'm not asking. I'm ordering you to leave her be, unless you want to find yourself tossed into the gutter outside."

Sir Huw flushed a dark red before holding up his fist. "Who do you think you are, sir, to threaten me? You stay out of this, or I swear I'll take you apart! This isn't your concern. Go back to your dancing, so we can finish our discussion."

Evan's gaze shot to her. "Do you wish to finish your discussion with this mannerless lout?"

Shamed to the very core by Sir Huw's public accusations, she couldn't speak, but only shook her head.

Evan turned back to Sir Huw, his fists clenched. "It appears that Mrs. Price considers your discussion over, so I suggest that you do as Mrs. Llewelyn asked and leave Mrs. Price alone."

When Sir Huw bristled and looked as if he would retort, Annie stepped in again, having fetched her husband and her new son-in-law. "Come along with me, Sir Huw." Though her tone was cajoling, it was clear she would have Sir Huw carried forcibly from the inn if he didn't behave. "You haven't had any of the roast goose in capers yet, have you? It's my special dish, and I'll be insulted if you don't sample it."

He hesitated a moment, looking from Evan to the scrappy little Mr. Llewelyn and then to the groom, a hulking farmer with hammy fists. Then his lips thinned into a harsh line, and he let Mrs. Llewelyn lead him away.

Catrin collapsed against the wall, unable to look at the staring, inquisitive eyes around her. A sudden dizziness assailed her, and her breath came in quick gasps as her stomach roiled.

Evan moved to her side at once. "Are you all right?"

"I . . . I think I may faint. I must get out of here," she whispered as she pushed away from the wall, then veered toward the side door leading from the inn into the garden. Evan caught her about the waist and led her through the door, closing it firmly behind them, cutting off the chorus of questions from the other guests who'd finally found their tongues enough to express their concern. With quick efficiency he led her to a wrought-iron chair, which she dropped into at once. White spots started to appear before her eyes as nausea assailed her.

"Put your head between your legs," he said tersely as he knelt beside her. "It will help."

Heedless of how unladylike the position might be, she did as he said. The dizziness and nausea did seem to lessen, although only a fraction.

"Breathe deeply," he urged.

He didn't have to tell her to do that. She was already sucking in great lungfuls of air. But she felt stupid and foolish in the bent-over position. She lifted her head and tried to sit up. Then her stomach lurched once more, forcing her to clap her hand over her mouth in fear that she'd disgrace herself further.

"Not yet," he murmured. "Give it a moment."

"I-I've never done this before," she stammered into the skirt of her gown. What a fool he must think her for acting this way! Oh, why was she such a coward? Grandmother would never have fainted in the face of Sir Huw's remarks. She would have cut him into pieces with her sharp tongue, then had him thrown bodily out the door. "I'm not the f-fainting sort, truly I'm n-not," she said, trying to convince herself as much as him.

"Don't worry about it." His voice was kind as he stroked her back with a surprisingly gentle hand. "Under the right circumstances, anyone is the 'fainting sort.' Besides, you scarcely ate anything at dinner and you've been dancing on an empty stomach in a crowded room."

She said nothing, but as she continued to breathe deeply and keep her head down, the fainting spell seemed to pass. Slowly, she became aware of the chill in the air, now that dusk was approaching, and the muffled sounds of revelry coming from inside the inn.

Then other things caught her attention . . . Evan's hand rubbing her back with soothing motions . . . his leg only inches from hers as he knelt on one knee at her side . . . his breath feathering her hair. It was more unnerving than her near faint.

Her awkward position was becoming uncomfortable. Fortunately, this time when she tried to sit up, he let her. Yet she was all too aware that he kept his hand on her back, his fingers still tracing circles on the silk of her gown while he regarded her with obvious concern.

Suddenly, his kindness was too much to bear, especially after the way he'd been forced to subject himself to Sir Huw's insults. Just thinking of it brought tears trickling down her cheek. "I'm so sorry I put you in such an abominable position."

"What position?" His tone was light. "This one? Kneeling at your feet? Personally, I find it far from abominable."

How could he joke about what had just happened? "N-no, I mean—"

"I know what you mean." The amusement faded from his voice. "Forgive my paltry jest, but I thought it might cheer you."

She couldn't look at him for fear of seeing something awful in his eyes. Though he was being more than kind, he must have heard what Sir Huw had said, all those terrible accusations. "I can only imagine what you must think—"

He touched his finger to her lips. "I think you're a woman unfairly maligned and little understood."

His words only made her feel worse. After all, some of

what Sir Huw had said was true. Once she'd accepted that the curse on her family was real, she'd been forced to admit that Willie's death had indeed been partly her fault, since she was the one accursed. The overwhelming load of her guilt made her choke out, "How can you say that when you don't even know me?"

When another tear trickled down her cheek, he rubbed it away with his thumb. But he didn't draw his hand back. Slowly, he traced the rise of her cheek, following the apple curve around, then stroking along the side of her face to her jaw, until his thumb came to rest beneath her chin. "You're right." His voice was low and husky. "I don't know you well at all. But perhaps it's time I remedied that."

She raised her eyes to his, her mouth going dry as she saw the way he looked at her. He wore an intent expression, his gaze trained on her as if somehow he could fathom the depths of her soul just by staring.

Suddenly, she was aware of how close he was, how intimate his thumb beneath her chin felt, how utterly vibrant and rich his eyes seemed in the dying light. He was scarcely an inch away from her, close enough for her to feel his warm, quickening breath on her face.

"Yes, it's definitely time we became better acquainted," he murmured only a second before he leaned forward the scant distance it took to touch his lips to hers.

Her first thought was that his kiss bore no resemblance at all to David's. It was light and undemanding, the merest whisper of a caress against her lips. She didn't know what instinct made her close her eyes or what urge made her sway toward him, but she did both. For a moment, they were frozen like that, only their mouths touching as their breaths mingled.

Then he drew back ever so slightly. His eyes registered surprise, before something more ancient and instinctual flickered in them. "So sweet," he whispered, "but it's not enough. I need more."

The plain, direct statement affected her like none of David's flowery phrases ever had. So when he clasped her chin and his mouth covered hers in earnest, she melted.

She scarcely noticed the taste of mulled wine on his breath or the rasp of his whiskery cheek against hers, for there was too much heady pleasure in the way he kissed her, with the authority of a man who knew exactly what he wanted and how to obtain it.

His hand now stroked her neck, his thumb trailing along her madly beating pulse as his lips rubbed hers apart so he could plunge his tongue deep into her mouth in a bold caress of terrifying intimacy. There was none of David's ruthless disregard for her in it, and yet Evan's kiss was hungry, even voracious . . . a raw, real thing. He devoured her mouth with shameless satisfaction, driving into it with long, hard strokes that seemed to say "I know what dark urges you have in the night. I can fulfill them. I want to fulfill them."

It ought to frighten her to the depths of her soul. Instead, it made her want to answer it with a kiss equally bold, to offer herself to him like a sacrifice to the ancient druidic gods.

He drove right out of her mind the memory of any other man who'd ever kissed her. It was as if it were the first time, the only time a man had touched her, for the pleasure of it was too intense for words. A silky heat rose from her belly to warm her throughout, to fire her hunger until it was a deep, aching pulse in her loins.

As he cradled her neck in his hand and ravaged her mouth over and over, she abandoned herself to that hunger, planting her hands on his broad shoulders and leaning into him to get more of the sustenance his wild kiss offered.

The next thing she knew, he was sitting on the ground and had pulled her off the chair into his lap. His arousal pressed into her bottom, but instead of rousing her panic, as David's arousal had, it made her blood run even hotter. The dusky evening was sweet and secret, the air filled with the summer scents of flowers, and she wanted to go on kissing him forever.

He seemed to want that, too, for his kisses grew more heated, more fervent. Nor was he satisfied with only kissing her mouth. A groan erupted from his throat as he rained kisses on her temples . . . her cheeks . . . her neck. Then he returned to plundering her mouth, stabbing deeply with his tongue until he'd reduced her to a puddle in his arms.

Only then did he tear his mouth from hers and stare down into her half-closed eyes. "Good God, you're enchanting." He caressed her face, then buried his fingers in her unruly curls. "I was right at the lake when I thought you weren't real. You can't possibly be real."

"Oh, but I am," she whispered. Without thinking, she took his hand and laid it on her heart. "You see? My heart beats like everyone else's."

Suddenly, she realized that she'd actually placed his hand on her chest. He realized it, too, for his eyes darkened to an oak brown. Never taking his gaze from her, he slid his hand down to cup her breast through her gown. At her startled, shocked look, he caught her mouth again with his.

She forgot that they were seated on the ground just a few feet away from a houseful of people. She forgot that it wasn't yet dark, and that anyone who came into the garden would see her nestled in Evan's lap. All she knew was that his kiss was the most glorious thing she'd ever tasted. And when he kneaded her breast with his palm until the nipple hardened into a tight, aching kernel beneath her silk bodice, she leaned into him with a sigh of complete satisfaction.

So engrossed was she in the wild, new sensations coursing through her body that she didn't at first register the sound of the outer door to the inn opening. But she couldn't miss the sharp intake of breath or the angry slam of the door.

And she didn't need the hissed words, "Unhand my fiancée, you bastard!" to know that the one person she hadn't wanted to deal with tonight had chosen this inopportune moment to seek her out.

David.

Chapter Seven

Who under my ribs put pain,
Girl I've long loved in vain. . . .
. . . she shall not keep with key
My love's due locked from me.
—Robin Ddu, "Invitation to Morfudd"

Evan moaned as Catrin scrambled out of his lap. It took a moment for him to clear his head. Kissing and caressing Catrin had driven all thought of where he was from his mind.

But as his wits returned, he recognized the man standing in the door. David Morys. The man had called Catrin his fiancée. But hadn't Catrin said she'd refused to marry him?

Evan looked to Catrin, but her eyes were riveted on David. "I'm not your fiancée, and you know it!"

Morys recoiled as if he'd been slapped. "Yes, but you *should* be! I won't stand by and watch some blasted nabob take advantage of you!"

Shifting his wary gaze back and forth between Morys and Catrin, Evan got to his feet, praying that the faint light would mask his heavy arousal. *Blasted nabob?* Well, the last thing this "blasted nabob" needed right now was a jealous suitor on his back. Clearly, Morys was confused about Catrin's betrothal status, and Evan didn't like being caught in the middle of it, even if the woman involved *had* just been firing his blood to unbearable heights.

That same woman was now thoroughly angry, although fortunately not at him. Her voice grew acid. "The man you're insulting is Evan Newcome. You've heard of Mr. Newcome, haven't you? The scholar from Oxford who wrote *The Development of Celtic Languages*?"

As Morys's face registered first fury and then resentment, Evan groaned. Why must Catrin throw Evan's credentials at the man? Weren't matters bad enough?

"He's here researching a book on folktales," Catrin added, "and he's asked me to help him with it."

Morys's embittered gaze shot to Evan. "Why would a scholar of your vast reputation ask for the help of a woman who's written only a few measly articles for small journals?"

When Catrin flinched, anger surged up in Evan. Hadn't the woman endured enough for one night? First she'd suffered through a wedding that had probably brought back terrible memories, then she'd been subjected to Evan's own unfeeling remarks, and finally she'd been badgered by a half-drunk idiot who thought she was a sorceress.

Now this. Deuce take them all, they were a lot of cruel fools.

He stepped between Morys and Catrin, his eyes cold. When he wanted, he could put on a superior air that would have cowed even his father. Justin had always called it his "Lord Newcome" air, and now he laced his voice with all the contempt the pose required. "I'd heard you were an intelligent man, Morys. But apparently you haven't recognized Mrs. Price's talent. She has an uncanny gift for description, and her ability to retell a legend in an interesting way is truly astounding. I'm only surprised I'm the first to seek her expertise."

Morys's hands balled into fists. "Really? Is that what you were doing out here with her in your lap? Seeking Catrin's expertise?"

"That's not your concern," Evan bit out. "Mrs. Price has made that perfectly clear, I think."

Ignoring Evan, Morys turned to look at Catrin. "My God, don't you see what he's after? I know his kind, always looking for a quick tumble from a country girl who doesn't have the sense to know she's merely a night's entertainment!"

Evan's temper was rapidly rising, and it took a massive effort to contain it. He didn't at all like being cast in the role of heartless seducer from the city. "Listen here, Morys—"

"*You* listen, you blasted London nabob!" The vitriol in Morys's gaze could have poisoned a hundred men. "I'll not have you mauling my Catrin—"

"I'm not *your* Catrin!" she shouted behind Evan. "You have no claim on me!"

"Only because of the curse!" Morys shouted back. "You said if it weren't for the curse, you'd marry me!"

The curse? Evan turned to look at Catrin. What the deuce was the man talking about?

Catrin wouldn't meet his eyes or Morys's. She shifted from foot to foot. "I didn't exactly say that. If you'll recall, I told you we weren't suited."

"Because of the curse," Morys insisted. "That's what you said."

"What curse?" Evan interjected.

A superior expression crossed Morys's face. Then he glanced at Catrin. "You haven't told *him*, have you? Is that because you know he's only interested in you for a quick tumble? You know he'd never marry you." Then his expression turned to one of alarm. "Unless you lied to me about the curse. Unless you invented the whole thing."

"I didn't—" Catrin began.

"Are you planning to make him your lover?" A muscle worked in Morys's jaw. "You kissed me, too, only yesterday. But you wouldn't make *me* your lover. You said you were worried about your reputation. What happened? What made you suddenly willing to play the whore for a blasted scholar?"

As shame slashed over Catrin's face, Evan's control over his temper snapped. In seconds he'd lifted David Morys by the collar and thrust him against the wall of the inn. "How dare you call the lady a whore! Apologize! Now! Or I swear I'll tear out your tongue!"

Morys pushed at Evan's unrelenting shoulders, but the schoolmaster's slender body was no match for Evan's farm-boy physique. "Let me down, you fool!" Morys growled, twisting his torso in a futile attempt to get away.

Evan applied pressure to the man's throat. "Not until you apologize!"

Then he felt Catrin's hand on his back. "Please, Evan, put him down and let's just go!"

Evan hesitated.

"Please," Catrin whispered as she dug her fingers into his coat, "It would pain me to see anyone hurt."

Those words brought Evan to his senses. She *had* suffered a great deal this evening, and he couldn't let her suffer more. Watching two men fight over her wouldn't make her feel better.

Evan sucked in breath after breath, fighting for mastery

over his volatile emotions. With some difficulty he put out of his mind Morys's inflammatory words and obvious snobbery, focusing instead on Catrin's small hand tugging at him.

Slowly, he lowered Morys to the ground, then released him and stepped back, breathing hard as he struggled to keep his temper. "You're lucky Mrs. Price has a kind heart, for I would have enjoyed giving you a thrashing."

"Let's go," Catrin said, pulling on his arm.

He turned toward her, so he didn't see the fist come sailing at him until it landed on the side of his jaw. Instantly, all his control snapped. In a rage he whirled on David Morys. "You bastard!" he barely had time to choke out, before Morys launched himself at him.

Morys's weight sent them both plummeting to the ground. Evan's mind registered Catrin's horrified scream, but his body reacted swiftly to Morys's attack. Although Morys was on top of him, his face contorted as he sent another fist toward Evan's jaw, Evan blocked the punch easily, using Morys's momentum to twist the man under him.

Then the fight began in earnest. To Morys's credit the schoolmaster proved to be quite a fighter, his slender frame masking a lithe strength that enabled him to fend off some of Evan's blows and get in a few of his own as they rolled over and over on the ground.

But no one was a match for Evan when he was angry. And at the moment he was furious. He hated men who insulted women or tried to bully them. He hated being punched when he wasn't looking. Worse, he hated knowing that Morys had kissed Catrin only yesterday. And the fact that he hated it infuriated him most of all.

As the rage swelled behind his eyes, he took it out on the schoolmaster, pummeling the man's body over and over. After a few moments Morys no longer hit back, but lay curled into a ball on the ground, groaning as he tried to avoid the punishing blows.

"Stop it!" Catrin screamed, but Evan went on driving his fist into Morys's side.

"Stop it!" she repeated, pulling at Evan's arm as he brought it back for another punch. "That's enough!"

When Evan hesitated a fraction of a second, she sank to the ground where he was kneeling and hung on his arm with all her strength. "Please stop! Please! Can't you see you've beaten him?"

The anguish in her voice reached Evan somewhere in the red haze of his anger, making him aware of where he was and what he was doing. He dropped his fists slowly to his sides, puffing heavily. As he surveyed the schoolmaster, he realized Catrin was right. He'd thrashed Morys thoroughly. The man was coughing, clutching his head as if to protect it from any more blows, and any sign of resistance had disappeared.

The rest of Evan's anger drained from him in an instant. Good God, what had he done? While the man had certainly deserved a beating, he hadn't deserved to be throttled within an inch of his life.

As always happened after Evan's temper had gotten the best of him, shame stole over his body, infecting his thoughts and making his stomach lurch. For a moment he'd been uncontrollable. If Catrin hadn't been there to stop him . . .

Morys had realized that Evan was no longer striking him, and now rolled to his side, still coughing. Evan scanned him, hoping none of the man's bones were broken. But though the schoolmaster appeared soundly whipped, it didn't look as if he'd suffered any permanent damage.

"We must go," Catrin whispered, tugging on his arm. "We must leave him with his pride at least."

Evan couldn't fault her logic. He knew too well how mortifying it was to face someone . . . anyone . . . after being beaten within an inch of your life. Facing the one who'd administered the beating was even worse.

Slowly, he stood, then dusted off his trousers. Something cold and wet trickled down the side of his chin, and he wiped it away. Blood. From somewhere. And he couldn't see very well out of his right eye, which meant the flesh around it was probably swelling from another punch Morys had given him. Good God, he was a mess, wasn't he?

Catrin touched her hand to his mouth. "Your lip's bleeding," she said, alarm in her voice.

"Only a little." He wiped away more blood and prayed she wouldn't pass out again. His former fiancée would have done so at the sight of even a drop of blood, and Catrin was more timid than Henrietta had been.

But Catrin surprised him. Though her face was ashen, she drew out her handkerchief and wiped his lip with a tenderness that made his breath catch in his throat. Then she touched the swelling above his eye. When he winced, she murmured, "You need tending."

He certainly did. He could use a compress for the swelling. Pray heaven he hadn't cracked a rib or two. He didn't think so, judging from the lack of pain when he breathed. He knew exactly how a broken rib felt, having had one when he was eleven after one of his father's particularly brutal beatings. This felt different.

But his leg hurt him, for when Morys had hurtled himself at Evan and they'd gone crashing to the ground, Evan had cracked the side of his knee on a rock.

"Come with me," she said. "I'll see that you're taken care of. You probably won't believe this, but I know a little about doctoring." She added softly, "I made sure I learned something about it after Willie's death."

He let her lead him away, trying not to show the pain that each step sent shooting up his right thigh. But when it became apparent she wasn't returning inside, he asked, "Where are we going?"

"To my estate."

He stopped short. That was the last thing he needed tonight . . . more time spent with sweet little Catrin. Despite everything that had just occurred, he still wanted her. Very badly. And acting on it wouldn't be wise at all.

He tried to drag his arm from her, but she wouldn't let go. "You don't want to return to the feast looking like that, do you?" she said. "It'll ruin Tess's celebration. And since going through there is the only way to reach your room upstairs, you don't have much choice. It's either go home with me and get your scrapes and bruises tended to or walk the streets of Llanddeusant until the celebration is over, which may be hours from now."

He hated to admit it, but she had a point. And going home with her was wise for other reasons. It might give him a chance to search the place for the chalice or the letter. It would also enable him to find out more about her and why that drunken man at the reception had accosted her. That is, if he could keep his hands off her long enough to ask the questions.

Nonetheless, it irritated him to skulk away from the scene of the fight like a criminal. "What about him?" He jerked his head toward Morys, who'd managed to sit up, though the effort had given rise to a fresh set of moans. "Don't you want to take care of his bruises and scrapes, too?" *After all, yesterday you were kissing him,* came the jealous thought.

How was it that the mere thought of her kissing Morys made him see red all over again? What had she done to him?

She didn't seem to notice the jealous edge in his voice. "I'll go inside and tell Annie about David. She'll make certain he's taken care of without creating a fuss." She nodded toward the alley that led along the outside of the inn. "You'll find my carriage out front. Bos insisted that I bring the carriage, since it would be dark on the road by the time everything was over. Sir Reynald, Sir Huw, and I are probably the only ones who brought carriages, so you shouldn't have any trouble finding it. Mine's the one without a coachman. John's inside with everyone else, celebrating."

When Evan merely stood there staring at her, she gave him a push and murmured, "Go on now. I'll be there in a moment."

She didn't stay to watch as he limped down the alley. Instead, she disappeared into the inn, leaving him to stumble toward the front of the building alone. As she'd said, her carriage was easy to spot, for the other two carriages held sleeping coachmen, and hers was empty, the horses tethered to a tree.

As he headed for the carriage, favoring his right leg, he couldn't help smiling. Only Catrin would let her coachman join the celebration instead of making the man wait outside alone as Sir Huw and Sir Reynald had done with their drivers.

With some difficulty he hoisted himself inside, then settled himself into a seat that was barely wide enough to accommodate his large frame. He propped his leg on the seat opposite him, wincing at the pain that shot through it.

Then he waited, unable to blot from his mind what had just happened. Had he really kissed her, despite all his warnings to himself? Oh, yes, he had. He still had the taste of her in his mouth, the warm, sweet taste of her. Her skin had been soft as rose petals, pure pleasure to kiss, and her thick, black curls had twined about his fingers like satin ribbons.

Was the skin—and hair—in other, more secret places of her body as soft and lush? Would he ever know?

Deuce take it, he thought as he grew hard again. Had he lost his mind? He couldn't think of her without wanting to bed her, just as he'd been unable to resist kissing her when she'd begun to cry.

A woman's tears had always affected him profoundly, ever since he'd been forced as a child to watch his mother sob after her beatings. Now that he was grown, whenever a woman cried, he had this almost painful urge to make the tears go away. But he didn't usually do it by kissing her senseless. Then again, no one like Catrin, with her soft, hesitant smile and her imploring eyes, had ever burst into tears in front of him.

Just thinking of her utter mortification after that drunken bastard in the inn had made his disparaging remarks roused Evan's protective instincts all over again. He could hardly belive what he was feeling for a woman whom he suspected of treachery. Yet no matter how much he told himself she'd acted suspiciously the night of Justin's death, he couldn't reconcile the scheming woman he'd expected with the shy, endearing one he'd kissed. How could she have had anything at all to do with the murder? She couldn't have. He couldn't believe it.

Then the carriage opened, and Catrin climbed in. She took the seat opposite him as the coachman mounted to the perch. He surveyed her face, wondering if she'd had to suffer any further embarrassment inside the inn. But if she had, she kept it well hidden, for she wore no expression at all as she thumped on the ceiling to signify that they were ready to set off.

When they were moving, she lit one of the lanterns inside the carriage and glanced at his propped-up leg. "Did you hurt it, too?" she asked in a voice laced with concern.

"I'm not sure. I knocked my knee on one of those boulders in the garden. It may only be bruised. Or I might have fractured it."

A stricken expression crossed her face. "Oh, I hope not. This is awful, truly awful! And it's all my fault!"

He cast her a wry smile. "I think Morys had something to do with it, too."

"Yes, but he would never have come at you that way if he

hadn't seen us . . . if we hadn't been—" She broke off, dropping her eyes from his. "It was wonderful of you to defend me like that when he was so abominable. And I do appreciate the lie you told him."

"Lie?"

"All that nonsense about my essays and how wonderful they were. I know it wasn't true, but it sounded lovely."

"How do you know it isn't true?"

She looked up. "Because you told me you only came here out of curiosity after what the Vaughans said about me."

"Yes, but I *have* read one of your essays, if you'll recall. And I found it to be exactly what I told Morys." Actually, he remembered very little about it, but it would take a trained torturer to wrench that confession out of him when his one invented remark had meant so much to her.

He hated the way she seemed to hold him in such awe. It made him feel like an impostor. He was surprised she hadn't guessed the truth about him after the way he'd laid into Morys like a common laborer. But if she ever did learn of his poor upbringing, she wouldn't be looking at him as she was now . . . with shining eyes and a smile that stopped his breath. No woman had ever looked at him like that before. Not a single one.

"It's all right," she murmured. "You don't have to pretend you know about my essays. I know you only sought me out because . . . well, you had me confused with Grandmother, whom you wanted to study, so to speak. Grandmother was a fascinating woman, so I can see why you would have been interested in her. I'm only sorry you had to be stuck with me instead."

Her gaze locked with his, and something twisted in his gut. Something very akin to guilt. "I want to study *you,*" he said. "And I find you every bit as fascinating as your grandmother may or may not have been. I don't regret being stuck with you, as you put it. Not for a moment."

"But so far I've ruined every moment of your stay."

"No, you haven't."

"I shouldn't have come with you tonight," she went on as if she hadn't heard him. "I should have known David would act foolishly when he saw me with someone else."

David. The jealous words were out before he could stop

them. "Especially when you were kissing him only yesterday."

A blush spread over her cheeks.

"I thought you told me earlier that you'd refused his offer of marriage."

"I did."

"Then why did you kiss him?"

"I didn't kiss him. He kissed me. There's a vast difference. I . . . I tried to make him stop, but he—"

"You mean the bastard forced himself on you?" Evan sat up straighter in his seat. "Now I wish I hadn't stopped beating him."

She shook her head. "Don't say that. It would have done no good. It would have only made him angrier than he already is. He can't seem to understand that I can't marry a man I don't love."

"That's why you refused his suit? Because you don't love him?" Evan asked, remembering what Morys had said.

"Of course."

"But I thought you refused it because of some curse."

Alarm lit her eyes. "Some curse?"

"Yes. The curse Morys kept blathering about. The reason he claims you refused to marry him."

She turned her face to stare out the window, saying nothing.

"Tell me about the curse, Catrin," he said. "Was it something you made up to get rid of Morys?"

"Not exactly."

When she offered nothing further, he frowned. She clearly didn't want to talk about it. But he bloody well had a right to know what insane story she'd told Morys to get the man so angry over Evan's involvement with her.

"Is there a curse?" Evan persisted. "I'd like to know what Morys was spouting off about before he knocked me to the ground for kissing you. I think I have a right to know."

She was silent a long time. When she spoke again, her voice quavered. "If I tell you, you'll think me mad."

"Perhaps. I'm already beginning to think you're a dangerous person to be around." He didn't know why he'd admitted that, but he was curious to see how she'd react.

When she spoke, her voice was laced with hurt. "You sound just like my father-in-law."

He stared at her in confusion. "Your father-in-law?"

"Sir Huw. The man who was shouting at me inside the inn. Willie's father."

Evan crossed his arms over his chest. This was getting interesting. He remembered Mrs. Llewelyn's mentioning something about her late husband's father. "Sir Huw was the man who said you were poison?"

She sighed, turning to stare at him. "Yes. How much did you hear of what he said?"

"Not much. I didn't notice him badgering you until the music stopped and he shouted something about your making his wife barren."

"It's not true, you know—all that about my casting a spell on her to make her barren."

"I didn't think it was." Remembering all the things Mrs. Llewelyn had told him about the rumors concerning Catrin, he added gently, "I don't believe in things like spells and curses, and I certainly don't believe you put a curse on Sir Huw's wife to make her barren or cast a spell that sent your husband to his grave. Is that the curse Morys was referring to?"

"Sort of, but—" She broke off, her eyes going wide. "How did you know that Sir Huw thinks I cast a spell on my husband if you heard only the part of the conversation after he accused me of making his wife barren?"

Deuce take it. That was a slip. He hadn't meant to let on that he'd heard things about her from Mrs. Llewelyn. Oh, well. The damage was done now. "Mrs. Llewelyn and I had a chat about you. She told me that Sir Huw, as well as others, thinks that . . . well . . ."

"That I put some enchantment on Willie." She sounded wounded. "Yes, I know what they think, but I didn't expect Annie to pass on such gossip."

"She wanted to set me straight before I heard the nonsense from anyone else. But she made it perfectly clear that it was all balderdash."

"Did she?" Her voice grew tight as she turned her head to stare out the window again. "Did Annie tell you I'm not the first woman in my family to be accused of such 'balderdash'? Did she tell you I'm descended from a long line of women who've all sent their husbands to early graves?"

How many was "a long line"? he wondered. "No, of

course not. She merely said you'd had a great deal of tragedy in your life."

She sucked in her breath. "Tragedy. Oh, yes, I suppose Annie looks at it that way. Everyone else, however, believes that the Ladies of the Mists marry their husbands for their wealth, then send them to their dooms with a spell or two."

"They're just superstitious fools, Catrin," Evan said, a hint of irritation in his tone. "You shouldn't take their words to heart."

"Oh, but I do." Her gaze shot to his. "You asked about the curse. Well, Sir Huw wasn't entirely wrong when he said we are poison. The female line of my family is cursed. It has been cursed for some time now, which is why all the husbands die young and their sons, when they have any, bear no heirs."

He stared at her, astounded that she could believe in such things. She'd struck him as an intelligent woman. Shy, but intelligent. Then again, a woman who chronicled folk superstitions was bound to be influenced by them. And somehow she'd persuaded Morys to believe in them, too.

"Cursed?" He couldn't help the indulgent smile that crossed his face. "Surely you don't believe that."

Her lips tightened. "I do, I'm afraid. I know it sounds ridiculous to a man with your education. I don't consider myself a credulous person either. Although I enjoy collecting folktales, my interest in them has always been academic. But even the wildest of tales has a grain of truth to it. And sometimes things happen that cannot be explained by educated minds. Sometimes the evidence of supernatural events is incontrovertible."

"What evidence?"

She tilted her chin up. "Did you hear the last thing Sir Huw said, about my mother and my grandmother and my great-grandmother being poison?"

"Yes, but—"

"You know why he said it? Because their husbands all died within three years of marrying them. My mother died along with my father, but in every other case, the women outlived their husbands by many, many years. As I am doing now."

Despite his avowed disbelief, a chill shook him. "Four

men? One after the other? Good God, that is a strange coincidence. How did they die?"

"It hardly matters, but if you must know, my great-grandfather died at sea, my grandfather was accidentally shot while on a hunting trip with a fellow squire, and my parents' carriage went over a cliff. And you know about Willie." She straightened her shoulders. "All of their deaths were accidental, and all of the men, except my father, left behind wealthy widows. A few had sons to inherit, but since the sons never produced any children, the men always left Plas Niwl to their daughters rather than entail it to a distant relative. Though all the wives inherited lands from their husbands, they preferred to remain at their own family estate. As did I."

He shook his head. "That's a fantastic story. And you truly believe those men died because of some curse?"

She stiffened at his faintly condescending tone. "I *know* they did. I found the curse written down in a diary. I'll admit that at first I was skeptical, but after looking at the family history and seeing how well it fit, I had to accept its veracity."

"You're saying that just because some diary claimed that your family is accursed and the family history seems to support it, you believe it? That's not evidence. Besides, why did it only start after four generations? What about the previous generations?"

She flashed him a defensive look. "It was only four generations ago that the female descendants stopped drinking from—"

She stopped short, and he went very still. He knew instantly what they'd stopped drinking from. A chalice. A druidic chalice.

"Drinking from what?" he prompted.

Turning pale, she glanced out the window. "Oh, look. We're here. Come. Let's get your leg tended to, shall we?"

When her words were accompanied by the jarring halt of the carriage, he gritted his teeth. He knew he couldn't keep her in the carriage, but he wasn't through with her yet. There was no way he was leaving here tonight until he got her to talk about the chalice.

But ten minutes later, as he sat in an uncomfortable wooden chair in the kitchen while Catrin, Bos, and a housekeeper named Mrs. Griffiths hovered over him, he wondered how he was supposed to get Catrin alone again to question her.

"We need to have a look at his leg," Catrin said as she put a cold compress on his eye. "He's not sure if it's broken or bruised or what."

"Then you will have to ask the gentleman to remove his breeches, madam," said Bos, his lips primly drawn.

Catrin went crimson. "Oh, yes, of course. I suppose you should look at it alone then. Mrs. Griffiths and I will leave for a moment."

"That would be advisable," Bos said, looking down his nose at Evan.

Evan took umbrage at being made the object of intense scrutiny. "Now see here, I think we should leave the tending of my leg to a physician, don't you?" *Or at least someone more competent than a butler,* he thought.

Bos's face reflected nothing of his thoughts, although his tone was laced with contempt. "As you wish, sir."

But Catrin explained, "Bos was the upper butler for the Earl of Pembroke, and one of his duties was to care for the earl whenever he was wounded while hunting or riding, which apparently was often. The earl is a dreadful rider, I'm afraid." Bos said nothing, although he obviously disapproved of his mistress's frank disclosure of his former employer's faults. "Really, Evan," she went on, "you should let Bos look at it. He knows more about such things than I do."

Though Bos raised one eyebrow at her use of Evan's Christian name, he made no other sign that he'd heard her.

It suddenly occurred to Evan that it might be useful to get Bos alone. If the butler had worked for an earl, Catrin's household must have represented a sad drop in his fortunes. Though Evan didn't have much blunt to spare, he certainly had enough to bribe a butler. And judging from the man's cold demeanor, Bos harbored little affection for his mistress.

"All right. If you think it's best," Evan said, and in seconds everyone had left the kitchen but he and the butler.

Bos turned his back to Evan. "Remove your trousers, sir, if you will."

Feeling awkward, Evan did so, then sat back in the chair, propping his leg up on a stool as he pulled his drawers up enough to expose his knee. "I'm ready."

Bos came to his side and bent over him, his lips pursing as he cupped Evan's kneecap in his hand, then moved it around. "Does that hurt, sir?"

"No."

He pressed none too firmly on the flesh around the knee-cap.

"Ouch!" Evan cried out. "Now *that* hurts."

Bos examined the spot, then straightened. "I would venture to say that it is merely a bruise. Its position near the kneecap is what is making it painful for you to walk, but by tomorrow, you should feel more fit. If you had indeed fractured a bone, I believe you would be experiencing pain in an entirely different area."

It had taken Evan all his effort to keep a straight face during Bos's cold recitation of his medical problem, but now he allowed a smile to cease his lips. "Thank you, Bos."

"You may don your clothing now, sir. I shall fetch the mistress."

"Wait!" Evan jumped to his feet, quickly pulling on his trousers. "I'd like to apologize. I see that I misjudged you."

"If you say so, sir," Bos remarked dryly.

"I mean it. I can see you're a competent butler. I'm sure you're an asset to Mrs. Price's household."

Bos turned to stare suspiciously down his long nose. "I certainly hope so."

Evan finished buttoning his trousers, then reached into his coat pocket. "And I want to offer you something for your services."

Bos's face remained perfectly bland. "That will not be necessary, sir."

"Nonsense. I know it's customary to offer a vail for special services." Evan withdrew a sovereign from his pocket and held it out to Bos.

The butler hesitated a moment, but that was all. Although Evan knew the amount was much larger than necessary, Bos showed not a flicker of emotion as he took the sovereign and tucked it into his pocket. "Thank you, sir."

Bos started to leave again, but Evan laid a hand on his arm. The butler turned, riveting his stare on Evan's hand until Evan withdrew it, stifling a chuckle. The man was certainly formal, wasn't he? "Bos, I'd be willing to double that sum if you might answer a few questions for me about Mrs. Price."

Bos fixed him with a steely gaze. "I beg your pardon, sir." If possible, his voice was even more chilly than before. "For no amount of money would I be willing to discuss my employer."

Evan was taken aback. Usually, servants delighted in talking about their masters, especially when money was involved. Not that he'd bribed any of them before. But he knew Justin used to bribe the maids to tell him what their mistresses liked in the way of presents. And other things, as well.

"I don't want to know anything personal," Evan protested. "I'm just curious about—"

"Then you must ask Mrs. Price, mustn't you?"

No doubt about it. The servant's tone was decidedly clipped. And there was a hint of protectiveness in it. Obviously, Evan had misjudged the situation entirely. In a way, it relieved him to know that Catrin inspired such loyalty in her servants.

He met the butler's stern gaze with a steady one. "I'm sorry if I offended you, Bos."

The butler said nothing, but merely turned toward the door.

"There's no need to mention this to your mistress," Evan called out as Bos left the room, but the butler didn't acknowledge the statement with so much as a nod.

"Deuce take it!" he muttered. He'd handled that badly. What insanity had made him think he could penetrate that cold Welshman's wall of silence? Now he could only hope the man's silence would extend to him. But when Catrin entered the room alone, an anxious look on her face, he feared that it had not.

She was carrying several folded cloths. Without a word she set all but one of them down on the table, then went to dip that one in a rain cistern outside the kitchen door. But as she came toward him with it, he could see the way her lower lip trembled, and he felt like an utter blackguard.

"Sit down," she said, and when he did, she placed the cool compress on his eye without another word. He watched as she moved to the stove to withdraw a steaming pot and dip another cloth in it. When she came toward him with that one, he stiffened, wondering what she intended.

But she merely began using the warm cloth to rub at his cut lip, her eyes avoiding his and her fingers shaking so badly that he couldn't stand it anymore.

He caught her hand, enfolding it in his. "What's wrong, Catrin? Why are you suddenly afraid of me?"

She wouldn't look at him. "Bos said you were asking questions about me. He said you wanted him not to tell me."

He sighed. "That's true."

"But why?" Her voice was the barest whisper.

"Why do you think?" he said as he drew the cloth out of her hand and tossed it on the table. This was his chance to get his questions answered, if he could make her think that his reasons for asking them were legitimate. "I'm interested in you and your strange curse. You roused my curiosity about it, then refused to finish the story, so I thought perhaps Bos would tell me."

"Bos doesn't know about it," she said. "No one knows but David."

When she said nothing else, he murmured, "You told Morys, but you won't tell me?"

A despairing look crossed her face. "Why do you want to know so badly?"

With a shrug he fell back on the argument he'd used earlier. "I just nearly beat a man to a pulp because of some dispute over that curse. I thought it might be helpful to know what it was all about." When she swallowed and didn't immediately answer, he added, "Besides, since you told Morys about it and he mentioned it in front of me, I assumed it wasn't such a dark family secret. *He* seemed perfectly willing to talk about it."

As he'd hoped, his implication that he could always ask Morys about it had the desired effect. With a sigh she drew her hand from his, then moved across the room to stare out the open door leading to the kitchen gardens.

The moon was rising beyond her, encasing her head in a white halo, and he thought to himself that he'd never seen a woman who intrigued him more. Or roused his lust so much.

Then she began speaking in a monotone. "The curse is chronicled in a diary I found four years ago. It stated that if any female descendant of a certain druidess refused to drink from a chalice she gave her daughter at her daughter's wedding, then that descendant's husband would die within three years of the marriage and any sons would be unable to have children. I am one of those descendants."

The chalice. He couldn't believe she was finally telling him about the chalice. "And I assume you refused to drink from the chalice at your wedding. Why? Because you didn't know about it?" He knew the answer, but he had to hear her say it.

"No. Even if I had known, I couldn't have drunk from the chalice. It was sold by my great-great-grandfather years ago."

Sold. That meant it had belonged to her family before it had belonged to Justin's. "To whom was it sold?"

She stiffened. "That hardly matters, does it? It's no longer in the family, so the curse is in effect."

"Yes, but you could get the chalice back, couldn't you, if you knew who had it? Then you could put an end to the curse." He held his breath, waiting to see what she would say.

She was silent a long time. Finally, she sighed. "I tried that, which is why David is so upset with me. He'd been waiting for me to return from London with the chalice that I thought I'd located. But the man in London who'd promised to sell it to me . . . never showed up. So I was left without a chalice, which means the curse is still in effect. That's why I refused David's suit."

Her words thundered in his ears. She'd never even met with Justin. Not at all. Justin had apparently been murdered on the way to meet her, and the thieves had stolen the chalice in the process. Then she had come home, and that was that.

It was just as he'd begun to suspect. She'd had nothing at all to do with the murder. Why had he assumed early on that she must be involved when her explanation made so much more sense?

Because of the missing letter. Still, it had been ludicrous of him to base his suspicions on something as flimsy as that. The letter could have fallen out in the struggle. For all he knew, Justin had kept it with the chalice, and the thieves had taken it. In any case, she wouldn't have just told him about going to London to buy the chalice if she'd had anything to do with the attack on Justin. Why would she?

Cursing himself for ten kinds of a fool, Evan wondered what he should do now. Tell her the truth—that he had come to Llanddeusant only to find out about Justin? No, he couldn't do that. She was already hurt that he wasn't interested in her scholarly work. He couldn't hurt her further by admitting that he'd lied to her about everything.

The only thing for it was to continue this pretense of gathering material for a book on folk legends. A few days of it, and he could return to London to get on with his life.

As if he could do so now that Catrin Price had whirled into his life.

"Now you know all about me," she said softly, turning to face him. "Now you know why I am considered poison to men."

There was an ache in her voice that tore at him. He recognized it well, for he, too, had spent years on the outside of society looking in, always the subject of speculation, rumor, and sometimes hatred. He knew what a vast, lonely world that was.

A surge of sympathy flooded him that was so intense he rose from the chair and went to stand before her. When she dropped her eyes from his, he slid his arm around her waist. "I don't consider you poison," he murmured. "Not at all."

After that, he didn't know whether it was sympathy or desire or an instinctual urge to communicate understanding, but the next thing he knew he'd pressed his lips to hers.

Chapter Eight

I burn with more than a fire
From the torch-light of her hair,
And yet, her touch as it fell
Was almost-virgin-gentle.
—Dafydd ap Gwilym, "In Morfudd's Arms"

"Ouch!"

Startled by Evan's cry, Catrin drew back, her surprise turning to concern when he gingerly touched his bruised lip.

"Oh, no, you're bleeding again!" she cried when she saw the smear of blood on his fingers.

"It's nothing to worry about." He flashed her a reassuring glance. "Really, it's nothing."

"Nonsense, you should sit down and let me put some salve on it."

That will give me a chance to gather my wits about me, she added to herself as she led him to the chair, then pressed him into it. With a sigh she went to the cupboard and drew out a bowl of salve that she kept there for emergencies.

She had let him kiss her again. Thank heavens he'd stopped or she'd have found herself in another disastrous embrace with him. She couldn't bear another of his shattering, devouring kisses, not when she'd just lied to him about the chalice.

She wouldn't have had to lie at all if he hadn't cornered her with all his questions about the curse. That wretched David had made it impossible for her to keep the tale secret, for if she'd refused to say anything, Evan would have asked David, who would have told him everything just for spite. After all, Annie had already told Evan a great deal more than Catrin would have expected.

"I don't need any salve," Evan grumbled as she returned to where he was sitting in the chair.

"Yes, you do. It's a folk recipe I came across in my

studies, and it'll lessen the swelling as well as stop the bleeding."

She scooped a dab of the stuff up with her finger and smeared it on his lip, but he took the bowl from her hand and tossed it to the floor. When she turned around to get it, he pulled her onto his lap—and groaned as she landed on his hurt knee.

"Stop that," she scolded, wriggling out of his grasp. "You're hurt, and you're only making it worse."

"I'm trying to make it better." With a rakish grin he clasped her about the waist and drew her between his legs. "Why don't you kiss it and make it better?"

She stared down into his face, at all the bruises he'd gained "defending her honor" like some knight out of a Welsh legend, and something melted inside her. Why did he do this to her? He wasn't the man for her. David had been right about that at least. Any interest Evan showed in her at the moment must stem from his boredom. The fact that he hadn't really been familiar with her writing only confirmed that.

He'd seen her half naked at the lake. Thus, he considered her a loose woman. And now that she'd given in so easily to his first kiss, he was determined to take advantage of it. But she wasn't the kind of woman he thought her.

"Kiss me, Catrin," he said in a voice too husky and seductive to be believed. His eyes smoldered now, not with anger but with a hunger that both frightened her and made her blood race.

She turned her face from him, trying to sound nonchalant. "Don't be silly. It'll hurt you."

"Not as much as holding you and not kissing you hurts me." He dragged her down onto his uninjured knee.

"Don't," she murmured, but he nuzzled her neck, and if it hurt him to do so, he didn't show it. The whisper of his mouth over her too sensitized skin sent a wild shiver through her. The only thing keeping her from giving in entirely was the scent of camphor from the salve on his lip, reminding her he was hurt. "You mustn't do that," she insisted, though she couldn't bring herself to leave his embrace.

"Why not?" He nipped her ear lobe with his teeth, eliciting a groan from somewhere deep in her throat.

"David is right." Though she said the words aloud, she

meant them to be a lecture to herself. "I shouldn't let you . . . I mean, you're probably used to women who think nothing of giving themselves to men. You see me as a diversion and—"

He uttered a soft curse in her ear, then grasped her chin, turning her face to him. "David's wrong. I'm not some smooth-tongued seducer of women. I'm a scholar. I spend most of my time buried in moldy books."

He was scowling now, and the scowl, added to his blackened eye, negated everything he was saying. He wasn't just a sedate scholar. Far from it. A fire blazed inside him that he always kept banked. Except when he was fighting. Or kissing her.

"Still," she protested, "I know you must think that since I'm a widow—"

With another curse he put a finger to her mouth. "I don't make assumptions about anyone, Catrin. But I also can't ignore that you're as attracted to me as I am to you."

Another wanton tremor passed through her as he smoothed his finger over her lips, sending sweet jolts of desire up and down her spine. When her lips parted as if of their own accord, he cast her a knowing look.

"What I feel for you is of no consequence at all," she said. She tried to rise, but he clamped his arm about her waist and wouldn't let her.

"Yes, it is. You know I'm the perfect lover for you."

Not suitor. Not husband. Lover.

In a panic she strained against his arm. This was going too far too fast and in entirely the wrong direction. "Let me go," she pleaded. Oh, why did it have to sound so pitifully weak, so uncertain?

"I won't hurt you." His voice was low and husky as he kissed her temple.

Of course he wouldn't, at least not in the way David had tried to hurt her. But she couldn't let him kiss her either, for he didn't mean anything by it.

"I just want a kiss," he added when she tried to rise. "That's all."

"I know, but—"

He stopped her mouth with his, and this time he didn't even make a murmur of protest at the pain, though she felt his body flinch.

She wanted to tear her mouth away. She truly did. It was the best thing to do. It was the right thing to do.

But she didn't. Instead she let him kiss her.

His lips were gentle, leisurely exploring the contours of her mouth without demanding anything. The very carefulness of it made her relax and turn her body toward his despite knowing she shouldn't. As his mouth shaped hers with exquisite tenderness and a warmth that cast rippling waves of heat through her body, she relaxed even more.

Just this one kiss, she told herself. *I'll let him have just this one kiss. What harm is there in it?*

But there was a great deal of harm in it. There was harm in the way he burst her resolve into tiny pieces like a bead of mercury suddenly shattered. There was harm in the way he roused strange aches in her belly, aches that until now she'd only felt late at night in the privacy of her room. And there was definitely harm in the way he coaxed her body into acting against her will.

Nonetheless, when he ran his tongue along the seam of her lips, she let him tease her mouth open with the tip of his tongue. She even touched her own tongue to his.

At once a groan erupted from his throat, and he drove his tongue inside her mouth, kindling flames in her. For a moment the coppery taste of blood—his blood—made her hesitate, but he wouldn't let her draw back. His fingers grazed her cheek before he curved them through her hair and about her neck, holding her still for his kiss.

And oh, what a kiss it was, mysterious and enticing as the waters of Llyn y Fan Fach . . . and just as fraught with danger. Yet she found herself slipping into the dangerous depths without a thought, letting him thrust his tongue over and over into her open mouth as he immersed her in the deep, treacherous waters of seduction.

She felt the effects of his hungry thrusts in the shift of his body that set her firmly down upon his aroused member. As he grew harder beneath her bottom, she grew softer everywhere. Soon his hands began to roam, at first over her waist and ribs, then higher until his thumbs skimmed the lower swells of her breasts.

When his thumbs traced twin lines from beneath her arms to her nipples, she shuddered all over from the sheer pleasure of it. Then she berated herself for giving in so easily.

She tried to draw back from him, but he murmured, "Don't. Not yet."

She threw out the first inane argument that came into her head. "The servants will wonder what we're doing in here."

To her despair he chuckled. "I don't give a damn. And I don't think you do either."

He buried his face in her neck and kissed her, then dragged his open mouth over her skin, lower and lower into the hollow between her breasts. Her hands were on his shoulders now, and she dug her fingers into the muscles as his rough tongue touched the exposed upper swell of her breast.

"But I-I should care . . ." she whispered. "I should."

He refused to answer that. Instead he drew down the thin white silk of her gown to bare one breast. She gasped and pressed against his shoulders, but when he closed his mouth over her nipple, she could no more pull away than plunge a knife through her heart.

It was all too enticing . . . the sweet swirl of his tongue over her skin, the way he flicked the nipple, then sucked it until he built the ache in her to a hot, urgent need. She clutched his head to bring him closer, to feel more of his mouth on her skin. The wicked thought occurred to her that she wanted to feel his mouth on all her hidden places, but she immediately chastised herself for even contemplating such a thing. Truly, these urges of hers were mad.

This was mad, this encounter with a man to whom she couldn't possibly mean anything. Yet she reveled in the madness, especially when his hand slipped beneath the silk to cup her other breast, kneading and teasing it until desire simmered in her belly.

"Evan . . . oh, dear Evan . . ." she whispered as she arched her head back to give him better access to her breasts.

He tore his mouth away only to murmur, "So soft . . . so adorably soft," as he filled both hands with her breasts. Then he took her mouth again, only this time his kiss was ravenous, and he showed no signs of pain. But she felt something almost like pain, a sharp hunger that gnawed at her most private places. His bold kiss only heightened the hunger until she ignored the taste of blood in his mouth and returned his kiss with more enthusiasm than sense.

Only when one of his hands left her breast to move downward and slide her gown up her legs did it dawn on her how insanely she was behaving. Here in her very own kitchen, she was letting a man seduce her!

It took all her strength of will, but somehow she dragged her mouth from his and whispered, "Stop. Please don't do this."

With a noise half moan and half growl, he tried to seize her lips again, but she jerked her head to the side, clamping her fingers around the hand that roamed up her thighs. "Evan, you must stop. I don't want you to . . . I can't . . ."

"Let me make love to you, Catrin," he said in a throaty whisper as he kissed her hair. "Please let me—"

"No!" Taking him by surprise, she pushed him away and scrambled off his lap. "I can't do this, Evan. I-I can't."

He stared at her, eyes glittering as his breath came heavy and hard. "Why not?"

She turned her face from his, drawing her gown up to cover her breasts. "It's . . . it's not right."

"The hell it isn't." He rose from the chair. "I want you. You want me. There's nothing wrong with that."

"But there is! We're not married!"

He went very still. "Is that what this is about? You're looking for marriage?"

"Yes!" Then she realized that her words contradicted what she'd just told him about the curse. "I mean, that's what I *would* want, if I *could* marry. Of course, with the curse and all, I can't—"

"Ah, yes, the curse." Did she imagine it or did he seem relieved? He stepped toward her. "So there's no problem, is there? You can't marry, and I can't marry. We're perfect for each other."

I can't marry . . . I can't marry. The words echoed hollowly in her mind.

In that second her hopes were dashed. It was only then she realized how ridiculously high her hopes had been. Though she'd never admitted it to herself, she'd been thinking of Evan as a suitor. What kind of fool had she been to assume that a man like Evan Newcome would ever relinquish a prestigious position as a fellow at Cambridge to marry a country sparrow like her?

Somehow she managed to make her voice sound normal.

"I know you said you're not allowed to marry. But surely you intend to marry someday, don't you?"

"No. Never."

"But why not?"

"I have my reasons." The clipped words made it quite clear he didn't intend to tell her what they were. "It doesn't matter anyway. If I'm not seeking marriage and you're not seeking marriage, then you and I can—"

"I can't simply leap into bed with a man who thinks no more of it than of eating a good meal."

"Good God, what gave you that impression?" he ground out, taking another step closer.

She sidled around the table, putting it between them. "You said you don't intend ever to marry."

"That doesn't mean I consider lovemaking nothing more than a good meal. I intend our . . . friendship to last much longer than that." His eyes glowed obsidian in the candlelight of the kitchen. "As I said before, you and I would make wonderful lovers." He gave a mocking smile. "It's quite the thing for widows to take lovers these days, or hadn't you heard?"

"But I couldn't! I want . . . I want . . ." *I want a husband,* she thought, but couldn't say that.

His mouth formed a hard line. "What do you want that I can't give you? What am I lacking that your previous lovers had?"

"Previous lovers?" she squeaked. This was worse and worse. Apparently, he thought she took a new lover every year! "I've had no previous lovers! I'm a virgin!"

He stared at her with narrowed eyes. "I realize that your husband died on your wedding day, but . . . Are you telling me you and he never indulged yourselves before you were married? Or that in five years of widowhood, you haven't taken a single lover?"

A blush stained her cheeks as she drew her gaze from his. "Never."

"I suppose I should have realized that. But you're twenty-five and passionate and I just assumed—" He lowered his voice to a soft thrum. "Don't you think it's long past time you took a lover?"

"No! I mean . . ."

"Don't you find it lonely here, Catrin, despite all the servants and your friends in Llanddeusant?"

The temptation in his voice was too much to bear. "Of course I find it lonely!" she burst out. "But I can't have what I want, a husband to comfort me at night, children to inherit Plas Niwl and care for all my tenants and servants." *I can't have it with you, anyway,* she thought in abject despair.

She tried to force some calm into her voice. "I can't have all that, and I won't take a sordid substitute."

His eyes blazed. "I promise you, Catrin, lovemaking between us would *not* be a sordid substitute."

The way he looked at her, as if he could offer her secret delights beyond her ken, threatened to incinerate her misgivings. "You mustn't say things like that!" She straightened her shoulders and met his intent gaze. "Just go, Evan. Please, go away and leave me alone!"

"Very well, I'll go. But I'm not leaving you alone." He cast her a dark smile. "Besides, you promised to help me with my research, remember?"

Her eyes widened. She'd forgotten all about why he'd come to Llanddeusant. But she remembered too well what he'd said yesterday in the inn, about how he had sought her out because she was interesting. And now she knew what he'd meant.

"You . . . you don't truly care about my help, do you?" she whispered. "You only asked me to help you because you wanted to . . . to . . ."

"To seduce you?" he said dryly.

She nodded.

"I never said that."

"But it's true, isn't it?"

A muscle twitched in his jaw. "No, it's not true. No matter what you think, I'd like your help."

Even if he meant it, she couldn't give it to him now. It would mean being constantly in his presence, all the while knowing that he wanted her and that it was fruitless, for she would never let him make love to her when he didn't desire marriage.

She came up with the only excuse she could think of. "But I've done a terrible job so far. Tonight I was supposed to make sure you learned all sorts of things at the wedding, and instead I got you embroiled in two fights."

"I didn't mind what happened tonight." The low thrum of his voice made it quite clear what parts of the night he didn't mind. "Not at all."

She didn't know what to say. After all, she *had* promised to help him. She couldn't very well back out if he truly wanted her help.

When she stood there in confusion, he said, "I'll be here tomorrow morning at nine. I hope that's not too early for you, but I've been told there's a man living near the top of Black Mountain who claims to be descended from the Lady of Llyn y Fan Fach. Since I intend to make the trek up there, we must get an early start."

She stared at him, dumbfounded that he simply assumed she'd do as he asked.

"Make sure you wear something for walking," he added, a faint smile tipping up his mouth.

That smile snapped her out of her astonishment. "Why do you need me if you already know what you're going for?"

He caught and held her gaze. "I need you to get me there, of course. Mrs. Llewelyn said you know Black Mountain like the back of your hand, and I know firsthand how good you are at giving directions."

Her heart sank at his blatant reminder that she owed him something for the way she'd lied to him at their first meeting. She would never get out of this. Never!

"I'd also enjoy having your company," he added softly. "Climbing mountains is lonely work."

Frantically, she searched her mind for a good reason to refuse to help him. "What if I have matters of the estate to take care of tomorrow?"

"Then I'll postpone my trip until the next day." He leaned forward, resting his fists on the table. "But be assured of this, Catrin. I'll return here every day until I get what you offered me." His gaze drifted down to her mouth and then farther, to her throat and the tops of her breasts. "*Everything* you offered me."

While she was still reeling from the boldness of that statement, he murmured, "Don't forget. Tomorrow at nine," then turned on his heel and left the kitchen.

Catrin sank into a chair, her pulse a maddening thud in her ears. What on earth was she going to do? He'd as much as implied that she'd offered him her body, but that wasn't true! It wasn't! Just because she'd let him kiss her . . . and fondle her breasts . . . and . . .

A blush stole over her face. By heavens, but she couldn't blame him for misunderstanding her actions. If it hadn't been for his cold words about matrimony, she'd probably have let him lay her out across the table and take her right there like the scandalous creature everyone believed her to be. The worst of it was, she still wanted him to. No matter how much she told herself it was wrong even to think about doing such a thing, she couldn't banish the swirling images of Evan sucking her breast . . . touching her thighs . . . bending her back over his arm so he could—

She shook her head to clear it. No, she mustn't allow these fantastic imaginings to consume her. It was fruitless to think of Evan in that way when he wanted only one thing from her, the very thing she should reserve for her husband.

The door to the kitchen opened and Bos entered, instantly cooling all her heated thoughts. He cast her a searching glance. "Mr. Newcome asked to borrow one of our horses until tomorrow. In light of the injury to his leg, I offered to have the carriage return him to his lodgings, but he insisted upon riding. He said he would return our horse in the morning, so I instructed the groom to lend him a horse. That *is* what you wished, is it not?"

She sighed. Evan was certainly making sure he had a reason to return, wasn't he? "Yes. That's fine."

Bos stared at her, a tiny frown creasing the already wrinkled skin between his eyebrows. "Are you well, madam?"

With a cry of sheer exasperation, she rose to pace the kitchen. "No, I am not well."

"Mr. Newcome did not harm you, did he?" Bos said, utmost alarm in his voice.

"Not exactly." She sighed. "Oh, Bos, I don't know what to do with the man."

"Must you do anything at all with him?"

"Yes. I owe him, I'm afraid. For lying to him and then landing him in not one, but two fights on my behalf tonight."

"On your behalf?" Bos regarded her with narrowed eyes. "Do you mean to say that the gentlemen's wounds were received while coming to your rescue?"

Casting him a helpless glance, she said, "I'm afraid so."

For the briefest moment he looked taken aback. Then he smoothed his features into his typically haughty ones. "That does alter matters a trifle. It almost makes me regret giving Medea to the gentleman for a mount."

"You didn't!" Her heart leapt into her throat. "Why, Medea is liable to run him right off the edge of a cliff! You know she's impossible to manage!" She wrung her hands, wondering if Evan was even now lying dead in some ravine. "Oh, Bos, why did you do that?"

For once, Bos appeared distressed by her criticism. "You came home with a gentleman who had obviously been in a fight. He then tried to pay me to betray your confidences. Surely you can understand why I thought it prudent to discourage any future visits from the man."

She dropped into a chair with a sigh. "Bos, sometimes I don't know whether to kiss you or throttle you."

"I take it that you didn't want me to discourage him?"

"No . . . Yes . . . By heaven, I don't know."

Bos stiffened. "It seems to me that if the gentleman has upset you to such an extent that you no longer know your own mind, perhaps you should not see him again." Then, realizing that he'd offered unsolicited advice, he added, "Of course, the entire affair is none of my concern."

Raising one eyebrow, she quipped, "Which is why you gave Medea to Mr. Newcome as his mount."

"A lapse in good judgment, I now realize."

She shook her head. "No. You were only protecting me from a man who appeared to be dangerous." *Who* is *dangerous*, she amended. "The trouble is, I don't know if I want to be protected from him."

A long, awkward silence followed the words she hadn't meant to say.

Catrin glanced at Bos, who looked as if he'd rather be anywhere but here, listening to her bare her deepest thoughts. Unfortunately, Bos was the only one she could talk to. And tonight, she desperately needed someone—anyone—who could give her a perspective on this situation with Evan.

"I . . . I like him, Bos," she added. "I like him a great deal."

Though Bos's expression remained bland, the faintest

tinge of pink touched the tips of his ears. "And does the gentleman share your . . . er . . . feelings?"

"I don't know." It was certainly true. She couldn't fathom what Evan felt. One moment he claimed he had a more than cursory interest in her, and in the next breath he insisted he never intended to marry.

But would he say differently if she told him the truth, that the curse was no longer in effect? Or was that wishful thinking on her part?

Now that she'd lied about the chalice, she didn't know what to do. If Evan truly had no desire to marry, then there was no point in telling him the truth about the chalice and revealing that she was indeed free to marry. In fact, there was no point in continuing in any friendship with him.

On the other hand, if he knew about the chalice . . .

"Bos?" she asked.

The servant was still standing rigidly at attention, not a muscle relaxed. "Yes, madam?"

"Please sit down. You make me nervous standing there like a statue."

Bos raised one eyebrow. "I shall leave you to your ruminations then."

"No, don't go. Please, Bos, I need your advice about . . . about something personal. I don't know where else to turn."

It was almost comical to witness the two sides of Bos warring with each other—the butler side protesting that it was inappropriate for a servant to listen to the personal woes of an employer while the human side argued for compassion.

She could tell when the human side won out, for Bos lowered himself into a chair, his features softening ever so slightly. "I will endeavor to advise you as best I can, madam. Proceed."

Not looking at him, Catrin recounted the entire tale of the chalice . . . how she'd discovered its significance and its whereabouts, how she'd gone to London to acquire it, how Lord Mansfield had been murdered shortly after selling it to her, and how her lies about the chalice had affected both David and Evan.

Bos sat silently throughout, merely muttering a "Hmm" or "I see" here and there. When she finished, she turned to look at him, wondering if she'd find condemnation in his eyes. Instead, she found compassion.

"I wish that you had confided in me sooner." His voice was a trace unsteady.

"Why?"

"Because I would never have allowed you to go to London. I would have insisted that you let me go in your stead." His lips tightened. "To think that you might have been murdered . . . or worse . . . by those ruffians. Only good fortune saved you from that, good fortune and your instincts. You should never have gone alone, madam. You must never do such a thing again."

The concern in his voice so overwhelmed her that she had to fight back tears. "So you don't think I was insane for wanting to acquire the chalice? You don't think I'm mad for believing in the curse?"

"I have no opinion whatsoever about the curse. *You* believe in it. That is all that matters."

She swallowed hard. "You don't think I was wrong to lure Lord Mansfield to that inn under a false name and try to circumvent his mother?" Her voice dropped to a whisper. "You don't think it's my fault the poor man was murdered?"

"Indeed not!" Bos's look of outrage warmed her. "I would say that you acted admirably to solve a knotty problem. You are certainly not to blame for the deplorable reign of the criminal element in London. You are fortunate not to have been murdered yourself."

She'd expected the levelheaded Bos to tell her she'd behaved like a fool. She'd almost wanted him to chastise her, so she could feel as if she'd received her punishment and could stop feeling guilty about having gotten exactly what she wanted while poor Lord Mansfield lay in his grave. "But I should have told the authorities about it, shouldn't I? I should have told them I was there. If they ever find out Lord Mansfield went to meet the Lady of the Mists, they may send someone after me."

Bos stared at her, tightness in every line of his wrinkled face. "I think I am beginning to comprehend your reasons for your actions over the past few days. Was your fear of having the authorities come in search of you what prompted you to shy away from Mr. Newcome when you first encountered him by the lake? Did you suspect that he might have come from London for such a purpose?"

"Actually, yes. After all, he came from London shortly after I left there, and he asked about the Lady of the Mists." She smiled. "But later he explained how he'd heard about me from the Vaughans, and it turned out to be nothing more than a coincidence that he was here."

"Hmm. Coincidence."

"Truly, Bos, that's all it was. Why would a scholar of his reputation act like a constable looking for the woman who'd met Lord Mansfield before his death?"

Bos scowled. "The more appropriate question is why would a scholar of his reputation travel all the way from Cambridge to meet a woman whose endeavors as a scholar are not . . . shall we say . . . on the level of his own?"

"I know, I know," she said without rancor. She wasn't on Evan's level, that was true, although it wasn't as if she hadn't tried to launch more ambitious endeavors. But as a woman without a university degree, her work in that area was largely disregarded.

Besides, to do any serious research on the subject of Welsh folktales would have meant leaving Plas Niwl and seeking out strangers who could tell her about particular customs. The very thought of doing such a thing terrified her. She much preferred to stay at Plas Niwl, running the estate and keeping to herself.

"All right," she said. "So we have established that he can't possibly be interested in my work. But I already guessed as much. It isn't that he came here to seek me out personally, however. The Vaughans confused him and told him all about Grandmother, so he decided to seek her out, to research her for his book. And . . . and he found me instead."

"And is now researching you. Is that it?"

She evaded his gaze, thinking that Evan had implied as much in the carriage tonight. "I suppose you could put it that way."

"Instead of gathering his folktales as quickly as possible from whatever sources he can find, he is waiting on your leisure . . . accompanying you to weddings . . . fighting battles for you—"

"He went to the wedding so he could hear folktales," Catrin protested.

"Oh, indeed. And did he hear any?"

"Well, no, but—"

"Madam, I believe you are allowing your . . . interest in

this man to overwhelm your good judgment. I find it highly suspicious that only a week after your return, a man should come to 'research' you, as it were."

Bos had a way of making it sound so suspicious. But she knew he was wrong about Evan. "I don't believe he came her for any other reason than to gather tales. If he did, he would have been put off by what I told him this evening."

Bos's eyes widened. "Surely you did not confess to him the same things about your trip to London that you confessed to me."

She shook her head. "I told about the curse, but I lied about the chalice. I said I never bought it, that Lord Mansfield never showed up."

"I see you have not entirely lost your wits," Bos remarked.

"In any case, if Evan *were* trying to find out something about the murder, he'd have taken what I said tonight to mean I wasn't involved, and he'd be planning to return to Cambridge on the morrow. But you said yourself that he's coming here tomorrow. He even took one of our horses. Why, he practically demanded that I go with him to speak to some descendant of the Lady of Llyn y Fan Fach. So you see, he really is researching a book, and he truly does want my help."

Pursing his lips, Bos rose to his feet. "Perhaps. Nonetheless, I find all of this highly disturbing." He drew in a heavy breath, then thrust out his chest. "You asked for my advice, madam. Here it is. I think you should avoid any future encounters with this gentleman. You were right to refuse to see him the first time, and you should follow that course from now on. Involvement with the investigation of that earl's murder could do you nothing but harm, and you must protect yourself."

Catrin agreed with Bos, though for different reasons. She didn't think Evan had come to spy on her or anything like that. It was clear, however, that he was determined to take her virtue. And if she continued in his presence much longer, she'd let him. What a mistake *that* would be! It would involve her in a sordid affair that could only end in scandal—and illegimate children.

She groaned. "I *want* to avoid him, Bos. I truly do. But he's very persistent. He says he'll come here every day until

I agree to accompany him and I . . . well, I'm not like Grandmother. I don't know how to send a man packing."

"There is no need for you to send him packing, madam." Bos straightened his perfectly straight cravat, his lips forming a thin line. "I shall make certain Mr. Newcome refrains from bothering you further. You leave him to me."

Chapter Nine

I am a man unwelcomed,
Disheartened, speechless, unloved, . . .
—David Llwyd, "The Fox's Counsel"

So this is hell, Evan thought as he prodded his horse through the mist up the now familiar path to Plas Niwl. *Two days of burning for Catrin, with no chance of quenching the flames.*

For two days he'd tried to see her. Both times he'd been rebuffed at the door by that bloody butler. The first day Bos had told him she was closeted with her solicitor and couldn't see him. Evan had let her have her little triumph, but he'd returned the next day as he'd promised, only to be told she was indisposed. When he'd refused to leave until he saw her, Bos had instructed the footmen to escort him back to Llanddeusant.

Evan could have fought them, but what would have been the point? Even if he'd seen her, she'd have been surrounded by her watchdogs, and Evan wouldn't have been able to talk any sense to her . . . to touch her . . . to kiss her.

Why was he behaving like such a fool? A hundred times over the past few days, he'd thought about leaving Llanddeusant. After all, he'd found out what he'd come here to learn. He'd discovered she couldn't have been involved with Justin's murder. So why not leave? The Vaughans had invited him to visit at Llynwydd. Why stay here?

Because he was in hell. Because every time he closed his eyes at night, he tasted her on his lips, felt the silken texture of her skin, and saw the glow beneath it whenever he fondled her. Her soft voice intruded in his waking thoughts, and she tormented him in sleep with hot, lustful dreams.

He desired her body, true, but he desired more than that. He liked talking to her as he had the day of the wedding. He liked prying opinions out of her, uncovering the complex woman beneath the shy facade.

He'd anticipated spending several days in her company, sharing ideas . . . and intimacies. Now that he'd not been given the chance, he was determined to take it for himself. It was madness, of course. It couldn't go anywhere. But maybe if he spent more time with her, he could shake this strange obsession. He had to try.

And she wanted him to try, no matter how much she avoided him. She desired him, too. She burned as much as he did, and it was absurd for them not to enter the flames together.

Some part of him knew why she hesitated. After all, Catrin had spent many years closeted in her estate, afraid to venture out because of the scandalous things said about her. With time, she'd obviously excelled at protecting herself by avoiding what was most frightening or hurtful. She'd avoided going to weddings so she wouldn't have to deal with her painful memories, she'd avoided Morys so she wouldn't have to hurt his feelings, and now she was avoiding Evan so she wouldn't have to face her own urges.

Well, he knew all about avoidance. He knew all about escaping into one's private world to avoid the rage that boiled inside. They weren't so different, he and Catrin. She had urges she didn't understand, and she refused to give in to them. He had urges, too, dark, murderous urges that made him flee into the blessed civilized world of scholarship.

But urges so intense would not be denied. Sometimes he thought if he could just loose them, could let his fury pour forth like acid to scorch the countryside, it would leave him forever. That was why he spent two or three hours a week at the Lyceum, the pugilist academy, sparring with whoever would fight him. But it only lessened his urges a little. The rest of the time he suppressed his uncivilized and very unacceptable urges.

Her urges were different, however. She didn't have to suppress her passion, no matter what she thought. She could give vent to all the desire that racked her senses. And she should. Before it ate her up inside.

He'd make sure she did. Oh, but his sweet girl was in for a surprise today. Morys might have rolled over and played dead for her, but Evan had no intention of doing so. This time he wouldn't give Bos the chance to deny him access to Catrin. Not for nothing had he spent his early childhood sneaking into Llynwydd so he could steal plums for his mother. He knew the ins and outs of estates. It would be an easy matter for him to sneak into Plas Niwl and find Catrin without being caught.

A grim smile on his face, he spurred his horse on. The mare he'd borrowed from the Vaughans was a skittish little thing, but not nearly so skittish as that deuced Medea Bos had given him to ride three days ago.

Evan's smile widened. Apparently, Bos had intended to wreak some petty vengeance on Evan for his ill-considered attempt at a bribe. Evan had thoroughly enjoyed thwarting that bloody butler. It had been worth his madcap ride down to Llanddeusant to see Bos's face the next day when Evan had brought Medea to a complete halt outside Plas Niwl. The butler had clearly not expected him to master the horse, and in truth, Evan hadn't been so sure he could either.

But all Medea had needed was a chance to vent her frustrations, to ride like the wind through the night–like her mistress.

Just as he was thinking that a ride through the night with Catrin would be a heady thing, he emerged from a particularly thick patch of fog to find two horses blocking the path. They were tethered to a tree, and he wondered fleetingly if they were from Plas Niwl.

Perhaps luck was with him. Perhaps he'd caught Catrin out trying to avoid him again. A faint smile crossed his lips as he stopped his horse next to the other two. If so, she was in for a surprise.

Tethering it to the same tree as the others, he followed the path that wound through the thick woods beside the road. As he topped a hill, he heard voices below him, but they were both male voices, one of them complaining loudly about "imbeciles and fools." Despite his disappointment, he went on, curious to see why two men were in the woods so close to Plas Niwl.

He moved more quietly now, creeping nearer until he reached the edge of a clearing. A few feet from him stood Sir Reynald, along with another man he didn't know. Behind them was a large dolmen, two upright stones supporting a third to form what looked almost like a table. Or an altar.

Wisps of mist swirled about it, giving it an air of frightening mystery, and at the foot of it was an animal.

At least it looked like an animal. A bull, he conjectured, though he couldn't be completely sure, since the head had been chopped cleanly off and the genitals were likewise gone. He must have made some shocked sound, for Sir Reynald and his companion whirled to face him.

"Show yourself!" Sir Reynald demanded. "You there, in the woods!"

With his eyes riveted on the butchered animal, Evan moved into the clearing.

"Ah, it is only you, Mr. Newcome," Sir Reynald said, his voice cold and angry. "I thought you might be one of the scoundrels who did this. Do come see. You shall probably find this evidence of insanity in our county quite intriguing."

Evan stepped forward, now noticing that the bull's hide was pierced in several places. "What in God's name is going on here?"

The man next to Sir Reynald muttered, "It's those idiots in Llanddeusant, the ones who dabble with druidry. They have some notion that the dolmen was once a druid altar, so they come here to perform their sacrifices under cover of darkness. But one day I'll catch them at it, I will, and I'll take a pitchfork to the lot of them!"

Sir Reynald raised one eyebrow. "Mr. Newcome, meet Mr. Parry. He is Mrs. Price's groundskeeper. We are standing on Plas Niwl land."

"Aye," said Mr. Parry. "They're trespassing, they are. And butchering fine animals on the estate."

"Fine animals indeed," Sir Reynald complained. "This is the second one of *my* cattle they stole and butchered. Do you know what a price a bull like that fetches at market? He had several more years of stud service in him. Now this. If I ever catch them, I shall strangle the lot of them."

"So will I," muttered Mr. Parry. "Now you see why I dragged you from your bed to show you this, sir. We must find a way to put a stop to it."

"Does it happen a great deal?" Evan couldn't tear his gaze from the horribly mutilated bull. He felt as if he'd stepped back in time a few centuries.

Druids, no less. Though he knew of the interest in druids shown by Iolo Morganwg and the others at the Gwyneddigion Society in London, none of them carried it this far. Oh, certainly, they arranged meetings of the Gorsedd and wore their white robes and called upon the ancient bards for inspiration, but animal sacrifice? Somehow he couldn't see Morganwg butchering a bull.

Yet here in this desolate place, with Black Mountain scowling down on them and the mist floating through the clearing, he could easily believe that druids in long white robes had come here in the night to perform strange rites. Too easily.

"It happens every so often," Mr. Parry was saying. "I've waited out here for them many a time, but I can't seem to predict when the devils will appear."

"I shall speak to Mrs. Price about this," Sir Reynald said. "She and I must lay a trap for them."

At Sir Reynald's mention of Catrin, Evan gave a start, remembering the tale of the druidess's chalice. Could Catrin have had something to do with this?

He laughed at himself for even thinking it. Imagine meek little Catrin presiding over such butchery. And butchery of someone else's cattle, besides. Even if she were given to performing rituals, she'd use less violent means . . . and her own livestock.

"You can't talk to Mrs. Price until tomorrow, I'm afraid," Mr. Parry remarked, jerking Evan from his thoughts. "The mistress ain't at home today. She's taken a jaunt to the mill in Craig y Nos to see about the wool prices. She left 'bout two hours ago and won't be back 'til this evening. But you may come talk to her then, if you wish."

Sir Reynald made some response, but Evan didn't hear it. He was too busy cursing Catrin. Gone to Craig y Nos for the day, had she? He should have known she'd do something like that. She must have realized he'd try another tack to reach her today and decided that the ultimate avoidance was not to be at home at all. The woman was driving him mad.

But she didn't know with whom she was dealing, he thought.

"Do you know which road Mrs. Price took to Craig y Nos?" he asked Mr. Parry. "I need to speak with her today, if possible." He held his breath, praying that Mr. Parry didn't know about all Catrin's attempts to avoid him.

Fortunately, the groundskeeper was apparently not a part

of the estate rumor mill. "Aye, I can tell you which way she went. If you've got a good horse and are willing to ride hard, you ought to catch up to her."

That was all Evan needed to hear. With a grim smile he made mental notes as Mr. Parry described the route to Craig y Nos. Then turning on his heel, he strode toward the path through the forest.

"If I see her before you do, I'll tell her you were looking for her," Mr. Parry called out behind Evan.

"Don't bother," Evan muttered under his breath. "She's not getting away from me this time, even if I have to follow her over half the countryside."

This is the last straw, Catrin thought as she sank onto the ground beside her Welsh pony.

Oblivious to his mistress's distress, Little Boy munched grass with utter contentment. Catrin stared up at the poor pony. No, it wasn't Little Boy's fault that he'd developed a saddle sore and refused to go another foot. If she'd been paying attention to what she was doing this morning when she'd saddled him, instead of letting her mind wander, none of this would have happened. If she hadn't been wholly absorbed in remembering a certain man's kisses and caresses . . .

"A pox on you, Evan Newcome," she muttered. She'd thought that keeping away from him would end her imaginings. Instead, it had made them worse. Just last night, she'd awakened to find her own hand caressing her breast. The very thought of it! Yet she hadn't stopped doing the scandalous thing right away. In her half fog of sleep, she'd pretended it was *him* fondling her, as he'd done so adeptly three nights ago.

So this morning, she'd decided to take a leisurely ride to Craig y Nos. She had told herself she would need to make the trip soon anyway, and this was the perfect time for it. She'd thought that another day away from Evan Newcome would lessen her wild imaginings.

Of course it hadn't. Instead, her mind had wandered from the moment she'd saddled the horse until the moment Little Boy had stopped moving. Thank heaven her woolgathering had resulted in nothing worse than a saddle sore for her sweet old pony. In this mist she might have driven Little

Boy into a ravine while her mind wandered to thoughts of hot, searching mouths and clever hands and . . .

She sighed. A lot of good this trip had done her. She couldn't evict Evan from her mind. And now she was stuck out here with her thoughts. She was still several miles from Craig y Nos, yet Plas Niwl was a good distance behind her as well. So what was she to do?

She really had only one choice—to lead Little Boy home. She certainly couldn't continue to ride him, not with that nasty sore, and she couldn't take the sidesaddle off and ride bareback, for her skirts were too tight for that. Grandmother, of course, would have hitched up her skirts and ridden the pony anyway, but even if Catrin could have brought herself to bare her legs in such an outrageous fashion, she couldn't have managed Little Boy bareback. She wasn't the horsewoman Grandmother had been, which was why she rode the gentlest horse in the stables.

Of course, if someone would come along to give her a ride and let her lead Little Boy . . . She sighed. How likely was that? This wasn't a well-traveled road. It might be days before someone came this way.

For once she regretted letting Bos embark on his plan for keeping Evan away. At the moment she would welcome Evan's presence. But he wasn't likely to turn up. By now, Bos had told Evan she'd gone on a trip to the mill, without telling him which mill. There were a number of wool mills around here, so Evan would never figure out which one she'd gone to. Of course, that was assuming he would try to see her today, and she couldn't assume that. After yesterday, he might have given up on her. And wasn't that what she wanted?

Refusing to think about that, she rose and dusted off her skirts. There was no point in sitting here and bemoaning her fate. The sooner she brought Little Boy home, the better. For both of them.

Unfortunately, Little Boy wasn't a young pony anymore, despite his name. He'd been Grandmother's mount as she aged, and he was getting on in years. So now that he was lunching on the fine grass by the road, he wasn't going to move anytime soon. He'd always obeyed Grandmother without even a quiver of his wide nostrils, but he would balk at Catrin's attempt to exercise control. Horses always knew she was a soft touch, and they never cooperated with her. She could tug on the reins until sundown, but Little Boy had found a patch of green and a sunny spot, and he wouldn't budge.

She'd have to use other tactics. Reaching into the bag of food Cook had packed for her lunch, she drew out an apple and held it under Little Boy's nose. "Here's a treat, my poor dear. Everything will be all right, I promise. I'll not mount you. But you must come along home with me, you know. I can't leave you here."

The pony lifted his head, his eyes bright as he nuzzled the apple. Slowly, she backed up, cooing to him the entire time. "Come on. Come along with me, and you shall have this apple. Come on then, Little Boy."

She was so intent on enticing Little Boy onto the road that she didn't hear another horse come up behind her until a familiar male voice rumbled, "I wouldn't listen to her if I were you, Little Boy. She's notorious for reneging on her promises."

"Evan!" she exclaimed, whirling around to find him astride his horse, a look of bemusement on his face. She couldn't hide her relief. "Oh, Evan, what are you doing here? However did you find me?"

With a wry frown he dismounted. "Why? What had you instructed dear old Bos to tell me today? That you had run off to America? That the Tylwyth Teg had taken you to fairyland?"

"You . . . you haven't talked to Bos?"

He shot her a cold glance. "No. I talked to your gamekeeper, who was much more forthcoming about where you'd gone." Before she could respond, he gestured to her pony and added, "What's wrong with your mount?"

She hung her head. "Saddle sore. I was in too much of a hurry to leave this morning, and I saddled him myself. I guess I didn't tighten the girth properly."

Without a word he went to the horse and examined the sore. "You can't ride him, you know."

"I know. I'm leading him home."

He turned toward her. "*We're* leading him home. You can ride with me. My horse is perfectly capable of carrying two riders."

The thought of riding with him quickened her blood—

unfortunately. "Th-there's no need," she stammered. "You go on, and I'll just walk home with Little Boy."

"Not bloody likely." He chuckled, his gaze warming as he looked at her. "Admit it, Catrin. I've caught you now. You can ride with me or walk with me, but there's no way in hell you're going to avoid me this time."

A tremor passed through her. They'd be astride together for hours in a most intimate position. How would she stand it? But she had no other options, not unless she wanted to walk all the way back to Plas Niwl, and that certainly didn't appeal to her.

Nonetheless, a few minutes later, when she found herself seated across the saddle in front of him with her shoulder against his chest and her bottom nestled in the juncture of his thighs, she wondered how she'd endure the ride home. She was all too aware of his corded thigh beneath her legs and his strong arms bracketing her body. His face was so close that all it would take was a half turn of her head to put her mouth to his.

By heaven, she must stop thinking in this vein! Evan had made it perfectly clear what sort of friendship he wanted to have with her, and it wasn't what she wanted. Not at all.

"How much longer had you intended to keep up this campaign of yours, anyway?" Evan said, breaking the silence.

"C-campaign?"

"Your campaign of avoidance. How much longer did you think you could avoid me?"

Oh, if only he weren't so close. But she knew he could feel the trembling that had started in her body. "I don't know what you're talking about. I haven't been avoiding you. I've simply been . . . very busy with matters of the estate."

His voice dropped to a husky rumble. "You mean, very busy inventing matters of the estate that would keep you from seeing me again."

She turned her head to stare at the mist-shrouded road. Must he always be so forthright? Must he always make her feel guilty?

"You've been avoiding me the way you avoided Morys," Evan went on. He paused. "Tell me something, Catrin. Is that why Morys was so angry with you that night? Because you gave him just enough of a taste of you to whet his appetite, then withheld the main part of the feast?"

Her face flamed in an instant as her gaze shot to his. "Never! I never let David touch me like that! I never wanted him to . . . I never . . ." She trailed off as she realized how much she'd just admitted.

His gaze dropped to her mouth. "Never wanted him to what? To make love to you?"

Ducking her head, she stammered, "I-I didn't say that."

"But you were thinking it. Admit it. Morys was angry at me because you let me take liberties with you that you had never allowed to him. Morys tried to beat me to a bloody pulp because he knew you wanted me . . . and that infuriated him."

"I don't want you," she protested feebly.

"Oh?" He nuzzled her hair and pressed a kiss to the tip of her ear. His breath tickled her skin, then warmed it until the heat spread clear to her toes.

"I don't," she repeated, trying to convince herself.

"Shall I prove that you do?" he murmured, then nipped at her earlobe, scattering pleasure through her.

"No . . . no . . ."

But Evan was already halting the horses. Before she could make another protest, he'd tucked the reins to his horse under her thigh, freeing his hands so he could turn her face up to his.

From that moment on, she was drowning, drowning in the soft kiss he pressed to her mouth . . . in the feel of his firm fingers cupping her jaw . . . in the musky scent of leather and wool that clung to him.

On a sigh she parted her lips, and he drove his tongue in deep, claiming her mouth in the same way he'd claimed her dreams, without apology or remorse. One of his hands wandered down her jaw to her neck, and she could feel the imprint of every finger splayed over her throat.

He shifted her so that she lay tucked in one of his arms and half reclining across the horse. The position forced her to cling to his neck, which meant she couldn't easily push him away.

Not that she wanted to. She'd lain alone three long nights anticipating this kiss, and her good sense wouldn't deprive her of what her body wanted. Thus when he slid his hand down her throat and inside her bodice to her breast, she made no murmur of protest, but arched up against the hand that caressed and teased the soft flesh exactly as she'd imagined in her dreams.

Only when she moaned low in her throat did he draw his mouth from hers, his eyes glittering with triumph. "Tell me you want me, sweet girl. Tell me you're not afraid of me."

When she stared up at him, wide-eyed and dazed, he thumbed her nipple and added in a husky voice, "There's nothing wrong with wanting me, Catrin."

Suddenly, she realized she was sitting across his lap on a public road where anyone could come along. She'd been so caught up in the pleasure of his kiss that she'd had no sense of her surroundings at all. And that realization terrified her.

With a soft cry she wriggled free of him and slid off the horse. As her face filled with horror at the thought of what she'd been about to let him do in front of God and everyone, she snatched up Little Boy's fallen lead rope and hastened down the road, wishing for the umpteenth time that she could simply leap onto Little Boy's bare back and race away . . . as far away from the dangerous seductions of Evan Newcome as she could get.

But she couldn't, and when he prodded his horse into a walk and came up beside her, she cursed the fact that she couldn't.

"Catrin," he said in a low, commanding voice.

"Please, just leave me alone, Evan. Leave me in peace."

"You don't want that."

"I do!" she burst out, though it wasn't true. What she wanted was for him to court her, to offer himself as a suitor, and he'd already made it clear he didn't intend to do that.

He prodded his mare into a gait that would keep him even with her. "You're merely afraid, Catrin, afraid to let your human urges overwhelm you. It's fear that makes you avoid me. It's fear that keeps you from taking a lover or marrying again after all this time."

"I couldn't marry because of the curse," she whispered.

"Not so. You know in your heart that the curse is all a lot of nonsense. But you've convinced yourself it's true because you're afraid."

She shook her head. He was wrong, so wrong. She believed in the curse because it was real. Of course, she had the chalice now, so it didn't matter anymore, but he couldn't know that.

He went on relentlessly. "You're afraid to let a man . . . any man . . . close to you, for fear he'll uncover the passionate side of you that you're so ashamed of."

"I'm not a wanton!" she protested. "I . . . I'm not."

"I didn't say you were." His voice thrummed with emotion. "But neither are you the passionless drone you think you are or the quiet, cowardly creature you seem to be."

"You don't know what I am."

"Yes, I do. I know you're not really a coward. I know you're stronger than you think, even though you're so convinced you're unremarkable that you hide from everyone who might see your supposed character flaws."

She wished she could stop up her ears against the things he was saying. There was too much truth in them. She increased her pace.

So did he. "But I know you better than you know yourself. It's not cowardice that keeps you from hurting people, but compassion. You're bright and beautiful and yes, remarkable. You have nothing to fear, Catrin, no reason to avoid the company of men. Any man would be delighted to have you as a companion."

As a companion, she thought. But not as a wife.

"I don't want to be a man's companion," she whispered. "I only want to be allowed to live my life in peace." *With a husband who loves me,* she added, wishing she could throw those words at him, but knowing she couldn't.

Why couldn't he see her as a wife? If she was as "remarkable" as he claimed, why didn't anyone want to marry her? Oh, certainly David wanted to marry her, but only because of her property. He'd made it quite clear that night behind the inn that he thought little of her intelligence.

Sometimes she suspected even Willie had married her only to strike back at his overbearing father. He'd liked her well enough, to be sure, but he hadn't been in love with her.

And Evan? Evan claimed to see her finer qualities, yet he had no desire to marry her either. Her property didn't even tempt him. Then again, he was probably from some fine family and needn't ever worry about such things anyway. No, he was only interested in her body, and while that was indeed flattering, it wasn't enough to prompt her to throw her virtue away.

She was so caught up in her thoughts that she'd gone several feet before she realized Evan was no longer at her side. Thank heaven. Perhaps he'd finally recognized that she meant what she said. Perhaps he would indeed leave her alone. She didn't even care that it meant she'd have to walk home. She'd never have survived a ride with him anyway.

But he called after her. "Catrin, stop! There's someone on the road ahead!"

She slowed down, lifting her head to look down the way. Indeed there was someone approaching, and with great haste. As she halted in the road, Evan came up beside her. "Quickly, mount the horse behind me. We must be able to flee if the man proves to be foe rather than friend."

She hesitated, and he said urgently, "Put your foot in the stirrup and mount behind me. Now!"

But she'd waited too long. Now the rider was so close, she could see it was a man, and as she got a good look at him, she relaxed. He didn't look like a highwayman or some other blackguard. He looked a great deal like a solicitor.

"Hallo there!" the man called out, and Evan muttered an oath under his breath. A few seconds later, the man pulled his horse up beside them, his face red from the obvious exertion of racing along the mountain road.

For a moment the man merely struggled to catch his breath. Then he fixed her with a pair of shrewd gray eyes. "I say, you wouldn't happen to be Mrs. Catrin Price, would you? I was told by your servant that you might be on this road."

Catrin glanced up at Evan, who said, "Who wants to know?"

The man drew out a handkerchief and mopped his jowly face, then said, "My name's Quinley, Archer Quinley. I've come from London to ask Mrs. Price a few questions. That's all."

Catrin's heart pounded in her ears. So they'd found her, had they? After all her worrying and her attempts at evasion, they'd found her. In a way, it was a relief. At least now she wouldn't have to spend all her time looking over her shoulder and wondering when someone from London would finally track her down.

Mr. Quinley reached into his pocket and pulled out a folded sheet of paper. "I'm an investigator hired by Lady Mansfield to look into her son's death. Here's the letter her solicitor sent when he hired me, setting forth what she wanted done."

Evan rode forward and held out his hand to take the letter, but Mr. Quinley shook his head and looked at Catrin. "You *are* Mrs. Price, aren't you?"

Evan shot her a warning glance. "You don't have to answer that."

She ignored him. It was one thing to avoid the authorities, but quite another to openly refuse to cooperate with them. And why did Evan seem not at all surprised to hear that an investigator wanted to ask her questions about a murder?

"Yes, I'm Catrin Price," she said, looking up at the investigator, who was regarding Evan with a wary expression.

Mr. Quinley handed her the letter, and she took it, though she didn't need to read it to know he spoke the truth. After all, she'd been expecting someone to search her out. But she scanned the letter anyway, noting that Lady Mansfield had immediately assumed a connection between Catrin's first letter to her about the chalice and her son's mysterious murder.

Then a line caught Catrin's eye. She had to read it twice to be sure she was not mistaken. But she wasn't.

A terrible pain threatened to engulf her as she read aloud the words, "My son's longtime friend, a respected scholar by the name of Evan Newcome, has already told the constable that a woman going by the name of the Lady of the Mists met with my son on the night of his murder. I suggest you focus your investigation on this woman, who I am sure must be Catrin Price. She may have seen something that night that would lead to the apprehension of my son's killers."

Catrin lifted her face to Evan, his betrayal slicing deeply into her too vulnerable emotions. And he knew exactly what she was thinking, for guilt was stamped in every line of his face.

"You didn't come here to do research for a book, did you?" she whispered. "You didn't seek me out because you'd read my essay."

He uttered a low oath, though he didn't look away from her accusing gaze. Then he drew in a heavy breath and said in a quiet voice, "No."

And her world crumbled.

Chapter Ten

The heart's gone cold, under a breast of fear;
Lust shrivels like dried brushwood.
—Gruffudd ab Yr Ynad Coch,
"Lament for Llywelyn ap Gruffudd, The Last Prince"

"Mrs. Price?" came a voice, drawing Catrin out of her torment. "Are you all right?"

She lifted her face to Mr. Quinley, who regarded her with some concern. She didn't dare look at Evan, or shame would engulf her. Here she'd been thinking he was interested in her, if only for her body. In truth, he hadn't been interested in her at all . . . not for her body or her property or even her help with his book.

His book. She scowled. Such a thing probably didn't even exist. He'd trumped it up to gain access to her so he could ask her questions. As she thought about it, her shame turned to anger. Why was she ashamed? She had nothing to be ashamed about. She'd drawn obvious conclusions from his behavior. *He'd* been the one to lie and mislead her, to treat her as if her feelings didn't matter.

"Catrin . . ." Evan began in his soft, low tone, and that was all it took to enrage her further.

"Mr. Quinley, meet Mr. Evan Newcome," she bit out with a curt gesture in Evan's direction. "He's been conducting his own investigation. A pity you came along so soon. He had almost dragged the entire story from me. But now I'm sure he's pleased to relinquish his onerous task to you."

"Catrin!" Evan said more firmly. "This is not what it seems."

She ignored him, addressing her remarks to Mr. Quinley. "I'm sorry you had to travel so far, but I'll be more than happy to answer any questions you have." Flashing Evan a quick glance, she added, "I'd have been more than happy to answer Mr. Newcome's questions . . . *if* he'd ever asked any."

It wasn't entirely the truth, for she had evaded him in the beginning when she'd thought he was an investigator, but it felt good to say it . . . and to watch a guilty flush rise over his face, staining his cheeks a dark red.

Mr. Quinley seemed uncertain what to make of the situation. "Are you telling me that this fellow here is Lord Mansfield's friend, the scholar?"

She nodded. She couldn't do more, for it had suddenly occurred to her why Evan hadn't been forthcoming about his investigation. He'd hidden his purpose because he'd thought she had something to do with his friend's murder. For the past five days he'd conversed with her . . . defended her . . . kissed her . . . while believing all the time that she'd taken part in a brutal crime.

The very thought of it made her sick. She swayed against the horse, and Evan was off his mount and at her side in an instant.

"Catrin, I'm so sorry—" he began as he took her arm to support her.

But she snatched her arm away. "Don't you *dare* touch me! After everything you said and did, you have no right to touch me!"

Mr. Quinley was off his horse now, too. "Perhaps we should pull the horses off the road and stop for a while." He cast Evan a suspicious glance. "Mrs. Price looks as if she's had a bit of a shock."

She shook her head, though she was fighting hard to keep from collapsing. This was no time to be weak or cowardly. She must keep her wits about her. She must tread carefully with these two men, neither of whom were friends. Otherwise, she'd find herself carted off to London for a crime she didn't commit.

"I'm fine." She straightened her shoulders and took a steadying breath. "I promise, I'm fine." She forced a smile to her face as she looked at Mr. Quinley. "However, unless you want to conduct this questioning as we trot along the road, we *should* probably pull off."

Mr. Quinley nodded. "There are some trees over there. Why don't we sit for a while, and you can tell me what you know of what happened the night of Lord Mansfield's death?"

"Certainly," she murmured.

She turned toward the trees, as did Evan, but Mr. Quinley stopped Evan before he could take a step. "Sorry, sir, but I think this would be better done without you there. You seem to upset the young lady."

Catrin laid her hand on Mr. Quinley's arm. "No, please. I want him to hear. I haven't done anything to be ashamed of. I have nothing to hide from Mr. Newcome, and I want him to know it."

With a shrug indicating his acquiescence, Mr. Quinley went to get his horse and led it to a tree a short distance from the road. She turned toward her horse and gathered up his lead rope.

But Evan came up beside her and closed his hand over hers, speaking in Welsh so the investigator couldn't understand. "Catrin, I know you're angry, and I don't blame you, but—"

"I told you not to touch me." She lifted her face to his as she struggled to pull her hand away. "It's bad enough that you pretended to care about me when all the while you were only spying on me." There was a catch in her throat. "Don't make it worse by continuing the pretense now."

With a stricken expression he tightened his hold on her hand. "Oh, my darling, it wasn't a pretense—"

"Stop it!" Her eyes welled with tears as she ducked her head to avoid seeing the fake sincerity in his face. How stupid did he think she was? And what did he think to gain by going on like this? "If you don't stop it, I swear I'll—"

"Is everything all right here?" came Mr. Quinley's voice at her side. She lifted her head to find him staring at her hand enclosed in Evan's. This time when she jerked it back, Evan released it, though she could feel his gaze imploring her.

She tossed back her head and tugged on the lead rope to Little Boy. "Yes, everything's fine. And it will be even better once we get this over with."

Then she led Little Boy to the tree next to Mr. Quinley's, painfully aware of Evan following behind her with his horse and of Mr. Quinley watching them both with his hawkish gaze. Her fingers trembled as she tied the rope around the tree trunk and tried not to think of the two men so close.

But even when they moved off a way to wait for her, her nervousness didn't ease. How was she going to get through this questioning? Enduring Evan's gaze would be bad enough, although her anger would help her through that. Enduring the investigator's questioning was a different matter, however. He was only doing his job, which made it even harder to talk to him, for he'd surely know if she told anything other than the truth.

The truth. She couldn't tell the truth, could she? Everything she'd done in London would sound suspicious. She was the last person to have seen Lord Mansfield, and she'd been mysterious in setting up their meeting. Even if she explained why she'd wanted the chalice, she couldn't explain the cowardly instinct in her that had made her flee the inn. She wasn't sure herself why she'd fled.

She had an even worse problem, however. She'd already told Evan she'd never met with Lord Mansfield. If she told the whole truth now, Evan would reveal to Quinley that she'd told him a different story about the chalice, and both men would find her conflicting stories suspicious. So what was she to do about this coil?

With a frown she turned from tethering Little Boy. There was only one thing for it. Give Mr. Quinley the same story she'd given Evan. She could tell the truth in every other respect, but she must continue in her lie that she'd never met Lord Mansfield. Otherwise, they'd not believe anything else she told them.

There was another consideration, too. If she told the truth about the chalice, Mr. Quinley would tell Lady Mansfield, who would no doubt demand to have the chalice returned. Then Catrin would find herself in the same position she was in before—without a husband or hope of a future for her and her servants and tenants.

When she faced the two men, her mind was set. She would tell them everything she could, but she refused to risk all by telling them the truth about the chalice, especially when she knew nothing about the murder to help them. Now if only she could manage to sound convincing when she wanted nothing more than to crawl into a hole and never come out.

What would Grandmother have done? she wondered as she strode to where the two men stood. Would Grandmother have lied? No, she'd have brazened it out. She'd have made all the suspicious things sound perfectly natural.

But then, Grandmother had always been bold enough for any aggressor. By the end of the questioning, she'd have had the investigator begging her pardon for his audacity, and there'd have been no talk of prison or of confiscating the chalice.

Usually thoughts of her grandmother's capabilities made Catrin all too aware of her inadequacies, but today it helped her to imagine Grandmother turning her steely-eyed gaze on Mr. Quinley. Mr. Quinley was just a man, after all. And Catrin had a perfectly good reason to lie—not only to save herself from jail but to save her lands from confiscation and the people dependent on her from losing their positions. Lying to Mr. Quinley was the only thing to do.

But what about Evan? Could she lie to him?

She squared her shoulders. She could do *that* perfectly well. He'd lied to her without a thought. He'd manipulated her and assumed the worst about her without any reason. From the moment he'd spun his tale about wanting her help with a book, he'd given up his right to the truth. He deserved to be lied to.

And she'd have no trouble giving him his just deserts.

His stomach fisted into a hard knot as Evan watched Catrin sit on the hard ground a good distance from him, ignoring the coat he'd spread out for her.

Good God, she was enraged. It was clear in every rigid line of her face, in the fury of her glance, in the tight tone of her voice. He'd never seen Catrin truly angry before, and it tore at him to know he'd been the one to provoke her.

What made it worse, however, was the pain he glimpsed behind the anger. He'd hurt her. He could only imagine how much. She sat there convinced that his interest in her had been purely prompted by his desire to learn the truth about Justin, with Quinley here, he couldn't even explain that everything had changed—that once he'd gotten to know her, he couldn't believe anything bad of her.

He must find a way to talk to her, to make her listen. She

must listen to him. How could he bear it if this was the end of things between them?

Quinley's first question—why hadn't she used her real name when she'd approached Justin?—was one Evan had wondered about as well. But Catrin's explanation showed him just how groundless all his suspicions had been.

Lady Mansfield hadn't wanted to sell the chalice to her, so Catrin had been afraid to tell Justin her real name, for fear he'd tell his mother.

Evan easily accepted that explanation. Justin's mother had always been miserly, which had prompted Justin's profligate spending. Although the chalice hadn't probably mattered a whit to her, once she'd learned that someone else wanted it, her first instinct had no doubt been to clutch it tight to her chest and pray she could find an even better buyer for it. He could even admire Catrin's resourcefulness in using her appellation of the Lady of the Mists to entice Justin to meet her. It had obviously worked, and looking at it through her eyes, he could perfectly understand why she'd done it.

As she answered Quinley's questions about the chalice, Evan's spirits sank lower and lower. She told Quinley the same things she'd told him when she'd thought she could trust him. She even told the investigator about the curse and why she'd wanted the chalice so badly.

Although Evan had decided three nights ago that Catrin couldn't be guilty, it still pained him to hear how blameless she was, for it made his subterfuge with her even more unconscionable. He could easily remember their last night together . . . how she'd told him about the chalice in such innocence . . . how she'd revealed her belief in the curse, which she'd apparently told no one else about but Morys . . . and how he'd had the chance to tell her the truth about his own motives then, but hadn't.

The knot in his stomach grew hard as stone. She would never forgive him for that. Never. And he couldn't stand the thought of her never forgiving him.

Quinley rubbed his heavy jowls. "So you say you never met with Lord Mansfield at all, eh?"

"I never did." Her voice shook as she met the investigator's too keen gaze.

She was suffering so, Evan thought, and he couldn't even comfort her. She wouldn't let him.

Arching one thick eyebrow, Quinley flipped through the notebook he'd been scribbling notes in. "Nothing I have learned so far either proves or disproves your assertion, Mrs. Price. The innkeeper and his wife admit to having directed you to the room where you were to meet Lord Mansfield, but they never saw Lord Mansfield enter the inn. Of course, if Lord Mansfield arranged for the private room as you have just told me, then he would have known which room to go to, and he wouldn't have needed to make his presence known to anyone. In fact, he might have chosen to pass through as inconspicuously as possible, as nobility often do when they are in less than reputable places."

"Yes," Evan interjected, "but surely someone would have seen him and remarked upon it."

Quinley looked over at him with eyes narrowed. "Denizens of such places tend to mind their own business, sir." He stared another long moment at Evan, as if trying to assess his interest in the entire affair, before turning his attention back to Catrin. "Now, Mrs. Price, I'd like to know why you left London without even seeking to discover why Lord Mansfield hadn't kept his appointment with you."

Catrin colored. "I-I didn't need to discover it. By the next morning the murder was in all the papers, and I read about it."

Again, Quinley's ubiquitous eyebrow quirked upward. "Oh? And did you not consider that you had information of relevance in solving his murder?"

"I did consider it. But I hadn't seen anything. I didn't know anything." Her voice lowered. "And to be truthful, I was afraid to come forward. I didn't know that anyone knew about our meeting, and I thought it best to leave it that way. I suppose that sounds awful, but it's the truth."

Those few words explained so much. Alone in an unfamiliar city, Catrin had probably been terrified at the thought of going to a constable, especially when she had no new insights to offer.

But while her words increased Evan's guilt even more, they apparently only piqued Quinley's interest. "Yes, I see," said the investigator in even tones. "I suppose you couldn't have known that anyone was aware of the meeting. How could you know Lord Mansfield carried the last of your letters about in his coat pocket? That is, unless you had something to do with the removal of the letter."

The look of surprise on Catrin's face was so genuine that Evan groaned. His poor darling didn't even know what Quinley was talking about, which only further confirmed her innocence.

"What do you mean?" she whispered. "I don't understand."

"It's simple, madam. When Lord Mansfield left his club, after showing your letter to Mr. Newcome here, he proceeded straight to the inn where he was to meet you. We can only assume that he had the letter on him when he was murdered, an assumption that Mr. Newcome made as well. Yet no letter was found on Lord Mansfield. I must admit I can see no reason for thieves to take it, whereas I can see any number of reasons for you to take it."

"Any numbers of reasons?" Her voice sounded hollow. "You mean only one reason, don't you? That I murdered him and wanted to hide the evidence of our meeting."

Quinley seemed faintly surprised by her straightforward assessment of his words. "That could be one interpretation of the events, yes."

When the blood drained completely from Catrin's face, Evan felt fury rise inside him. "This is absurd! The letter could have fallen out in the scuffle . . . or Justin might have left it in his carriage or—"

"He didn't take a carriage, Mr. Newcome," Quinley interjected. "As you may recall, he walked."

"Fine," Evan bit out. "But that still doesn't prove anything."

"You seemed to think so at one time," Quinley said pointedly.

Evan groaned, especially when he noticed Catrin's face grow even more ashen. He had started all this, but God help him, he wished he hadn't. If he'd known when he came here he'd find a sweet, shy gentlewoman instead of the greedy schemer he'd thought to discover. . . .

Somehow he had to find a way out of this for Catrin. The investigator's evidence against her was flimsy at best. Surely Quinley knew that.

Apparently, he didn't. Quinley leaned forward, taking

Catrin's hand in what to all outer appearances looked like a gesture of comfort. But Evan knew it wasn't that at all.

"Have you anything to say, Mrs. Price?" Quinley asked in a voice deceptively gentle. "Do you have any idea where the letter might have gotten to?"

She shook her head, her distress plain in the way her gaze darted from bush to tree as if she searched for some rescuer. "Truly, I don't know anything about the letter, Mr. Quinley. I-I mean, I wrote it, but I have no idea what might have happened to it later."

"And you know nothing about what happened to Lord Mansfield the night you were to meet with him?"

She swallowed. "No." Her gaze locked with Quinley's, her eyes brimming with tears. "But I *am* sorry he was murdered."

Evan noted with grim satisfaction the discomfort that spread over Quinley's face. The man wasn't blind. Obviously, he was beginning to realize that Catrin Price was a genteel innocent and not at all the sort of woman he'd been led to believe, who could arrange a man's murder without a thought. Still, would that be enough to keep him from bothering Catrin? It was clear he had no evidence against her, but then that didn't always matter in English courts.

Suddenly, a rumbling sound came from down the pockmarked road. The three of them looked up in time to see a carriage hastening toward them. Though Evan didn't immediately recognize Catrin's coach, he knew it was hers because of the man whose head was stuck out the window, scanning the road ahead. Catrin's watchdog, Bos.

Catrin rose quickly as the carriage came to a shuddering halt on the road and the servant leapt out. "Bos! What are you doing here?"

Bos's gaze lingered a moment over Evan and then Quinley. Then he said through tight lips, "I have come to fetch you home, madam. There is an emergency, I'm afraid."

"An emergency?" Alarm suffused Catrin's face. "What kind of an emergency?"

"The kind only you can deal with. I would rather not speak of it here."

For once, Evan was pleased Bos took his responsibilities so seriously. No doubt, the "emergency" was simply a way to get Catrin out of Quinley's clutches. The investigator had gone first to Plas Niwl, and Bos had thus been alerted to the fact that a stranger was causing trouble for his mistress. It didn't surprise Evan at all that the butler had taken it upon himself to rescue Catrin. It was more than Evan himself could do at the moment.

But Catrin was apparently oblivious to Bos's ploy and seemed to take it at face value, for her anxious expression looked genuine. "I suppose I must come then. We'll have to tether Little Boy to the back of the carriage. He has a sore and can't tolerate a rider just now."

"There is no time for that," Bos said. "I shall send a groom back for him."

Suddenly, she seemed to remember her companions. Turning back to Quinley, she asked, "May I go now, sir? I've told you everything you wish to know. I can't tell you any more, and as you see, I have pressing duties at my estate."

Quinley's exasperation was clear. "Yes, you may go." When she murmured thank you and headed for the carriage, he called out, "But I may think of other things I need to ask you. If I do, you will be at home, won't you?"

"Yes, of course," she said, letting Bos help her into the carriage. She stuck her head out the window and fixed Quinley with a steady gaze. "Rest assured, Mr. Quinley, I am willing to help you in any way I can." Then without even a glance at Evan, she told the coachman to go, and they were off in a cloud of dust.

With a mixture of emotions Evan watched her ride away. On the one hand, he was pleased to see her escape Quinley's questioning. On the other, a sharp despair filled him at the realization that she was once more inaccessible to him, surrounded by her servants and her fears.

He didn't realize how much of his feelings showed in his face until Quinley cleared his throat, then said in an acid tone, "Next time, sir, I think you should leave the investigating to professionals."

Evan swung around to face him. "What is *that* supposed to mean, Quinley?"

The investigator faced him with a calm countenance. "It merely means that you are quite obviously inexperienced at eliciting the truth from an unwilling subject, especially when that subject is a pretty widow."

Evan gritted his teeth. "I came here as convinced as you

that she'd had something to do with the murder. But only a fool could learn what I've learned of Catrin and still persist in believing her guilty."

"And what have you learned?" Quinley drew a pipe from his pocket and busied himself with filling it. "Or have you gone over so fully to the young woman's side that you aren't willing to tell me?"

Evan was rapidly losing patience with the man. "I'll tell you whatever you wish to know, Mr. Quinley, but I assure you none of it paints her guilty." He drew a deep breath. "First of all, she is indeed very shy, certainly shy enough to be afraid to face a magistrate."

Quinley lighted his pipe with a nonchalant air. "Yet that 'very shy' woman traveled alone to a strange city and agreed to meet a strange man in an inn without knowing a single thing about his character."

"Because she wanted the chalice very badly. She truly believes in that curse of hers, you know. She even refused to marry the local schoolmaster because she believes marriage to her is a death sentence. You should talk to him. He's thoroughly convinced of her belief in it. And so am I."

Drawing deeply on his pipe, Quinley regarded Evan with narrowed eyes. "You're saying she was desperate for that chalice, so desperate she would have swallowed her innate shyness to obtain it."

"She wasn't desperate enough to have a man murdered, if that's what you're implying."

"What if she couldn't meet Lord Mansfield's price? I began my questioning this morning in Llanddeusant and discovered that she recently sold a painting for a hundred pounds, probably to ensure she could purchase the chalice. Yet that amount is only half of what she offered Lord Mansfield. What if she couldn't raise the other half? What if he'd refused to sell it to her for less, so she'd had it stolen from him?"

Evan rolled his eyes. "Even if she's lying and her meeting with him went as you say, she could hardly have arranged to have footpads attack him between the time he left the inn and the time he reached the alley down the street. And surely you don't believe she did the deed herself."

"Of course not. But we have no idea how long Lord Mansfield remained in the inn before he ventured into the street. Nor do we know if Mrs. Price brought anyone with her. She might have brought two companions along for the very purpose of relieving Lord Mansfield of the chalice if he didn't agree to her price."

Uttering a frustrated sigh, Evan stared off down the road. "Then why kill him? Why not just have him robbed?"

"Because he would know who'd done it. She would have had no other choice but to be rid of him."

He tried to imagine Catrin plotting to gain the chalice . . . hiring footpads and stationing them outside the inn so they could accost Lord Mansfield—or not—according to her signal. But he couldn't. The idea was ludicrous. It wasn't in her character. He knew it, and any number of people in Llanddeusant could attest to it.

He groaned. Of course, there were the few who would claim she cast spells and created havoc, people like her father-in-law. Good God, he could only hope that Quinley was too good an investigator to listen to such hogwash.

Suddenly, it occurred to him that he had a piece of evidence in Catrin's favor. "I don't know if you realized this from Catrin's words, but before you arrived, she told me about the chalice and her trip to London to acquire it. If she'd done something as awful as you think, why would she have told me about her trip at all? I was a stranger to her. If she was guilty, she risked a great deal in telling me. Yet she did."

Mr. Quinley drew deeply on his pipe. "That is indeed curious. I take it she didn't know of your part in the investigation?"

"No. She believed me when I said I was in Llanddeusant doing research." Evan leaned forward. "And consider this—in telling me of the chalice, she made it quite clear that her trip was unsuccessful. Her story to you and her story to me were exactly the same, yet when she told me of it, she didn't know who I was. If she'd managed to acquire it after all, why wouldn't she have said so while she was being so open?" Evan smiled in triumph. "She didn't say so because she doesn't have the chalice, because she has nothing to hide, because she is blameless. Only the innocent are so open about their actions."

"Actually, that's not true," Mr. Quinley said with a puff on his pipe. "Guilty men—and women—often have a need to confess to someone. Their dark deeds eat at them until they spill out the truth at unwarranted moments. We catch many a criminal because of an unwise word said here or there."

"Oh, for God's sake, she's not a criminal. Surely you could see that in five minutes of talking to her." When Quinley merely shrugged, Evan's exasperation turned to fear for Catrin. "So what will you do now?"

"I've done all I can do, since I have no hard evidence of wrongdoing on Mrs. Price's part. But I do intend to report my findings to Lady Mansfield—and the constable in London—upon my return. If they choose to pursue the matter further, they may. In the meantime, I shall spend the rest of the day finishing my questioning of the townspeople of Llanddeusant before I leave on the morrow."

"And those you've already questioned. What do they tell you about Catrin Price?" Evan awaited the man's answer with held breath.

Quinley glanced away, his face inexpressive. "If you must know, a few ignorant folk claimed she's a witch and such nonsense. I suppose that's to be expected in Wales." He shot Evan an arch glance. "But most of them hold Mrs. Price in high regard, probably because she lends her assistance to charitable institutions."

Evan hid his relief. "Does that count for anything with you?"

A puff of smoke escaped Quinley's lips as he fixed Evan with a level gaze. "Of course. It will go into my report with everything else, including the observations you have made. I am merely trying to get at the truth, Mr. Newcome. And unlike you, I am not easily swayed by soft words and sweet looks."

Evan ignored the subtle insult. "Just be sure you *do* get at the truth, Quinley. Because if you hound Mrs. Price to jail on the basis of nothing but a few conjectures and my own early speculations about that letter, I'll find a way to prove your incompetence in this investigation. Though that may not sound like much of a threat, I do have many friends in positions of power. No doubt, more than you."

Quinley didn't even bat an eyelash. "You will do what you feel you must. But if I were you, sir, I'd hesitate to place my trust in a woman, even a woman of Mrs. Price's obvious background. Women are natural deceivers. Remember, 'twas the sweet-faced Eve who tempted Adam to sin . . . and Adam's lust that brought about the downfall of man."

Leaning close, Evan stared Quinley down. "As I recall, Lucifer, the serpent, tempted Eve first, and he was decidedly male." He lowered his voice to an angry hiss. "What's more, if God hadn't wanted Adam to lust, why did He create Eve in the first place?"

That bit of unorthodox theology must have taken Quinley aback, since he said not a word as Evan stalked off toward his horse. But Evan could feel the man's speculative gaze on him, and much as he hated to acknowledge it, he knew he should heed Quinley's cautious words.

Catrin had taken hold of him in an alarming way. It frightened him how badly he wanted her and how quickly he'd come to believe her version of what had happened in London. Yet he couldn't help but think her innocent, for to think anything else meant forsaking his instincts, which told him she was falsely accused.

He ought to leave her alone. He'd already hurt her too much. He'd never convince her that everything he'd said to her wasn't a lie.

He sighed as he untethered his mare and wondered what to do. A glance at Catrin's pony decided him. Quickly, he mounted his horse, then reached down and loosened her pony's tether. With the rope in his hand, he prodded his horse forward, leading her pony behind him.

He must see her again. He couldn't leave her feeling wounded and betrayed. Somehow he had to convince her that he believed in her. But he feared that would prove a far more difficult task than convincing the investigator of her innocence.

Chapter Eleven

My choice is to share with and be with a girl
privately, with secrets and with gifts. . . .
You are my choice. How do I stand with you?
Why are you silent, my pretty silence?
—Hywel ab Owain Gwynedd, "Ode to a Chosen Girl"

The rain drummed against the window in Catrin's study, the storm blowing it nearly horizontally against the house. Catrin sat in the window seat, watching the fat drops bombard the many-paned glass, and wishing they could somehow beat her traitorous thoughts out of existence.

No matter how much she told herself that she was well rid of Evan Newcome, that he'd betrayed and manipulated her, other soft thoughts of him intruded to torment her. He'd come to her defense so gallantly that night at the wedding. He'd given both Sir Huw and David a piece of his mind, and then he'd comforted her with the tenderness of a lover.

More insidious thoughts plagued her, however . . . thoughts of how he'd kissed her and fondled her and offered to make love to her. Was it all a sham? Or was it as he'd tried to tell her this afternoon—that things were not "as they seem?"

She pressed her head to the glass, welcoming the cool hardness of it against her too warm skin. What was she to do? How could she drive this man from her mind?

With a sigh she left her seat at the window, going to the bookshelf and opening the secret compartment. The chalice was still there, of course. She stared at it. Had it been worth it, gaining the chalice? This afternoon's discussion of the murder had reminded her of how high the cost of acquiring it had been. Lady Mansfield had lost a son. Evan had lost a friend. She'd been lied to and manipulated and—

A knock at the door drew her from her thoughts. "Yes?"

"May I have a word with you, madam?"

She relaxed. Bos. Dear, sweet Bos. "Come in," she called

out as she gave the shelf a little push to move it back into place, then turned to face the door.

It opened to reveal Bos wearing an expression of thinly veiled sympathy. Seeing her loyal servant made her feel better. Yes, her pursuit of the chalice had been worth it. It wasn't her fault, after all, that Lord Mansfield had been robbed, and she needed the chalice, for herself as well as the people depending on her.

Those people cared about her a great deal. Bos had demonstrated that dramatically when he'd come to her rescue that afternoon. The "emergency" he'd referred to had proven merely a ploy to get her out of the London investigator's clutches. When Mr. Quinley had appeared at Plas Niwl and stated his credentials, Bos had grown alarmed. He'd thought it unwise to be as protective and vague about her whereabouts with Mr. Quinley as he'd been with Evan, for he didn't want her to look guilty. Nonetheless, Bos had been determined to make sure Mr. Quinley didn't badger her. So he'd come after her. For that, she would always be grateful. She couldn't have borne a long walk back to Plas Niwl with Evan and Mr. Quinley at her side.

Now, however, Bos seemed extremely uncomfortable. He stood immobile for a long moment before he cleared his throat. "I am sorry to disturb you, madam, but we have a problem."

Alarm skittered through her. Had Mr. Quinley come to question her further? What more could she say? How else could she allay his suspicious?

"It concerns Mr. Newcome."

Bos's voice held an unmistakable edge of contempt. In the height of her anger and hurt that afternoon, she'd told Bos everything that had transpired in her interview with the investigator. To his credit Bos hadn't said, "I told you so," when informed of Evan's betrayal, but he'd been as irate as she.

"Yes?" She tried to make her voice sound calm. "What about him?"

"He wishes to see you, I'm afraid."

His words shattered all her attempts at calm. She stepped forward. "He's here? Downstairs?"

The merest raise of his eyebrows demonstrated Bos's surprise. "Not downstairs. Really, madam, you did not think I would allow the man entrance into the house after what he had done to you, did you?"

She tried to hide her disappointment. "Oh, I see. You sent him away. That was the right thing to do, of course."

Bos's lips tightened. "I attempted to send him away, madam, but he refused to leave. That is why we have a problem."

As it dawned on her what he was trying to tell her, she ran toward the window. "You mean, he's sitting outside in the rain?" She rubbed away the condensation on the window and peered out, trying to see if he was there, but it was too dark and the rain too heavy to see anything.

"Precisely. I had assumed that the mountebank would leave when the storm worsened, but he is still rather stubbornly sitting on the entrance steps."

"How long has he been there?" she asked in alarm.

"I believe it has been nearly two hours now. He says he will not leave until he is allowed to converse with you."

Two hours! The storm had begun nearly an hour ago, yet he'd been sitting in the tempest all this time?

A shaft of lightning tore across the sky, and she jumped. "We can't leave him out there in the rain! It's dangerous! He might be struck by lightning!"

"One can only hope," Bos said dryly.

"Bos!" she scolded as she lifted her skirts and strode to the door.

"You must admit it would solve a few of your difficulties if Mr. Newcome were to . . . shall we say . . . expire of natural circumstances."

She circled around Bos when he tried to block her path to the door. "Oh, yes, that would certainly help. Then Mr. Quinley could blame me for *two* deaths that aren't my fault, instead of one."

Bos followed her as she left the room and hurried down the hall. "Surely, you do not intend to let him enter the house."

"I'm not going to leave him out in the rain to be struck by lightning or catch his death of an ague." She hastened down the stairs. "I could never forgive myself if something were to happen to him."

Bos struggled to keep up with her mad flight down the stairs. "Then let me fetch him in and see that he is cared for.

You need not deal with him. He can stay here until the storm ceases, and then I shall send him on his way."

"Yes, on crazy Medea, no doubt." She stopped short on the landing, turning back to look at Bos, who was coming on stiff legs down the stairs. "I appreciate your concern, Bos, but if I let you take care of him, he'll probably find himself boiled in oil."

Bos shrugged. "But if *you* care for him, madam, you may find yourself in jail. After all, he came to Llanddeusant to discover a way to have you arrested."

She bit her lip. "I know. Don't you think I've told myself all that?" She cast him an imploring glance. "But I can't let him perish in the storm either, don't you see? It would make me no better than him."

Bos sighed. "You are too kindhearted. It will be your downfall one day."

"No doubt." When Bos looked so forlorn, she added, "Don't worry. I won't let him hurt me again. This time I know what he really is. I'll make sure he's taken care of, then leave him in the servants' capable hands. All right?"

"Whatever you wish."

She ignored the skepticism in his expression and hurried down and into the hall. As she headed for the door, she called out to the footman to fetch the maids and tell Mrs. Griffiths to start boiling water for a bath and to stoke up the fire in the Red Room. Then waiting only long enough to allow Bos to help her into her hooded coat of oiled twill, she rushed outside.

It took her a few minutes to find Evan. The rain blinded her at first, stinging her face with nettled drops. Then she spotted him seated at one end of the steps, his back against the marble side in a futile attempt to protect himself from the driving rain. She hastened to his side as quickly as she could on the slick steps.

He'd drawn his knees up to his chest and had bent his head, so he was almost curled into a ball against the rain that beat relentlessly against him. A pang of guilt hit her, and she immediately cursed it. The man deserved such treatment after all he'd done to her. It wasn't as if she'd asked him to sit out in the rain like a fool.

Nonetheless, when she went to his side and tugged at his

arm, untold relief washed over her when he lifted his head and murmured, "Catrin? Is that you?"

She pushed her hood back a little so he could see her face. "Yes."

There was no reproof in his eyes, though he said in a low voice, "You've taken pity on me at last."

"Come inside," she urged. "Come. You mustn't sit here."

He glanced up at her window. "I thought you'd left the window because you'd grown bored with witnessing my suffering."

"Don't be absurd," she hissed as she pulled on his arm again. "I didn't realize you were out here, or I'd have told Bos to let you in at once."

This time he stood, a hulking form against the flash of lightning that suddenly lit the sky. "And all this time I'd supposed you were punishing me. Since I deserved it, I had no quarrel with it."

"Hush," she murmured, his self-deprecating words striking her hard. "Come inside where it's warm. You must be soaked through and freezing to death."

Now that he was standing, she noticed he was shaking all over. But through chattering teeth, he managed to say, "It's not so bad. I've been through worse."

"They're preparing a warm bath inside," she said as she clasped his arm to lead him up the steps. "My servants will get you out of those clothes and into the bath before you take your death of a chill."

"Your servants? You will have no part in it?" He halted on the top step. "You're going to send me inside and disappear? Because if that's the case, I'd rather stay out in the rain. At least here I can watch you in the window."

"Oh, you . . . you fool!" She yanked at his arm, but he didn't move, merely watching her with eyes grim and silent. How could he be so stubborn and arrogant even when soaked to the skin and on the verge of catching his death of a chill? "You can't stay out here in this weather!"

"I must talk to you, Catrin. And until you're willing to talk to me, I'll stay anywhere I bloody well please."

She hesitated, and even briefly considered leaving him out there. But she couldn't. "Oh, very well. You may talk to me, though I promise it won't make a whit of difference." She planted her hands on her hips. "*Now* will you come inside?"

Though he gave a great shudder, a smile stole over his face. "I am at your command. As always."

By the time she'd gotten him in the house, her cloak was soaked through. Ignoring Bos's scowl, she handed her cloak to the footman, then told another of the men to take Evan to the Red Room and get his clothes off him.

"I shall attend to it," Bos interrupted, placing a hand on the footman's shoulder.

"Bos—" she began in a warning tone.

But he murmured, for her ears only, "I promise not to boil him in oil, madam. I think, however, that someone with a firm hand should make sure that this is managed properly."

But Catrin knew that what Bos really meant was "to make sure Mr. Newcome doesn't run loose through the house or harass you." She wasn't sure whether to be pleased or irritated by Bos's protective instincts.

"Catrin?" Evan said as Bos took one of his arms and gestured to a footman to take the other. "I want to talk to you. You said I could talk to you."

She was painfully aware of all the servants listening to every word. "Yes, of course," she told him as the two men dragged him away. "As soon as you're more . . . er . . . comfortable, I'll be there."

Surely the man didn't think she was going to watch him be undressed and take a bath, did he? That was carrying things a bit far, even for him.

After arranging for one of the larger footmen to lend Evan some of his clothes, she found Mrs. Griffiths, who assured her that the bath was almost ready and would be brought up to the Red Room momentarily.

As her servants scurried off to follow her commands, Catrin paced the hall. What was she going to do? She'd have to let Evan speak his piece, since she'd promised to do so. Yet how could she bear to listen to him, not being sure if what he told her was lies or truth? He'd lied to her from the beginning, the wretch!

Her conscience reminded her that she'd lied, too. She was still lying. But it wasn't the same, she told herself. She'd lied to ensure a future for herself and the people who depended on her. He'd only lied to . . . to . . .

To discover who'd murdered his friend. With a sigh she thought of Lady Mansfield's letter. Evan had not only been

Lord Mansfield's friend, but his closest friend. When she thought of the horrible manner of Lord Mansfield's death, she could almost understand why Evan had gone to such extremes to unmask the killer.

Almost. His urgent need to find a murderer still didn't excuse his methods of investigation. If he'd been suspicious of her from the beginning, why not say so? Why not come right out and ask her questions, instead of playing all those terrible games . . . making her think he had an interest in her, making her like him?

Nothing he could say excused that, and he must know it. So what did he hope to gain by talking to her? Besides, he knew everything now. Why hadn't he returned to London with his newfound knowledge and left her alone?

She didn't know the answer to that, but one thing she did know. She couldn't bear to be alone with him, to be reminded of the last time they'd been alone and he'd kissed her with a lover's fervency. Being reminded of all that would kill her.

By the time Bos came to inform her that Evan had completed his bath and wished to speak to her, she'd made up her mind—she would give him the audience he'd requested, but not a private one. He could say what he wished, but he'd have to say it with Bos present.

As she'd expected, Bos was more than happy to oblige her. He was obviously uneasy about letting her speak to Evan at all. But if he was uneasy, she was even more so. Nor did her uneasiness improve when she and Bos entered the room to find Evan wearing only a shirt and a snug-fitting pair of breeches.

A blush instantly stained her cheeks. "I thought one of the footmen had loaned you some of his clothing!"

Evan shrugged. "This is the best he could do. None of his waistcoats or coats fit me. Your housekeeper says it will take a few hours to dry my clothes, so you're stuck with me until then, I'm afraid."

"I see." By heaven, this would be even harder than she'd thought. He looked so different without his fine clothes, more like an adventurer than a scholar. His wet hair slicked back from his face and his grim expression lent him a dangerous air, at once more frightening and more tempting.

This wasn't the Evan Newcome who'd spoken cordially to

her of Celtic languages and Greek poetry. This was the Evan who'd beaten David Morys to the ground . . . and who'd kissed her with wild passion in the kitchen.

She clenched her fists. She wouldn't think of that, she simply wouldn't!

When she spoke again, she managed to make her voice cold and formal. "You said you wanted to talk to me, Mr. Newcome."

Evan winced at her formal tone. Then his gaze flicked to Bos, who was standing rigidly beside her. "Yes, but not with your watchdog here. I want to talk to you alone. Send him away."

She tossed back her head in a gesture that she hoped looked confident and arrogant. "Whatever you have to say can be said in front of Bos."

"You promised to hear me out," he said through gritted teeth.

"I didn't promise that our discussion would be private, did I?"

Evan's eyes narrowed. "If you don't send him away, I shall be forced to remove him myself."

When she gasped at his effrontery, Bos said coldly, "I should like to see you try it, sir."

"Stop this!" she protested. "Mr. Newcome, you wouldn't dare pick on an old man—"

"I am not an old man, madam," Bos remarked. "I am perfectly capable of taking care of myself in matters involving fisticuffs."

"You see, Catrin?" Evan cast her a dark, mocking smile. "We can settle the matter easily between us. And I shall try not to hurt him too badly—"

"Oh, a pox on you both!" she burst out. "All right, Mr. Newcome. You shall have five minutes. But Bos will be right outside the door, do you hear?"

Evan shrugged. "If that's what you want."

But Bos wasn't so amenable. "Really, madam, I cannot believe you would allow this scoundrel to intimidate you. We should both leave together—"

"No, I can't," Catrin interjected, turning toward her servant. "I promised to let him speak to me, and I must keep my promise. So you have to leave."

"But madam—"

"Please go, Bos," she whispered. "I-I just want this over with. Please."

For a moment he hesitated, his eyes shifting to Evan, and she feared the matter would end violently. Then he looked at her and sighed. "As you wish. But I shall be just outside if you need me."

"Thank you," she murmured. As soon as he'd passed through the doorway, however, she shut the door and whirled on Evan. "You are a bully, Mr. Newcome!"

Her words seemed to strike a chord, for anger flared in his eyes. But he merely said, "So I've been told. Still, it seemed the only way to get you alone."

"And why did you want me alone so badly?" She glared at him. "What did you think to accomplish? I don't even understand why you're here. This afternoon, you succeeded in finding out everything you sought. You now know what I did in London. What more can you want from me?"

"I want you to understand why I behaved so abominably. I want to explain. And to apologize."

"There's no need for that," she bit out as she turned away from him. She was cold, so very cold. She shivered and moved to the fireplace, putting her back to him as she held her icy hands to the flames. "I understand what you did. You wanted to find out who murdered your friend, and you assumed that I did it, so you came here to spy on me. It's all perfectly clear."

She felt him come up behind her, and she groaned. By heaven, if he so much as touched her, she'd crumble. She truly would.

But he didn't touch her. Instead, he began to speak in a low tone. "There's more to it than that. It doesn't excuse my actions, but I want you to know why I stooped so low." He drew in a ragged breath. "Justin—Lord Mansfield—was my closest friend. We'd known each other since I was twelve years old, so his death hit me very hard."

She clamped her eyes shut, wishing she could do the same with her ears. Merely speculating about his reaction to his friend's death hadn't affected her, but hearing it from his own mouth, hearing the pain in his voice, couldn't fail to touch her sympathies, and she hated herself for being so weak.

"The constable treated it as a simple case of thievery,"

Evan went on, "but I knew more than he did. Justin had shown me your letter—and the chalice—before he left to meet you, and I'd found it curious even then that you hadn't signed your real name. Justin treated it as a lark, so I didn't think any more about it. He invited me to go with him to the inn, but I couldn't because I had another engagement. When my companion didn't show up, I walked to The Green Goat on the chance that I might still find Justin there."

Catrin opened her eyes, turning to face him as dread for what he would say next built in her. He was so close, she could see the strained lines about his mouth and the growing memory of horror in his eyes.

He sucked in a breath, as if he were drowning and couldn't get enough air. "As I passed one of the alleys near the inn, I happened to glance down it. The moon was bright that night, as you may recall. I saw what looked like a body and went to investigate."

Despite everything, her heart went out to him. "You found him? It was you who found him?"

He went on, his face now grim. "There was a . . . great deal of blood, of course. Seven stab wounds produce an astonishing amount . . . of blood."

His breath came quickly now, and his eyes looked past her. She couldn't help herself—she laid her hand on his rigid arm.

But he didn't even seem to notice. "I called for the watch, and they came. I told them what I knew of why he was there, and they searched the body, but they didn't find any money or the chalice, so they assumed he'd been murdered in the course of a robbery."

He swallowed. "I found the whole thing very strange, however. He'd gone to meet a mysterious lady who wouldn't sign her real name. And the letter she'd sent him, which he'd carried on his person that night, was gone. Though I tried to believe the constable when he said the Lady of the Mists couldn't have had anything to do with it, the thought that I knew something that might lead to justice for my friend plagued me, until at last I decided to come here. I didn't even tell his mother my suspicions. I didn't want to upset her during a difficult time. That's why I didn't know who you were when I came. Everything she told Quinley about you after hearing of my suspicions from the constable . . . I didn't know any of that."

"All you knew was that I was a murderess," she whispered, her throat tight.

He shifted his gaze to her. "Nay, I wasn't such a fool as to leap to that conclusion. But I did have some vague idea that you might have . . . I don't know . . . had the chalice stolen from him so you wouldn't have to pay for it."

She stared at him incredulously. "You thought I hired men to rob and kill him?"

"Yes." When she gasped, he added, "I know it sounds farfetched, but it's not as strange as it seems. Quinley still considers it a possibility."

The blood drained from her face. "What do you mean?"

His eyes were steady on her. "After you left this afternoon, Quinley informed me that he found your story . . . suspicious. He thinks you might have had the chalice stolen . . . perhaps because you couldn't offer Justin as much money as you'd said and Justin had refused to take a lesser offer."

"But I ga—" She stopped short, her heart pounding. "I *had* the two hundred pounds. Why would he think otherwise?" By heaven, she'd nearly revealed that she'd given the money to Lord Mansfield, which would have shown that she'd lied about not having met with him. She must be more careful.

"Quinley's been talking to people in town. He knows you sold a painting to raise a hundred pounds to buy the chalice, and he wonders where the other hundred came from."

She stiffened. "He should have asked me. I would have told him it came from the hard-earned rents of my tenants, which I'd just collected." Terror filled her. "It's those very tenants whose livelihoods he'll jeopardize if he arrests me. Oh, Evan, if he takes me to jail—"

"He won't take you to jail." There was assurance in his voice . . . and something else—determination. "I made sure he knew you didn't have the chalice. I pointed out that you'd told me everything when you didn't even know who I was. I think I convinced him that was a sign of your innocence."

Catrin turned her face from him, sure that her guilt must be blazing in her face. If Evan ever learned that she *did* have the chalice . . .

Then the enormity of what Evan had done for her struck

her. Her voice dropped to a whisper. "Why did you try to convince him I was innocent? You didn't have to do that."

"Of course I did." There was distress in his voice. "I'll admit that when I first came here, Catrin, I believed you'd played some part in Justin's murder. And when you were so evasive at the lake, I was even more convinced of it. I was afraid to confront you with my questions because I thought you might flee. That's why I pretended to need your help with a book . . . so I could be around you."

Her gaze shot to his. "So you could spy on me."

"Yes, I admit it. So I could spy on you. There's no way I can deny that."

With a little sob she tried to move past him, but he clasped her shoulders to stop her. He went on relentlessly, his lips so close to her that she could feel his breath on her cheek. "Then things changed." His voice dropped a notch. "The more time I spent with you, the more I saw what you were really like, the more I *wanted* to be with you. And after a while I could no longer believe you had any part in Justin's murder."

She glanced up at him, her eyes accusing. "Oh? Then why didn't you tell me the truth once you decided to believe in me? Why did you go on lying?" She didn't even attempt to hide the tears that welled in her eyes. "For pity's sake, you let me think I . . . I was someone worthy of your attention when all the time you were merely trying to find out what I knew."

He dug his fingers into her shoulders. "Deuce take it, Catrin, you *are* someone worthy of my attention."

But she ignored his protest. "You didn't have any intention of writing a book about folk legends, did you? That was only one more way to soften me so I'd . . . tell you what you wanted to know. You probably never even read my essay." All her insecurities came rushing in at once, as she remembered how she'd thought he cared for her. "You must have thought me such a fool to actually believe you'd go one foot out of your way to visit me . . . to care about my opinions . . . to—"

"I *did* care," he protested, a stricken expression on his face. "I *do* care. Don't you see? That's why I couldn't tell you the truth once I realized you were innocent. I knew it would hurt you as it's hurting you now. And the last thing I wanted was to hurt you."

She averted her face, unable to bear the pity in his words. "I-I'm not a complete coward, you know. I could have borne the truth. I would have wanted to hear it."

"I didn't say you're a coward." There was no contempt in his voice, or even condescension. "If I've learned anything at all about you, Catrin, it's that you're brave about things that matter. Despite your fears and shyness, you do what must be done. But even brave women have feelings, and I simply couldn't bear to wound yours. If anything, 'tis I who am the coward. I knew if I told you the truth, you'd hate me . . . and I couldn't bear having you hate me. As you hate me now."

She shook her head. "I don't hate you. But . . . but you didn't have to take your game so far. You didn't have to pretend to desire me or—"

"Good God, Catrin, you're mad if you think I'm that good at pretending." He lifted his hand to turn her face to his. His eyes glittered as he moved his gaze slowly over her face, his expression growing more stained. "The desire wasn't pretended, I assure you. Not for one moment. Surely you could tell that I wanted you, that every time I kissed you, I could hardly keep from tearing your clothes off. Even when I wasn't sure what you'd done, I wanted you."

His words shocked her. Since this afternoon, it hadn't once occurred to her that his sensual overtures had been anything but part of his "mission" to find the truth. Could he mean what he said? Or was it one more way to spare her feelings?

She couldn't bear to find out. Steeling herself against the desire she surely imagined in his face, she tried to pull away from him. He dropped his hand from her chin, but only to slide his arm around her waist and draw her close.

"Does it frighten you to hear that?" he asked hoarsely. "Because it frightens me half to death that I desire you more than I've ever desired any other woman."

She averted her face from his, wishing she didn't want to believe what he said.

"Why do you think I came here tonight?" he persisted. "I didn't have to. I didn't have to wait in the rain and pray you'd give me the chance to explain."

She turned her face up to his as she blurted out, "Then why did you?"

Cupping her cheek with his free hand, he fixed her with eyes tempestuous as the storm he'd just left. "Because I couldn't bear the thought of never seeing you again." He rubbed the pad of his thumb over her lower lip, sending a traitorous tingling through her. "Because I couldn't stand the thought of never touching you . . . or holding you . . . or kissing you. . . ."

He said the last words on a breath, giving her full warning he was going to kiss her again. Yet she seemed incapable of doing anything but waiting for his lips to touch hers.

And when they did, a shudder broke over her, the shudder of a person finally given exactly what she wants. Her eyes slid closed as she parted her lips and let him drink of her mouth in a slow, sensuous kiss that stole her breath . . . her strength . . . her will.

It was probably only seconds before he lifted his mouth from hers, but it felt like an eternity. When it was over, she felt confused. How could her body betray her like this, accepting the kiss of a man who'd sought to have her arrested?

He must have wondered the same thing, for he pressed his forehead to hers and murmured in an incredulous voice, "You truly don't hate me."

She couldn't say a word. She had no earthly idea what to say.

"I know I had no right to that kiss," he whispered in a husky voice, "but I've spent three sleepless nights remembering that time in your kitchen and wanting you. I couldn't help myself."

And wanting you. The words echoed through a heart already torn by all he'd said to her. It was true he had no right to kiss her. It was also true she'd wanted him to, despite all her hurt and anger.

"Catrin?" he murmured, his mouth so very close to hers.

"Yes?"

"Can you ever forgive me for lying to you?"

She looked at him, swamped by a whirl of emotions. The warmth was giving her a headache and making it hard for her to think, the warmth of the fire . . . and of his breath . . . and of his body—

With a groan she moved out of his embrace and went to

stand by the window, pulling aside the heavy drapery as she looked out at the cooling rain and tried to think instead of feel.

But no matter how much her mind told her he'd behaved in a manner unbecoming of a gentleman, her heart urged her to consider what she would have done in his place. If Bos had been murdered, she'd have told any number of lies to search out his killer. And she'd only known Bos two years, whereas Lord Mansfield had been Evan's friend for much longer.

"Catrin?" Evan prompted. He hadn't moved from his stance by the fire. "Can you forgive me or not?"

She hesitated, but she knew what her answer would be. "I suppose I can."

He let out a breath. "Thank you."

Then she felt rather than saw him move to stand behind her, but she didn't realize how close he was until his hand stroked her hair, which had tumbled down about her shoulders when she'd taken her sodden cloak off. He swept the mass aside, then bent to plant a kiss against her bare shoulder.

She dropped the drapery as an instant surge of desire slammed into her, panicking her. It was one thing to forgive him, but quite another to let him stay here and kiss and caress her . . . and do things that might lead to other things . . . and . . .

He kissed further up her neck, and she whispered in a futile attempt to stop him, "Now that you have my forgiveness, you can leave here with a good conscience."

"I don't want to leave." He slid his hand about her waist and nuzzled her hair. Then his lips brushed her ear as he added in a husky whisper, "And I don't think you want me to leave either."

Her body, her traitorous body, trembled all over. "It . . . it doesn't matter what I want."

"Ah, but it matters to me." He turned her around to face him. She'd never seen him look so solemn. "It matters a great deal to me."

They stared at each other in silence. His hands rested lightly on her waist, but he made no attempt to do more. Still, the light in his eyes promised so many things. It reminded her that he'd been the only man who'd ever aroused her desire, the only one who could transform her into a wild woman with one long kiss.

Suddenly, a knock at the door made them both jump. Evan dropped his hands from her waist, though he didn't shift his gaze from her for even a moment.

"Madam?" called Bos through the door. "It has been more than five minutes. Shall I come back in?"

Catrin froze, unable to tear her eyes from Evan. His expression shifted subtly. He made no unusual sound or gesture, yet she could see the faintest flicker of fear in his eyes, fear that she would send him away.

"Madam?" Bos repeated. His voice now held a note of urgency that wasn't there before.

"I hear you, Bos," she called out. Oh, what to do? She didn't want to end this moment with Evan, yet she knew she should. And if she said, "Yes, Bos, we're finished here," it would be over. At least for the moment.

"I'll make this easy for you, Catrin," Evan said in a low voice. "If you call your watchdog back in, I will leave. I swear I'll leave and never disturb you again."

His eyes burned into hers as his voice dropped even lower. "But if you send him away, be assured of this. I will make love to you. I'll lay you down on that bed there and show you all the wanting that's built up in me from the day I saw you emerge from the lake."

The promise was clear in his eyes, in his aggressive stance, in the firmness of his tone, and it roused her like nothing ever had before.

"Those are your choices," he continued. "Those are the only two I'll give you. Perhaps it is unfair of me to give you such an ultimatum, but I know I can't continue here in this in-between state . . . I can't stay and spend night after night desiring you with every breath of my being. If I cannot have you, then I must leave. It's your choice."

She sucked in an aching breath. What a choice . . . to send him away and never lay eyes on him again or to give him everything. He asked so much . . . too much . . . without offering either marriage or any permanent agreement. He offered only temporary pleasures. And after it was over, she would be spoiled for any other man. She might even find herself pregnant with his child.

She should chide him for his arrogance and send him

away. She should flee him as fast as her legs would carry her. And yet . . .

Yet night after lonely night stretched ahead of her. What good was it that she could now marry when there was no man who came even close to affecting her the way Evan did . . . no man she could respect . . . no man whose company she enjoyed as much as his? What did it matter if he spoiled her for any other man, when she didn't want any other man? In truth, he'd already spoiled her for any other man, because after him, what other man could she tolerate?

Her eyes fixed on Evan, she called out, "Bos? Come in, please."

Evan closed his eyes, an expression of pain crossing his face. Then Bos entered the room, and Catrin said to the servant, "I no longer require your services this evening. You are dismissed for the night."

Evan's eyes shot open. He stared at her disbelievingly as Bos sputtered, "But madam, do you mean you wish me to leave you alone with this—"

"You are dismissed," Catrin said more firmly, unable to tear her eyes from Evan. But inside she prayed, *Please, Bos, for once behave as my servant and not my guardian.*

There was a long silence. She thought she could hear every drop of wax hitting the sconces and every slight shift of the logs on the hearth, it was so silent.

Then Bos sighed. "As you wish, madam." And he left, closing the door behind him.

Chapter Twelve

Her poet-prisoner, frail
In her wine-sweet body-gaol,
So I, though I do not tell
All truth of the miracle.
—Dafydd ap Gwilym, "In Morfudd's Arms"

Evan could hardly believe it. They were alone. She'd made her choice, and after everything that had happened, after he'd lied to her, she'd still chosen him.

"Good God, Catrin." He lifted his hand to stroke her face, still scarcely able to fathom what had happened. "I thought when you called Bos in—"

"If I hadn't let him see I was unharmed, he wouldn't have left."

"I'm glad you sent him away." He trailed his fingers in wonder over her blushing cheek. She was his now, *his* by her own choice. "I don't know what I would have done if you'd . . . sent me away instead."

"I should have." Uncertainty filled her face. "I shouldn't have agreed to see you or—"

He kissed her, muffling whatever else she'd been about to say. He wouldn't let her have any regrets, not tonight. Drawing her close, he kissed her thoroughly, relieved that though her mind still vacillated, her body knew exactly what it wanted. She lifted her arms to cling to his neck and pressed her body against him with the guilelessness of a woman who has no idea how much she was about to relinquish.

But he knew. He knew what she was giving up—her innocence. And though she believed she couldn't ever marry and thus would never need it, he felt a stab of guilt at what he was going to take from her.

The guilt was fleeting, however, as his body began to respond to her nearness, her sweetness, her untutored response to his kiss. Never had he held a woman whose passion mirrored his. His former fiancée had lacked passion entirely, only allowing him an occasional peck on the lips. When he'd tried to do more, she'd been outraged.

There'd been other women, of course. Though he'd never been able to afford a mistress, there had been plenty of women to warm his bed if he'd wanted—women seeking pleasure at the parties Justin dragged him to . . . the discontented wives of university staff . . . the married sisters of his students.

Yet that kind of meaningless lovemaking had never appealed to him as it had to Justin. He'd only resorted to it when he was desperate. And then none of the women he'd bedded had made him feel like this, driven and hot, eager to do almost anything to have them.

With Catrin, desire was a golden, glittering promise of fulfillment. When he smoothed one hand over the lovely curves of her hips, then up her waist to cover one of her rounded breasts, she groaned and arched into his hand, like a seagull lifting its white body into the wind.

The discovery that she wore no stays fired his memory of how she'd looked emerging from the lake, her rosy nipples showing through her muslin chemise. How he wanted to see her like that again. Or better yet, with all her clothes off, so he could stroke her white thighs and the sweet cleft between her legs.

Instead, he contented himself for the moment with kissing her long and deep, exploring every secret of her warm, wet mouth as he kneaded her breast through her gown. Only when he had her trembling in his arms did he move his lips down over her chin and the long slope of her throat to her collarbone, planting kisses everywhere he touched. Pushing down the neck of her bodice and chemise, he found her breast with his mouth and drew on the tight, pebbled nipple, feeling her dig her fingers into his shoulders as he did so.

"Oh, Evan . . ."

Her soft, shaky whisper drove him on until he had both of her breasts bared and was lavishing attention on one delicious crest and then the other, reveling in the way she twisted her body blindly against him in the urgency of her need.

His need was as urgent as hers. He wanted to have all of her, to bury himself between her pale thighs and feel her legs clamp about him in her eagerness. Oh, the wicked things he wanted to do with her . . . to taste her everywhere . . . to have her taste him. . . . And he would do them all eventually, but he must be careful, oh, so careful with his darling. She wasn't used to passion. It would frighten her, and the last thing he wanted to do was frighten her off.

Slowly, he drew his hand from her breast. Her eyes were closed and her lips parted. The sight of it inflamed him. "Catrin?" He bent his head to press a kiss to her arched throat. "I want to see you naked. Will you let me remove your clothes?"

Her eyes flew open, and she blushed a deep rose. "I . . . I . . . oh, Evan, I don't know. I have no idea what I should do and what I shouldn't."

With a low chuckle he turned her around and began to undo the buttons and ribbons that held her gown closed in back. "Don't worry. I know exactly what you should do."

She flinched, going very still as he pushed her gown off her shoulders. "I know you do. You've probably done this with countless women and—"

"Not countless," he interrupted. Good God, she wore no petticoats either, only her chemise. He knew it was the fashion, but seeing her in next to nothing made him grow unbearably hard. "And no one whom I've ever wanted as much as you."

He turned her back around to face him. She was so embarrassed, she couldn't even look at him. He cupped her cheek, feeling the heat of her blush against his palm. "Would it help if I let you take *my* clothes off, too?"

Her eyes went wide. "That would make it worse! Oh, Evan, I shouldn't be doing this! It's wrong!"

"Does it feel wrong?" he asked as he tugged loose the ties of her chemise, then dragged the thin muslin slowly off her shoulders until she stood there naked.

"Yes . . . no . . ." She trailed off as he raked his gaze slowly down her body to the pert breasts . . . the trim waist . . . the slender hips.

Her blush spread over her body when his gaze reached her triangle of silky hair. She tried to cover herself with her hands, but he caught them, murmuring, "Please, let me see all of you. I've dreamed of it in the night, my darling."

The endearment seemed to affect her, for although she ducked her head, she let him hold her hands aside and made no move to stop him as his gaze drifted down over her long legs, with the well-turned calves encased in stockings.

A faint hint of lilacs lingered on her body, reminding him that she was of a higher class than his . . . one that bathed daily in lilac-scented water and wore clothes of the finest muslin, like the ones he'd just removed.

As a boy he'd watched her kind come and go from Llynwydd. From a distance he'd marveled at their cleanness and beautiful clothing, for on the farm he'd been lucky to have a bath once a week and his clothes had been rough wool and homespun.

Now, of course, he could have baths when he wanted and dress in fine clothes and mingle with the same beautiful people he'd admired from afar. But inside, a little voice nagged him that he was a farmer's son pretending to be something better.

That voice clamored at him now, telling him he had no right to this exquisite woman with her blushes and innocence—no right to take a knight's daughter to bed. Firmly, he squelched the voice. Catrin wasn't the kind of woman to care about his class.

And she wanted him. He knew she wanted him. That was all that mattered.

He bent on one knee to untie her ribbon garters, then drew each of the stockings down until he'd removed both them and her dainty shoes. He slid his fingers up the inside of her leg, feeling her quiver as he did so. "Tell me, Catrin, does it feel wrong to have me touch you like this?" He swallowed convulsively, his throat raw with need. "Because it feels right to me. I've lain awake every night since the day I met you, wondering if your skin could be as soft as it looked or your legs so long and lovely."

He rose to his feet, but he kept his hand on her thigh, moving it higher until he was stroking the inner skin so close to her thatch of curls that they brushed his hand.

When he covered the springy hair with his palm, she gasped, but he gave her no time to protest. He took her mouth again, this time more roughly and thoroughly to distract her as he ran his finger along the silken folds.

She was damp and warm and quivering, and he moaned in sheer pleasure just to feel it. She wanted him. She was afraid, but she still wanted him.

When he first began to caress her cleft, teasing and rubbing, he thought she'd jump out of his arms, but as he stroked her more boldly, she groaned and pressed up against him.

"It feels right, doesn't it, dear girl," he murmured against her mouth.

Catrin scarcely knew what to answer as he moved his hungry mouth from her lips to suck her breast. It did feel right . . . and wonderful and thrilling. His mouth roused an ache that she'd never felt before, even in the loneliness of her bed.

And his fingers! They were magical beyond description! When one suddenly delved inside her, she shuddered at the intimacy, the outrageousness of it. But as he continued to stroke and fondle, rubbing and smoothing her fluid warmth over her skin until she tingled all over, her shock turned to an absolute pleasure so stunning she thought she'd die from it.

No one had told her it would be like this. On the night before Catrin's wedding, Grandmother had termed lovemaking a "sometimes pleasant duty," but had warned her there'd be pain the first time. From what her practical-minded grandmother had described of the act, Catrin could easily see how there'd be pain, for she couldn't imagine how anyone could plant anything inside her the way her grandmother had described.

But there was no pain yet. No pain at all, just the consuming need he roused that made her fist her hands in his shirt, then flex her fingers against the linen-draped muscles.

Suddenly, she wanted to touch those muscles more fully, to stroke his bare chest. Feeling a bit foolish, she nonetheless pulled loose the ties of his shirt. She'd never undressed a man before and wasn't sure how to do it, but the moment he felt her hands at his shirt, he helped her, drawing back only long enough to pull the shirt over his head.

He didn't stop there, however. With quick, urgent motions, he jerked his breeches, drawers, and hose off. Then he was naked, too.

She swallowed at the sight that greeted her. His was not the body of a scholar, though she'd guessed as much from the fine figure he'd always cut in his tight swallow-tailed coat and snug breeches. She wondered how he'd gotten such muscular shoulders and arms. Or the broad chest with its trickle of hair passing down between more well-defined muscles to a lean waist and then down to . . .

She jerked her gaze back to his face, the blood flooding her cheeks, but his eyes glittered now, and she knew he'd give her no respite from her embarrassment.

He confirmed that when he rasped, "Am I the first man you've seen naked, Catrin?"

"Yes."

"Maybe you should do more than look." With a dark smile he took her hand and placed it on his chest.

The thought of touching him shot a thrill through her that made her hand tremble as she ran her fingers down the sculpted chest and the ridges of his stomach. When she moved her hand over his belly with its deep, shadowed navel, his muscles bunched and tightened, and he shuddered.

She stopped, but he groaned and moved her hand lower until it actually rested on his jutting member. She tried to pull her hand away, but he wouldn't let her. Somehow his hand over hers, pressing her against him, freed her to explore him with all the curiosity she'd been ashamed to admit to. He gave a great shudder as she stroked the silky skin and ran her finger over the rounded tip.

Then she made the mistake of looking down at it, and she froze, her hand still on him. So this hard shaft was to go inside her? But how? It was too big. It would surely cleave her in two!

In a panic she jerked her hand from him, but he caught her fingers, lifting them to his lips and kissing them one by one. "Listen, darling," he murmured, "has anyone told you what lovemaking is about, what a man does to a woman in bed?"

Unable to look at him, she nodded.

"Then you've probably been told that it hurts."

She nodded again, more insistently.

He rubbed her hand against his whiskery cheek. "I assure you the pain is fleeting."

Shaking her head in disbelief, she tried to back away, but he caught her head in his hands, forcing her to stare into his fathomless eyes.

"I wouldn't lie to you about this, Catrin, not even to gain my own pleasure. It will hurt at first, but you must believe me when I say the pain fades quickly. And after that, you'll enjoy it. I'll do everything I can to make sure you enjoy it."

As she stared at him, eyes wide and uncertain, he brushed kisses on her cheeks, her nose, her brow. "*Everything* I can do," he added in a husky voice. Then before she could say another word, he lifted her in his arms and carried her to the bed.

She kept her eyes fixed on him as he laid her down. She didn't know how to contain her fear, and she wanted to protest that she hadn't really meant him to do this at all. But she couldn't do that after she'd asked him to stay. In any case, if she said no, he would leave her, and she didn't want that either.

He seemed to recognize her fears, for he lay down beside her and began to caress her body with gentle, soothing strokes as he stared down into her frightened face. "You must tell me what feels good and what doesn't. You must help me find your pleasure places."

She turned her face away, feeling exposed and embarrassed, but he covered her breast with his hand, then rubbed his thumb along the circumference of the nipple in teasing circles. "This is no time for shyness, Catrin. Outside of the bedroom you may be reticent, but here, with me, you must be bold. How else will I know how to please you?"

He thumbed her nipple, his voice dropping to a sensuous murmur. "Tell me, darling. Does this please you?"

When she remained silent, he started to pull his hand away, but she covered it and pressed it to her breast, giving him a mute look of entreaty.

He gave her a dark, provocative smile as he resumed his caresses. "Yes, that's it. You need not use words. Let your body speak for you."

What he said ended her reluctance. There was something less shameful about speaking to him in touches, drawing his hands to all the places of her body that had burned for touching in the middle of the night.

And he obliged her every wish. When she pulled his head down to hers, he took her mouth again, with tender delicacy at first, and then with more ardor, plunging his tongue inside to mate with hers. When she timidly pushed his hand below her waist, he needed no more provocation to run his hands over her belly, but he soon found secret places to caress that she had never dreamed were so sensitive . . . her navel . . . behind her knees . . . inside her thighs to coax her legs apart so he could settle his hard body in the juncture of her thighs.

That in itself gave her an unexpected pleasure that was only enhanced when he settled his hand there, too, rubbing between her legs until she thrust her hips boldly against those maddening fingers in an urgent need for more.

She could tell he wanted more, too, for his hand shook as he caressed her and a sheen of sweat broke out on his forehead. But he was patient and slow, only slipping his finger inside her when she prompted it by widening her legs.

"That's it, darling," he murmured against her lips. "Open yourself for me. Let me in."

She clutched at his shoulders, crying out as his fingers drove inside the tight, wet passage, deeper and deeper and more intimately. . . . Suddenly, he lifted his body slightly off hers, and it was no longer his fingers there but something harder, bigger—inching up insistently inside her.

In that instant her haze of pleasure shattered. Panicking, she bucked against him, as if to throw him off, but that only succeeded in driving him farther inside her. Then he came up against something and paused.

She gazed at him in wide-eyed fear as the feeling of invasion intensified. "Evan? Are you sure that this is the way? Are you sure?"

He gave her a strained smile. "I am quite sure."

His arms were tense as they bracketed her body. He seemed to be controlling himself only with the greatest effort. Though she appreciated his concern for her, it didn't lessen the strange feeling that she was his captive, her thighs widening to receive him . . . her breasts pressing beneath his chest . . . and that hard part of him delving into her as if to reach her soul.

She was his captive, and he would never release her. That was what his glittering eyes seemed to say, and his hard mouth, too, as he bent his head to take her mouth in a long kiss.

Suddenly, he began to move again, pushing, probing inside her. He groaned, then gave a hard thrust that planted him fully inside her.

There was indeed pain, just as he'd said. But she'd expected it to be terrible. Instead, a fleeting feeling, as of something tearing inside her, came and then was gone.

She wiggled her hips, curious to see if that was all, and he seemed to take that for an invitation, for he drew out and drove in again, his mouth now devouring hers. He was marking her as his, and she felt it in every thrust of his hips, every stab of his tongue.

And she wanted to be his, she discovered as his movements began to warm and then excite her. She didn't understand why the feeling of him inside her sent hot, melting pleasure spreading from her loins throughout her body, but she didn't stop to think on it. She simply let the enjoyment of it overtake her, push her on and up toward some height she could only glimpse.

"Ah, darling, you feel so good," he muttered against her mouth, scattering kisses over her cheeks and jaw before he lifted his face. "You can't know . . ."

"I . . . I can . . . I do . . ." she whispered as she met his thrusts, at first timidly and then with abandon. He felt wonderful, as if he belonged inside her, as if she'd been waiting all her life for him to join her in this incredible dance.

As he plunged deeper and harder and faster, each thrust carried her higher, like a runaway coach racing up the slopes of Black Mountain toward the brilliant sky. The brush of his taut belly against hers, the tantilizing look of hunger in his face, the delicious slide of him inside her made her insensible, until she no longer thought of anything but opening to him, pressing against him more and more and more. . . .

Then everything seemed to explode around her. "Oh, Evan!" she cried. She clutched him to her, feeling wave after wave of bliss inundate her in a swirl of light. "Yes, oh, yes!"

"My darling!" he cried out as he drove into her with one mighty thrust. She felt something warm and liquid fill her as they strained against each other. Then he sank against her body, burying his face in her neck. "My sweet . . . sweet . . . Catrin . . ." he whispered.

He lay atop her, his body twitching a little as she shook beneath him. Then as her body calmed, she dropped into a contented peace, warmed by the feel of him against her and the aftermath of what they'd just shared.

After a moment she felt him nibble at her earlobe. "Are you all right?" he whispered.

At the sound of his voice, so calm and normal, her innate shyness reasserted itself, and all she could manage was a nod. Then it hit her. She'd done it. She'd given her innocence to Evan, despite all the reasons she shouldn't have. By heaven, she was a ruined woman.

Yet she didn't feel ruined. Not at all. She felt alive and full of joy. Was this what she'd missed all these years? No wonder widows took lovers after their husbands died. Once they'd tasted this, they weren't likely to want to abandon it.

Then again, she couldn't imagine sharing this with anyone but Evan. It wouldn't be the same. She was sure of it.

Evan slid off to lie at her side, resting one hand on her belly as he propped his head up on the other. "Was there very much pain?"

"Only a little," she whispered.

"Good." Not looking at her, he traced circles around her navel, leaving tiny shivers of sensation everywhere he touched. "And was I right? Did you enjoy it despite the initial pain?"

His tone was so uncertain it gave her a start. Didn't he know? Couldn't he even guess? He always seemed so sure of himself that it surprised her to find he had doubts about how thoroughly he'd pleasured her.

It drove away her shyness. As she covered his hand and squeezed, she stared up into the features she'd come to know so well in the past few days. "It was the most wonderful thing I've ever felt."

When he met her gaze, his eyes shone. "I've never had that with any woman before. It's never been like that." He bent to press a swift kiss to her lips. "But from the moment I saw you, I knew it would be special with you."

Special, she thought with a little stab of disappointment. Yes, it had been special for her, too, special but so much more than merely special. Now what was to happen between them? Now that they'd shared this "special" thing, this glorious experience, what would he do? Leave her? Stay?

She didn't want to ask, to ruin the pleasure of the moment. But as he covered her mouth in a soft, tender kiss, only one thought played through her mind.

After this, what next?

Chapter Thirteen

A North Wales girl was once my passion.
She'd got two costumes, both in fashion,
Two matching hats as well, the peach,
And two false faces under each.
—Anonymous, "Two-Faced Too"

As the first streaks of dawn brightened the room, Evan quietly slid from the bed. He stood there staring down at Catrin. She slept so blissfully, her lips curved in a secretive smile and her hands clutching the blanket up around her shoulders. Her hair lay scattered across the pillow like crushed ebony silk.

He wanted to touch it, to twine each curl around his fingers as he had countless times last night, but he didn't want to wake her. He would have slept longer himself if he could have, but his early years of rising before dawn to tend to chores had made him an incurable early riser. Though he was still tired, he wouldn't be able to sleep again until evening.

Catrin, however, looked as if she might sleep for a while, and that was good. She needed the rest. He'd greatly taxed her strength. He shouldn't have taken her the second time, sore as she must have been from the first time.

Yet once had not been enough for him . . . nor for her either if he were to judge from the enthusiasm she'd shown the second time they'd made love. He bore marks on his shoulders where her fingernails had dug into him as she'd writhed and cried out her enjoyment.

The very thought of it aroused him all over again, and he muttered a low curse. He must give her body a chance to adjust to him. For all her passionate involvement in their lovemaking, she'd nonetheless been a virgin. This had all been new to her.

The thought doused his arousal as surely as a cold bath. A virgin. He'd never taken a virgin before. He'd never stolen a woman's innocence. But he'd certainly stolen hers. Now what was he to do with it?

Pulling on the drawers he'd borrowed from the footman, he went to the door and peered out into the hallway. As he'd expected, his neatly pressed and folded clothes sat on a stool outside the door. With a quick glance to make sure he wasn't noticed, he stuck one hand out and snatched them up, then shut the door.

He dressed quickly, keeping an eye on the slumbering Catrin. He had to think. He had to decide what this meant, and he couldn't think here in this room, with Catrin in that bed, looking so luscious. If he stayed here and watched her, he'd want to touch her . . . kiss her . . . make love to her again. No, he couldn't stay in this room. He would find somewhere quiet, where the servants wouldn't notice him and he could ponder what he'd done.

As he slipped from the room, easing the door closed behind him, his mind raced in circles. Last night when he'd come here, he hadn't thought about the consequences of his actions. He'd had one thought only—to see Catrin and beg her forgiveness for having deceived her.

But once he'd seen her, he'd known it wasn't enough. He couldn't simply gain her forgiveness and walk away. He didn't want to leave. He didn't want to think of never seeing her again, of never talking to her or holding her.

Why did she have this effect on him? he wondered as he walked down the hall to the stairs. Though he couldn't deny the appeal of her elfin looks and lithe body, he'd met women more beautiful.

But none of those women had made him feel like a king. The women of her class whom he'd known had always been aware of his inherent unsuitability as a companion. London society was small, and he'd been classed as "Justin's friend, a genius but a farmer's son." He'd once overheard a man describe him as "not a bad chap really, if he weren't a penniless Welshman. You know what I mean."

Evan had known exactly what the man meant. "A penniless Welshman." That was akin to saying "an immoral, lying scoundrel who'll sooner steal your sheep as buy them." How did that popular English rhyme go? "Taffy is a Welshman, Taffy is a thief." It didn't matter that his work was highly respected by critics, that he behaved as a gentleman, that he had friends among the gentry and nobility. As soon as he came around their daughters, his background was all that mattered.

Indeed, the only reason he'd captured the affections of beautiful, genteel Henrietta, was that her father, a Welsh merchant and a Londoner of some wealth, had been an odd old man who'd liked both Celtic scholarship and Evan. Mr. Williams had been determined to see his daughter married to a man of intellect and not to some unscrupulous fortune hunter.

Of course, unlike Henrietta, Catrin knew nothing of Evan's background. She didn't know that only twenty years ago, he would have watched her from afar. To her, he was a great scholar to be admired.

Was that why he wanted her so badly, because she represented the unobtainable? he asked himself as he strode down the stairs, thankful that no servants were in sight. Was it only his wounded pride that drew him to her for solace? Perhaps he simply longed to have someone respect him for what he was instead of what he had been. Perhaps he merely liked her for what she saw in him.

But no, he didn't think so. Even before he'd known who she was, she'd intrigued him. Catrin emanated a captivating blend of intelligence and shyness. She was bright, but didn't know it . . . pretty, but uncertain of her appeal . . . wealthy, but didn't care.

What's more, despite her class, she'd grown up in that same limbo he'd lived in all his life, never quite fitting in and trying to hide how much it mattered to her. Watching her bravely navigate those treacherous waters brought out all his protective instincts. He found himself wanting to shield her from the ignorant and uncaring.

That was the trouble. Now that he'd taken her virginity, he felt responsible for her. He ought to do something about the situation he'd put her in. He ought to offer marriage. That was the right thing to do. Even if she refused him and insisted on clinging to her ridiculous belief in that curse, he should at least offer marriage.

He paused on the stairway as his mind wandered to imaginings of life with Catrin as his wife, and a quick smile touched his lips. Not only would she be the rare woman who understood his work and his absorption with it, but she would be the perfect wife in every other way . . . considerate, passionate, refined.

His smile faded as he strode more quickly down the steps. Refined, yes. And wealthy. How could he offer marriage to a woman like that? He had no fortune to speak of. She might think he wanted to marry her only for her fortune.

Besides, there were other, more important considerations. With a shudder he thought of what could happen if he ever lost his temper with Catrin, shy, delicate Catrin. It would destroy her. She'd seen him angry, but not at her. He couldn't imagine ever being angry at her, but what if it happened? And what if he couldn't control it?

He forced himself to remember what had happened with Henrietta. His former fiancée had thought she was getting a gentlemanly scholar when she'd allowed him to court her. She'd always shown a liking for him, from the time she was a young girl and her brother had been one of his students. Evan, too, had fancied himself in love, though he now knew he'd only been responding to Henrietta's dazzling beauty and his disbelief that such an angelic creature could tolerate him as a suitor.

Everything had been perfect. When he'd offered for her, her father had been pleased, stating that he would bring Evan into his business, since Evan would have to leave the university to marry. Evan had started making plans to leave the college.

It had all changed the night Evan stopped at Henrietta's house unexpectedly and found Henrietta on the balcony in the arms of a strange man. Evan hadn't known the man was her cousin who'd just returned from years of military service. Nor had Evan stopped to ask. In a jealous rage he'd jerked the man away from her, striking him over and over until Henrietta's screaming had brought the servants.

That had been the end of his engagement. His actions had so appalled Henrietta that she'd wanted nothing further to do with him. He still remembered her tearful words—"I thought you were a good man, but you're a wild beast! And I cannot marry a beast!"

He winced at the memory, still a painful one. No, marriage wasn't wise . . . to Catrin or to anyone. In any case, Catrin didn't expect or want him to marry her. She truly believed she couldn't marry because of that bloody curse.

So what other choices were available to them? Ending his liaison with her wasn't one of them, to be sure. She'd crept into his heart, and he couldn't tear her out. He had to be with her. Nonetheless, could he stand being her sometime lover, coming here when he could, living from visit to visit as he carried on his real life in London?

He didn't think he could do that either. Yet the only other choice was to persuade her to come with him to London. He paused at the bottom of the stairs, glancing around him at the well-appointed manor that was all hers. How could he persuade her to leave all this to live in a scholar's lodgings, sneaking about like a pariah? No, that wasn't for Catrin either.

There was a choice he hadn't considered—to give up his position as fellow and live here with her. He shook his head as he moved away from the stairs toward a series of doors that looked as if they might lead to a parlor or a study or somewhere he could be alone.

Live here with her. Oh, certainly. Ask her to risk more approbation from the community, to be considered a whore by all who knew her and to bear him bastard children. That was impossible. Even if she agreed to it, he could not.

In fact, marriage did seem the best choice. Of course, he was assuming she would want to marry him, that their lovemaking had meant as much to her as to him.

What was that line from Farquhar? "The best security for a woman's soul is her body." He'd certainly done his best to secure her soul last night, hadn't he? But he wasn't sure it would be enough for Catrin. And suddenly he wanted very much to secure her soul.

He opened a door and found what appeared to be a study. Quickly, he slipped inside and stared around the room. A smile touched his lips. Catrin's study. It had to be. A half-knitted shawl lay draped across what looked like a sewing box. There was a desk and chair as in any man's study, but the desk was a delicate writing table with slender little legs and the fragile-looking chair would probably collapse under the weight of a man Evan's size.

The bookshelves, however, had a more masculine appearance. They'd probably been built long ago, when the men of the family hadn't been quite so scarce. Curious to see what kind of books she preferred, he moved to the shelves.

It pleased him to find she did indeed have a copy of his book, *The Development of Celtic Languages.* She also owned other scholarly works, mostly ones about myths and legends. She even had copies of the short-lived Welsh journal, the *Cambrian Register.*

As he moved along the shelves, taking out a book here and there, fascinated by this glimpse into his lover's interests, he suddenly came to a shelf that was slightly out of kilter. When he pushed on it, it swung in just a fraction.

A secret compartment. Good God, a secret compartment, of all things. He smiled at the thought of Catrin having such an archaic safe in her bookshelves and wondered if she even knew it was there.

Prompted by curiosity, he pushed it in all the way. The shelf slid open on well-oiled hinges, and as it came around, sunlight glinted off something metal. No, something bronze, he realized as the contents of the shelf were revealed. When the shelf shuddered to a stop, he stared at the object, his blood running cold. Before him sat a massive bronze chalice.

Memory slammed into him, of the night Justin had been murdered and had shown him the chalice Catrin wanted to buy. An ancient chalice. *This* chalice.

The one she'd claimed never to have bought.

"Oh, God," he groaned as he took the chalice from the shelf and stared at it, praying he was wrong and knowing he wasn't. He would have recognized the hideous thing anywhere, even after having seen it only briefly. It had the same strange etchings, the same unusual coded letters. Besides, if this wasn't *the* chalice, then why was Catrin keeping it hidden? No, it was the right chalice. Of that, he was certain.

A sense of betrayal sliced him so deeply, he reeled from the pain. Catrin had the chalice in her possession, which meant she had indeed met with Justin. Nonetheless, she'd lied about it, so thoroughly and so convincingly that he'd abandoned all his suspicions of her as a result.

His sweet, shy Catrin was not what he had supposed at all.

The ramifications of his discovery so overwhelmed him that at first he didn't hear the door open. But when a soft voice asked, "Evan? Why are you in here?" he whirled around, the chalice clutched in his hand.

Catrin looked like an angel in her white satin wrapper, her

raven curls lying in a tangle on her shoulders . . . her lips full and red . . . her eyes still dazed from sleep.

But she wasn't an angel, he reminded himself with a curse, and that fact was confirmed when she caught sight of what was in his hand and went pale as death.

The look of guilt on her face drove a stake right through his gut. "Come in and close the door," he commanded. "It's time you and I had a more honest discussion of what happened in London."

Catrin stepped across the threshold, but kept her hand on the doorknob. Her heart raced madly. This was horrible. First, she'd awakened to find him gone from bed. All sorts of thoughts had passed through her mind as she'd swept through the house looking for him. But she'd never expected to find him here with the chalice.

Drawing her wrapper more tightly about her, she whispered, "I know what you must be thinking, but I—"

"Shut the door!" he hissed.

Without another protest she shut the door behind her. How would she ever explain this to him? How would she reach him through his obvious fury?

He shook the chalice at her, his eyes glittering like the hot coals of hell. "This is the one, isn't it? This is the chalice you claimed you didn't buy from Justin."

She bit her trembling lip and swallowed. She'd never seen Evan like this. Even when he'd fought David, he hadn't been so angry. "Yes. It's the one."

With a curse Evan hurled the chalice across the room, knocking a painting off the wall as he did so. She jumped back a step. By heaven, what was he going to do?

She heard the patter of steps running down the hall toward the study, and then voices whispering, but Evan didn't even seem to notice them.

"Let me see if I've assessed the situation correctly," he bit out, advancing on her with his hands clenched at his sides. "Obviously, you lied about failing to acquire the chalice."

Crossing her shaky arms over her chest, she backed away. She couldn't speak. His anger terrified her. Facing David's anger had been bad enough, but facing Evan's was like staring into the open mouth of a dragon.

When she continued to watch him silently, he swept his arm across the surface of her flimsy writing desk, sending papers and quills and an ink bottle flying. Then he pounded his fist on the cleared top. "Answer me!"

"Y-yes," she whispered. "I lied."

"Did you lie about never meeting Justin as well? Did you actually buy the chalice from him? Or is it worse than that? Did you have it stolen from him before he could reach the inn?"

It took a moment for her to realize what he implied, but when she did, a wave of nausea assailed her. "Stolen from him? Surely you don't think I could have done such a thing!"

"Yesterday I didn't." He gritted his teeth and walked up to her. "But that was before I knew how easily you can lie. That was before I discovered what a two-faced deceiver you are."

The unfair words tore her apart. "How dare you! You lied to me from the moment you came here. You pretended to be something you weren't and—"

"I was trying to get at the truth," he spat out. "You, on the other hand, were covering up an abominable crime, which is ten times worse than anything I did!"

"Abominable crime?" She couldn't believe this. How could this man have spent such a beautiful night with her and then accuse her of . . . of . . . "What are you saying? That I murdered your friend?"

The word "murder" seemed to bring him up short. Pain spasmed over his face before he shook his head. "I don't . . . think you drove the knife in yourself." He took a shuddering breath. "But I think you could have hired someone else to murder Justin. Either you had him waylaid before he reached the inn or you sent men after him when your meeting didn't work out as you'd planned." His gaze hardened. "You wanted that chalice very badly. I've known that all along."

She reeled away from him, shocked by what he was saying. She could tell from the hard set to his jaw that he was perfectly serious. "You're insane. . . ." she whispered. She must escape him and his crazy accusations. Turning toward the door, she tried to open it, but before she could open it more than a crack, he'd slammed it shut.

Then he turned the key in the lock and pocketed it as he faced her, rage inscribed in every line of his face. "Insane? I was insane to believe you innocent! I ignored all the questionable evidence and listened to you when you claimed you'd had nothing to do with it!"

His voice grew bitter. "Even Quinley said I was a fool to believe you, but I was so . . . bloody enamored of you that I . . ." He speared his fingers through his hair. "For God's sake, I even threatened to use my influence to have him dismissed for incompetence if he tried to have you arrested. What an ass I made of myself!"

That he had defended her to Quinley gave her pause. She watched as he rubbed his neck in a distracted gesture, his eyes haunted. He didn't believe this horrible thing about her. He couldn't. He was angry and confused right now because he'd found the chalice, but once his anger passed he'd realize she was innocent. He must!

A hesitant knock came at the door. "Madam?" someone said timidly. "Is everything all right in there?"

Evan's head snapped around as Catrin recognized the voice of one of the maids. He glared at her, his breath coming quick and heavy as his eyes dared her to call out to the maids for help.

Briefly, she considered it. She felt as if she'd been locked up with a crazed beast. Yet she knew that somewhere in his confusion Evan must sense the truth about her. She must help him find it. She must make him see she could never have done this terrible thing he accused her of.

In the meantime, however, she must tell the maids something or they'd fetch Mrs. Griffiths or Bos to open the door. Catrin forced her voice to sound calm as she called out, "I'm fine. I . . . accidentally knocked over something. Why don't all of you go tell Mrs. Griffiths to see about the preparation of breakfast? I'll be down to the kitchen soon."

She could hear soft murmuring on the other side of the door. Then the same maid who'd spoken before said, "Perhaps we should call Mr. Bos—"

"No!" She could only imagine what Bos would do if he found out what was going on. "All of you! Go! I won't hesitate to summon you if there's a problem."

There was a moment of silence outside the door, then the sound of whispers as the servants conferred with each other. But a second or so later, she heard footsteps moving away from the door, and she breathed a sigh.

Evan leaned forward on her rickety writing table and cast

her an insolent look. "You're good at lying, aren't you? I wonder what your servants would say if they knew what you'd done. I wonder how much your precious butler would strive to protect you if he knew the truth."

She flinched, but refused to let him see how his words lacerated her. "Bos already knows what happened in London."

Evan looked taken aback. "Oh? Does he know everything? What you did to acquire that chalice?"

"I'll tell you exactly what he knows." She strove for calm. She would never make Evan believe her if she lapsed into hysterics. "He knows I traveled to London with two hundred pounds. He knows I went to The Green Goat to meet Lord Mansfield. I felt uneasy in the road outside the inn." She drew a steadying breath. "After I purchased the chalice from Lord Mansfield, some instinctive fear of danger made me leave the inn through a back door and return to my lodgings."

Evan averted his face, a muscle working in his jaw. "So you told Bos lies, too."

Tears burned her eyes. She moved up to the writing table. "They're not lies, Evan. That's exactly what happened, and the only difference between what I told you at first and what I'm telling you now is that I did meet with your friend and buy the chalice. But everything else is the same. I swear I never did anything wrong."

Needing to feel some connection with him, she laid her hand on one of his.

"Take your hand off me!" he hissed, jerking back from her as if he'd been burned, then edging away from the writing table that stood between them.

Desperation clawed at her. "Evan, I didn't have anything to do with Lord Mansfield's murder! You must believe me!"

"How can I?" His face filled with pain. "Everything shows your guilt. The missing letter . . . the lies to me and Quinley . . . the way you fled London without a word to anyone about your meeting with Justin!"

"I don't know what happened to the letter, but I fled London because I was afraid everyone would jump to the same conclusions that you are!" She gripped the top of the chair that sat behind the writing desk. "I admit I lied. I did buy the chalice. I did meet with your friend. But Evan, when he left me, he was whole and healthy and in possession of two hundred pounds. I swear it!"

Whirling away from her, he crossed the room to the chalice. "Then why didn't you tell me the truth about this?" He kicked the bronze object. "If you were so bloody innocent, why did you lie about the chalice even when you didn't know why I was really here?"

That wretched lie again. Why *had* she lied? Because as usual, she'd been afraid to risk revealing too much of herself to anyone. But this time her reticence had served her ill.

"I didn't mean to tell you about it at all," she said, "but once I started . . . I was afraid to tell all the truth. You see, I feared from the beginning that you might be an investigator who'd come from London to find out what had happened. I guess I didn't want to take any chances."

"You didn't want to take any chances? Guilty people fear taking chances, not innocent people. And the innocent don't lie. They don't run." He gestured to her bookshelf safe. "They don't hide things in secret compartments."

What was eating at him was obviously the thought of her lying to him. Remembering how betrayed she'd felt yesterday when she'd discovered his deception, she could almost understand that, but it didn't alleviate the knot of cold hurt festering in her belly. After everything they'd done . . . after all the sweet things he'd murmured last night, how could he think so ill of her?

"Innocent people can still be afraid," she whispered. "You know people are often sent to prison on little more than a supposition. Don't you think I realized how my presence at that inn looked in light of Lord Mansfield's murder? Don't you understand why I had to protect myself?"

He scooped up the chalice. "I don't even understand why this bloody chalice is so important to you, so how do you expect me to understand any of your actions that night?" He held it up so that the morning sun flooding through the one window glittered off the aged bronze. "For God's sake, Catrin, it's not even worth the money you paid for it!"

"It was worth more than that to me," she protested. "Without it, I couldn't marry and have children, not if I wanted them to have a father who could be there while they were growing up. I couldn't ensure the future of my tenants and my servants. Women of property are rare in England, I know, but they have the same needs as men of property. They have tenants and servants that rely on them, so they must have heirs to maintain the property when they're gone."

He cast her a hard look. "So you made sure you gained the chalice at any cost."

"No!" She bent over the chair as frustration gripped her. Shaking her head back and forth, she cried, "No . . . no . . . no! I could never see anyone hurt for it. You should have realized that about me by now." She lifted her face to him. "Did last night mean nothing to you? After last night how can you think me capable of having your friend murdered?"

His eyes met hers, and for a moment she glimpsed the turmoil he must be feeling. Then he wrenched his gaze away. "Last night you lay with me . . . you shared every intimacy a woman can share with a man, and you did it knowing that you had lied to me. Last night you made me . . . beg your forgiveness for *my* lies when you knew your lies were far worse." He sucked in a ragged breath. "You aren't the woman I thought you to be. I no longer know *what* you are capable of."

She rounded the table, her voice an aching whisper as she went to his side. "That's not true. You know me as I really am. Deep in your heart, you do. I'm sure of it!"

He turned a glittering gaze on her. "You think that because I desire . . . desir*ed* you, you can make me dance to whatever tune you set. You think my cursed attraction to you will blot out everything. But it won't!"

She couldn't help herself. She laid her hand on his chest. "Please, Evan, you must—"

"I won't listen to more of your lies, do you hear?" He grabbed her hand and twisted it behind her back, pulling her up close as he did so. "You can touch me, you can murmur your soft, false words, but it won't work. I won't be made a fool of anymore!"

In his eyes shimmered a vast darkness, like the bottomless lakes that were rumored to hold demons in their depths. She had glimpsed the darkness a few times and known there was an edge to his seemingly easy accord with life, but she'd never had to look into it so deeply. Suddenly, she knew there was more to his distrust than his anger over her lies or his determination to avenge his friend's death. Something that went to the roots of his being flickered in his eyes.

Her arm began to hurt where he had twisted it behind her back, but she ignored the pain. Meeting his gaze with hers, she tried to reach into that encompassing darkness, to pull him out of whatever depths he'd sunk into. "Evan, I'm sorry for not telling you before, but you know what a coward I am. I was afraid to tell *anyone* what had happened."

"A coward," he echoed. The cool distance in his tone struck fear in her. "A coward who marched off to London all alone to gain her property, to do whatever it took to make sure she could marry again."

He'd been holding the chalice in his hand. Now he released it, letting it fall with a thud on the carpet inches from her feet. With indrawn breath he lifted his hand to stroke the side of her face. But though his touch was almost a caress, his expression was hard.

"I should have listened to Quinley when he warned me about you," he murmured. "I should have listened to all those who termed you pretty and deadly. But all my life I've been taught to revere women like you . . . to protect them from the cruel world." His tone grew brittle. "I've spent a lifetime apologizing for what I am to your kind, but I can see it's a habit I must break."

She couldn't imagine what he was talking about. "What do you mean, 'your kind'? How am I any different from you?"

His face grew even fiercer as his hand at her back tightened on her wrist, threatening to cut off her circulation. "Oh, there's a great deal of difference between us, my dear. Didn't you know? I'm a farmer's son. I'm not fit to kiss your boots and certainly not to bed you." He dragged her against him until she could feel every muscle in his unyielding body. "But that doesn't mean I'm completely blind. Even I can see the corruption that lies at the core of all your beauty and gentility."

His words took her aback, but only for a moment. Though she'd assumed he was of a more refined background, she didn't care if he was a farmer's son. None of that meant a thing to her. But it obviously meant a lot to him.

Frantically, she struggled to find the words that might reach him through his confused ideas about her. "It's true

I'm not the kind of woman to revere. But then I know of no woman who is, no matter what her class. Like you, I'm simply trying to muddle through life as best I can, Evan, and I make mistakes. I made several in the past two weeks, but none so heinous as you seem to think."

When he closed his eyes as if to close her off from him, she lifted her free hand to stroke the hair back from his temple. "Must I be either an angel or a devil? Can't you see I'm just a woman, and I made mistakes like everyone else?"

He groaned. His head moved infinitesimally against her hand as if to meet her caress. Then with a low curse he thrust her away from him. "You are not 'just a woman,' I assure you." His eyes snapped open. With a frankness bordering on insolence, he let his gaze trail down her thinly clad body. Despite her fear of him, the heat of desire rose again in her belly. How could he have this effect on her, even after every terrible thing he'd said?

His voice shook when he spoke again, but whether with anger or desire, she couldn't tell. "I don't know what you are yet, but you could never be 'just a woman.' "

They both stood there frozen. She could hear his tortured breathing even from where she stood, and the wild light in his eyes made a quick shiver ripple over her.

What would he do with her now that he believed her to have been involved in Lord Mansfield's murder? She couldn't simply stand there and wonder. "What happens now?"

He stared at her in silence a moment, then said, "You and I shall go to town."

"To town?"

"Quinley is staying at The Red Dragon. We'll take the chalice, and you'll tell him your new version of what happened. Then he will have to decide what to do with you."

Terror gripped her. When he bent to pick up the chalice, she dropped to the floor, grabbing it at the same time he did. "Evan, you can't do this to me! I'm innocent!"

He lifted one eyebrow, fixing her with a gaze so cold it froze her heart. "Then you'll have no trouble convincing Quinley of that, will you?"

She couldn't believe it. He would drag her before Quinley on the basis of nothing but his wild suspicions. He wouldn't even give her the benefit of the doubt.

Tugging the chalice free of her numb fingers, he stalked to the window and looked out. "You have two choices. Call for your servants and have them throw me out, in which case, I'll tell Quinley everything and leave it to him to have you dragged from your home. Or go with me to Llanddeusant of your own free will and tell him what you've told me."

He turned from the window, his eyes boring into her. "But no matter what you choose, I will make sure Quinley hears the entire story."

"You mean, your distorted version of the story!" she protested. She rose from the floor, heedless of the way her wrapper had fallen open to expose her thin shift. "How could you do this? After last night, how could you?"

Paling, he stared at her. Then his gaze moved down her throat to the swells of her breasts that showed above the lacy edge of her chemise. He swallowed convulsively, one of his hands tightening on the chalice as his hungry gaze moved lower.

With an oath he tore his gaze from her, striding past her to the door. He unlocked it and bit out without looking at her, "For God's sake, go upstairs and put some clothes on. I'll give you ten minutes to dress while I see to the horses. If you're not down here when I'm ready to leave, I'll leave without you." He paused, then added in an icy voice, "But I'll be back. And I'll have Quinley with me." Yanking the door open, he strode from the room.

Catrin drew her wrapper closed with shaky fingers. He'd left her no choice at all. He knew quite well she wouldn't let him go to Quinley alone with his suspicions. Nor could she risk having Quinley come here and subject her servants to the ignominy of having to defend her or hide her. No, she had to go with Evan.

She wanted to cry. She wanted to scream and rage against the unfairness of it all. She wanted to linger here and nurse the devastating wound Evan's accusations had inflicted on her pride . . . her heart . . . her soul.

But she had no time for that. He'd given her ten minutes. That was all. So she pulled her wrapper tight and squared her shoulders, tamping down on the pain.

He thought he could bully her into a jail cell and thus destroy everything she held dear. Well, he was in for a surprise if he thought he'd get away with that. She was the Lady of the Mists and the descendant of a druidess. She'd been a coward in the past, but she couldn't afford to be one anymore. Somehow she must find a way to beat him. And somehow she would.

Chapter Fourteen

They are doomed with the art
which the fates impart
of turning men to stone
with a glance alone.
So young and old take care,
don't fall into love's snare.
—Anonymous, "Against Women"

Evan urged his mare to quicken her pace as they reached the outskirts of Llanddeusant. He didn't need to look to know that Catrin was increasing her pace to keep up with him. After all, he'd already won the first half of the battle when she'd agreed to come with him.

He still wasn't sure how she'd convinced the servants that nothing was amiss, but he didn't really care. She excelled at lying. No doubt, she'd given them some innocuous reason for why he'd spent the night and why she'd felt a sudden urge to accompany him to town at dawn.

He stole a glance at her, then instantly regretted it. Good God, how did she manage to look so angelic all the time? It wasn't just her gown of pink spotted muslin or her lace-trimmed spencer. It was the delicate blush of her cheeks, as pink and fragile as the pink satin lining of her snowy bonnet, and the sweet trembling of her lips as she set her face stoically forward to the road. She could make him feel like a monster even when he knew he was in the right.

Deuce take the woman! he thought as he tore his gaze from her. She'd lied to him! She'd misled him purposely, leading them all in a merry chase! What right had she to look like an affronted virgin goddess as she rode sidesaddle on another of her gentle ponies?

Quinley was right. Even women of her class could be deceitful and unworthy of any man's trust. Even women of her class could plot murder.

His fists tightened on the reins. So why didn't she look

like a murderess? Why did she sit her pony so proud and silent, her very manner proclaiming her innocence?

Because she was determined. He pressed his knee against the bag slung over his saddle that held the chalice, reminding himself that she'd been desperate to obtain it, desperate to make sure she could marry someone—anyone.

Yet she'd refused Morys's suit, even after she'd gained the chalice. That thought brought him up short. He hadn't even considered that until now. It was odd, wasn't it, that she would go to such lengths to obtain the chalice, then refuse to marry the one man in Llanddeusant who was most appropriate as a husband?

I can't marry someone I don't love, Evan remembered her saying. An odd sentiment for a woman whose blood ran cold in her veins.

Not that it ran cold all the time. He couldn't help but remember how warm she'd been in bed, how passionate and responsive. For the first time he wondered why she'd let him bed her. It made no sense. If she'd had a whit of sense, she'd have sent him away, secure in the knowledge that she'd escaped detection forever.

Then he remembered what Quinley had said yesterday: "Guilty men—and women—often have a need to confess to someone. Their dark deeds eat at them until they spill out the truth at unwarranted moments."

Is that why she'd let him stay? Had she been secretly hoping he'd find the chalice? Is that why the bookshelf had been slightly ajar, enough so that he could discover the safe? But then why did she still profess her innocence? If she was consumed by guilt, why hadn't she broken down and told him everything?

He rubbed his neck wearily, wishing that last night he'd slept more and made love less. He couldn't think anymore. He didn't know what to think. Every part of him ached when he thought of how dear and innocent he'd found her and how duplicitous she'd proven to be. All that time he'd been worrying about how to make amends for taking her virginity, not even realizing that the only innocent part about her was her body.

And yet . . . He groaned. He mustn't think about it anymore or he'd go mad. He must leave the sorting of truth from untruth to Quinley. At least the investigator could be objective about the whole matter.

To his relief The Red Dragon appeared at the end of the street. At last he could give this over to someone else. If he spent much more time brooding over it, he'd start to make excuses for her again and believe her lies.

A few moments later, they rode into the inn yard, and one of the hostlers rushed out to take his horse, casting a speculative eye first on him and then on Catrin. "Good morning, sir. Mrs. Llewelyn has been in a tizzy worrying about you. With the storm last night, she thought you might have lost your way or fallen into a ravine hereabouts."

Evan forced a smile to his face. "I did lose my way, but Mrs. Price was kind enough to give me shelter for the night."

He dismounted, unhooking the bag with the chalice and slinging it over one shoulder. When he looked up at Catrin, whom the hostler was helping down from the horse, she wore a look of faint surprise. What had she expected? That he'd proclaim her guilt to everyone he saw?

Apparently so, for when he took her arm to lead her into the inn, she murmured, "Thank you for lying to the hostler. I have enough problems with my reputation as it is."

Her gratitude irritated him. "I didn't do it to save your reputation, I assure you. It doesn't suit my purpose to have the entire town up in arms about the stranger who has come to hand Mrs. Price over to the authorities."

She blanched, then pulled her arm out of his grasp. "I see." Her voice was low and cutting. "I'd forgotten that the courteous Evan Newcome of these past few days has been replaced by a madman bent on vengeance."

Before he could answer her, she'd swept through the door ahead of him. He followed at a leisurely pace, eyes narrowing. So the shy recluse had claws, did she? Well, she'd best keep them sheathed if she wanted to enlist Quinley's sympathies. She was in enough trouble already.

He surveyed the common room while Catrin took a seat, her spine straight as she perched on the edge of the chair. He'd expected to find Quinley eating breakfast, but no one was in the room. Apparently, Quinley had slept late.

He'd scarcely finished scanning the room when Mrs. Llewelyn swept through the door from the kitchen, wiping her hands on her apron. Her face beamed as she caught sight of him and Catrin together. "Good day, Catrin. And Mr. Newcome, too. I had the devil of a time last night worrying about what you were enduring out there in that wretched storm, but the hostler tells me that—"

"I . . . we have come to speak to Mr. Quinley," Evan bit out. He wasn't in the mood for polite conversation with Mrs. Llewelyn. He wanted to see Quinley and be done with this whole nasty business.

Mrs. Llewelyn's face fell at his aloof tone. "Mr. Quinley?"

"The investigator from London who's staying here."

She glanced from him to Catrin, confusion in her face. "But . . . but he left," Mrs. Llewelyn said.

A chill stole over Evan. "What do you mean, he left?"

She shrugged. "He left this morning. He said he didn't want to miss the ship from Carmarthen that leaves this evening, so he had me rouse him before dawn."

Before dawn, Evan thought. It wasn't long after dawn now. "Then he can't have gotten far."

Mrs. Llewelyn watched him with a wary gaze. "He's been gone more than two hours."

"Deuce take it!" Evan muttered. He turned to Catrin, expecting to see triumph on her face, but she was staring woodenly into space, as if she no longer cared what happened.

With a twinge of an emotion he didn't want to explore too deeply, he returned his attention to the now scowling Mrs. Llewelyn. "Thank you. Then I shall be leaving, too." He fished in his pockets and drew out some coins, which he handed to the woman. "This is for my lodgings, and there should also be enough to send my belongings on to Cambridge. I don't have time to pack."

Mrs. Llewelyn stared down at the coins. "You're going after the man, are you?"

That evoked a response from Catrin, who looked at him, her eyes echoing Mrs. Llewelyn's question.

"Mrs. Price and I are both going after him," Evan said as he went to Catrin's side. Meeting Catrin's gaze, he murmured, "Come on. We'll have to ride like the devil if we're to catch up to him."

Her face paling, Catrin rose from her chair. "I can't ride

like the devil. My pony can't possibly keep up a killing pace."

"Then you'll ride with me." The words were out before he could stop them. He certainly wasn't leaving her behind, and though riding two to a mount might slow them, at least it would ensure she didn't purposely lag behind or try to escape.

Nonetheless, the thought of having Catrin in his arms for a day's ride to Carmarthen bloody well terrified him, even if it was the only way to ensure that he got her to Quinley before Quinley boarded the ship in Carmarthen.

Mrs. Llewelyn, who'd been listening avidly to the interchange, said in a strained voice, "Mrs. Price is going with you to London?"

Evan went very still. All Catrin had to do was protest that she didn't want to go to London, and Mrs. Llewelyn would rise to her defense.

Thus it surprised him when Catrin answered Mrs. Llewelyn in a steady voice. "Mr. Newcome and I need to speak with Mr. Quinley. If that requires our journeying to London, then I suppose we shall do so."

Mrs. Llewelyn's eyes narrowed. "Does this have anything to do with all the questions the Quinley fellow asked about you last night?"

Catrin colored and ducked her head. "Yes."

"He says you might have been involved in a murder and a theft in London," Mrs. Llewelyn remarked. "Of course, I told him that was nonsense." Then her eyes went wide as if something had just occurred to her, and she shot Evan an accusing glance. "Mr. Quinley asked me about a chalice, just as you did, Mr. Newcome, the first time we spoke."

Evan became very conscious of the bag he carried in his left hand. Instinctively, he tightened his grip on it.

As he was wondering how to answer Mrs. Llewelyn, however, Catrin said with an edge to her voice, "Mr. Newcome and Mr. Quinley are very anxious to learn the truth, Annie. That's why Mr. Newcome insists that I speak with the investigator."

"That Quinley man told me he'd questioned you and Mr. Newcome yesterday, so why are you running after him all in a rush today?" Annie planted her hands on her hips and glared at Evan. "Surely, Mr. Newcome, you don't think our Catrin had anything to do with this crime, do you?"

Catrin faced him, her gaze steady as she lifted one eyebrow in question.

He averted his gaze from her. "This is none of your concern, Mrs. Llewelyn. We're leaving now, and you have no say in it."

But as he took Catrin's arm to lead her from the room, Mrs. Llewelyn stepped forward to clasp Catrin's other arm. "She don't have to go anywhere she don't want to go, Mr. Newcome. I don't know what made you up and decide our Catrin could take part in a murder, but I'll not let you carry her off to be hanged for no good reason."

The word "hanged" stunned him. Hanged. He hadn't thought as far as considering what would happen to Catrin if indeed she was found guilty of conspiracy to murder.

Hanged. The very word blew an ominous wind through him.

But though Catrin paled at the mention of hanging, she covered Mrs. Llewelyn's hand with her own and murmured, "It's all right. Mr. Newcome is only doing . . . what he believes he must. I'm going with him because I choose to. I'd like a chance to clear my name, and I can't do that if I stay here. Don't worry. It will all come right in the end. I know it."

She squeezed Mrs. Llewelyn's hand before she removed it from her arm with the faintest of smiles. "But I do appreciate your loyalty, Annie. It means a great deal to me."

Mrs. Llewelyn reddened. "Oh, Catrin, I would never have told Mr. Newcome a thing about you if I'd known he would use it in this despicable manner . . . I can't bear to think—"

"We have to go," Evan interjected. He couldn't take much more of this. He must escape all these people who thought well of Catrin, who believed her a sweet innocent. It was having an effect on him . . . a very telling effect.

"But you must take provisions at least," Mrs. Llewelyn cried out. "You don't know how long it will be before you catch up to Mr. Quinley, and you both look as if you've done without breakfast—"

"We're leaving now!" Evan insisted and led Catrin out the door.

He could hear Mrs. Llewelyn crying behind him, but she

didn't stop him. Shaken to the core by what he'd just witnessed—and by the talk of hanging—he had to pause to gather his bearings before calling for the hostler.

Then he grew angry at himself for his sudden attack of emotion. If Catrin was guilty, she deserved to be hanged. And if she was innocent, the whole truth would out. He would make sure of that.

The hostler halted his mare in front of them, and Evan explained that Catrin was riding with him. Then Evan mounted the horse and waited while the hostler helped Catrin into the saddle in front of him.

Mrs. Llewelyn rushed out of the inn, a wrapped bundle in her hand, which she thrust into Catrin's hands. "Here's a bit of cold mutton and a loaf of bread." She cast Evan a fierce glance as if daring him to refuse it. "The girl has to have something."

"Thank you, Mrs. Llewelyn," he managed to say. Then he dug his knees into the horse's flanks and rode from the inn yard. Seconds later, they were on the road to Carmarthen.

At first, he concentrated on remembering the route he'd taken when he'd come to Llanddeusant, then on making sure the horse kept up a punishing speed that might enable them to overtake Quinley. But they couldn't continue that way for long, and when after an hour's hard riding they hadn't spotted the investigator, Evan was forced to let the horse slow its pace.

By then the silence between them had become almost painful. Nor did it improve matters that every jounce of the mare made Evan dramatically aware of Catrin's body. There was no way to escape it, not with her thighs draped over one of his and her face only inches away. Her lilac scent eddied between them with the changing shifts of the air. Once he even caught himself breathing more heavily to take it all in. She'd pinned her hair up beneath her bonnet, but their ride had tugged a few tendrils loose, and one of them tickled his cheek whenever the wind caught it a certain way.

He tried to concentrate on what he would say to Quinley when they reached him, but all he could think of was the slender woman whose straight back pressed against his arm and whose luscious bottom was nestled snugly between his legs. Had it been only last night that he'd tasted every lovely inch of her? Had it been only a few hours since he'd thrust into her, relishing the way she met his thrusts with wanton cries of pleasure?

The memory of it made him hard in an instant, so hard he wondered if he'd ever find satisfaction for his desire again. He'd certainly never be able to bed Catrin. Yet he didn't know if he could find fulfillment with any other woman, not after Catrin had shown him what mutual enjoyment really was.

Deuce take her! Obviously, he was destined to be plagued by unfulfilled urges, at least for the duration of this journey.

He caught a glimpse of her stoic, unyielding expression, and his irritation intensified. Must he also be tormented by her reproving silence, which made him feel guilty despite his belief in the rightness of his position?

This wasn't what he'd expected. She should have collapsed under the strain by now, admitting the truth with tears and pleading, begging him not to bring her to the authorities. But ever since they'd left Plas Niwl, she'd maintained an almost tragic calm, as if she were being martyred to some cause.

How could she be so aloof, so ladylike when her world was falling apart? And why did it make him feel like the basest man alive?

"That was a very noble scene you played back there in the inn," he snapped, determined to break through her maddening calm. "You were quite the tragic heroine."

Her face betrayed nothing, although her voice quavered as she retorted, "I could tell you were impressed."

"You must remember that I know the whole story, so I'm less inclined than Mrs. Llewelyn to think you a saint."

With a slow turn of her head she met his gaze. "No, you're more inclined to think me a thief and a murderess, which is why we're taking this madcap journey. You do nothing by halves, do you?"

"If you don't want to be regarded as a murderess, my dear, don't behave as one."

He knew he'd struck a nerve at last when she flinched and looked away. "Yesterday, you didn't think me capable of murder."

"Yesterday, I didn't know that a calculating heart beat beneath that fine facade."

She sighed. "Tell me something, Evan. Who was the

woman who taught you that fine facades always hide treachery? Who of 'my kind,' as you so nicely put it this morning, convinced you that a woman of position and wealth can either be a saint or a sinner, but never something in the middle?"

He thought of Henrietta, so amiable and sweet until she'd decided he was beneath contempt. Then he thrust that thought from his head immediately. Henrietta had never betrayed him. If anything, he'd betrayed her. "What on earth makes you think this has anything to do with another woman?"

With a shrug she shifted in the saddle. "I'm just trying to understand how you could make love to me one night with such tenderness, then pronounce me a murderess the next day." Her voice shook. "I can't quite reconcile two such vastly different reactions."

"Believe me," he muttered, "I've never before met a woman of the gentry who behaved as duplicitously as you. I think my reaction is perfectly normal, given that your deception was wholly unexpected."

"It couldn't have been 'wholly unexpected' or you wouldn't have hidden your purpose in coming to Llanddeusant in the first place. You must have been suspicious of me from the very beginning." She sucked in a deep breath. "Perhaps you never lost your suspicions of me. Perhaps you merely pretended to have lost them last night because you wanted to bed me before you packed me off to the authorities."

"Deuce take you!" he exploded. "You know I meant every word of what I said last night! You know I thought you a . . . a . . ."

"An angel," she finished for him, turning her head to look at him. "Yes, I do know. The question is, what made you suddenly decide I was a devil?" She lowered her voice to a whisper. "How could my foolish mistakes so blind you to my true character if not because some other woman has betrayed you before?"

He fixed her with a fierce gaze. "Not that it's any of your business, but the only other women of your class I've had substantial dealings with truly were angels. One of them you know—Lady Juliana, who very nearly saved my life. The other was my former fiancée, Henrietta, who could never even contemplate an act of such deception as you perpetrated."

"Your former fiancée?" she echoed in a small voice. "You were once engaged?"

With another curse he tore his gaze from her to stare out at the grass-carpeted slopes they were riding through. He shouldn't have mentioned Henrietta, but he'd had enough of Catrin's foolish suppositions. "Yes, I was once engaged. We didn't suit, however."

"Why not?"

"That's none of your concern," he snapped.

"She's the one who made you distrust 'my kind,' isn't she?"

"No, she is *not*!" He clenched his fists on the reins, wishing it were her lovely throat instead. "Henrietta broke off our engagement because of something *I* did. Trust me, I well deserved her approbation."

"Why? Did you show her the same distrust you show me?"

His gaze swung to her. Her blue eyes held his, solemn and calm, and he flinched from the unswerving steadiness of her gaze. In a sense she was right. He *had* shown no faith in his fiancée when he'd assumed she was in the arms of another man for the wrong reason.

But that wasn't the issue, he told himself. "Yes, I showed her distrust. I behaved like a jealous fool once and scared her off. But there's a vast difference between what happened between me and Henrietta and what happened between me and you. Henrietta didn't deserve my distrust. And you certainly do."

She didn't answer, but turned her head, her lips tightening as she stared at the road ahead. After a long silence she asked, "What will you do if we don't reach Carmarthen before Quinley sails?"

"Perish the thought," he muttered. He'd never last an entire journey to London with Catrin close at hand.

"Will you take me to London then?" she persisted. "Will you drag me across the country in your thirst for vengeance?"

"It's a thirst for truth." He cast her a grim glance. "And the only way to find out what really happened is to present

Quinley with the new evidence and see if he can corroborate your story."

"Or prove me wrong." She was silent a long moment, her spine rigid against his arm. "What if . . . what if he decides I'm as guilty as you think? They *will* hang me, you know."

There was that horrible word again. And she was using it on purpose to unsettle him. Unfortunately, it was working. He tried to keep his voice even as he said, "You have nothing to worry about if you're innocent."

She laid her small hand on his chest. "How can you, a Welshman, have such faith in English law? When did the English begin thinking of the Welsh as anything but thieves and criminals?"

His gaze shot to her. She was staring at him with an earnest expression, her blue eyes dark as the night waters of Llyn y Fan Fach. The fear that haunted those eyes struck an answering fear in him.

She had a point, one he'd not considered. The English had always been quick to judge harshly, even with their own people, but when the offenders were Welsh or Irish or Scottish, it took little evidence to gain a conviction.

"What if you're wrong?" she whispered. "What if everything happened the way I said? Once you give me to Quinley, it will be out of your hands. Even if they find no witnesses or evidence that proves I took part in the murder, they'll convict me, because they have no one else to blame. After all, why not blame it on the Welsh witch? Why not rid the world of one more of our race?"

A vivid image abruptly entered his mind, of a hooded man lowering a noose about Catrin's neck. Good God, how could he endure seeing her hanged? He forced himself to remember how Justin had looked lying in his own blood in that alley, but the picture blurred next to the one of Catrin on a scaffold.

A violent shudder coursed through him. Then he cursed it. She was playing on his fears, and he mustn't let her rattle him. "Stop talking of hanging. All we are doing is presenting the facts for Quinley. He may decide you're telling the truth."

"I don't see how, when you've already tried and sentenced

me, based on nothing more than the lies I told to protect myself from men like you who leap to conclusions."

Her quiet words held a fatalistic calm that chilled him to the marrow. What if he *was* wrong? Good God, what if he was? What if it had been as she said, that she'd merely been afraid to tell the truth in the beginning? What if all she was guilty of was hiding the truth?

The refrain tormented him as he urged the horse into a gallop once more. *What if? What if?*

With a foul curse he tightened his fingers on the reins. He couldn't go on the entire journey this way or he'd go mad.

The only way to survive this was to fall back on what had kept him sane as a child, through his father's beatings. Literature. Other's people's words to drown out his thoughts and feelings.

Shakespeare, he thought. *I'll recite Shakespeare. I know all of* Othello.

Then he groaned. *Not* Othello, *a story of lovers betrayed. No, Shakespeare is too wrought with emotion.*

Tacitus, then. Yes, that's it. Something from the histories.

So while the horse rocked beneath them, and Catrin's scent assailed him, he tried to think of himself anywhere else as he began to recite in his mind, *Etiem sapientibus cupido gloriae. . . .*

Annie paced the common room a few minutes after Catrin and Mr. Newcome had left. She wrung her hands as she thought of how Mr. Newcome had looked when he'd pulled Catrin from the inn. Who'd have guessed the man was a betraying wretch? After the way he'd brooded over his inability to see Catrin for the past few days, Annie had assumed he'd taken a fancy to the girl.

Then there was the thrashing he'd given David Morys. Catrin had related the sketchiest account of what had happened in the inn garden, not venturing to explain why Mr. Newcome had fought with David, but Annie had guessed why. She hadn't been so caught up in the celebration not to notice Mr. Newcome and Catrin disappear out the garden door together.

No doubt David had come across a little scene he hadn't liked and had lost his temper. Knowing David's tendency to insult one and all when he was angry, she could only imagine what had provoked the fight. Oh, she'd have liked to have seen it. David was too pompous by half. He needed to be taken down a peg or two.

But after all that, she'd assumed that Mr. Newcome had honorable reasons for his pursuit of Catrin. She'd never dreamed he might have been planning to carry the poor lass off. And under suspicion of having committed a murder, no less!

"What a piece of dastardly work!" she muttered, thinking of how Mr. Newcome had deceived all of them by pretending a concern for Catrin. "Why, the lass is no more a murderess than I am!"

Something must be done about it. But what could she do? Mr. Llewelyn, bless his soul, wouldn't approve of her trying to thwart the law, even for Catrin. There *were* people in Llanddeusant who liked the young woman, but no one would take on Mr. Newcome and a London investigator for her. Despite his scholarly talk, Mr. Newcome was a mountain of a man and not to be considered lightly. The only person who'd presumed to fight the London Welshman was—

She brightened. Of course! If David was so enamored with Catrin that he'd fight for her, then surely he'd be willing to stop this nonsense before it got out of hand! He'd wanted to marry the lass, after all, and he was a clever sort. Much as she disliked David's snobbery and his pretensions, he was the perfect choice for someone to go after Catrin and make sure she was treated properly.

Her mind made up, she rushed out the door of the inn toward the cottage that served as Llanddeusant's school. Pray God that David was there now and not on one of his visits to the gentry.

Bursting through the entrance to the cottage, she ignored the astonished looks of the children and their tutor. "Where's Mr. Morys?" she cried.

"In his study," said the tutor.

Hurrying through the cottage, she found the study in seconds, relieved to see that David was indeed at his desk, scowling as he pored over a pile of papers.

"Thank heaven you're here!" she exclaimed as she entered the study, careful to close the study door behind her. "Something awful has happened!"

David sighed. "This is not a good time, Mrs. Llewelyn—"

"But Mr. Newcome had taken Catrin off!"

That got his attention at once. He dropped the papers he'd been perusing and leaned forward. "What do you mean, he's 'taken Catrin off'?"

She gulped in a great breath. "You know that investigator who was here yesterday asking all the questions? He talked to you, didn't he?"

"Yes, of course," he muttered with an impatient wave of his hand, "but what's this about Newcome and Catrin?"

"That investigator thinks she had something to do with a murder in London, and apparently Mr. Newcome is the one who set the man on her. I can't be sure of all the details, but Catrin and Mr. Newcome showed up at the inn this morning, looking for the investigator. When I told them the man had already left for Carmarthen, Mr. Newcome said he and Catrin were going to follow him. Then he rode off with her on his horse!"

David's face was ashen. "Did she want to go?"

"I don't think so. I think she went because she felt she had no other choice."

With a curse David opened one of the drawers to his desk and pulled out a flintlock pistol.

"David!" she exclaimed. "What in the devil are you doing with a pistol?"

He checked to be certain it was loaded. "It was my father's." He stuffed it in his waistband, then drew out a bag of what must be powder and shot and thrust that in his waistcoat pocket.

She leapt to her feet. "What are you planning to do with it?"

"Get Catrin back, of course." He stood up and rounded the desk, going to where his hat lay on a table.

"Yes, but if you shoot Mr. Newcome, they'll come looking for you next!"

"I won't have to shoot him." Taking up the hat, he reached inside it and drew out a pair of riding gloves. "If I wave this pistol in his face, he'll give her up, don't you worry. That bastard won't be so smug when facing down the barrel of a flintlock." He donned his hat and gloves, then left the study.

She ran after him. "Yes, but what will you do once you wrest her away from Mr. Newcome? Will that do any good when they can simply send someone else here after her?"

He paused to stare at her, and she shivered at the hollow coldness shimmering in the depths of his black eyes. "And what would *you* suggest, Mrs. Llewelyn?"

"I . . . I don't know. Go with her to London, I suppose, and make sure they treat her fairly."

Shaking his head, he said, "If she makes it to London, no one will treat her fairly. You can be sure of that." He stalked off across the schoolroom, between the aisles of students straining to catch every word.

She hurried after him with a frown. The pistol worried her. She hadn't meant to send David out to kill anyone. Mr. Newcome had behaved abominably, it was true, but she wouldn't want him murdered. Even though David said he meant only to brandish the weapon, she knew well enough that an angry man might fire without thinking.

She held her tongue until they were outside and out of earshot of the students. Then following David to the back of the cottage where the horses were kept, she said, "Perhaps you shouldn't take the pistol." She thought quickly, then said, "What if you get into a fight and he gets the pistol away from you?"

It was the wrong thing to say. A muscle ticked in David's jaw as he glared at her. "He won't get the pistol away from me, I assure you." With angry movements he dragged a saddle off a hook in the stable, then tossed it onto the horse.

"But what if—"

"Enough!" David interrupted. "You came to me with this problem, Mrs. Llewelyn, and I shall take care of it. I'll have Catrin back, make no mistake." He cinched the saddle up, then mounted the horse. Looking down on her, he gathered up the reins. "And that bastard will rue the day he was born once I'm through with him."

Then with a click of his tongue he rode away.

Annie stared after him with an uneasy feeling in the pit of her stomach. She had hoped he would care enough about

Catrin to go after her, but she hadn't thought he'd consider violence. Now she wondered if it had been wise of her to arouse his fury. A jealous man with a pistol could be a very dangerous thing.

She prayed he knew how to use it properly and that he could indeed intimidate Mr. Newcome merely by threatening him with the weapon. Because if not, they might be carrying Catrin home in a coffin. And Annie couldn't bear even to think of that.

Chapter Fifteen

Sun on hillsides, wind on seas,
And grey crags instead of trees;
Instead of men, the gulls' lament—
God! how should not my heart be rent?
—Anonymous folk verse, "Desolation"

Catrin stared ahead at the road, despite the ache in her neck that came from spending the entire day in that rigid position. The ache was preferable to the alternative—looking at Evan.

Unfortunately, although she couldn't see Evan, she could feel him . . . every virile, unyielding inch. She couldn't escape his arm that occasionally brushed her spine or his rigid thigh under hers or his rock-hard chest pressed against her shoulder. Nor could she escape the memory of how that chest had felt beneath her splayed fingers last night, how that thigh had parted her legs so Evan could—

A pox on the man! Couldn't she forget what they'd shared?

Oh, but how could she? It was all she'd thought of for the last few hours. She'd had nothing to do *other* than think of what they'd done, since they'd spent the day in total silence.

Normally, she welcomed silence. It had always been her haven from her grandmother's constant harping and from their neighbors' whispered comments. But this silence wasn't a haven. It was a brutal, awful chasm stretching out between her and him, a horrifying contrast to their wordless communication last night.

There was no way to breach this silence. What could she say that wouldn't be a repetition? Polite conversation was impossible, for he couldn't be polite to her and she couldn't bear hearing the contempt in his voice.

A tear snaked down her cheek, and she wiped it away furiously, praying he hadn't seen it. She hadn't cried once today, although how she'd managed it, she didn't know.

She'd tried to lose herself in the scenery, since the day had been fair, with sunlight skipping off the rain-speckled rocks and Black Mountain for once looking more like a benevolent regent than a scowling tyrant. But the very beauty of it seemed to mock her, for who knew how long it would be before she experienced it again, if ever?

Another tear trickled down her cheek, and she didn't bother to wipe it away. She knew why she was crying. Despite the scenery, the ride had been long and tiring. Evan had pressed on at a killing pace, obsessed with reaching Carmarthen before Mr. Quinley left. He'd stopped only to let her relieve herself. There's been nothing to eat but the mutton and bread Mrs. Llewelyn had given them, which they'd devoured hours ago, so now her stomach rumbled continually.

Evan showed no signs of hunger, however. Didn't he feel it? No, she supposed he didn't. A man who could snuff out any soft emotion without a thought couldn't possibly feel something so mundane as hunger.

That was what had made the day most horrible—Evan's eerie control. After their first brief discussion he'd shown no more awareness of her presence than the trees they occasionally passed. She might have thought him carved of oak, so stiffly and quietly did he suffer her nearness.

While she couldn't move without remembering their ill-fated lovemaking, he apparently had cast it from his mind. What kind of man was he? She could hardly believe he'd once held her so tenderly. How could this cold statue of a man have made love to her with fire and fury?

As she had several times before, she wondered about the man who she'd discovered was a complete stranger to her. A farmer's son, he'd said. How had a farmer's son become a renowned scholar and a fellow at Cambridge University? It was unbelievable.

Then she remembered how he'd behaved at Tess's wedding. He had fit in there as well as any of the farmers and laborers. Yes, he might have been a farmer's son once, though he seemed to have eradicated most traces of his humbler origins.

Still, some things never faded. As a farmer's son, he had most likely resented those with more wealth and position than him. That would explain his eagerness to believe wrong of her.

That wasn't what he'd told her, however. He'd said he'd been taught to revere women like her. She frowned. If this was how he showed reverence for a woman, she hated to see how he showed contempt.

Well, she'd had enough of his silences and brooding. The journey had been interminable, and now night was falling. They seemed nowhere near Carmarthen, and surely Mr. Quinley had already boarded his ship. So how long did Evan intend to continue this?

"Where are we?" she asked, wondering if he'd deign to answer the question.

He flinched, as if her words had brought him out of some other place. Then he drew in a deep breath. "Two hours from Carmarthen."

The deep rumble of his voice hit her hard, so familiar and yet so capable of rousing pain. She struggled to force any emotion from her own voice. "You intend to go on even after dark."

The rumble turned to a growl. "I intend to go on until we reach Carmarthen."

"Yes, but surely it's dangerous to ride at night, with highwaymen and—"

"Trust me, there's never been a highwayman on this stretch of road. Rhys Vaughan makes sure of that. He makes it well worth the while of his tenants and staff to work honestly so they don't have to resort to such drastic tactics to survive."

He seemed to know a great deal about his friends, the Vaughans. Then again, he'd originally come from Carmarthen, hadn't he? At least, that's what he'd said. "We're near the Vaughan estate then?"

"Llynwydd. Yes." His words were clipped and remote, but she could hear the weariness behind them nonetheless. "We just passed the drive leading to it."

She craned her head back, looking past his shoulder. In the dying light she could just make out a road cutting off from the main one. "Don't you want to stop and visit your friends?" She didn't know if she could stand two more hours of being so close to him . . . and so very, very far.

But he dashed her hopes. "No. I want to reach Carmarthen tonight on the slim chance that Quinley is still there."

"Yes, but the Vaughans would at least have food and—"

"No! We'll eat in Carmarthen!"

That was the last straw. She refused to endure another moment of his punishing silence or his cold words or his inhuman ability to ignore hunger. Before he could realize what she was doing, she grabbed the reins out of his hand and began to turn the horse to go back the way they'd come.

"Deuce take it, Catrin, what are you doing?" he growled as he closed his hands over hers.

Somehow she maintained control of the reins as the words spilled out of her. "I'm hungry, I'm tired, and I'm not moving another inch without something to eat!"

"You'll do as I say!" he bit out, snatching the reins from her.

She glared at him, gripping his wrist with her hands to make it more difficult for him to control the reins. "Don't be so stubborn! You know quite well that Quinley will be gone by the time we reach Carmarthen. The ships set sail before sundown, and it's sundown now. There's no reason to continue on this journey without sustenance or respite!"

"Deuce take you, Catrin, let go!" Evan hissed as he wrenched his hands from hers, still gripping the reins and thus jerking them wildly to the left. The horse hesitated, confused by the conflicting commands. Then he danced a few steps to the left.

They were both so intent on their struggle that they didn't hear the sounds of hoofbeats on the road from Llanddeusant until a voice called "Ho, there! Stand to!"

Instantly, Catrin froze, her hands going limp. "I thought you said there were no highwaymen on this road," she hissed as the rider approached.

With a low oath Evan fought to reestablish control over his horse, but by the time he'd done so, the man who'd hailed them had caught up to them and it was too late to run.

As the man halted a few feet from them in a swirl of dust, Catrin strained to see his face in the dying light. Then the dust cleared, and relief flooded her. "Oh, thank heaven, it's only David."

Instantly, Evan slipped one of his hands around her waist in a protective gesture and muttered under his breath. "What the deuce is *he* doing here?"

"I don't know," she whispered.

David swept his gaze over them both, scowling as he took

in the intimate way Evan held Catrin pressed to his chest. "You've led me a merry chase today, I'll have you know. My horse isn't used to such hard riding."

"So why did you follow us?" Evan snapped.

"Because I couldn't let you take Catrin off. I've come to bring her home."

She could feel every muscle in Evan's body grow rigid. He shifted in the saddle, cradling her more firmly between his thighs. "What makes you think she wants to go home? She rejected you once already, you know."

The jealous edge to Evan's voice came as a shock to Catrin. From his behavior today, she'd assumed he no longer had any feelings for her.

"I know everything, Newcome," David bit out, "so stop pretending yours is some lover's elopement. I know where you're taking her and why. She isn't here because she wants to be, that's for certain. You're taking her off to be hanged. So I'm sure she'll be more than happy to come with me."

Evan pulled on the reins, turning the horse back toward Carmarthen. "She's not going to be hanged, and she's certainly not going anywhere with you," he stated calmly as he urged the horse into a walk.

David rode up ahead of them and blocked the road. To Catrin's shock he drew a pistol from his coat, pointing it straight at Evan's head. "I'm afraid you don't have a say in this, Newcome," he announced with a deadly glint in his eye.

Evan froze, halting the horse at once.

"No!" Catrin cried as David held the pistol steady. "David, you can't mean to shoot him! Surely not!"

"Get off the horse, Catrin," David said. "I won't risk shooting you."

"I don't want you to shoot anyone!" she exclaimed.

"Get off the horse." This time the command came from Evan.

In total shock she glanced up into his stony face. "Wh-what?"

His eyes never left the pistol. "I don't know if Morys can use that thing, and I can't risk him hitting you."

Yet he would apparently risk being shot himself. She shook her head. "I'm not getting off. He'll kill you—"

The next thing she knew she was sprawled on the ground

at the horse's feet. Evan had pushed her off the horse and was now dancing the horse away from her.

She sprang to her feet. A terror gripped her such as she'd never known in her entire life. Without her on the horse, David would surely fire the pistol. Expecting any minute to hear a shot ring out, she lunged at Evan's horse and got close enough to grab Evan's leg.

"Deuce take it, Catrin!" Evan said in a tortured voice as he tried to shake her loose. "Let go!"

David swung the pistol back and forth, his face ashen as he gauged the shot.

If only Evan carried a weapon himself, Catrin thought as Evan struggled to pull the horse away from her. If only he had a sword or a pistol or—

Something hard swung against her arm and she gave a start. She stared at the bulging saddle bag. The chalice, she realized. She could use it as a weapon if she could get close enough to David to hit him with it.

Hooking one arm firmly around Evan's leg, she slid her free hand under the flap of the saddle bag and withdrew the chalice, praying that David wouldn't notice what she was doing.

Fortunately, David was too busy paying attention to the horse swerving from side to side in his sights. "Move away from the horse, Catrin!" David called out. "Blast it, I can't get a clear shot with you there! Move away from him!"

Her heart leaping into her throat, she released Evan's leg and skittered away from the horse, thrusting the chalice behind her back. As her fingers tightened on the cold bronze, David steadied his aim on Evan.

"Wait!" she cried. "Don't shoot!"

David paused a moment, his gaze and his weapon both trained on Evan. "And why not?"

Frantically, Catrin tried to think of a plan. She'd never been in a situation like this, and she hadn't the faintest idea what to do. Grandmother would have managed some spectacular maneuver to get David's weapon away from him and protect Evan, but she wasn't Grandmother.

All she could think of was to get behind David and hit him with the chalice. But he'd have to dismount first, and how on earth would she get him to do that?

Still, she had to do something. Keeping a wary eye on

both men, she sidled toward David. "I'll go with you, David! Just don't shoot Evan!"

"The bloody bastard deserves to die!" David spat out, but to her relief he didn't fire.

"I know he does," she said, trying to sound soothing. "But it'll be worse for us if you kill him. They'll hound us through the hills. If we let him go, maybe they won't come after us. It won't be worth tracking us into the mountains."

She hardly knew what she was babbling, but she prayed it would keep David from shooting until she could get him off that horse.

It didn't help that David was suspicious. He shot her a questioning glance. "You would go with me into the mountains? You'd run away with me?"

She forced a smile to her lips. "Yes, of course."

"I thought you didn't want me," David said.

"That was before I knew what a . . . a low bastard Mr. Newcome would prove to be. And before you so bravely came to rescue me."

Evan's eyes were the color of black ice as he watched her edge ever closer to David. "Running away again, Catrin? Afraid that this 'low bastard' might get the truth from you eventually?"

She ignored his cutting words, forcing herself to concentrate on sidling nearer to David. Her heart pounded so fiercely she thought sure it drowned out every other sound on the road, but she kept moving. She kept her movements slow and easy so she wouldn't spook David's horse. A step to the left. A half turn. Another step. David couldn't watch both her and Evan, and as long as he kept his eye on Evan, she might reach him.

"Tell me, Catrin," Evan continued, his voice low and harsh in anger. "Was Morys one of the men you took to London with you? He seems awfully eager to use that pistol in your defense."

"What is he talking about, the men you took to London?" David asked as his gaze flickered to her for a moment, then back to Evan. "I thought you went alone."

Mentally, she cursed Evan. "Of course I went alone." She forced tears to her eyes. It wasn't hard to do under the circumstances. "Oh, David, you don't know what a beast Mr.

Newcome has been. He's been saying all these awful untruths. . . ."

David steadied his aim again, muttering, "The bastard! I'll kill him!"

"No!" she cried, taking the last few steps to his horse. Grabbing the horse's rein with her free hand, she looked up at David. "Please, just take me away from here." She forced a petulant pout to her lips. "If you shoot him, I won't run away with you. I won't risk being linked with a known murderer, not in my situation."

David hesitated, glancing down at her, then at Evan. "Come on then," he murmured noncommittally, holding his free hand out to her.

She could tell that he thought to have her safe in his grasp on the horse before he shot Evan. She must get him off that horse! "You'll have to dismount and help me up. I can't mount by myself."

David looked at her, then at Evan. *Please, God,* she thought, her fingers growing clammy on the chalice. *Please let him be arrogant enough and certain enough of my incompetence to think I can't mount without his help.*

Apparently, he was. "Oh, very well," he muttered. He kept his eyes trained on Evan. Throwing his leg over the side of the horse, he slid smoothly to the ground with the pistol still clutched in his hand.

In that moment, when he was slightly off balance, she struck, swinging the chalice with all her might down on his head.

Then everything happened at once. David growled, "What the hell?" as he turned toward her. At the same time Evan rode up and vaulted from his horse onto David. The two men crashed to the ground, struggling for the pistol as she screamed and circled them, trying to find an opening to hit David again.

Suddenly, there was a thunderous noise, and Evan fell back, clutching his shoulder. "Evan!" she screamed as the horses bolted, running off down the road.

David rocked back on his heels, staring down at the smoking pistol with astonishment. In that moment a murderous rage consumed her. Without even stopping to think, she came up behind David and struck him on the back of the head with the chalice over and over until he keeled over senseless.

A wrenching moan to the right of her drew her out of her mindless fury. In an instant she dropped the chalice and ran to where Evan sat on the ground, his hand splayed over his coat as if to somehow halt the red stain spreading across the wool.

"My God, Evan!" she cried as she knelt beside him and stared blindly at the blood seeping through his fingers.

I failed! she thought, her heart twisting in her breast. *David has killed him!*

Then she heard him utter a choked word that sounded like her name. He lifted a face racked with pain to her, his eyes wide with shock.

"Please don't die," she whispered as she pushed his hand aside and tried to open his coat to examine the wound. "Oh, please don't die, Evan!"

Evan's eyes focused on her. "I . . . I don't think . . . it's fatal," he managed to say. "And that bastard Morys might hurt you if you don't—"

"Hush," she cried, pressing her fingers to his lips as tears welled in her eyes. She glanced over to where David lay slumped over on the ground. "He can't do anything. But we've got to get you help."

He clutched at her arm as she struggled to drag his coat off him. "The . . . the pistol," he rasped. "Must get the pistol . . . first. Before . . . he can . . . use it on you."

Tears coursed down her cheeks. Thanks to her, his life's blood was draining away, and all he could think of was protecting her. "He won't use it on me. He doesn't want to hurt me."

He winced as she tugged his coat sleeve off his right arm. "He might . . . want to . . . now that you hit him . . . over the head."

"I'm not worried about that," she said, pulling the other sleeve off as gently as she could to keep from hurting him. "You said that Llynwydd was a short distance away. Do you think you can walk that far if I support you? I'm afraid we've scared off the horses."

With a groan he dug his fingers into her arm. "Get . . . the pistol first."

"A pox on that thing!" she told him in despair. Then she

heard another groan, but it wasn't Evan's. She turned and saw David lift his head.

"The pistol!" Evan hissed, his lips drawn from the pain.

This time she obeyed, rising to her feet, then moving the few steps to where the pistol had fallen just short of David. She snatched it up as David slumped back down with a low moan.

Hurrying back to Evan's side, she knelt down and held out the pistol. He took it from her and opened the chamber. "Deuce take it, he's used . . . the one shot."

"Of course he's used the one shot!" she cried. "It's buried in your chest! Pray God it's not buried in your heart!"

Evan looked up at her, then ran his tongue over his lips. "I'd be dead . . . if it were." He swallowed twice. "Catrin . . . you must get . . . another ball."

"Another ball?" she said uncomprehendingly.

He raised the pistol an inch.

"Oh, yes, a ball for the pistol." She glanced over at David. Once again, he was stirring. Without stopping to think about it, she went to his side and used her foot to turn him onto his back. Then she searched through his pockets until she found a bag containing the balls and powder.

Swiftly, she returned to Evan and handed them to him. Though his rigid mouth showed the pain it caused him, he reloaded the gun and handed it to her.

"What am I supposed to do with this?" she cried as she held the hateful thing in her hands.

"Catrin . . ." growled a voice behind her.

She whirled to find David struggling to his feet. Her heart began to beat triple-time, and she instinctively moved in front of Evan to block him.

David rubbed the back of his head as he scowled at her. "What happened to me?" Then he caught sight of the chalice lying a few feet away from him. As she watched helplessly, he picked it up and stared at it.

"This is it, isn't it?" he said hoarsely as he turned it over and over in his hand. "This is the chalice, isn't it? It has to be. It's exactly as you described it."

When she didn't answer, he said, "You hit me with the chalice, didn't you?" He glanced up, eyes hard. "Didn't you?"

"Yes," she murmured.

"You've had it all this time."

She hesitated before answering, but there was no point in denying it. "Yes."

Anger suffused his face with scarlet color. "You deceitful bitch," he hissed. "You lied to me! You . . . you hit me!" With determination in his eyes he stepped forward. "I'm going to make you regret that, my sweet. You and Newcome both."

Her hands shook as she raised the gun. "Stay back, David!"

He paused, a taunting smile crossing his face. "It's been fired once. You can't fire it again."

"Evan reloaded it," she said. Keeping the pistol level on him, she knelt and picked up the bag she'd taken from his coat. She held it up with her free hand. "See? It's reloaded now. And I *will* shoot you if you come any nearer."

His handsome features hardened into a nasty mask. "You wouldn't dare!"

"I would! I won't let you hurt either of us. I'll shoot if I must!" Brave words, she thought, but false. She could never pull the trigger, not in a million years.

With a snarled oath he took another step forward, but she cocked the gun as she'd seen him do earlier. Pray heaven that the dusk concealed the way her hands shook.

Apparently, it did. He stopped short and scowled first at her, then at Evan, before his expression evened out. "Come now, Catrin. You can't think I'd hurt you. As for Newcome, how can you defend the man who would see you hang?"

"How can I let him die by the side of the road?" she countered.

David sneered. "He'd let *you* die."

She swallowed. "Perhaps. But it doesn't matter. I can't do it."

David stared at her, his face sullen. "I tell you what, Catrin. Come with me and we'll send someone back here for him."

"You should . . . do as he says, you know," Evan choked out behind her.

"Don't be a fool, Evan," she muttered. "I'm not leaving you." Her arms were beginning to ache from having to hold the pistol so steadily on David, and she knew Evan was losing blood. She must get David away from here. But how? What would Grandmother have done?

Whatever it took, she answered herself, and that gave her courage. "Listen, David." She forced her voice to be even. "I don't know why you would want me to come with you when I don't care for you, but—"

"It's only your infatuation with this bastard that keeps you from seeing we're meant for each other," David put in.

"No! I don't want you! And it's pointless for you to stay and try to persuade me to go with you. I'm not leaving Evan. So you might as well hunt up your horse and return to Llanddeusant, before I tire of holding this pistol and shoot you in the leg." She lowered the pistol until she was aiming at his crotch. "Or shoot you somewhere else more important. Believe me, after what you just did to Evan, I'd have no compunction at all about leaving *you* here to die."

It was a bluff, of course. Aside from the fact that she had no intention of pulling the trigger, she could also never leave even a wretch like David to rot on the road. But he didn't know that.

Paling, he glanced from her to Evan, then down at the chalice in his hand. With a grimace he finally muttered, "Very well, then. I'll go. But you'll regret sending me away when he dies of his wounds and they blame you for his murder. What will you do then? You'll need me to tell them the truth about what happened. So I'm not going far, I promise. I'll be close by, waiting for him to die, and you to come crawling to me."

He held up the chalice. "Besides, I have this, don't I? And I know how much it means to you. You'll come to me, if only to get it back." Then he turned and walked off.

"No!" she cried as she watched her precious chalice being taken from her. "You drop that chalice, David! Drop it now!"

But he kept walking, acting as if he hadn't heard her. A pox on him! He knew her too well. He knew that while she might shoot him to protect Evan, she'd never shoot him over the chalice, and certainly not in the back. There was nothing she could do about it, not unless she left Evan's side, and she didn't dare do that.

She watched despairingly as David strode in the direction the horses had gone, but the minute he disappeared over a hill, she uncocked the pistol and went to Evan's side. "We must get you away from here at once in case he returns."

Unbuttoning his waistcoat, she peeled it back to examine the wound. The light had almost faded completely, and she could make out little to nothing in the darkness, but she could feel the damp blood against her fingers. Ignoring the utter fear that gripped her in its claws, she moved her fingers as gently as possible over his chest until she found the place where the ball had gone in.

It seemed high enough to have missed his heart and lungs, but she couldn't be sure. After Willie's death, she'd made a point to learn something about life-threatening injuries, for nothing had been so horrible as sitting there with Willie's head in her lap, wishing she could do something to help, praying that he would live.

But a person could learn only so much from talking to apothecaries and surgeons. She'd never had to care for a wound of this consequence. As despair seeped into her, she tried to consider what would be most important. She couldn't get the ball out, not here in the darkness. But perhaps she could stop the bleeding.

Trying not to move him unnecessarily, she unknotted his cravat and folded it into a pad. She pressed it against his chest to stanch the blood, then glanced around for something to keep it in place and put pressure on the wound.

She looked down at the scarf that crossed her bosom. Yes, that would do. Untying the knot she'd tied so hastily that morning, she drew off the scarf and threaded it under his arms and around his chest, tying it as tightly as she could manage.

"Catrin," he said hoarsely as he covered her hand with his. "The walk to Llynwydd . . . is too long. I won't make it . . . there, even with your help." He sucked in several deep breaths. "You . . . must go there . . . and fetch someone."

"But I can't leave you here unprotected!"

"Give me . . . the pistol . . . and help me move . . . off the road." He glanced up at the sky. "It's getting dark . . . no one will find me."

She wanted to argue, but she knew he was right. He had no chance at all if she didn't move swiftly, and she couldn't move swiftly with him so badly wounded.

She rebuttoned his snug waistcoat over the wadded-up

cravat and her scarf, hoping that would provide added pressure against the wound to slow the bleeding. Next she stuffed the pistol into the pocket of his coat along with the bag containing the ball and powder, then donned it so she wouldn't have to carry it.

Moving behind him, she bent to clasp him under the arms, but she realized at once that she'd never be able to lift him. Fortunately, he had enough strength left that between her frantic tugging and his halting attempts to rise, she was able to maneuver him to a stand.

Quickly, she looped his arm over her shoulder, supporting him with her body as she clasped him around the waist. Then they began the long, tortured walk that took them off the road and into a wide field.

"A . . . tree," he groaned. "Find a tree to . . . prop me against."

She glanced around and spotted a tree about a hundred paces from where they stood. Praying that he could make it that far, she moved doggedly forward, though she felt him shudder with pain at every step.

After a few minutes her right arm and shoulder ached from the effort of supporting him, and she could feel that he was growing weaker, for he seemed to lean more heavily on her. Only sheer force of will drove her on to the tree. Though it required a few more torturous steps, she half-dragged, half-carried Evan around to the side of it away from the road.

Then she lowered him to the ground as gently as she could manage, given the inequity in their sizes. As it was, he slipped through her grasp and fell the last few inches, landing on the ground with a terrible grunt of pain.

"Oh, Evan, I'm so sorry." She knelt beside him. "Are you all right?"

"I'll . . . manage," he said. "Give me . . . the pistol."

She drew it out of his coat pocket and pressed it into his hand. His fingers were cold and clammy against hers as he closed them around the handle of the pistol. She removed his coat, then tried to make him comfortable, drawing him slightly forward to place the coat around his shoulder.

Loath to leave him just yet, although she knew she must, she slid her hand inside his waistcoat, checking to be sure the wadded cravat was still in place. "I'm so sorry about this, Evan. If not for me, you'd never have gotten shot."

He covered her hand with his. "If . . . not for you . . . I'd be dead now."

She shook her head, tears stinging her eyes. He could still die, out here in the night all alone. "It's such a mess, such a horrible mess. But I promise I'll do my best to get you out of this alive."

She started to rise, but he tightened his fingers on her hand. "Tell me something . . . before you go."

"What?"

"Why didn't you . . . leave with him when . . . you had the chance?"

"I couldn't let you die—"

"Why . . . not?" He drew in a ragged breath. "I was taking you . . . to London against your will . . ." The faintest hint of guilt tinged his next words. "I was risking . . . *your* life. You had the right . . . to risk mine."

That he really believed she would have left him to die tore at her, and she couldn't hide the hurt in her voice when she answered. "What you and I did together last night . . ." She swallowed. "It may have meant nothing to you, but it meant something to me. I couldn't leave you to die."

He clutched at her hand. "Ah, Catrin . . . I wish last night had . . . meant nothing to me. Then I wouldn't have been . . . in hell ever since it . . . happened."

He angled his head up toward hers, and though she couldn't see his features, she could feel his difficult breathing on her cheek. Had he been in hell today? She wouldn't have guessed it. But she'd certainly been in hell, and there promised to be no salvation in sight until she could see him safe.

Afraid she'd betray how much she cared, she turned her face away. "I-I have to go now, before you lose any more blood."

But he clung to her hand a moment longer. "Thank you," he whispered. He rubbed her hand against his cheek, which after two days of not shaving had the surface of a wire brush. "Thank you for looking after me."

The gesture was so intimate, it made her throat constrict. Why must he always do this to her, turn her inside out when she least expected it? "I must go now," she choked out and extricated her hand from his.

It took every ounce of her will to leave him lying there alone against the tree, knowing that when she returned he might be dead.

No! she vowed as she took one last look at his shadowed form. *I won't let him die. I won't!* She had already watched one man she cared for die. She was *not* going to watch another one do so.

She paused to memorize every facet of the landscape, praying she could find the spot again. Then she turned and rushed off into the darkness.

Juliana and Rhys Vaughan had just sat down to dinner when their youngest footman rushed into the dining room. "Excuse me, sir. I hate to disturb you, but there's a madwoman out here begging to speak with you and Lady Juliana."

Rhys stifled a smile at James's tendency to exaggerate. With a knowing glance in Juliana's direction, he set down his glass of wine. "A madwoman?"

"She says you know her, and she gives her name as Mrs. Catrin Price, but she looks a terrible sight. You want me to send her away?"

Rhys cast Juliana a glance as he wondered what Catrin Price would be doing here. And did this have anything to do with Evan's visit to her?

He turned to the footman as he rose from the table. "Don't send her away. We do know her. Of course we'll speak to her." With a worried expression Juliana rose from her place, too, and they walked from the room together.

When they passed into the hall, they found Mrs. Price pacing, her face distraught. As she whirled toward them, Rhys could almost understand why James had thought her a madwoman. Blood was spattered all over the poor girl's muslin gown. Her hair was a disordered mass, and her eyes shone with a wild light.

"Thank heaven you're home!" she exclaimed. "I don't know if you remember me, but—"

"Of course we remember you," Rhys said. "But what in the devil has happened?"

"Evan has been shot," she said. "You must help him. You must send someone—"

"Evan Newcome?" Juliana asked.

As his heart began to pound, Rhys turned to see his wife's face go ashen.

"Yes!" Mrs. Price turned to Juliana with a pleading expression. "He said you were friends of his—"

"Where is he?" Rhys asked as he clasped Mrs. Price's shoulders.

"Up at the road, close to the entrance to your estate. I had to leave him, because he couldn't make it this far with his wound."

"How badly is he wounded?" Juliana asked.

Mrs. Price's distress was clear in every line of her pretty, young face. "Very badly, I'm afraid. The ball is lodged in his shoulder, and he's lost a great deal of blood." She gripped Rhys's arm. "If you don't hurry—"

But Rhys was already drawing on his coat and barking orders—calling for a wagon and horses and telling the footman to send someone to Carmarthen for a surgeon.

Juliana drew on her coat, too. "I'm going with you."

"No, you're not," Rhys said. When she flashed him a mutinous glare, he added, "I don't know who shot him and if they're still lurking out there. Besides, you need to get a room ready and find someone on the estate to help with patching him up. It'll be hours before the surgeon from Carmarthen arrives."

Apparently seeing the wisdom of his words, Juliana gave a curt nod and hurried off to find the housekeeper.

Rhys turned to Mrs. Price. "Let's go," he said as he gripped her arm.

Together they hurried down the steps to where two saddled horses already awaited, along with a wagon drawn by a cob. Rhys helped Mrs. Price into the sidesaddle before mounting his horse. Then he took off like a shot, praying that the girl was as good a horsewoman as her grandmother and could keep up with him. After all, he needed her to tell him where Evan was.

Evan had been like one of his own sons almost from the day Rhys had met him. To think of him lying alone and wounded made Rhys's gut wrench painfully.

To her credit, Mrs. Price matched his pace, and they soon

left the wagon far behind. Although he could tell from the way she sat the horse that horsemanship wasn't one of her stronger points, her face wore a look of such determination that he doubted anything could stop her.

In record time they reached the place where the drive to Llynwydd met the main road to Carmarthen. She turned onto the road, but went only a few feet before she halted her horse and dismounted, peering into the shadowy land bordering the road. "I left him propped against a tree." A note of fear entered her voice. "We have to find him before David comes back."

"David?" Rhys asked as he got down from his horse and left it to graze by the side of the road.

"The man who shot him," she explained. "He said he'd be back."

Rhys wanted to ask more, but she'd already left the road to enter a field. After a moment he made out the shape of a tree silhouetted against the night sky. He hurried to it in time to see her round the tree and kneel on the ground. As he came around the tree himself, he saw a hulking figure slumped against the trunk.

The sound of the wagon lumbering from the drive onto the road behind them caught his attention, and he rushed out to fetch the groom who was driving it. It would take two men at least to get Evan into the wagon, and he was grateful that the groom had brought a stable boy with him.

By the time he'd returned to Evan's side, Mrs. Price was rocking back and forth, rubbing Evan's hand in hers as she sobbed, "Please, Evan, wake up! Please don't die and leave me!"

Rhys knelt beside her and groped along Evan's neck until he found a pulse. "He's not dead yet," he murmured reassuringly. He half-turned toward the road. "Bring that light here!" he called out, and the groom approached with a lantern.

He almost wished he hadn't asked for a light when he saw Evan's face. It was so pale in the glow of the candle that he feared the worst. When he opened the coat and saw the blood-soaked shirt, he sucked in a harsh breath. They must get him back to Llynwydd at once.

When he and the groom and the stable boy lifted Evan, Rhys was relieved to hear his friend moan, for that meant at least he was still enough in this world to feel pain. They tried to be as careful as they could with his shoulder as they carried him to the wagon, but Evan was a giant of a man, and they had to struggle to carry him.

He wondered for the first time how Evan had come to be lying against a tree several feet from the road. Surely Mrs. Price hadn't moved him there alone. Why, the woman was a little slip of a thing!

It took some work, but at last they had Evan in the wagon, propped against a feed sack. Rhys helped Mrs. Price into the wagon, then climbed up beside her while the stable boy scurried off to collect the horses. As the groom started the horse moving back toward Llynwydd, Mrs. Price eased herself between the wagon side and Evan, then pulled him down until his head was cradled in her lap.

Rhys watched with interest as she stroked the hair away from Evan's face, whispering that he must not leave her yet, that he could not die, that they would have him fixed up fine if he could just hold on.

Rhys waited until she'd fallen silent, her hand absently caressing Evan's face. Then he moved a little closer. "Tell me, Mrs. Price, how did he come to be shot?"

She looked up at him. For a moment her face looked blank, as if she hadn't even realized he was there. Then a stricken expression spread over it. "Oh, Mr. Vaughan, it's dreadful! It's all my fault!"

"I doubt that," he said soothingly.

But she shook her head back and forth. "It is, truly it is!"

He heard a sob catch in her throat and murmured, "You said a man named David shot Evan. Who is he?"

"David Morys," she choked out, wiping away a tear from her face. "The schoolmaster in Llanddeusant."

A schoolmaster, Rhys thought. This grew increasingly curious. It was odd enough that Evan should have been near Llynwydd with Mrs. Price in his company, though from the way Juliana had tried to throw the two of them together, it shouldn't surprise him. Still, Evan had left Llynwydd only a week ago.

"Why did a schoolmaster shoot Evan?" he continued, praying that she wouldn't collapse into tears before he could get the entire story from her. If this Morys fellow was running loose shooting people, Rhys wanted to be prepared. Besides, focusing on finding Evan's attacker kept him from thinking about that bloodstained shirt and the bloodless face of his friend.

Mrs. Price choked back a sob. "Please, it's very complicated, and I promise to tell you all of it eventually, but I . . . I can't talk about it right now."

"I understand," he said, reaching over to pat her hand. "Under the circumstances, your first concern has to be making sure Evan lives."

She bobbed her head.

"Nonetheless, I must know if this David Morys would come to the estate after Evan or you."

"He might," she whispered. "The only way I got him to leave was by threatening to shoot him with his pistol, and—"

"You threatened him with a pistol?" Rhys asked, incredulous.

"Yes. I had to."

"Where's the pistol?" he asked.

She pulled it out of Evan's coat pocket and handed it to him. "Here. I never want to see another pistol as long as I live."

That brought a faint smile to his face. "I imagine not." Rhys tried to imagine the shy Mrs. Price facing down a man with a pistol, but he couldn't. Damn it all, the woman had changed considerably since he'd met her the first time. Juliana would be surprised.

"Anyway, when David was leaving," Mrs. Price went on, "he said he'd be back. I think he assumed we had nowhere to hide. That's why I had to pull Evan off the road. I was afraid David might find him before I could return."

Rhys stared at her. "*You* pulled him off the road? Alone?"

"He could still stand, but I did have to support him while we left the road, and I was afraid I wouldn't make it." She sighed and lifted her face to him. "I had to do something. I . . . I couldn't let him die."

Rhys took her hand in both of his as they neared the squire hall. "You did well, Mrs. Price. If he comes through this, it will be largely due to your efforts."

In the light blazing from the squire hall, he could see the tears filling her eyes again. She sucked in a heavy breath.

"If it hadn't been for me, he wouldn't be in this predicament!"

"Nonsense. It sounds as if it was this Morys fellow's fault entirely."

She hid her face from him. "Oh, but you don't know . . ."

She trailed off when the wagon halted at the foot of the entrance. As servants scurried down the steps, followed by an anxious Juliana, Rhys squeezed Mrs. Price's hands. "He'll be all right, Mrs. Price. He's in good hands here. Evan's strong. He's survived many things in his life, and he'll survive this. So don't worry about him. All right?"

She managed a smile through the tears that shimmered in her eyes. "Oh, I do hope you're right. I couldn't bear it if . . . if . . ."

Though she didn't finish, Rhys knew exactly what she meant. And he shared her sentiments entirely.

Chapter Sixteen

Then came a mist at close of eve;
Wide o'er the path by which I passed,
Its mantle dim and murk it cast.
That mist ascending met the sky,
Forcing the daylight from my eye.
—Anonymous, "The Mist"

Layers of mist clung to Evan like damp cotton, dragging him into a dark swamp. He flailed his arms. The mist swirled tighter . . . closer. . . . It suffocated him. He sucked in air, but it was fetid and damp, poisonous.

And cold. Bone-chilling cold. Alien and clammy, drowning him in a terrible, black emptiness.

"No . . . No . . . Please help . . . me," he choked out.

"I'm here" came a voice out of the mist.

A soft, gentle voice. Catrin. He stopped flailing and turned, looking for her. *I must find her. She's here, somewhere. Catrin, Lady of the Mists.*

Once before she had come to him out of the mist, out of the fearful, tainted mist. Only Catrin could part the dangerous vapors. Only Catrin.

"Catrin," he croaked out as the mist wrapped his legs and arms in spidery tendrils. "Catrin!"

Then he saw her, cocooned in a halo of light. Catrin. His Catrin, coming to him with a smile.

"It will be all right," she said as she stepped closer, holding out her hand to him. "I'm here. It will all be fine."

He strained against the blackness threatening to swallow him up. He strained toward Catrin, toward her light. The cold trickled out of him, seeping away like the vapor that vanished in her light.

He stretched out his hand, fighting the pull of the mist. His shoulder ached from the effort of reaching, of fighting. But he ignored it. Catrin. She would rescue him from the darkness. If he could only reach her . . . if only his shoulder didn't ache so much, so very much.

Her hand closed around his . . . warm, supple fingers and strength greater than his . . . stealing into him, warming him.

Relief rushed through him as he gripped her hand.

Suddenly, the mist faded, and he realized he was lying on his back in a soft bed. His mouth was dry and hot, but his skin was drenched in cold sweat, making his breeches and shirt cling to him. His shoulder ached terribly. He tried to move it, but discovered it was bound in bandages, as was his arm, which lay on his chest beneath the loose shirt.

"It will all be fine," came a hoarse whisper from somewhere to his right. "It has to be. You can't die. You can't!"

His eyes fluttered open, and for a moment he was completely disoriented. Sunlight streamed through the windows of a lavishly appointed room, and a woman was gripping his hand, pressing it against her cheek as tears slid down her face.

No, not any woman. Catrin. A very pale, very anguished Catrin. The dark smudges under her eyes attested to a lack of sleep. Her hair was a wild mass of tangled curls and her gown was stained and creased.

And she looked like an angel.

Suddenly, everything came back to him. Catrin crowning Morys with the chalice. His own fight with Morys. The pistol going off and Catrin struggling to save him. Their torturous walk to the side of the road that ended with him alone, staring at the sky and wondering if he was going to die.

He obviously hadn't died. He glanced at his arm. It must be in a sling, he thought, since the left arm of the shirt he was wearing hung down empty from his shoulder. Someone had patched him up very well.

His eyes widened as he stared at Catrin. How had she gotten him here? And where was here? He remembered her talking about getting him to Llynwydd. Had she managed that? Is that where he was?

Licking his dry lips, he tried to speak. At first only a pitiful rasping noise escaped his lips, but it was enough to draw Catrin's attention.

She lifted her head to look at him with glistening eyes. "Evan?"

He swallowed, then croaked, "Good . . . morning."

At first shock filled her face, but the shock soon turned into a brilliant smile. "Oh, Evan . . . you're awake . . . you're awake and alive and—" She broke off as tears streamed down her face. "When you had such a bad fever last night, I thought—By heaven, it doesn't matter. Nothing matters now that you're all right." Then her face fell. "You *are* all right, aren't you? I mean, I know you must be feeling pain, but—"

"I believe I'm through the worse of it." He flexed his legs and his unbound arm experimentally, pleased to discover that he'd maintained control of his other limbs. "As you said, there's pain . . . but everything seems to be intact."

She clasped his hand to her chest with a sob. "I'm so sorry about David's shooting you. I have this knack for getting you hurt."

"It doesn't matter." He squeezed her fingers weakly. "As you said, nothing matters but . . . that you're here and . . . I'm here. Safe."

A shy smile lit her face as she ducked her head. That smile devastated his insides. He tightened his grip on her hand, then ran his thumb over her knuckles, savoring the texture of her skin. Her fingers were so delicate and dainty, the skin so soft. Something flickered in his mind, something about a mist and a hand held out to him, but the effort of thinking about it made his head hurt, so he stopped.

Besides it felt wonderful just to hold her hand, to feel her warmth against the cold clamminess of his skin. It seemed as if he'd wandered in the darkness for an eternity, waiting to hold this hand. "How long . . . have I been here?"

"Two nights and a day. The surgeon removed the ball successfully, but you had lost a great deal of blood and you didn't wake up." Her mouth tightened. "Last night during the storm you were so still and your fever so high that I feared—" She squeezed his hand. "Oh, Evan, I thought for sure you would die. We've all been frantic with worry."

"We?"

"The Vaughans. That's where you are. At Llynwydd. Don't you remember what happened after David shot you?"

Running his tongue over his parched lips, he murmured, "Some. Not all." He remembered asking her why she'd stayed with him. What had she said? Because their lovemaking had meant something to her, even if it had meant nothing to him.

Lovemaking. Ah, yes, the beauty of lovemaking with Catrin. And he had thought to give that up simply because—

Other things came back to him then, all the accusations he'd thrown at her, all the lies she'd told him. Justin's murder seemed a lifetime away now. Strange how none of it mattered as much as it once had.

What mattered was that he was alive, that he was whole, that he hadn't perished by the side of the road. What mattered was that Catrin hadn't left him, even when it had been to her advantage to do so. She'd nearly killed herself to save him. Surely that proved her innocence, didn't it?

"Evan," she whispered, drawing his attention from his unsettling thoughts. "Mr. Vaughan and Lady Juliana are nearly beside themselves with worry for you, so I really should tell them you're awake. It will only take a minute. All right?"

He nodded, though he watched her leave the room with a quick spurt of panic, the same panic he'd felt when she'd left him propped against the tree. He had to remind himself how irrational his panic was now. When she'd left before, matters had been more dire. He'd even feared she might not come back . . . or might not come back in time. The menacing darkness had clawed at him, reminding him of nights as a boy when his father's fury and beatings had driven him to hide in the woodshed, when he'd lain in the dark, hearing rats scrabble along the floor as he waited for morning and the abatement of his father's anger.

After Catrin's departure, he'd struggled to stay conscious enough to use the pistol if Morys came back. But his struggles had been fruitless, for somewhere in that horrible night, he'd slipped into unconsciousness and a black morass of—

He wouldn't think of it. It was over now. He was safe. The darkness was banished, and Catrin was here. She was bringing his friends, and everything was right with the world.

A need to look not so helpless and weak suddenly assailed him, and he struggled to push himself into a sitting position. But that was all he could manage before the door to the room opened, and Lady Juliana thrust her head inside. Her face lit up when she saw him propped against the pillows. With a little cry she rushed into the room, followed closely by Rhys and Catrin.

Evan noticed that Catrin stood back, watching shyly as Lady Juliana fussed over him and Rhys teased him about being a "damned sight too big to carry." It took all of Evan's will not to call Catrin over to his side. After what had happened, he needed her even more than before. He needed to feel her warmth, her strength, her will. Yet he knew that Rhys and Lady Juliana, especially Lady Juliana, would make much of any sign of his urge to have Catrin at his side, and he didn't want to embarrass Catrin.

Instead, he turned his gaze to the squire. With a smile he said, "I'm afraid I lost the horse you loaned me, old chap."

Rhys laughed. "As if I would care. But you didn't lose it. She showed up at the stables yesterday, a little ragged and weary, but otherwise whole."

"Good."

"The surgeon said your shoulder would heal well if you lived through the loss of blood and the fever," Lady Juliana put in, settling her hip on the edge of the bed. "Thank heaven you got through all that."

"Yes, thank heaven," Rhys quipped. "I don't think the university could stand to lose an instructor of your caliber."

Rolling her eyes, Lady Juliana said, "Don't listen to him. He doesn't give a whit about the university. *He* would have been destroyed if something had happened to you. He's paced the floors ever since the night he and Mrs. Price went to fetch you in the wagon."

As Rhys smiled at him, a lump formed in Evan's throat. It was good to have such loyal friends. "Thank you, all of you, for looking after me."

Lady Juliana patted his hand. "Yes, well, it's not over yet. You must get your strength back. You need lots of rest and plenty of food in that bottomless pit you call a stomach. I'm having Cook prepare some savory broth for you right now."

"It sounds wonderful," Evan murmured.

Lady Juliana rose. "I suppose we shouldn't tire you too much, so we'll let you rest for a while."

She turned toward the door, but when Catrin did the same, he blurted out, "Will you stay, Catrin?"

"Of course," she said, her eyes bright as she stepped toward the bed.

But Lady Juliana checked her with one hand. "Evan, you need rest. And so does Mrs. Price, I'm afraid. She hasn't slept since she and Rhys brought you here, except for dozing in that chair over there." She pointed to an uncomfortable-looking chair.

"If Evan wants me to stay with him—" Catrin began.

"No, it's fine," Evan broke in. Good God, he was such a dolt. Of course Catrin needed rest. "I am indeed . . . quite tired. I think I shall sleep a while."

Catrin cast him an anxious glance. "Are you sure? If you need me, I'll stay."

He looked at her, at the weariness evident in the stoop of her young shoulders and the worry lines about her mouth, and cursed himself for not thinking sooner of what she must have been through. Thanks to him, she hadn't had a good night's sleep in three nights. And she'd probably drained her strength in her struggle to get him here.

The enormity of what she'd done struck him once more. After he'd threatened to turn her over to the magistrate, she'd saved his life at great personal hardship. It was amazing. *She* was amazing.

Amazing and tired. Despite his irrational and very selfish desire to have her with him, he couldn't ask it of her, not at the moment.

"I'll be fine," he said, keeping his eyes averted from Lady Juliana, who was watching the interchange with avid interest. "Truly, Catrin, I do need sleep."

She nodded, but stepped forward to lay her hand briefly over his. "If you need me, just call." She lifted her hand, as if to stroke his cheek, then seemed to think better of it and dropped her hand abruptly. "I'm so glad you're doing better. Sleep well."

Long after she and the others were gone, he thought about her aborted gesture and wondered how she felt about him now. She must have cared some for him to save him from Morys. But was it merely the kind of caring one showed another human being or was it a sign of something deeper?

Had he so alienated her affections with his accusations that he'd never again feel her hand against his cheek? Good God, he hoped not. He fervently hoped not.

He's going to be fine, Catrin thought as they left Evan's room. *Thank heaven he's going to make it. I didn't cause his death.* Blinking back the tears of relief that stung her eyes, she followed the Vaughans down the hall to the stairs.

Lady Juliana was insisting that Catrin eat something, and Catrin was too tired to protest, so she let them lead her down the stairs to the dining room. Her joy at seeing him well seemed to have roused her appetite, and she was looking forward to a meal.

Still, the prospect of sharing that meal with the Vaughans unnerved her. The only words she'd spoken to them since she'd arrived had concerned Evan's condition, and even those had been sparse. Despite Lady Juliana's attempts to get Catrin to leave Evan's room, Catrin had refused to leave his side, for fear he would wake up and no one would be there to help him.

Now she felt out of place, a definite outsider in this house where everyone knew Evan so well—not only the Vaughans but all the servants, too. When Evan's sister, Mary, had joined Catrin at his bedside yesterday, Catrin had learned why Evan was so close to the Vaughans. Even though he was only the younger son of one of their tenant farmers, they had paid for his education and had treated him like one of their own children for twenty years. They'd seen in Evan what no one else would have taken the trouble to see—a genius who needed only nurturing to blossom.

No wonder they'd been so distraught over his wound. No wonder they were kind to her for having saved his life. She swallowed the lump in her throat. If they knew how much she'd been responsible for his near death, they wouldn't be so kind to her, would they?

Worse yet, she was here under false pretenses. If it hadn't been for David's heedless act, Evan would never have exposed his benefactors to the shameless woman he thought her to be. That was probably the real reason he hadn't wanted to stop at Llynwydd on the way to Carmarthen.

She sighed as the Vaughans ushered her into the dining room, their expressions so considerate and friendly. Like Evan's just now. He'd looked at her with such tenderness, it had made her heart beat faster. It was like the way he'd looked at her the night he'd made love to her.

Had he forgotten why they'd been traveling this road in the first place? Or was he simply filled with a temporary gratitude that would fade as he grew stronger? She almost didn't care, she was so happy to see him alive and well and smiling at her like a man who has found good fortune at last.

"Why don't you sit here by me?" Lady Juliana said as she took a seat and patted the chair next to her. "Cook has prepared enough food for an army, although I honestly believe we'll have no trouble eating it all."

As Catrin sat down, she scanned the Vaughans' tired faces and realized they were probably as weary and hungry as she. They, too, had waited through Evan's frightful fever, hoping he would survive it. And they, too, had missed meals and sleep to be sure Evan was cared for.

"Where are the children?" Mr. Vaughan asked Lady Juliana.

His wife smiled. "Owen was up before dawn to go in to town for me, and Margaret is still asleep, but they'll join us for lunch." She cast Catrin a kindly look. "I think, however, that our guest won't be at lunch to meet them, since she'll probably spend the next several hours sleeping."

Catrin looked down at her plate. "Yes, if Evan doesn't need me."

"He can do without you for a few hours," murmured Lady Juliana, though Catrin could feel the older woman eyeing her with curiosity.

The food came then, blessedly ending all attempts at conversation, for they were all too ravenous to do anything but eat. Catrin surprised herself by the amount of food she devoured. Eggs and sausage had never tasted so good, nor simple baked bread so exotic. Thankfully, her host and hostess shared her hunger and ate as much as she did.

When they'd all eaten their fill, Mr. Vaughan leaned back in his chair with a sigh of contentment. "I tell you, Mrs. Price, there is nothing so wonderful as a good meal when one is hungry."

She nodded. "I'll have to agree with you there, sir."

Lady Juliana said gently, "Except perhaps a good night's sleep when one has been without, don't you think?"

As Catrin nodded again, the smile faded from Mr. Vaughan's face, and he leaned forward to cover his wife's hand. "Yes, dear, I know Mrs. Price needs a long rest. But before we send her off to bed, I need to ask her a few questions." He looked at Catrin. "If that's all right with you, that is."

She sighed and nodded. The time had come. Ever since she and the squire had carried Evan to Llynwydd, she'd been waiting for him to question her more thoroughly about the circumstances of the shooting.

Thus, she was surprised when his first words weren't a question at all, but a statement. "A man calling himself Mr. Price showed up here yesterday."

For a moment she simply stared at him. "Mr. Price?"

"Yes. I suspect it was David Morys, since he asked for you and Evan."

Fear clutched at her heart. "What did he say?"

Mr. Vaughan settled back in his chair, casting her a shrewd look. "He said that his wife, a pretty young woman named Catrin Price, had run off with some mountebank from London, and he wanted to know whether they had stopped here. He said the . . . er . . . mountebank had stolen his pistol, too."

Her fear was rapidly replaced by outrage. "Why, that wretched liar! To call me his wife! I assure you I am *not* his wife, nor ever have been!"

Mr. Vaughan smiled. "Yes, I know. I was aware that Willie Price died six years ago, and the likelihood of your having married two Mr. Prices was slim. Obviously, your Mr. Morys was lying. He must have realized you would use your real name to gain help, and he couldn't very well pose as your husband with a different last name, could he?"

A shudder racked her weary frame. "What did you tell him?"

"That I hadn't seen the couple, of course. I did remark that a coach passes this way late at night on its way to Carmarthen and perhaps you had taken it."

"Very quick thinking," Lady Juliana said with a smile at her husband. "As I recall, that particular coach goes on to other parts before returning to Carmarthen. It will be days before he can speak to the driver and find out that the man didn't pick up Evan and Mrs. Price."

Mr. Vaughan nodded. "And that storm we had yesterday ought to slow him down even more. The roads are still difficult to traverse. Besides, once he learns that Evan and Mrs. Price didn't take the coach, he'll no doubt assume they made it onto a ship to London. With luck, his pursuit will end there."

"I think it will," Catrin interjected. "I don't think David would try to follow us to London." Catrin flashed Mr. Vaughan a grateful smile. "Thank you so much for misdirecting him. After what he did to Evan, I never want to see him again."

Mr. Vaughan steepled his fingers. "I can understand that." He paused and drew in a deep breath. "Mrs. Price, I hope you don't mind if I ask you why this Mr. Morys is going to so much trouble to find you. You said you'd tell me the whole story eventually, and now that Evan is doing better, I thought perhaps you—"

"Yes, of course." She'd been expecting this, but it had come too soon. How much should she tell Mr. Vaughan? How much would Evan want him to know?

As she hesitated, Mr. Vaughan added, "When Evan stopped here on his way to Llanddeusant, he mentioned that he thought you might have been the last person to see his friend Justin alive. At the time, Evan said he was on his way to question you. Can I assume that all of this had something to do with what he said?"

So Mr. Vaughan knew that much, did he? If that was the case, there wasn't much point in keeping the whole truth from him. Obviously, Evan confided in him, so even if Evan hadn't yet told him everything, he would soon enough.

"Yes, it has everything to do with that," she said.

Then she began to relate the whole story . . . or most of it anyway, for she left out the details of why she'd wanted the chalice. All she said was that it was a family heirloom she had thought to regain. They didn't prod her for more, which was fortunate since at the moment she didn't much feel like explaining about the curse and trying to convince them of its veracity.

She also left out any mention of her physical relationship with Evan. Apparently, however, they deduced some of that, for Lady Juliana began to regard her with a speculative gaze.

But when Catrin came to the part about Evan's finding the chalice and accusing her of all manner of duplicity, she dropped her eyes to her plate, unable to see the condemnation that must necessarily rise in their faces.

It was all she could do to relate everything without tears, especially the events leading to David's shooting Evan.

Somehow she managed it, ending with, "And that's what happened. That's why David is after us."

The long silence that ensued tormented her, for it told her nothing of what they thought. At last she could bear it no longer, and she lifted her head to find Mr. Vaughan looking speculative and Lady Juliana intrigued.

Mr. Vaughan caught her eyes on him and cleared his throat. "That's a very interesting story. You say Evan was carrying you to London to be questioned by this Mr. Quinley?"

She nodded. "Evan . . . well, you see he thought that—"

"He thought you might have been part of some sordid conspiracy to murder his friend." Lady Juliana snorted as she shot Mr. Vaughan a glance. "Men! They always look at the 'evidence' and never at their hearts. I should have known Evan was as bad as all the rest, jumping to conclusions and making assumptions based on the flimsiest of facts."

Catrin looked at Lady Juliana, surprised to find an ally where she hadn't expected it.

But Mr. Vaughan raised an eyebrow and said dryly, "I don't think these are the flimsiest of facts, Juliana. Perhaps you are letting your own . . . ah . . . past experiences color your assessment of the situation."

Lady Juliana drew herself up, casting him a haughty glare. "Perhaps. But it seems to me that a guilty woman wouldn't risk death to save the man who planned to have her arrested for a supposed treachery. Nor would she stay by his side when she could run off and leave him to die."

"No, of course not," Mr. Vaughan said. "But when Evan accused Mrs. Price, he didn't realize she was going to come to his rescue so valiantly. So you can't entirely blame him for being suspicious." He cast Catrin a solicitous glance. "In any case, I think we've discussed this enough for the moment. Mrs. Price looks as if she might fall asleep sitting up if we don't allow her to get some rest."

Catrin was indeed more than happy to end the discussion. She wanted sleep more than anything.

"I agree," Lady Juliana said, smiling broadly at Catrin. "I know you haven't spent much time in it, but you do know where your room is, don't you?"

"Yes." Catrin rose from the table. "And please let me know if . . . if Evan needs me or calls for me."

Lady Juliana's eyes sparkled. "Of course, my dear, of course."

Then Catrin left the room and started up the stairs, feeling the weariness in every muscle of her body. When she reached her room, which was directly across from Evan's, she hesitated, wondering if she should check on him. But she decided against it, for she didn't want to risk awakening him from his much-needed sleep.

Instead, she entered her own room, closed the door behind her, and glanced at the bed, only to discover that a beautiful night rail had been left for her. With a sigh of pleasure she went to the bed and lifted one sleeve of the delicately wrought muslin gown, with its lace-edged sleeves and neckline. What a shame that after three days without a bath she was so grimy. She winced to think of soiling such a lovely piece of work.

She had just decided to forgo the generosity of her hostess and sleep in her shift, when a knock came at the door. She went to open it, surprised to find a cherry-cheeked young maid standing there with two footmen carrying an empty tub.

The girl curtseyed. "Good morning. My name's Sally. Milady said you'd be wantin' a bath. And I'm to be your maid while you're here."

A hot bath. It sounded lovely beyond words. Tears welled in Catrin's eyes. Lady Juliana had to be one of the most thoughtful women in Wales. "Thank you so much," Catrin murmured as she stood aside to let the servants in.

Sally took over, telling the footmen where to put the tub and directing the servants who came afterward bearing pails of hot and cold water.

As they prepared the bath, Sally turned to Catrin. "Milady has chosen a few of her gowns she thinks you might be able to wear, with a little tuck or two taken here and there."

A little tuck or two, Catrin thought wryly, remembering Lady Juliana's voluptuous figure and comparing it to her own less curvy one. It would take more than a tuck to make those gowns fit. But at least she wouldn't have to wear her own blood-stained gown anymore.

A few minutes later, when she was immersed in hot water up to her chin, she thought of how many things one took for granted in life—sleep, clean clothes, baths, good food. With a lurch she realized that if she *were* arrested for Lord Mansfield's murder, she would lose such simple things as that.

Reaching for the soap and wash rag, she tried to put such terrible thoughts from her mind. But she couldn't. No matter how fiercely she scrubbed her skin or her hair, she couldn't help dwelling on the uncertainty of the future.

What was to happen to her now? Once Evan was well and able to travel, would he continue in his purpose? Surely, the fact that she'd stayed by his side would sway him to believe in her . . . at least a little. It had seemed to sway the Vaughans, so perhaps it would affect him, too.

All at once the pain hit her, the pain she'd been fighting so hard to ignore. Evan had thought her a criminal, a monster. She clutched at her stomach. How could she bear it if he still believed all those dreadful things about her? How could she stand another long trip with him silent and condemning, watching her as if she were a criminal?

Yet if he did still doubt her, she had no other choice but to go with him. Escaping into the hills, that farcical solution she'd posed to David, was exactly that—farcical. What would be the point of escaping into the hills if it still meant losing her lands and condemning her tenants to the ownership of an uncaring landlord? At least if she went to London and spoke in her own defense, everything might come out all right or new evidence might be found to exonerate her.

What if, however, Evan decided to believe her? It was possible, after all, that he might. Just now, he'd looked at her with gratitude and even something like affection. What if he did take her side? What then?

She would return to Llanddeusant, of course, and go on with her life. Evan would probably go on to London, and . . . and . . .

The thought of separating from Evan gave her pain, but she tamped it down ruthlessly. He'd made it clear from the beginning that he didn't want to marry. Even as she had given herself to him, she'd known that. And although he now knew she owned the chalice—

Her heart sank. But she *didn't* own the chalice, did she? David had stolen it. He would never give it back to her either, not unless she married him, and it would be a cold day in hell before she agreed to that.

Despair crept through her in icy trickles. It was so unfair! The only man she wanted to marry thought she was a criminal, and the only man she *could* marry without risking the curse thought she was a whore and wanted to treat her thus.

Feeling defeated, she rose and stepped from the tub, catching up the towel that Sally had left for her before Catrin had dismissed her for the day. She couldn't think about all this right now or she'd go mad.

She must sleep and prepare herself for whatever terrible things were thrown at her next. She must put the pain aside for a while, or she'd never make it through this.

Yes, she told herself as she donned the soft nightdress and slipped between clean sheets. She must gather her strength, as Grandmother had done when she'd lost first her husband and then her daughter and son-in-law. She must be brave.

There was no more place for reticence in her life. Her reticence had made her lie to Evan and thus lose him. Her reticence had made her lie to David and thus lose the chalice, for David would never have come after her three days ago if she'd been honest with him about why she didn't want to marry him.

It was time to rid herself of reticence, before anything else dreadful happened. That was her last thought before she drifted off into a blessedly numbing sleep.

Chapter Seventeen

Futile the frantic plotting
Of weak clay, dead in a day.
From bare earth he came, dark cold,
Coldly he goes in ashes."
—Siôn Cent, "The Vanity of the World"

The White Oak was crowded with people eating lunch. Scowling blackly, David bent over his steaming plate of mutton, ignoring the other genteel travelers who frequented the well-appointed inn on the outskirts of Carmarthen.

When David had left Catrin and that damned Newcome on the road two days ago, he'd thought for certain they'd be unable to go anywhere. It had taken him an hour to find his horse and return. He'd planned to watched Catrin in secret until Newcome died, but in the time he'd been gone, the two of them had vanished without a trace.

That whole night he'd ridden the road, looking for them, and when daybreak had come, he'd gone to every cottage along the way, asking about them. It had taken him only a few minutes to discover that Newcome was from Carmarthen and well-known by many, who refused to tell a stranger whether they'd seen the man wandering the roads.

Fortunately, the squire at that huge estate had told David about the coach that came through there at night. Otherwise, David might never have figured out how they'd vanished.

A coach, of all things. Catrin and Newcome had found themselves a blasted coach.

Perhaps if it hadn't been for the storm that had set in after David had left that squire's estate, he might have caught up to them anyway. But the storm had forced him to beg shelter from a sheepherder for the rest of that day and that night. He'd only reached Carmarthen this morning.

Devil take that coach! The innkeeper had said it was well on its way to the west coast by now. David had thought about following the coach on its route, but he felt sure

Catrin and Newcome hadn't continued on with it. Though the innkeeper didn't remember seeing a wounded man get off in Carmarthen, Newcome might have been smart enough to have the coach stop before he reached the inn.

Catrin and Newcome were sure to be in Carmarthen. After all, they were on their way to London, and this was the closest port. David would have to scour the town for them, but this time he'd be sure not to mention Newcome's name. He'd simply ask about Catrin and a wounded man. Blast it all, the very thought of having to spend more time searching for them gave him a pulsing headache!

He rubbed the back of his head and cursed. No, that wasn't what gave him a headache. Catrin had raised a lump on his head the size of an egg. Even after two days, it still pained him. If he ever found her, he'd make her regret that particular act.

Glancing down at the burlap bag on the seat next to him, he gave a grim smile. At least he'd paid her back in part for what she'd done. The chalice. He had it, and she wanted it. She wouldn't stay away, not without the chalice. If she managed to escape Newcome on her own, she'd come for it, and he'd give it to her only if she agreed to marry him.

"Good day, Morys," growled a low voice behind him.

David froze. He would recognize that voice anywhere. Blackheart, as David privately referred to his father's old friend. But what was he doing here?

When Blackheart skirted the table and took a seat across from him, David fought to keep from showing his panic. The chalice was on the chair between them. If Blackheart saw it, he'd take it. David couldn't let the bastard have it. It was his only hope of getting Catrin back.

Yet how could he hide it without Blackheart noticing?

"I told you to keep me apprised of all developments between you and Catrin," Blackheart said in a voice threaded with menace. "Then I had to hear from Mrs. Llewelyn that you had taken off for Carmarthen without telling me a word of your plans."

"There was no time to go through that nonsense of leaving a message at the cottage and waiting for you to pick it up. I had to catch up to them."

Blackheart leaned back in his chair, folding his arms across his chest. "Indeed. Mrs. Llewelyn told me that Newcome was carrying Catrin off to Carmarthen to hand her over to that London investigator who came to find out who killed Lord Mansfield. Apparently, they suspect our shy little Catrin of that. I can only imagine what you thought when you heard it. Your sweet 'love' a murderess."

"She's innocent!" David exploded. "You know quite well Catrin could never kill anyone!"

"I know that you think her incapable of it, in any case." Blackheart lifted his hand and turned it under his gaze as if to examine his well-manicured fingernails. "Mrs. Llewelyn said she sent you off to rescue Catrin." He glanced up, his eyes cold. "Obviously, you were unsuccessful in catching up to them, or Catrin would be sitting here with you."

David debated lying about what had happened. He didn't want to give Blackheart any reason to stay, but he knew Blackheart well enough to know that the man wouldn't take only David's word for what had happened. Somehow he'd find out about the questions David had been asking.

"Actually," David said at last, "I did catch up to them."

Blackheart fixed him with a shrewd gaze. "Did you indeed? So where is she? And where is Newcome?" He gave a mocking laugh. "Perhaps I should have approached Mr. Newcome instead of you about keeping an eye on Catrin. From the gossip I heard in Llanddeusant the day they left, Mr. Newcome has managed to ingratiate himself with the young widow."

A rage poured through David so scalding, he could hardly refrain from leaping over the table and throttling Blackheart. All too easily he remembered finding Catrin in Newcome's arms the night of the wedding. Then last night, she'd defended the bastard despite what he was doing to her. She'd even protected him with David's own pistol! Devil take that woman!

And devil take Blackheart, too, for his snide insinuations! "Even if that's true, Mr. Newcome won't be long in her affections, I assure you. I shot him, and it will only be a matter of time before he succumbs to the wound I gave him."

"You shot him?" Blackheart said incredulously. *"You?"*

"Aye! I put a ball in his chest that should cause him a good deal of trouble!"

Blackheart's eyes narrowed. "*Should* cause him trouble? Don't you know? What did you do? Shoot the man, and leave him for dead? And what about Catrin?"

David glanced away from the contemptuous expression on Blackheart's face. "She and Newcome . . ." Blast, he hated having to tell Blackheart of his humiliation. "They escaped me. That's why I'm here. I'm trying to find them."

Blackheart gave a bark of laughter. "A woman and a wounded man? They escaped you when you had a pistol on them? How did they manage that?"

"Never mind," David said sullenly.

"Where's the pistol?" Blackheart asked.

David kept his head averted from the mocking countenance of his father's friend and said nothing.

With a chuckle Blackheart shook his head. "They got it away from you, did they? That is the only way they could have escaped. Christ, what a fool you are."

David's gaze snapped back to Blackheart. "Look here, they won't be missing long, especially with him so badly wounded. I know they're in Carmarthen somewhere. I'll find them."

"You had better." All amusement faded from Blackheart's face. "I need Catrin to lead me to that chalice, and if Newcome carries her off to London to hang, I shall lose my only hope of gaining it."

At the word "chalice," David cast a nervous and wholly involuntary glance at the chair next to him. Too late, he realized what he was doing and jerked his gaze away.

But Blackheart had already leaned forward to stare down at the chair that was pulled out a few inches from the table. At the sight of the burlap bag, he glanced up at David. "You had time to pack a bag for this unplanned trip, Morys? Or is this something you acquired on your journey?"

Blackheart reached toward the bag, but David snatched it up before he could get it. "It's . . . provisions I gathered for my search."

A twisted smile touched Blackheart's lips. "Oh?"

"Yes. I . . . I thought I'd search the town, so I bought some bread and cheese to carry with me."

"I see." He cast a meaningful glance at David's plate of mutton. "I suppose the provisions are for your dinner, since you have already had a substantial lunch."

"Er . . . yes. For dinner. I shall spend the rest of the day looking for them."

For a moment he feared that Blackheart didn't believe

him. Then the old man shrugged. "Well, then, get to it. Do not sit here chatting. I shall take a room and wait for you to find them."

David couldn't believe his luck. He'd lied to Blackheart and gotten away with it. A giddy sense of relief swirled through him as he hurried out of the inn. Things were looking up indeed if he could fool Blackheart.

It wasn't as if David wanted to thwart the man. Not at all. Once David found Catrin and Newcome, David needed the chalice only long enough to accomplish his marriage to Catrin. After they were married and they'd drunk from the chalice, Blackheart could have the blasted thing.

But David didn't dare let the bastard have it now, since Blackheart had never said why he wanted it. David refused to let Blackheart stand in the way of Catrin's marrying, even if the man *had* promised David money . . . and Catrin's body.

David had higher aims. He wanted marriage. He wanted to live the life of a country gentleman with Catrin at his side. First, however, he must find the betraying wench.

As he scanned the streets, he wondered where to start looking. He looked up the road from Llanddeusant and thought of his conjecture that Catrin and Newcome might have left the coach before they reached Carmarthen. Perhaps he should start questioning people in the cottages on the outskirts of town, then work his way in.

That seemed as good a plan as any. He sauntered along the road, trying to remember if he'd passed any small dwellings when he'd thundered into town on horseback a few hours ago. But there seemed to be only forest lining the road. As he rounded a bend and stopped to scan the roadside ahead, he thought he heard a rustling behind him, but when he whirled to see what it was, he saw nothing but a muddy road lit by the afternoon sun.

A shiver whispered over his skin, but he ignored it. Blackheart's appearance at the inn had upset him, of course, but that needn't make him start at every wayward sound.

He turned in the direction of Llanddeusant again and nearly jumped out of his skin. Blackheart stood in front of him, blocking the road.

"Blast it!" David cursed. "You frightened me half out of my mind! What are you doing here?"

"I followed you." Blackheart gestured to the burlap bag that David clutched in his hand. "I believe you have something that belongs to me."

David tightened his grip on the bag. "I don't know what you're talking about."

"You have the chalice. Give it to me." When David hesitated, Blackheart stepped closer and added, "I'm not an idiot. I know you have it. So give it to me."

"Why should I?" David stared at Blackheart, whose countenance seemed strangely threatening. So threatening that David found himself having difficulty breathing. "What will you do with it? Because if you hope to keep Catrin from marrying by taking it, then I'll not let you have it. She shall marry me, whether you allow it or not."

Blackheart's uncanny laugh seemed to rustle the leaves in the forest around them. "Do not be absurd, Morys. I know what you want of the chalice. And you shall have what you deserve from it. As shall I. Do you want to thwart me and risk losing Catrin? All I need do is tell her of your little peccadillo with that student in Merthyr Tydfil, and she will choose to be a widow all her life rather than marry you."

Helpless anger surged in David, but he tried not to show it. Devil take Blackheart! He would always get what he wanted, wouldn't he?

With a heavy sigh David handed the burlap sack over, but to his surprise Blackheart turned and strode into the forest with it, moving with surprising speed for a man of his age.

David hurried after him. "Where the devil do you think you're going?"

Blackheart said nothing, pushing farther into the forest and stopping only when he'd reached a spot well-hidden from the road. "I want to examine the chalice to make sure it is the right one, and I am not going to risk doing that on the road where anyone might see me."

Then Blackheart drew the chalice out of the bag, holding it up to the thin light that filtered through the overhanging beech trees. The smile that passed over his face at that moment was like nothing David had ever seen, a mixture of pleasure and pride and something else, something almost evil.

"*Siprys dyn giprys dan gopr,*" Blackheart muttered as he

turned the chalice over and over in his hands, running his fingers over the markings with eerie delight.

David didn't recognize the words Blackheart spoke. They sounded like Welsh, but no Welsh he'd ever heard. As Blackheart continued to murmur other nonsensical phrases and stroke the chalice, David grew uneasy.

When he shifted his feet in the leaves, Blackheart started, as if he'd forgotten that David was there. Then he turned to fix David with eyes brightly burning in the dim light. "So you thought you could keep it from me, did you?" he whispered. "You thought you could find Catrin and force her to your side with this. You were planning to ignore my claim to the chalice."

"What claim? You have no more claim to it than I. Besides, I don't see why we can't both have it. I need it only for as long as it takes to court Catrin and marry her. You can have it after that."

Blackheart scowled and took a step toward David. Instinctively, David backed away.

"What makes you think I want you to marry Catrin?" the older man hissed.

When Blackheart moved forward again, David stepped backward and stumbled, cursing as he regained his balance. "Even . . . if your aim is to k-keep her accursed," he stammered, "even if you won't let me use it to marry her, it could serve another purpose. She'll do anything to get it back. She'd certainly give herself to me for it. That's all I want . . . to have Catrin in my arms for one night—"

"That is all you want, eh?" Blackheart said with a sneer. "What a stupid liar you are. You want Catrin to marry you so you can get your hands on her land. That's why you tried to hide the chalice from me."

"No!" David exclaimed, alarmed by the menace in Blackheart's face. "I would have given it to you eventually! I swear it! Once Catrin and I were married. . . ." He trailed off as Blackheart withdrew a dagger from inside his coat.

Numbly, David stared at the dagger. Judging from the strange markings and S-shaped blade, it was an antique weapon. And Blackheart clearly meant to use it on him.

He lifted his face to Blackheart's cold one. "You can't mean to . . . No, no. You don't understand—" As Blackheart advanced on him, David shook his head. "You wouldn't have gained the chalice at all if it wasn't for me!"

"True, but you have served your purpose now."

David took another step back, only to find himself up against a tree. He threw up his hands. "You can have the chalice! Take it with my blessing! I'll never trouble you about it again. I'll go my way and—"

"And tell Catrin where the chalice is. Oh, yes, I know what you will do. You will do anything to get it back so you can marry her. You shot a man for it yesterday. I'm sure you would betray me to her for it as well." Blackheart's eyes flickered like two ghastly lights in his stony face. "But I cannot have you link me to the chalice. My possession of it must remain utterly secret, and that is impossible with you alive."

Blackheart smiled as he paused to let the reality of what he was saying sink in. In that instant David darted from between the man and the tree, whirling back toward the road, his mind in a panic.

Dear God, Blackheart plans to kill me! He is mad, completely mad!

David weaved his way frantically through the trees, his heart pounding in his ears. Surely he could escape the older man running after him. If he could only reach the road, he'd be safe. Yet he heard steps closing on him as he veered around trees and stumbled through the underbrush.

Suddenly, a sharp pain tore through his back, knocking him to his knees. "Oh, God," he cried as pain radiated outward and something warm and liquid soaked the back of his shirt.

Blood. With a gasp of horror, he realized that Blackheart had thrown the knife, that it was lodged in his back.

In a panic he tried to rise. He got one foot planted on the ground, but before he could stand, a savage kick from behind sent him crashing down. Fear clutched at his gut as he pushed himself up and started to crawl blindly forward, but a foot came down on his back, and he heard a tearing sound just as another horrible pain wrenched him and blood gushed forth.

With surprising strength for a middle-aged man, Blackheart kicked him onto his back, and David stared up at him in disbelief. Blackheart held the dagger in his hand again, only this time it was sheathed in blood. David's blood.

David tried to raise his arms to cover his face, but he couldn't make them work. He could barely feel the dry brush scratching his palms. He tried to speak, but could manage only a gurgle.

"Your poor father," Blackheart said as he casually knelt on David's belly with one knee, causing David a sudden fire of pain. "To have his younger son set upon by thieves on the road while running to the rescue of a damsel in distress. A fitting end to a disappointing life, is it not?"

The face of his father loomed in David's mind, always scowling, always disapproving. Then his father's face inexplicably became that of the schoolgirl in Merthyr Tydfil, the one David had debauched and abandoned. He could see her pretty cheeks drenched in tears as she'd stood trial for the crime his father and Blackheart had blamed on her. He saw her pale when the sentence of transportation was announced.

With a sob David closed his eyes. He didn't want to die thinking of all that. Catrin. He would think of Catrin, of her shimmering eyes and soft lips.

But as Blackheart lifted the dagger and brought it down over and over into David's chest, all David could see was the face of the young girl in Merthyr Tydfil. It was the last thing he saw before the light died.

Chapter Eighteen

So, in the bonds of the bright
Of her arms, all snow-drift white,
She was imprisoning me
All courtly, lightly, gently.
Who would want to stir
Out of her hold and halter?
—Dafydd ap Gwilym, "In Morfudd's Arms"

Muted golden light from the dying sun spilled into Evan's room, rousing him from what had been a deep and satisfying sleep, his first in three days. As he came awake, he once again experienced some disorientation, but this time it took only seconds before he realized he was at Llynwydd.

His shoulder still ached, and his head still throbbed an insistent beat, but the pain was easier than before, and he felt stronger, thanks to the broth and cider Juliana had forced him to drink that morning. As he crooked his knees, pressed his feet against the mattress, and pushed, he discovered he also had less trouble maneuvering into a sitting position than he'd had before.

And he felt hungry. Quite hungry. It was to be expected, of course. He'd had little to eat in the last few days. Still, hunger was a good sign he was feeling better. In fact, he was eager to leave his bed, to flex his muscles. But first he must regain his strength, and that required food.

A quick glance around the bed revealed a pull rope close at hand that would ring in the servants' quarters. He yanked on it with his uninjured arm, hoping that it worked and that someone would respond to his summons.

To his surprise scarcely ten minutes had passed before someone opened the door to his room. The person who entered wasn't a maid, however, but Rhys himself.

The squire looked hesitant as he came through the doorway, but as soon as he saw Evan sitting up, a jovial smile crossed his face and he settled into a chair next to the bed.

"One of the servants said that you rang downstairs. I thought for sure they were mistaken, but since Juliana was out seeing to one of the cottagers, I decided to check. And here I find that Mr. Lie-a-Bed is awake at last."

"Mr. Lie-a-Bed," indeed. Evan had to stifle a laugh. Rhys's concern for Evan seemed to be inversely proportional to the amount of teasing he subjected Evan to. Rhys wasn't the type to become maudlin, and Evan had to admit he preferred Rhys's way of dealing with the crisis. Juliana's fussing embarrassed him at times.

"I'm awake, alive, and starving," Evan said, matching Rhys's light tone. "I want a real meal tonight, not that broth your wife gave me this morning."

Rhys shook his head with a mock expression of disappointment. "One day's rest and already you think you're cured. I'll admit, however, that your voice sounds stronger. This morning you could barely wheeze your demands, and now you're actually voicing them. That's promising, very promising indeed."

"Promising enough to gain me a joint of mutton and a pudding or two?" Evan asked hopefully.

Rhys laughed. "You don't waste any time with such mundane tasks as recovering from being shot, do you, Evan? Juliana will be delighted. She has peeked in here ten times today, convinced that your protracted sleep must indicate a relapse. Only the sound of your snores and your healthy color kept her from sending after the doctor again."

"I'm surprised she didn't take my snores for moans of agony and bring the doctor in anyway," Evan grumbled. "Sometimes your wife is overly diligent in seeing to my health."

"Someone has to be," Rhys said with a raised eyebrow, "especially when you go about the country throwing yourself at madmen with loaded pistols."

Evan met Rhys's now serious gaze with surprise. "You know what happened? Catrin told you?"

"Yes."

"What did she say?"

"That she knocked a certain Mr. Morys over the head with a family heirloom, thus enabling you to launch yourself at him and his pistol."

"Did she also tell you why Mr. Morys was there in the first place and why we were on our way to Carmarthen?"

Rhys fixed him with a steady gaze. "She said you were taking her to talk to an investigator who believes she had a part in Lord Mansfield's murder."

Evan digested that, unable to determine whether Rhys approved or disapproved of his actions. "She must have told you about the chalice, too."

"You mean, the one she bought from Lord Mansfield? As a matter of fact, she did."

"Did she mention her reasons for wanting it?"

"She said it was a family heirloom."

Evan gave a faint smile. A family heirloom. Well, he would hardly have expected her to tell the Vaughans about the curse, since it sounded so unbelievable. Then again, he was surprised she'd told them everything else.

What did her candor mean? Oh, deuce take it, what did any of it mean? Why had she fought so hard to save him? Why had she chosen him over Morys, the one man who would have done his best to keep her from being arrested?

"Tell me something, Evan," Rhys said, breaking into his thoughts. "Do you really suspect she had something to do with Lord Mansfield's death?"

Evan stared at his longtime friend, trying to assemble in his mind all the evidence that had pointed to her complicity. None of it seemed very convincing now. "I suppose I did once. Two days ago, I was almost sure of it."

Leaning back in his chair, Rhys eyed him with interest. "And now you're not?"

"I'm not sure about anything anymore." Evan laid his head against the headboard, his gaze distant. "I'm not sure why Catrin saved my life or why she sent Morys packing when he only wanted to help her. I'm not even sure why she explained the situation to you and Juliana, especially when it reflected badly on her."

A long silence ensued, punctuated only by the regular beat of the clock in the hall and the whisper of the covers as Evan restlessly shifted his legs.

"You know," Rhys said at last, "if I might venture an opinion, it seems that Mrs. Price's lies and her fleeing the scene are perfectly understandable, given her shyness and her lack of experience in dealing with London officials. And

I find it hard to believe a woman like her would go to such lengths merely to acquire a family heirloom."

Evan stared up at the ceiling, thinking of the ugly bronze object that had caused so many people so much grief. "Yes, well, the chalice is . . . more than a family heirloom. Believe me when I say she thinks she has pressing reasons for acquiring it."

"Pressing enough reasons to have a man robbed and murdered?"

Evan thought of everything he'd seen of Catrin . . . her kindness to her servants, her generous spirit, her willingness to put aside her natural reticence when it was necessary . . . like the time she'd done it to save his life.

That one act transformed his entire picture of her. Or was it that he'd had the right picture of her from the beginning? Had he merely allowed his rage at her lie about the chalice to blind him to her true character? The Catrin who'd saved his life was not the Catrin he'd imagined plotting to steal a chalice from an innocent man.

He came away from the pillow, turning an unsettled gaze on Rhys, who was still waiting for his answer. "I'm not sure that anything in this world could compel Catrin to hurt someone."

"Except a threat to your well-being," Rhys said dryly. "She certainly routed Morys, didn't she?"

"She did, indeed." He smiled. "You should have seen that pompous bastard's expression when he realized she'd hit him. He was astounded. He never for one moment expected sweet Catrin to crown him." He shook his head. "For God's sake, *I* never expected Catrin to crown him. Or hold a pistol on him. When I handed her the loaded pistol and told her she'd have to defend herself with it, she looked utterly appalled, as if I'd asked her to handle dog dung with her bare hands."

His smile faded. "But she did it. She did it to save my life, to pay me good coin for the bad I had given her." He didn't remember much about her stand-off with Morys, for the blood had been roaring in his ears at that point, but he did remember her standing there with that cocked pistol, willing to defend Evan to the death if Morys didn't leave.

Why had he been so ready only a few nights ago to think that Catrin had conspired against Justin? The very idea was preposterous. The woman who'd risked her life to save him, who'd shown courage and kindness time and again, couldn't be part of such a horrendous act.

"You're in love with her, aren't you?" Rhys said quietly, breaking into Evan's thoughts.

Evan stared at his friend as the question thundered in his ears. Was he in love with Catrin? Was love this feeling of being in a permanent state of waiting for her to return to his side? Was love the crushing ache he'd felt when he'd believed her guilty of involvement in Justin's murder? Was love what had made their ride from Llanddeusant to Llynwydd a torment unmitigated even by his absurd attempts at reciting Latin?

Was love what made him cringe whenever he thought of the difference in their backgrounds?

"If I am in love," Evan said morosely, "fate has certainly played a devilish trick on me, hasn't it? She has wealth and position, she can marry anyone she wants, especially now that—"

He stopped short before he mentioned the chalice. What *had* happened to the chalice after Catrin had hit Morys with it? Evan tried to remember if she'd picked it up, but everything from that time was hazy. She and Morys had discussed it. That was all he'd managed to absorb. Still, she'd had the pistol, so she'd never have let Morys have the chalice. It meant too much to her.

"Now that what?" Rhys asked when Evan simply sat there, staring into space.

"Nothing. Anyway, you see what I mean, don't you? A woman like Catrin Price with a man of my background? It's impossible."

"Not if she loves you." Rhys leaned back in his chair. "I would never have thought to marry an earl's daughter either, but Juliana proved that a good woman doesn't care about such things. And you've just been telling me what a good woman Mrs. Price is, haven't you?"

"That's the trouble," Evan murmured. "Catrin is too good for the likes of me." He thought of Henrietta. She'd been a good woman, too, and when she'd witnessed his violent side, she'd recoiled from him.

Still, hadn't Catrin seen him at his worst that day in her

study? Was it possible she could consider him someone to love?

Rhys was watching him with concern. Evan briefly considered telling him about his fears, but couldn't bring himself to reveal his dark urges to the man he respected more than anyone. Instead, he pasted a smile on his face. "In any case, I don't even know how she feels about me, do I?"

"You could ask her."

Evan's smile faded as he thought of how devastated he'd be if he asked and she spurned him. "I don't know, Rhys." He sighed. "But perhaps I will."

Rhys took one look at his expression and rose from his chair. "I'm sorry, Evan. It wasn't right of me to meddle in your private life." He smiled. "I'm becoming as bad as Juliana. Here I am tormenting you with questions when all you wanted was a joint of mutton." Rhys was back to his light tone, for which Evan was secretly grateful. "In any case, I'd best go downstairs and see to getting you some sustenance before you're forced to summon someone else. Juliana will take a stick to me if I leave you starving."

He walked to the door, then paused there. "Oh, I almost forgot to tell you. That Morys fellow came here looking for you and Mrs. Price yesterday."

Evan scowled. "What did you tell him?"

"I sent him on a wild-goose chase. He won't be back here for a while, so don't worry about him."

"Thank you, Rhys. One of these days I must figure out how many centuries it will take me to repay you and Juliana for everything you've done for me."

"Nonsense. You're a friend. You owe us nothing." Rhys opened the door and grinned. "I take that back. Give us an autographed copy of your next publication, and we'll be content."

Evan managed a smile as Rhys walked from the room, but as soon as his friend was gone, he lay back against the pillow with a sigh. The muddle in his head was giving him a great deal more trouble than the pain in his shoulder. His thoughts twisted and turned, yet they always returned to one place. Catrin. The woman who'd captured his soul. And yes, the woman with whom he was in love, wonderfully, horribly in love.

What was he going to do about Catrin?

Marry her, the thought instantly came to mind. That's what people did when they were in love. And marrying her was the only way to keep her. He knew that.

But did he dare marry her? Even if she would have him, did he dare risk seeing his marriage degenerate into the kind of marriage his parents had lived in, where love was twisted up with explosive violence and loathing?

He closed his eyes, remembering what his mother had endured because she'd loved his father. Memories assailed him . . . of his father's vicious temper and subsequent tearful apologies . . . his claiming to love his wife even though he beat her and their children regularly.

Love. They'd both claimed to love each other. Yet the love Evan felt for Catrin wasn't a violent thing. He'd only come close to hurting Catrin physically when he'd thought she was lying to him, and he'd resisted the urge even though he'd had great provocation.

He couldn't imagine striking her because she spilled his glass of wine or spent too much on a gown or talked too loudly in church, all things for which his father had beaten his mother. He certainly didn't want to make Catrin fear his every mood and cringe whenever he raised his voice. The idea of Catrin watching him with constant wariness repulsed him.

And children. Oh, God, if he ever had children with Catrin, he'd never hurt them. If he was ever fortunate enough to have her as wife, he'd cherish any child that came of their union. How could he not?

For the first time in his life, hope flickered within him. Perhaps he wasn't like his father entirely. Yes, he'd lost his temper in the past, but he had never hurt anyone he loved nor anyone more helpless than himself. And he especially couldn't imagine doing so now. His near brush with death had made him see that life was too sweet to waste in anger, and people too precious to torment needlessly.

It had made him realize something else, too. He needed Catrin. He wanted her in his life, but more than that, he wanted her for the rest of his life. He wanted her to be his totally, and there was only one way of ensuring that—by marrying her.

His decision made, he straightened on the bed. Then he slowly moved his legs over the side, bracing his hands on either side of his hips. He must find Catrin. He must ask her to forgive him for his deplorable lack of faith in her earlier.

If she forgave him, he would tell her how he felt and ask her to marry him. But first, he would explain what she was taking on if she agreed. It was only fair to let her know of the dark possibilities, of the violence that simmered in his breast. Once before, he'd tried to hide it from the woman he wanted to marry, and that had ended disastrously.

This time he'd make sure that the woman he loved married him with her eyes open. He would tell her everything, even if it meant that she refused him.

He only prayed that she didn't.

Chapter Nineteen

What mischief is it, or spite,
That damns me in their sight?
What harm to a fine-browed maid
To have me in deep glade?
No shame for her 'twould be
In a lair of leaves to see me.
—Dafydd ap Gwilym, "The Ladies Of Llanbadarn"

As the last slivers of fading daylight crept in splintered designs across the rich carpet, Catrin paused outside Evan's room. Should she go in or wait until she'd heard from one of the servants that he was awake?

She glanced down at the simple muslin gown Lady Juliana had loaned her. The gown hung on her. Catrin wished she had the lush curves it took to fill it out, but she'd not been blessed with Lady Juliana's figure. Unfortunately. Despite all she and Evan had gone through in the last few days, she had this inexplicable need to look beautiful for him.

She smoothed down the muslin that puffed out too much at the neckline. Oh, well. Evan would have to settle for clean and presentable.

The sound of footsteps in the carpeted hall made her drop her hand, embarrassed to be seen touching her bodice. But the maid coming toward her seemed more concerned with balancing a tray of food than looking at her.

"Good evening," Catrin called out.

The maid brought her head up. "Oh, good evening, Mrs. Price. We didn't know you were awake." She approached Catrin, then stopped beside her.

"Is that for Mr. Newcome?" Catrin asked.

The young woman nodded. "The master says Mr. Newcome wants food." She glanced doubtfully at the tray, which was heaped with assorted plates holding bread and cheese and what looked like a joint of mutton. "If you ask me, this is too much food for a sick man, but the master laughed at Cook when she tried to tell him so, and milady isn't here just now to set him straight."

"I suppose it can't hurt to offer it to him," Catrin said. "But if you don't mind, I'd like to bring it in to him myself."

"Certainly, miss." The maid handed over the tray, then opened the door for Catrin.

As Catrin slipped inside, she found herself suddenly reluctant to face Evan. She couldn't bear it if he had returned to his cold stance of before. Staring down at the loaded tray, she hesitated inside the door. "I waylaid the servant and stole your meal. I hope you don't mind."

"Only if you don't intend to give me any of it," Evan quipped.

The rumbling amusement in his voice made her look up to see him sitting on the edge of the bed. She dragged in a sharp breath at the sight of him looking so wonderful in his breeches and the large shirt that covered his bandaged shoulder and arm. Despite everything he'd been through, his color was better, and he smiled at her with such devastating effect she couldn't do anything but smile back.

As she watched, he pushed himself into a stand, and her smile faded. "What are you doing?" She set the tray down on a nearby table, then hurried to his side. "You shouldn't be up yet! You'll hurt yourself!"

As she clasped his waist, he laid his free arm about her shoulder and leaned on her. "I'm really much better. And I don't want to eat in the bed like an invalid."

"Yes, but—"

"You're not getting me back into that bed just now, Catrin, so don't even think about it." He took a step forward, forcing her to move with him. He did seem stronger, for he barely put any of his weight on her at all as they headed toward the table where she'd set the tray.

"Besides," he continued in a husky voice, "I don't mind struggling out of bed when it allows me to hold you."

The tender note in his voice was almost painfully familiar. She lifted her face to find him watching her, his eyes burning with a fire she'd never thought to see in them again. She couldn't breathe or move.

Apparently, neither could he, for they had come to a complete halt in the middle of the room. He turned toward her, dropping his good arm from her shoulders to her waist so he could pull her close. When he brushed a kiss to her forehead, she let out a sigh and slipped her arms about him.

"Catrin," he whispered. "I've been thinking about doing this ever since I woke up this morning."

"So have I," she said before she could stop herself.

He nuzzled one of her temples. "You mean, you haven't been cursing me for distrusting you, for hauling you across the country on the basis of my foolish suspicions?"

She pulled back to stare at him uncertainly.

His eyes filled with remorse. "I've been the greatest fool. I must have been mad to think you were involved with Justin's murder. I don't know what came over me, but I swear I know better now. I know in my heart you'd never do such a thing."

A rush of emotion hit her so quickly she had to turn her head to keep him from seeing the tears of relief that spilled down her cheeks.

He believes me, she thought. *By heaven, he believes me at last.*

He pressed his lips to her cheek, then whispered soothingly, "Don't cry, darling. Please, don't cry. I've made you cry enough. I don't ever want to make you cry again."

Darling. He'd called her *darling*. That made her tears flow even more freely. "I'm sorry . . ." she stammered, wiping the tears away. "I . . . I just didn't know what to expect . . . I thought maybe once you got better, everything would go back . . . to the way it was before."

His voice dropped to an aching whisper. "You mean, when I let my stupid anger blind me to what should have been obvious from the start—that you could never commit a crime . . . any crime? When I sat on a horse, holding you in my arms while every step closer to London tormented me? Good God, it nearly killed me to think I'd never kiss you or caress you or make love to you again."

She lifted her face to his, scarcely daring to believe his words. "But you were so . . . cold that day. I thought you'd dismissed me totally from your mind."

"Only a eunuch could have done that, and I think even a eunuch might have had trouble." He tightened his arm about her waist, then closed his eyes, a grimace of pain crossing his face. "I don't know how you can ever forgive me for not trusting you, for all the things I said and the wretched way I dragged you off. I didn't even bother to consider your version of events. I was horrible to you. Morys recognized one thing at least. I deserved to be shot for the way I treated you."

His remorse and guilt so touched her that it blotted out her hurt over his earlier distrust. "It wasn't entirely your fault. I did lie to you. You had a right to be angry about that. And it's easy to see why you might have thought I'd done something—"

"No, it's not easy to see," he interrupted, his voice tortured. When he opened his eyes, they glittered like gems at the bottom of a night stream. "I behaved like a deuced idiot. It was one thing to be angry at your lie, but I took it too far."

His breath came quickly now, as if it took all his strength to speak. "After my tantrum, I should have stopped to consider the absurdity of my accusation, instead of hauling you off like some common criminal. If I'd used half a brain that morning, I wouldn't have gotten myself shot later and put you in danger."

A perverse desire to comfort him overwhelmed her. She cupped his face in her hands. "And if I hadn't been such a coward and told you the truth in the first place, none of it would have happened and you wouldn't have gotten shot either."

"Coward?" His voice held a note of incredulity. "I wouldn't call any woman who does what you did the other night a coward. You saved my life. Morys would have shot and killed me if it hadn't been for you."

"Yes, but if not for me you wouldn't have—"

"Enough. We both were at fault." His jaw went tight. "If it makes you feel better, I'll lay some of the blame on you, but only so we can forgive each other and put it behind us." He splayed his hand across the small of her back as his expression shifted from remorse to something more powerful. "Besides, I can think of a hundred more important things to do just now than fight over who was more guilty of getting me shot, especially since I survived it anyway."

The look in his eyes drained all breath from her. Understanding . . . caring . . . desire . . . all shone forth where once there'd been nothing but condemnation and hurt.

"In fact," he added in a raspy whisper as his gaze trailed down to her lips, "I can think of one very important thing I want to do just now." Then he brought his mouth down on hers.

Such a kiss he gave her, sweet and light like whipped cream, the kind of kiss befitting a vow to abandon the past. She'd almost forgotten how soft his lips were, how snugly they fit with hers. She'd almost forgotten, too, how he could make her blood leap and race with just the tender press of his mouth to hers.

He drew back, his eyes wide and wondering. "How could I have ever thought to give this up . . . to give you up?"

This time when he bent his head to kiss her, he wasn't content to merely taste her. His mouth coaxed hers open. Then he began a ravening possession that sent wild shivers over her skin. His tongue mated with hers in a mesmerizing rhythm, as if he had an unquenchable thirst for her, as if he sought to find the very secret to her soul in their kiss.

She knew she shouldn't let him kiss her. There was no point to going on with him like this. He wouldn't offer her marriage, and even if he did, she couldn't marry him without the chalice.

But he needs me right now, she rationalized as his kiss enveloped her in his scent and taste and essence. *I can't turn him away. Not now.*

She needed him, too. Oh, how she needed him to wash away the terror of the past few days. She strained against him, wanting to feel more of him, and he drew her hard against his body until his arousal pressed against her through his breeches.

"Oh, Catrin," he murmured against her lips, "you are such a wonder. You see what you do to me? I've barely left the sick bed and I want you beyond endurance."

His words, enticing though they were, reminded her of where they were and what he'd been through the past two days. She drew back from him. "Evan, you should sit down. You shouldn't be standing like this."

"I want to hold you," he whispered as he brushed kisses along the upward sweep of her cheek. "I need to hold you."

"You can hold me while you're sitting down. I'm not going anywhere, I promise." Not yet, anyway, she told herself. She had to have more time with him.

With a groan he let her lead him to the chair next to the table that held his tray of food, but as soon as she had him seated, he tugged her into his lap and buried his face in her neck. "You were right," he murmured, "this is much better."

He kissed a path down the part of her shoulder that was bare, along her collarbone to the cleft between her breasts.

Closing her eyes, she lifted her hand to clasp his shoulder. Then she felt the bandages swathing his shoulder beneath his shirt, and she went still. By heaven, what was she doing? He was ill! He shouldn't even be out of bed! "No, Evan." She pushed his head away. This isn't the time or place. For heaven's sake, you've only just recovered. You need time to regain your strength. I'll die if you fall ill again. It nearly killed me watching you languish from that fever."

His eyes darkened as he trailed his gaze over her flushed cheeks, her half-parted lips, her gaping bodice. "Good God, I don't know how I'll ever wait."

She said nothing, turning her face from him for fear she'd burst into tears if he said many more seductive things like that. He leaned forward to kiss her, but she broke away and slipped off his lap.

As he stared at her, his breath coming hard and fast and his eyes gleaming, she forced herself to meet his gaze. "You should eat some of this food you called for. It'll help you recover your strength."

Apparently sensing the change in her mood, he watched her solemnly. "I'll eat, don't worry, but first I have things to talk to you about. Important things."

She was afraid of what those things might be. Although he'd said he believed her about what happened in London, he probably still wanted her to tell the constable what she had or hadn't seen, and she couldn't bear the thought of it.

"We'll talk after you eat," she said brightly. "You really should get some sustenance in you."

He arched an eyebrow. "You certainly want to hasten my recovery, don't you?"

"You were the one who asked for food." She went to the tray and looked at it. "Still, I don't know what possessed Mr. Vaughan to send you so much. By heaven, there's even a joint of mutton here."

"Don't you touch that joint of mutton," Evan warned. "I asked for that. And in a few minutes I shall eat the entire thing. I might even make you feed me, since you obviously think I'm not strong enough to lift a fork."

When she looked at him askance, he grinned. Then he reached over and took her hand and his grin faded. "But right now, I need to talk to you."

"Evan, if this is about Quinley and the investigation and—"

"It's not about Quinley or the investigation. As far as I'm concerned, that's all behind us. If I took you to London to speak to Quinley now, I can't predict the outcome, so I can't risk it."

When she lifted her head in surprise, he said gently, "You saved my life. What kind of man would I be if I made you face those hostile men who don't know you . . . who might jump to the wrong conclusions?"

"But what about your friend's death and—"

"It was thieves. You said you had nothing to do with it, and I believe you, so that leaves only one other possibility—that he was murdered by thieves. Since that's the case, there's nothing you can add to the investigation, and much you'd risk by speaking out. So there it stands."

She slumped in relief. She hadn't admitted even to herself how much the thought of going to London again had terrified her. It had been easier to face once Evan said he believed her, but she'd still wondered if she could endure it. Thank heaven he wasn't going to make her.

"No," he added, "that's not what I wanted to discuss." He drew her by the hand until she was standing between his spread legs. Then he nodded his head toward his knee. "Will you sit with me again?"

Out of consideration for his weakened condition, she ignored his knee and sat instead on the floor at his feet.

Although he didn't protest, he sighed as he laid his free hand on her head, then threaded his fingers through her hair and began massaging her scalp. "Do you remember the night you first told me about the chalice?"

She tensed beneath his hand. She remembered that night all too well, for that was when she'd lied to him. "Yes."

"We talked about marriage that night."

That wasn't what she'd expected him to say, though it was true. They had indeed talked of marriage, and he'd said he would never marry. She'd said the same. So why was he bringing it up now when nothing had changed, especially since she no longer had the chalice?

"Yes," she murmured as she lifted her face to his, "You told me you couldn't marry because of your position at Cambridge."

His lips tightened into a thin line, but he held her gaze. "That was a lie, I'm afraid." When her eyes widened, he added, "I mean, it's true that fellows at the university aren't allowed to marry. But that wouldn't stop me if I chose marriage. I'd simply leave the university and do something else." He gave a faint smile. "Be a schoolmaster in a town like Llanddeusant, for example."

"Oh, of course," she said with a trace of bitterness. "I'm sure you'd prefer the scintillating conversation of scruffy children to the intellectual stimulation of Cambridge."

"University fellows are more like children than you'd think." He stroked her hair absently. "They're as likely as children to snub someone who's different. They're jealous of anyone who is more successful, and like children, they can be inordinately cruel, except that their sophisticated minds enable them to find more subtle ways to ostracize the unusual . . . the brilliant . . . the misfit."

When he glanced away, she realized with surprise that he was speaking of himself. She'd assumed that a genius would be perfectly at home at Cambridge, but she'd forgotten he was not only a genius, but a Welsh tenant farmer's son. She understood only too well what it meant to be outside the community one has chosen as one's own. With a pang of sympathy she rested her cheek against his knee, wishing she knew how to comfort him.

When he continued, his jaw was rigid. "Intellectual stimulation doesn't feed the heart, Catrin. Leaving Cambridge wouldn't trouble me in the least, I assure you."

She chose her words carefully. "Then why did you tell me you couldn't marry?"

He stopped stroking her hair as he glanced down at her. "Do you remember when I told you about Henrietta, my former fiancée?"

She nodded. She shouldn't let him tell her all this, especially if it was leading to a discussion of marriage. But she couldn't help wanting to know.

"I had known Henrietta for years when I became enamored of her. Her father was a rich Welsh merchant who liked me and was pleased when I offered for her. We even made plans for me to work with him in his business since he had no sons."

He stared off across the room, his face shadowed with remembrance. "One night I found Henrietta alone on a balcony with a man. He was holding her close, and I . . . I went insane with jealousy. I jerked him away and began hitting him while she screamed and begged me to stop. Of course, that only made it worse, for I thought she was defending her secret lover."

A self-deprecating smile touched his lips. "She was defending her cousin, whom she hadn't seen in several years. I happened to come across them just as she was hugging him . . . the same way she would hug any cherished relative who'd just returned from the war."

He brought his gaze back to her. "In my fit of temper, I broke his nose and bruised him badly." He let out a heavy sigh. "She was furious. She called me a 'beast' and ended our engagement, and that was that."

Catrin stared at him incredulously. That was all there was to it? After the way he'd hinted of the terrible thing he'd done to make his fiancée hate him, Catrin had imagined a number of more horrible things. "You mean, she ended your engagement simply because you made a mistake?"

"Not because I made a mistake, Catrin." He clasped her chin and lifted it until she was staring straight up at him. "Because she saw for the first time what I really was. Unreasonable. Ill-tempered." His voice grew tight. "And violent. I couldn't blame her for breaking the engagement. She was refined and beautiful and civilized, and I was exactly what she'd called me—a beast."

"Oh, but you're not a beast!" she cried, wishing she could tear the very word from his memory. "One slip does not make you a beast. Besides, many men would do the same thing if they saw their fiancées in what looked like compromising positions!"

"I doubt it. Another man would shout a little. He might even challenge the man to a duel . . . a challenge he would withdraw once he realized the circumstances. But a gentleman, a civilized man, would never lose his temper to the extent that he beat someone to a bloody pulp without even knowing the situation."

"Perhaps. Yet you've learned from what you did, haven't you?" she said. "And I doubt you would do it now."

"I don't know—" he began.

"*I* know," she broke in. "I know you're not a beast."

A half smile touched his lips as he stroked her jaw with the back of his hand. "What a prickly little minx you are, so fierce in my defense even when what I did was inexcusable." He shrugged. "Perhaps you're right. Perhaps I'm not quite the beast Henrietta once thought I was."

He brushed her hair back from her face and turned serious again. "You're nothing like her, you know. Nothing at all, even though you're of similar wealth and station. She was always just so . . . every hair in place . . . every word completely proper . . . the epitome of perfection—"

"No, that's not me at all," she said, a trace of envy in her voice. "I am definitely imperfect."

"Thank God for that."

She glanced up at him in confusion.

"Perfection is for porcelain statues," he added, "not for human beings with whom you wish to share your life. Perfection doesn't feed the heart any better than intellectual stimulation, and after a while, it can be bloody intimidating."

He leaned forward, his eyes boring into hers. "You, my darling, are imperfect and warm and full of surprises. I wouldn't trade a thousand Henriettas for one of you." He'd barely given her the chance to revel in the sweet statement before his face hardened and he said, "Anyway, that's why I told you I couldn't marry. I've been afraid of what might happen if I ever . . . lost my temper with a woman I cared for. I couldn't bear the thought of striking a woman, and the fear of doing that has kept me from marrying."

"But you lost your temper with *me* the day you found the chalice and you didn't strike me, although I'll admit you wreaked havoc on my study." She shifted until she was kneeling in front of him, her arms resting on his knees. "If ever you had provocation, it was then."

"I know. I've told myself that." Anguish filled his face as he glanced away. "Still . . . good God, Catrin, you don't know how quickly I can lose my temper . . . and how violent

I can be when I do. I'm terrified I might hurt my wife if I ever marry." He swung his gaze back to her. "Especially now that I've found someone I want to marry . . . someone I love."

Her heart twisted. She couldn't mistake his meaning, but she should never have let him speak of it. Marriage to Evan would be heaven . . . until the day she watched him die because of the curse.

She rose to her feet and turned away, trying to conceal her turmoil. Didn't he remember about the curse? Of course he did, but he didn't believe in it, so it didn't matter to him. And if she gave him any encouragement at all, he'd seduce her into believing it didn't matter to her either.

But it did. Deep inside, she knew it was real. She couldn't marry him without the chalice. She couldn't watch him die. These past few days had been bad enough, but if she ever had to watch him die, knowing it was her fault . . . she couldn't bear it.

Not when she loved Evan. A groan escaped her lips. She did love him, too, with all the breath in her body. Her gentle friendship with Willie paled by comparison. Watching Willie die had been heart-wrenching, but watching Evan die would be like splitting herself in two.

There was only one thing for it. She must give Evan a firm refusal. No explanation, no soft words of regret, nothing but a no. That was the only way to make him see how impossible it was. She wouldn't make the same mistakes with Evan that she'd made with David. No more evasions.

Oh, but how could she stand to tell him no?

At her long silence, Evan broke into her thoughts. "Catrin, I know I'm not much of a prize. I can bring nothing to a marriage but myself and my willingness to work hard." He dropped his voice to a whisper. "Yet I'd like to try. I—"

A knock sounded at the door, and they both started. Catrin whirled toward the door, thankful for the reprieve.

But Evan cursed under his breath. He couldn't believe this. Here he'd been in the midst of telling Catrin how he felt, and some idiot had come to spoil it. "Go away, I'm resting!" he shouted at the door.

Unfortunately, that did no good. The door swung open and Lady Juliana breezed in. "Resting, indeed. Your sister's here and—"

She broke off as she caught sight of him in the chair and Catrin standing a few feet away. "I'm sorry, Evan, I didn't realize you had company."

"I brought Evan his tray," Catrin said.

Evan tried not to scowl, but it was hard. Catrin seemed suddenly distant, and he could only hope it wasn't because of what he'd said. He wanted to finish their conversation. He wanted to know how she felt about marriage.

Lady Juliana eyed the untouched tray with raised eyebrows. "I see your appetite hasn't yet returned, Evan. I'll call and have a servant take this away."

"If you touch that tray, Juliana, I'll bite your hand off," Evan muttered. "I called for that food, and I intend to eat it."

"Is that Evan?" came a familiar voice from the doorway, and he looked up to find his sister standing there.

A wave of feeling gripped him as his gaze met hers. Mary, his sweet Mary. He'd missed her more than he knew.

Tears welled in her brown eyes, and she hurried to his side with a little cry of joy. "Oh, Evan, look at you! You're . . . you're . . ."

"He's nearly back to his old self," Lady Juliana finished for her. "Ordering people about and scowling at everyone."

Mary wiped the tears from her eyes as a smile spread over her ruddy face. "Oh, as long as he's awake and breathing, I don't care if he orders me about."

"It's good to see you," he whispered as his own eyes grew misty.

Though it had been only a week since last he'd seen her, he'd gone through hell since then, and it made him appreciate his family more than before. He rose from the chair, eliciting a flurry of protests from the three women, but he ignored them to lay his good arm about his sister's shoulder and pull her close.

She hugged him, though he noticed she was careful not to press against his bandaged arm and shoulder. "Oh, my dear boy," she whispered, "I can't tell you how glad I am to see you well. And standing up, no less!" Drawing back to look at him, she said, "I feared I'd not see you again in this life, and here you are, looking quite fit for a man who's been shot."

Belatedly, Evan remembered Catrin standing there and said, "You must thank Catrin for that. She saved my life."

Still leaning a bit on his sister, he angled his body toward Catrin and murmured, "I'd like to introduce you to my sister—"

"Oh, we've already met," Mary said brightly, casting Catrin a shy glance, "haven't we, Mrs. Price?"

When Catrin nodded, Evan stared at Mary. "You were here before?"

"Oh, yes, while you were so bad off with the fever," Mary said. "Mrs. Price and I kept a vigil over you until I had to go home and see to my own family. She and I became rather cozy, as a matter of fact." She squeezed him with a smile. "I told her all about the scrapes you got into as a boy, and she told me what a hero you were to throw yourself in front of that madman with the pistol."

It was all Evan could do to keep his expression even. He dared not let Mary see how her matter-of-fact words devastated him. How much had she told Catrin? What scrapes did she mean? The many times he'd stolen plums from the Llynwydd orchard until he'd been caught by the gardener and then rescued by Juliana? Or more horrifying things, like the punishments his father had inflicted on him?

He didn't think Mary would speak of the latter, but at the very least, she must have told Catrin that his father had been no more than a tenant farmer to the Vaughans. He'd planned to tell Catrin himself eventually, but he'd thought that if he first told her how much he loved her, the other wouldn't matter so much.

Now he wondered if her unsettling reaction to his talk of marriage signaled that it did indeed matter to her. She might have decided that a man of such background, especially one with the kind of violent nature he'd described, wasn't a man to marry.

Though she was probably right, he didn't think he could bear it if she rejected him. He tried to catch Catrin's eye, but she refused to look at him, which made the dread build in his chest even more. Had he completely misread her kisses, the way she'd melted in his arms, the sympathy she'd shown him when he was telling her about his broken engagement? Had he misunderstood everything?

"In any case," his sister was saying, "it looks as if our vigilance has been repaid, for here you are, looking much better for all our efforts. Don't you think he looks well, Mrs. Price?"

"Yes," Catrin whispered. She glanced at him, then cut her eyes away when she saw him watching her.

That one little movement spoke volumes. And he feared what it said. He feared it terribly.

"Oh, dear, Evan," Mary suddenly exclaimed. "I'm forgetting everyone who's waiting for me downstairs. George is here, and I brought Robert and the girls. They're all eager to see you. Do you think you can endure a few more visitors?"

Somehow he managed a smile for his sister, even though he felt as if a hollow chasm was opening up beneath his feet. "I'd love to see them. By all means, tell them to come up."

She beamed at him. "Wonderful. I'll hurry down and fetch them. I'll be only a moment." Then she left his side and hastened out the door.

Deprived of her support, he felt a little weak, but it was Juliana who came to his side and helped him back to the chair, not Catrin. And when he sat down and released a heavy breath, he looked up to see Catrin headed toward the door.

"Catrin? Where are you going?" he asked, his throat feeling raw and tight.

She paused at the door, not looking at him. "To my room."

"Don't leave." He was begging and he knew it, but he couldn't let her go. If she left, it meant that his talk of marriage had alarmed her. It meant she didn't want him. "Please stay and meet the rest of my family," he said, knowing it was a shameless ploy and not caring.

But even his ploy didn't work. She met his gaze, then said in gentle tones, "I don't think that would be wise. I wouldn't want to intrude."

"It's can't you stay an intrusion, Catrin."

She looked on the verge of tears, but shook her head. "I'm sorry, Evan. I can't stay." She swallowed, then stiffened, as if gathering her courage. "I shall be in my room if you wish to speak to me later."

"Why can't you stay?" Juliana asked, clearly puzzled by the strange interchange.

Catrin left the room without answering, but Evan didn't need her words to know what her answer was. She couldn't stay because she knew he was going to ask her to marry him. And she was going to refuse him, so she didn't want to meet his family or further the connection with him in any way.

He'd lost her, and he wasn't even sure why.

"Evan?" Juliana said. "What's going on? What happened between you and Catrin just now?"

He closed his eyes, marshaling all his resources to endure the pain. "Nothing. Nothing at all."

"If this is about Justin's murder—"

"Deuce take it, no!" he cried, opening his eyes to glare at her. "You're as bad as she is! It had nothing to do with that! I'd be an idiot to still believe she had any part in that after she saved my life, wouldn't I?"

"Then what—"

"It's none of your concern, Juliana. Good God, haven't you meddled enough? Don't you ever stop meddling?"

When her body stiffened with hurt, he instantly regretted his hasty words. "I'm sorry, I shouldn't have said that."

She ignored his apology and leveled a wounded gaze on him. "How have I meddled? What have I done to make you snap at me?"

He bit back another angry retort. Juliana had been a second mother to him, and he wouldn't hurt her for anything in the world, but her questions were driving him mad. "Nothing. I shouldn't have said anything."

"No, I want you to tell me what terrible thing I've done!"

He glared at her. "Well, for one thing, you let me believe when I came here the first time that Catrin was an old woman. I've had plenty of time to think about that, and I finally figured out why."

Juliana's anger seemed to dissipate like smoke in a sudden rain. She turned away from him, wringing her hands. "Oh? And what did you decide?"

"You wanted me to see her without any prejudgment. You wanted me to see her and fall in love with her." He clenched his fists as all his hurt over Catrin's rejection of him came to the fore. "You thought I'd take one look at her and be lost, and then it wouldn't matter if she was the Lady of the Mists or not. It wouldn't matter what part she had in Justin's murder."

Slowly, Juliana turned to face him, quiet, waiting.

"And you were right," he added bitterly. "You were absolutely right. You know me so well. I lost my heart to her the second I saw her." He lifted his anguished face to her. "But you forgot to take her feelings into account. You assumed she'd fall in love with me, too. Well, Juliana, I hate to disappoint you, but she didn't." The pain wrenched at him as he added in a choked whisper, "She just didn't."

"What makes you think that? That girl sat by your bedside night and day, crying and praying that you'd wake up, not eating, not sleeping . . . merciful heavens, Evan, how much more proof of her feelings do you need?"

"I need her not to leave when I start talking about marriage." He gave a shuddering breath. "Before you came in, I was on the verge of asking her to marry me. She knew it, and that's why it 'wouldn't be wise' for her to stay and meet the rest of my family. She's planning to refuse me, and it would have been too hard for her to meet them all, knowing what she intended."

"I don't believe that." Juliana planted her hands on her waist and stared at him. "If that girl isn't in love with you, then I'm deaf and blind. I tell you, if you could have heard the way she spoke about you, the way she fretted over you—"

"Yes, but that was *before* she found out from Mary that I'm only a tenant farmer's son by birth!" He couldn't stand hearing Juliana talk about how well Catrin spoke of him. "That was before I told her why my engagement to Henrietta failed. Now that she knows I'm not the kind of man who'd make a good husband—"

"Men!" Juliana said, an expression of disgust passing over her face. "You're all such fools! When it comes to love, do you think women care about things like position and money?" She came up and laid her hand on his shoulder. "Catrin is a good woman, a wonderful woman, and I don't believe she cares at all about your background. I just don't believe it."

"Then why did she refuse to meet my family? Why did she leave just now?" he ground out. "She knew what I was going to say to her. A woman in love would have remained with me until I got the words out."

She shrugged. "Maybe. Maybe not. But I wouldn't assume she is rejecting you. If she really means so much to you, go find out what's troubling her, instead of sitting here sulking."

He glared at her. "Thank you for your unwanted advice, Juliana, but I know Catrin better than you do."

With a shrug she headed toward the door. "Fine. Do as you wish. Give up on the one woman who suits you and who cares for you." She stopped in the doorway and fixed him with a haughty glance. "But don't blame me for your broken heart. I don't regret meddling, and I believe wholeheartedly that I picked the right woman for you. I just underestimated your ability to hold on to her." Then she stalked from the room.

Evan let out an explosive curse. He should never have told Juliana what had happened between him and Catrin. Deuce take Juliana! She was wrong, utterly wrong! Catrin had obviously stayed by his bedside out of an overdeveloped sense of guilt for what had happened to him. But if she'd been in love with him, as Juliana claimed, she wouldn't have left when he'd started talking about marriage!

He settled into the chair with a scowl. This was one time Juliana would be forced to acknowledge that she'd made a mistake.

Unfortunately.

Chapter Twenty

O may I with myself agree
And never covet what I see;
Content me with an humble shade,
My passions tamed, my wishes laid;
For while our wishes wildly roll
We banish quiet from the soul. . . .
—John Dyer, "Grongar Hill"

Juliana had done her best not to meddle. She truly had. After her talk with Evan last night, she'd managed to do nothing when Mrs. Price had sent down a message saying she was too ill to come to dinner. Juliana had kept her peace when Evan spent the evening brooding in his room and not eating any of the food he'd called for so eagerly. She'd gone to bed and tried not to think about it, determined not to give Evan any more excuse to be angry at her for interfering.

She'd even restrained herself from acting this morning when a servant told her that Evan had called for a bottle of brandy in the middle of the night, "to dull the pain in his shoulder and help him sleep." To dull the pain indeed. She knew exactly what pain he wanted to dull, and it wasn't the pain in his shoulder.

But now Sally stood before her at the breakfast table, telling her that Mrs. Price was preparing to return to Llynwydd and wanted her old clothes back.

Juliana decided she'd had enough.

She rose from her seat. "Thank you, Sally. I'll take care of it. Why don't you see if you can help Beatrice with the silver?"

Sally nodded and left.

"What are you going to do?" Rhys asked as Juliana turned toward the door.

"Talk some sense into Mrs. Price."

"Maybe you should keep out of it," Rhys said in a warning tone. "Let the two of them work out their problems."

She glared at him. "I'm surprised you noticed that they were having problems or even that they were interested in each other." Her irritation with Evan got the better of her. "Men are usually stupid about such 'petty' things as love."

Rhys raised an eyebrow. "Not always. And yes, I've noticed that Evan turns into a puddle of mush whenever Mrs. Price is spoken of. And vice-versa, I might add."

"Well, turning into puddles of mush is all very well, but at the moment those two puddles are being rather stubborn, and I think it's time a third party made certain they don't go their separate ways and live the rest of their lives in misery."

"You're the third party, of course," he said, skepticism in his voice.

"Don't even think of trying to stop me, Rhys." She shot him a quelling glance. "I left it up to them yesterday, and they bungled it. Now it's my turn to see that matters come out right." She paused, then added, "Oh, and you'd best prepare to go to town."

"To town?" He looked blank. "Why?"

"Because when I get through with those two, they'll need some privacy. So we're going to Carmarthen for the day. The whole family. Margaret has been begging for a new dress, and Owen has been itching to visit with Edgar now that he's home from the university, so we might as well get that done."

After that pronouncement she swept from the room. Although she heard Rhys laugh behind her, the fact that he didn't try to persuade her any further demonstrated that he knew she was right. Something must be done about this situation.

When she reached the hall between Evan's room and Mrs. Price's, she hesitated, but it was clear which one she must work on first, for she'd said her piece to Evan last night and it had done no good. So she knocked on Mrs. Price's door.

When Mrs. Price opened it, her face reflected surprise at seeing Juliana standing there, but she quickly recovered. "Good morning, Lady Juliana."

Juliana took one look at Mrs. Price's tear-swollen face and knew she'd made the right decision. "May I come in?"

Mrs. Price hesitated a fraction of a second. Then she nodded and stepped aside to let Juliana enter.

Juliana closed the door behind her. "Sally told me you

want to leave this morning, so I thought I'd see if everything is all right."

Turning away, Mrs. Price said in a strained voice, "Everything . . . is fine."

"I can tell. Your eyes are the color of poppies, a sure sign that matters are going well in one's life."

Mrs. Price's shoulders stiffened. "Please, Lady Juliana. I prefer not to talk about it."

"Very well. But I thought you should know that Evan is sitting in that room across the hall, convinced that you won't marry him because of his lowly background."

There. She'd done it. She'd meddled to the highest degree. And she didn't care.

This time it took Mrs. Price several minutes to speak, but Juliana could tell she was crying as she did so. "It's better that way," she whispered.

Juliana's temper rose. Merciful heavens, the woman was as stubborn as Evan. "Better that way? You listen to me, Mrs. Price, it is *not* better. You can't let Evan go on thinking he's not worth marrying, especially if you have some other reason for refusing him."

Mrs. Price turned to her with eyes awash in tears, but her expression was resolute. "As I said before, Lady Juliana, I don't wish to discuss it."

Juliana exploded. "Oh, but *I* do. Sit down, Mrs. Price."

"I will not di—"

"Sit down!" Juliana ordered.

Recoiling from the determination in Juliana's manner, Mrs. Price obeyed and perched on the edge of the bed. Then she lifted her face with a mutinous expression.

Juliana crossed her arms over her chest. "I'm going to tell you some things about that young man that I have never spoken of to anyone, even him. He would no doubt hate me if he learned that I'd told you these things, but he's like a son to me, and I refuse to stand by and watch him suffer for no good reason."

She sucked in a heavy breath. "When I'm through speaking, you may do as you wish . . . break his heart . . . suffer in silence . . . I don't care, but first, you will hear me out."

Mrs. Price gave her a stony stare.

"Evan Newcome is an incredible man," Juliana said, "but then you must have already realized that. And yes, he is the son of one of our tenant farmers, Thomas Newcome, who passed away this year." When a faint flickering of sympathy shone in Mrs. Price's eyes, Juliana added, "But in case you pity Evan for losing his father, don't. The man regularly beat Evan and would have kept him out of school and ignorant if Rhys and I hadn't intervened."

Mrs. Price's rigid composure cracked a little.

"Evan has never spoken of what he suffered from his boorish father," Juliana continued, "but I saw plenty of evidence of it during the years I tutored him. He used to come to lessons covered with bruises. Several times he had black eyes that he claimed came from fights he'd gotten into with other boys. The first one appeared when he was only seven, so I was suspicious of that explanation, especially since his father rarely gave him time to consort with other children."

As Mrs. Price's face filled with horror, Juliana's voice hardened. "And then there was the time Evan broke his ribs 'falling out of a tree.' He wasn't yet eleven, and could climb like a monkey. Oddly enough, when his mother came to tell me he wouldn't be coming to lessons, she was also sporting a black eye.

"In fact, he was often not the only one in his family with bruises. His mother . . . his sister . . . his older brother . . . I saw all of them with injuries at one time or another, although they always had an explanation for how the 'accident' occurred."

The tears began streaming down Mrs. Price's face again as she held the back of her hand over her mouth to stifle the sobs.

"You met Mary," Juliana went on relentlessly, "so you know what a little dear she is. But that little dear didn't shed a single tear at her own father's funeral. Not one, although she cried copiously at her mother's funeral. And her brother . . . Evan's brother . . ." Juliana glanced away. "Let's just say that George is the angriest man I know. His family wears a good many bruises, too. I guess it's difficult to grow up in a household like the Newcomes' and not learn a few of the wrong things."

She swung her gaze back to Mrs. Price. "But Evan rose above all that. Despite his wretched father, he fought to wrest an education for himself from a system designed to keep out the Welsh. Evan made something of himself, and that takes a very strong and brave man. But he still believes what that horrible man beat into him—that he's not worthy of love—and if you walk away from him like this—"

"Please, Lady Juliana, no more!" Mrs. Price cried. Tears streamed down her face. "You don't understand! I know what a good man Evan is! I'd be honored beyond words to marry him!" She gave several small gasps in an obvious attempt to stem the flood of tears. "But I can't, and he knows why!"

"Does he?"

"Yes!" She clenched her fists. "He knows I don't have the chalice anymore!"

Juliana looked at Mrs. Price in complete confusion. "The chalice? You mean that . . . that chalice you went to London to get from Lord Mansfield?"

Catrin nodded.

"What in the name of God does the chalice have to do with anything?" Juliana asked.

Mrs. Price swallowed. "It's a long story, and you'll not believe it."

Juliana forced some patience into her voice as she sat down on the bed next to Mrs. Price and took her hand. "You don't know that. Why don't you tell me?"

For a moment Juliana thought Mrs. Price would refuse. Then the woman mastered her tumultuous emotions and began speaking in a low murmur. "There's a curse on all the Ladies of the Mists. If I marry without drinking from the chalice on my wedding day, my husband dies. It's as simple as that. That's why Willie and my father and my grandfather and my great-grandfather all passed away within three years of their weddings. That's why I went to London to purchase the chalice."

Staring off into space, she whispered, "But David Morys took it, and he'll never give it back to me. So if I marry Evan, he'll die." She fixed Juliana with a dark gaze. "I can't watch Evan die the way I watched Willie die. I can't! I almost caused Evan's death once. I *can't* do it again!"

Juliana felt as if someone had punched her. This was a new development entirely. All this over some chalice? "But Evan didn't mention anything about a curse—"

"He knows about it. He just doesn't believe in it. Yesterday, when I realized he was going to ask me to marry him and obviously hadn't taken the curse into account, I didn't know what to do. I knew if I reminded him of it, he'd not consider it a valid reason for not marrying me, and he'd pursue me until I gave in." She ducked her head shyly. "I can't resist Evan, you see, when he . . . I have no will at all where he's concerned."

Juliana bit back a smile. She'd known she was right about Mrs. Price's feelings for Evan.

"So I decided I would refuse him without explanation. But I never got the chance, and after you came in and he wanted me to meet his family—" She broke off with a sigh. "I couldn't meet them, knowing I was about to refuse him. And I did tell him to speak to me later, but I confess I was grateful that he didn't. Evan knows me well enough to know I was about to refuse him. I don't know why he acquiesced so easily, but I am content to let matters lie."

She lifted her face to Juliana. "He has obviously realized I will not marry him. So I shall leave and let him get on with his life."

"But how can he get on with his life? He thinks you have contempt for what he is . . . or was."

Mrs. Price gave a shudder, then mastered it. "That will pass. If I tell him once more that the curse governs my actions, he will never let the matter drop. And if he presses me into marriage, he will die. So I must avoid that at all costs."

The curse. A shiver passed through Juliana despite herself. It was all so medieval, yet Juliana had enough belief in the unknown to wonder about such things. And had four men in Mrs. Price's family really died after three years of marriage?

She shook off the uncomfortable chill. Even if such a curse existed, there must be a way around it. And if anyone could find it, Evan could, no matter what Mrs. Price thought.

"Now you understand," Mrs. Price said, a catch in her throat. "So you must help me leave. You must!"

Juliana squeezed Mrs. Price's hand. "Yes, of course," she lied. "I shall go see about having your clothes brought and a horse saddled for you."

Mrs. Price nodded, but as Juliana left the room, she heard the sound of weeping. With a grim expression she went straight across the hall. Mrs. Price was suffering, poor woman, and Juliana couldn't just stand by and watch it happen. Evan must be reminded of this . . . curse business. This time, she suspected he'd welcome her meddling.

She tapped lightly on his door, not wanting to alert Mrs. Price to what she was doing, although she doubted the woman could hear anything over her crying.

"Who is it?" a voice snarled on the other side.

She smiled. Good. He was clearly as unhappy as Mrs. Price. Maybe he was unhappy enough to end this foolishness. "It's Juliana," she said in a low voice. "I must speak to you."

She heard the low curse he muttered on the other side. "Go away! I'm . . . I'm getting dressed!"

If he thought that would keep her out, he'd forgotten how stubborn she could be. Besides, she already knew he'd summoned one of the servants earlier that morning to help him dress. She tried the knob. It was unlocked, thank heaven.

"I'm coming in!" she said, in case he truly did need the warning. Then she opened the door and entered the room. As she'd suspected, he was as fully clothed as he could be, given the injury to his shoulder, and was standing by the window with a scowl on his face.

"Can't a man have any privacy around here?" he growled.

"You will have all the privacy you want an hour from now." She took note of the half-empty bottle of brandy and the filled glass in his hand. "In fact, that's what I've come to tell you. Rhys and I and the children are going to Carmarthen for the day. We may even spend the night, depending on how long it takes us to finish our business there."

"Fine," Evan bit out as he turned back to the window. "Have a wonderful time. Now if that's all . . ."

With a glance across the hall, she said, "Mrs. Price is planning to leave today as well."

That got a reaction from him. He went very still, and even from where she stood, she could see his fingers clench the glass of brandy. "Where's she going?"

Juliana shrugged. "Back to Plas Niwl, I suppose. I didn't ask."

A distinct bitterness crept into his voice. "I hope she has a wonderful time, too. I hope you *all* have a wonderful time."

Barely suppressing an irritated oath, Juliana said, "And

one more thing, Evan. What's all this business about a chalice and a curse?"

He gave a heavy sigh. "She told you about the curse?"

"Mrs. Price says that's why she won't marry you."

He whirled on her. "Then she lies! She has the chalice now, so that bloody curse is no longer a problem between us!"

Aha. So *that* was the source of the problem. Thank heaven. She would have been very disappointed in Evan if he'd been so oblivious to Mrs. Price's feelings that he hadn't thought of how much the curse might affect her. "Oh, but she doesn't have the chalice. Didn't you know? That Morys fellow stole it while she watched over you with the pistol."

The look of astonishment that spread over his face was rapidly replaced by one of fury. For a fleeting instant she feared she'd gone too far and that he was angry at *her.* But when he swore, then stalked past her, pausing only to hand her the glass of brandy, she heaved a relieved sigh.

She turned and watched as he crossed the hall, threw open Mrs. Price's door, and entered the room. Then she set down the glass of brandy and strode blithely down the hall.

Her work was complete. She'd done everything she could to get those two to recognize they were meant for each other, and if they couldn't carry it on from here, then she washed her hands of both of them.

But she had a sneaking suspicion that all would be well from now on.

When the door behind her slammed shut, Catrin jumped. She hadn't heard the door open, and she whirled away from the window, wondering if Lady Juliana had returned.

But as she came face-to-face with Evan, who was glowering at her like a demon in human form, she froze. "You . . . you shouldn't be here. You're not well enough to—"

"I'm much better than one would expect, given that I spent the last fifteen hours barely able to sleep or eat. I did manage to drink, though it did nothing but remind me that even liquor can't dull some pains." His gaze burned over her swollen eyes and red nose, and the faintest softness touched his features. "Answer one question for me, Catrin."

"What?" she whispered.

"Did Morys take the chalice?"

The question took her by surprise. "Of course he did. You saw him—"

"For God's sake," he exploded, "I was half-conscious when all that happened! I dimly remember the two of you discussing it, but by that point I could barely see, and all I could hear was the blood roaring in my ears!"

"I thought you knew." She took a shaky breath. "I thought you were just ignoring the fact that it was gone, since you don't . . . believe in the curse anyway." If he hadn't known, then obviously Lady Juliana had told him. Catrin wanted to be angry at the older woman for doing so, but found that she couldn't.

"Yesterday when we were talking, you didn't bring up the curse," he said, his voice tight with emotion. "Why? Or did you indeed have some . . . other reason for not wanting to discuss marriage?"

She should lie. She should do as she'd planned and simply tell him she didn't want to marry him, didn't love him more than life. But faced with his pain—and remembering all Lady Juliana had told her—she couldn't bear to hurt him more.

When he'd told her about his violent nature, she hadn't known it came from years of abuse, of witnessing a marriage fraught with violence. She hadn't known how deep his scars were, how much he hurt. Lady Juliana had certainly done her work well, hadn't she? Now Catrin couldn't stand to heap new suffering on him.

"The only reason I could ever have for not wanting to marry you is the curse," she stated, turning away from him to stare once more out the window. "And I knew you . . . wouldn't accept the curse as a reason, so I let you think whatever you wanted about how I felt."

As he came up behind her, she held her breath, wishing he'd go away and leave her alone. No, she didn't want that either. Oh, how would she ever bear this?

"So you don't care that I'm a tenant farmer's son," he murmured, "that I have a temper, that I'm not fit to kiss your dainty little foot?"

"Of course I don't care!" She continued in a halting voice, "Besides, I'm the one who's . . . not fit. I'm accursed, Evan."

"It doesn't matter to me," he whispered as he slid his

good arm about her waist and drew her against him. "You were absolutely right—I refuse to accept the curse as a reason not to marry you." He bent his head to press a kiss against her hair, rousing a thousand tremors in her wayward body. "And I do want to marry you, Catrin. I want to be part of your life at Plas Niwl, whatever part you see fit to allow me. I want to spend every night of my life in your arms. I want to see you grow big with our child. And no curse will keep me from that."

Every word was like a glittering promise dangled just far enough in front of her that she could see but not touch it. She had known this would happen if he ever pursued her in earnest. She had known he wouldn't relinquish her easily, and still she felt powerless before the force of his will.

"Please, Evan," she whispered, "don't say these things to me. There's no point to it. Nothing can come of it."

He dragged her around to face him, his eyes solemn. "Tell me you don't want the same thing as I do, and I won't discuss it anymore. I'll let you go wherever you wish, even if it means spending the rest of my days wanting you." When she tried to glance away, he caught her chin and made her look at him. "Tell me you don't love me, and I'll end this now. It's all you need do to be rid of me."

All? Oh, unfair, she thought as she gazed into the fathomless depths of his black eyes, knowing she couldn't lie about this. *You are too, too cruel, my love.*

His face shone with expectation and perhaps the faintest hint of uncertainty.

"It doesn't matter if I love you—" she began.

He swore. "That's not what I asked. *Do* you love me, Catrin? Tell me one way or the other!"

She stared at him, at the man who'd endured a hellish childhood and a lonely adulthood, who'd defended her even when he thought she was a criminal . . . who'd become more precious than life to her. It wasn't in her to lie to him. Not anymore. "There is no point to saying this, but I do love you. You know I do."

She had no time to utter anything else for he was kissing her as if she were his only answer to living, as if the world might end if he didn't kiss her. And God help her but she gave herself up to it without a protest, opening her mouth to the wild stabs of his tongue, twining her arms about his waist, letting him do whatever he wished so long as she could kiss him forever. One kiss, she told herself, one kiss and then I will make him see sense.

Oh, but that one kiss! His brandy-scented mouth tempted her to taste more and more, and his thrusting tongue emphasized his possession of her, his absolute determination to have her no matter what. The overwhelming force of his need—and of her own—alarmed her.

As if he sensed her fear, he brought his fingers down her throat with a silken touch, stroking her neck like a horse trainer soothing a skittish colt. But when he slid his questing fingers along her collarbone to the neckline of her dress, she backed away with a soft protest, only to come up against the deep windowsill.

Although hampered by the fact that one of his arms was in a sling, he nonetheless pressed closer, pinning her between the window ledge and his body. His gaze bore into hers as he lifted her with his good arm to set her on the deep ledge, then bent his head to kiss her again.

She twisted her head away. "No, Evan, we can't . . . we mustn't. . . ."

"We will," he affirmed as he kissed a path from her ear down the long slope of her neck, turning her insides to liquid with every touch of his lips against her skin.

She lifted her hands to push him away, but he'd already dragged the neck of her gown down to bare her breast, and when his mouth found one of them and began to work an incredible magic, she found herself clutching his shoulders instead, anchoring him to her.

"That's it, my darling," he murmured against her breast. "Show me your sweetness . . . let me love you." He tugged at her nipple with his teeth, sending a hundred shocks of pleasure through her, weakening her will even further.

This is insane, she told herself. *I can't let him do this.*

It was just as she'd feared . . . he was using her desire against her . . . and winning. And she couldn't let him, for in the end they'd both lose.

Somehow she found the strength to resist the heady strokes of his tongue and his hand sliding down toward the hem of her gown.

"Evan," she whispered, shoving against his chest, "stop

this. Stop it now! This won't change anything. It will only make it worse. I can't marry you. You know I can't!"

He straightened, looming over her like the thunderous god Zeus as his eyes glittered. "You can. You can and you will, if I have to abduct you to be sure of it!"

She curled her fists against his chest, despairing of ever making him understand. "I won't watch you die! It was torture watching Willie die, and I didn't even love him! But I love you! Don't you see? I can't sit by your bedside again, knowing that you'll die! And without the chalice, I assure you that you *will* die!"

"I won't!" he proclaimed. "Now that I have you, I won't allow it!"

Tears of frustration flooded her eyes. "A pox on you, it's not a matter of your choosing!"

Her distress seemed at last to affect him. He caught one of her fists in his hand and lifted it to his mouth, kissing it until her fingers uncurled. "If you are so sure of the power of your curse, my love, then we'll get the chalice back. We know who has it. All I have to do is take it from him."

"Oh, certainly!" she said with heavy sarcasm. "I'm sure David will be delighted to hand it over to you, his rival, so you can marry me. He'd destroy it before he'd give it to you or me."

"Then we'll go to the authorities. We'll charge him with theft."

"Yes, we'll go to the authorities. And he'll tell them how I came by the chalice, how I'm suspected of taking part in a murder. Is that what you want?"

Grim determination crossed his features. "All right, then I'll take it from him by force."

She gripped his hand as a tear coursed down her cheek. "That's what I'm afraid of. You'll try to take it from him, and he'll shoot you with another pistol. Only this time he'll kill you. You'll be dead even before we are married."

He brought their joined hands up to rub away the tear. "You don't understand, Catrin. There are many kinds of death. You say you don't want to watch me die, but if I don't have you, I'll die for certain. Not physically. Oh, I suppose I'll continue to teach and write my books, for I know nothing else. But I'll find no joy or purpose in it. My life will be over as far as I'm concerned."

With a faint smile he released her hand and began stroking her cheek with the backs of his fingers, a gentle caress meant to soothe. "And if, my love, you consign me to *that* death, I promise to rub your face in it for the rest of your life. I'll become a schoolmaster in Llanddeusant, right under that deuced Morys's nose, and I'll either provoke the bastard until he kills me or I'll pine away before your very eyes. What will you do then? Will you close yourself up at Plas Niwl to avoid the sight of me grown pale and thin?"

His voice dropped to a whisper as he painted the scene. "Will you lie in bed wanting me, all the while knowing I am only a mile away wanting you? If I come and sit outside in the rain as I did before, will you tell Bos to let me in? Or will you watch out the window and know I'm thinking only of you, that my every breath is for you, that I'm slowly dying with want of you?"

She closed her eyes, unable to face the force of his too poignant words. "You . . . you wouldn't do all those things—"

"I would."

"You'd find another woman to love—"

"I wouldn't." He clasped her chin and kissed her closed eyes. "You underestimate me if you think I'd give you up without a fight. Even last night, when I was convinced you didn't want me, I was already trying to find a way to make you want me, to make you love me. I'd already decided I'd rather spend a short, torturous time with you, my love, than an untroubled eternity without you."

She opened her eyes to find him wearing a look of such sincerity that she couldn't doubt his words. And before she even knew what she was saying, she whispered, "I could be your mistress. You . . . you said before that I should take a lover. Well . . . I could do that. We could live as husband and wife without ever marrying. The curse couldn't touch us then."

As soon as she said the words, she thought, *Yes, I would do that for you, my love. I would.*

But his eyes hardened. "Live as husband and wife without marrying? In Llanddeusant, I suppose? Where every man, woman, and child already gossips about you with glee? You would raise our children as bastards and subject them to the same whispers and veiled glances that you have suffered all your life . . . that I, too, have endured?"

When she paled, he went on relentlessly. "Or perhaps you'd leave your estate to the management of a steward and travel with me to Cambridge. Of course, I'd have to hide you from the prying eyes of my superiors."

She groaned, and he growled, "No, that wouldn't work, would it, not in a university town. All right then, we could live in London, where I could travel to Cambridge with ease, always hiding the existence of my mistress. Or I could leave the university entirely and claim that we're married. But though we live in London, we could never be part of that place, and you know it. We're Welsh, we're peculiar . . . we're the kind of people who are invited to social occasions for our curiosity value."

He was right, but the truth was painful, and she averted her face to hide the effect his harsh words were having on her.

"You spent a few days in London, didn't you, Catrin?" he continued fiercely. "Tell me, did you enjoy it? Did you find yourself longing to live amidst all that grime and misery? Because I tell you I hate it. I hate the refuse in the streets, both human and inhuman . . . the black grind of poverty . . . the corruption of the nobility. I don't want to raise children there."

He turned her face toward him with a touch of his finger on her chin. "I want to raise my children in a secure home in a community where I have at least some friends. And I want to raise them with the woman who is my wife. I know I said I'd be your lover, but that was when I thought I dared not marry. I don't feel that way now. I want to marry you, love, and I think you want to marry me."

"Every choice you give me is terrible," she whispered as she gazed up into his black eyes. "What am I to do?"

"You're to trust me. We'll find a way around the curse. We'll get the chalice back, I swear it. But we must do it together. We must."

"I . . . I don't know, Evan. I don't know what to do anymore."

As if he sensed her weakening, a dark smile lit his face. "Then let me show you, darling." He dropped his hand to her thigh and began drawing her gown up her legs. "Let me show you what you would be missing if you refused me."

When the hem of her skirt cleared her knees, he parted her legs with his muscled thigh and pulled her forward until the juncture of her legs rested against him. Dragging his knee over her most secret of places, he watched as she sucked in a sudden breath, then another and another as he repeated the caress until she was damp and aching.

"My Lady of the Mists," he whispered. "My sweet, sweet lady . . . you want me . . . you know you do. And that's all that matters."

"No, it isn't—" she protested, but broke off with a gasp when he slipped his hand beneath her skirt and fondled her warm, wet cleft with knowing fingers. Another gasp escaped her lips and he caught it with his mouth, opening his lips over hers, then trailing his open mouth over her chin and down her throat in a series of new, blood-firing caresses. His tongue darted out to taste her wherever his mouth touched, leaving fire in its wake.

It was too much pleasure to bear. With a sigh she clutched his shoulders as he ran his tongue down the hollow between her breasts. Waiting expectantly for the touch of his mouth on her breast, she arched her head back and closed her eyes as he moved his mouth down her body. But he stopped only briefly to tease her nipples with his tongue. Then he drew back and knelt between her legs.

Her eyes shot open, and she stared down at him in shock as he held her gown up to bare her patch of ebony hair to his hungry gaze. "What are you doing?"

"Making you burn, my darling girl," he said as he cast her a knowing glance. "Making you burn."

Then he parted her hair and pressed the most intimate kiss she could ever imagine against the soft petals of skin between her legs. Every part of her body leapt to life at the incredible touch of his tongue, and when he caressed her with his mouth, finding all the places where she ached for his touch and indeed making them burn, she whispered, "By heaven . . ."

His mouth was both fire and frost, arousing, then soothing, then arousing again. Heedless of his wounded shoulder, she dug her fingers into his arms, but though he groaned, he didn't stop what he was doing. His tongue darted inside her, and she closed her eyes with a drawn-out moan, leaning back instinctively to give him better access.

She couldn't believe what he was doing . . . it had never occurred to her that mouths could be used in such amazing ways, yet she wouldn't have wanted him to stop for anything in the world. Heat and want built within her in equal portions, making her move against him to get more, ever more of his mouth.

Then his mouth left her, and she sagged weakly against the window, feeling unfulfilled and ravenous. He stood, still holding up the hem of her gown with the back of his hand. Then he darted his hand beneath it and between her legs to continue doing with his fingers what he'd been doing with his mouth, all the while watching her.

"Do you want more of this, sweet Catrin? Would you like to have more?" He stroked her roughly, then found the hard little kernel that seemed to be the center of her pleasure and rolled it between his fingers until she cried out at the surge of molten wanting that poured over her.

As her body shuddered from the exquisite, wanton joy, she twined her arms about his neck and buried her face in his shoulder, too ashamed to say how badly she indeed wanted more, though she knew her body proclaimed it quite loudly.

Her gown was draped over his arm, hiding the subtle movements of his fingers, but she felt every one to the depths of her being and each seductive touch shook her to the core. Then he slid one finger deep inside her slick passage, eliciting a gasp from her. "Do you like that, my love?" His voice was hoarse with his own desire. "Do you want to see what it can be like between us when there's no pain, when there's love instead of mistrust?"

"Yes," she whispered, unable to help herself, "Oh, yes."

"I want you, love. I want to bury myself inside you. Will you let me?"

He was already unbuttoning his breeches, and she realized with a little shiver of horror and fascination that he intended to take her right there, against the window in broad daylight. "Evan, you can't . . . someone might see . . ."

"No one will see," he said as he pulled his breeches and drawers down far enough to expose his rigid shaft. "No one's home. The Vaughans have gone to town for the day."

He slid his hand down her thigh, then curved it under her knee. Drawing her leg up along the outside of his, he pulled her toward him until her bottom rested on the edge of the window sill and his shaft nudged her wet heat.

She glanced over her shoulder through the window. "But the servants—"

"—are not standing outside staring up at your window," he finished for her, "and in any case, they'll see nothing but your respectably clothed back."

"But, Evan—"

"Hush," he growled, spreading kisses in her disordered hair. "I want you so badly . . . and I'm afraid that with my arm in a sling, the conventional position will be hard to manage." He nipped at her ear, then whispered, "Please, Catrin . . . if you want me, do as I say."

She groaned and turned her face up to his, pressing a kiss against his mouth. "You know I want you."

He sucked in a harsh breath. "Then guide me in, love."

It took her a second to understand what he meant, but though she blushed, she did as he asked, intoxicated by the thought of having him inside her again. There was some shifting of bodies and the position was a little awkward, but when he drove himself in deep, she forgot all that.

"Good God, Catrin," he said as his breath quickened. "You are . . . oh, my love, you are exquisite."

When he bent her back against the window and began to move, some urge deeper even than hunger or thirst made her loop her arms about his neck and curl her legs behind his until she was open fully for him, wide-open and aching to feel him buried in her to the hilt.

Evan could scarcely believe it when he felt her clamp her legs about his. He'd won part of the battle at least. She did want him, and as long as he kept her wanting him, he had a chance to break down her fears about their marrying.

She shifted her body, allowing him to sink even further into her, and he groaned. God, she was heaven . . . so tight and warm. The sensation of entering her body was indescribable . . . beyond anything he'd ever felt, and he knew it was because of who she was . . . what she was . . . the kindest, most generous woman he'd ever known.

She hadn't cared at all about his past. She'd made that perfectly clear. And he wouldn't let her regret giving herself to him. Not now. Anchoring her with his good arm, he bent his head to taste her mouth, stroking it in the way he knew she liked as he thrust into her.

He could feel the tension build in her body as she writhed against him with undulating movements that drove him mad. Pray heaven he could restrain himself long enough to let her find her release, for this was his only way to keep her, to "secure her soul," as Farquhar had put it.

He wanted to caress her breasts, but with one hand in a sling and the other holding her, it was impossible. Instead, he used his mouth on her lush lips, her delightful ears, her enticing neck, nipping and sucking and kissing all the places he thought would thrill her, all the places he adored.

Soon, however, the animal in him took over. He'd been without her for too many days, and she felt too good. Before he knew it, he was losing himself in her, driving her hard, trying to immerse himself in her sweetness as he buried his face in her neck and rode out the storm.

But she didn't seem to mind, for she clamped her legs about him and strained to join her body more closely to his, making soft, mewling sounds that brought him to the edge of sanity. "Catrin . . . my love . . . my life," he whispered as he quickened his pace.

Holding back became nearly impossible, for she ground her hips against him enticingly, and his need for her built to mind-numbing heights. So when her thighs tensed around him and she cried out, he exploded into her in a shattering release, joining his cries to hers as her spasms wrung him dry.

Afterward, it took some time for the thundering of his blood to subside and his muscles to relax. He was clutching her against his body as if to fuse her to him, and when she sighed and rested her head limply on his shoulder, he began to feel a painful throbbing near the site of his wound.

Still, he was loath to move. To have her body draped around his was all he could ever want for contentment, and if it weren't for his waning strength, he could have stayed there forever.

He managed to wait until she stirred against his chest before he drew her face up to his and pressed a lingering kiss to her reddened lips. "What do you say, love?" he whispered. "Shall we move to the bed? I confess I got little sleep last night, and I can think of nothing more perfect than sleeping in your arms."

His words seemed to draw her out of some enchanted place, for she gave a start and gazed up at him. "The bed? But it's daylight and . . . and the servants will wonder. . . ."

He laughed. "For a woman who has spent her entire life as part of the upper classes, you have the most extraordinary concern for what the servants might be thinking. Trust me, the servants here are most discreet. And I suspect that Juliana ordered this part of the house off-limits for the day anyway."

With a blush she trailed her fingers down his chest. "Surely you don't think she was encouraging us to . . . to—"

"Make love? Of course she was." He rubbed his hand against her warm cheek. "I assure you that the Vaughans don't make a practice of running off to town when they have guests."

"She's a very unusual woman, isn't she?" Catrin ventured.

"No more unusual than you, my love." When she seemed pleased at that statement, he added, "And I want to spend the day and most of the night making love to my unusual woman."

"Evan, you wicked man!" she scolded, but she didn't protest when he turned her around and unhooked her gown, then drew it off her. Even when he had trouble doing so with only one hand, she helped him.

"This is not the way it's usually done, you know," he murmured as he pulled off his own drawers and breeches, then somehow managed to get his shirt off over his head. "Most people undress *before* they make love."

He rested his hands on her shoulders, then dragged her chemise off very slowly. She trembled as he pressed a kiss to her bare shoulder.

He led her to the bed. "But I suppose a little . . . deviation from the usual is acceptable." He lay down on the bed, then pulled her on top of him with a smile. Naked and splayed across his body, she looked like a goddess, and he felt himself hardening once more. "Let's try another deviation, shall we?"

With his thigh he nudged her legs apart and watched as her eyes widened. "I'm not finished making you burn." He ground his hips up against her, letting her feel his burgeoning arousal. "By the time I get through with you, you'll be begging me to marry you."

He covered her breast with his hand and teased the nipple until she gasped. "*Begging,* I tell you."

Either that or he'd be dead, he told himself, and not from her bloody curse either. She was enough woman to send a man to an early grave.

Oh, but I'll die happy, he thought as she realized what he intended and then settled her body experimentally on his. *I'll certainly die happy.*

Chapter Twenty-one

For her sake this prayer I offer,
For her who gave me passion to pain me:
As none was so dear to me as she was,
May she not know pain, may Peter protect her!
—Einion ap Gwalchmai, "Elegy for Nest,
daughter of Hywel, of Tywyn, Merionethshire"

In the middle of the night Catrin awakened with a start. She'd been dreaming that the Vaughans had discovered her and Evan together in bed and had thrown her out of their house. The shame of it lingered in her mind, and she glanced over at Evan, sleeping peacefully at her side.

How could he feel so little guilt about consorting with her beneath the very noses of his benefactors? It was true that the Vaughans weren't in residence at that moment, but who knew when they might return? The servants had insisted that they often stayed overnight at their town house in Carmarthen, but Catrin still felt uneasy about the scandalous things she was doing in their house here.

Not Evan. A pox on the man, but he had indeed kept her in bed most of the day. She sat up and stared along the shaft of moonlight to the window where Evan had taken her the first time. A blush stained her cheeks to think of it, and the blush increased when she remembered the subsequent times they'd made love.

It surprised her how much she'd enjoyed being on top of him. Once she'd gotten past the embarrassment of being so blatantly exposed to his gaze, she'd enjoyed having some control over their lovemaking. Oh, the things he'd shown her! No wonder he'd been amazed that she hadn't sought a lover before. She'd never dreamed of what she was missing . . . the wonderful cresting pleasure of being in the arms of the man you loved.

In the evening, when they'd decided to go down to dinner and find out whether the Vaughans had returned, they'd exchanged pleased glances to hear that their hosts were staying in Carmarthen for the evening.

But that had seemed to give Evan a license to behave in the most disgraceful manner. She still couldn't believe what he'd done throughout the meal. He'd had her sit next to him, but only so he could tease and fondle her under the table where the tablecloth hid them from the eyes of the servants. Evan had insisted that to any undiscerning eye, they looked just like two friends enjoying an evening meal, but she'd been certain that the evidence of their scandalous behavior was stamped on their faces.

The strange thing was, although she'd been terrified of being discovered, she'd found the most awful thrill in what they were doing. How she'd made it through that meal she didn't know. She couldn't remember what she'd eaten or drank or even what they'd talked about. All she remembered was the secret excitement she'd felt as his hand lay on her thigh, drawing her gown up bit by bit until he could slip his hand between her legs to find the already damp place and touch it with heated fingers. He'd stroked and caressed her so deftly that he'd had her aching for him in a matter of minutes.

Then she'd thought to fight fire with fire, so between one of the courses she had slipped her hand inside his breeches to clasp his member. She'd meant it only to provoke him, but when she'd tried to withdraw her hand, he'd clamped his over hers and murmured in her ear, "Leave it there, love." Only when the next course had come did he let her pull her hand away, but by that time he was as hard as iron. After that, they'd made short work of their meal, so aroused that they'd barely made it up the stairs and to the bed before falling upon each other.

Later in their room when she'd remonstrated with him for doing something so outrageous, he'd told her with a grin that this was what she must endure from a man with lusty appetites. And he'd made love to her again with his mouth until she'd begged to have him inside her. Only then had he pulled her atop him.

By heaven, what a night. What a beautiful, glorious, exciting night.

Now she turned her head to watch him. He was sleeping on his back with his head resting on his uninjured shoulder.

Such an angelic face, she thought. From looking at him asleep, no one would ever guess the fierceness of his passions . . . or the mischievousness he hid well beneath his scholarly facade. Last night at dinner, it had been as if he wanted to draw her with him into a conspiracy of desire, where she chose him over the strictures of society.

A faint smile touched her lips. That had been an easy choice, for she'd never really fit into society. Maybe that was why she'd enjoyed their secretive caresses under the table. All her life, she'd been gossiped about for things she hadn't done. It was nice, for once, to do something that merited gossip . . . and to get away with it.

Nonetheless, stolen caresses were one thing—a lifetime of flouting convention was another. He had known her better than herself when he'd disparaged her suggestion that they live as man and mistress. Despite his sometimes uncivilized soul, he desperately wanted to be part of civilization, and he knew she did, too. They would always be oddities, people who didn't quite belong. Yet neither of them desired the condemnation that would come of their living together outside of marriage.

So that left only one choice. She must get the chalice back. Alone. If Evan came anywhere near David, David would hide it forever rather than risk her marrying someone other than him. But if she approached him alone, perhaps she could change his mind and get him to return it.

The only problem was that she didn't think after having rejected David twice, she could persuade him to trust her. Still, she must try. Otherwise, either Evan or David would do something foolish. It was up to her. This was her curse, and she must be the one to take control of it.

And the sooner the better. There was little point in waiting. By morning the Vaughans would have returned, and then getting away without being noticed would be near to impossible. Much as she hated to leave Evan right now, she could never feel wholly comfortable about what they were doing as long as their future together was in limbo. She'd learned that at least from her dream.

Slipping from the bed, she went to the chair where lay her own clothes, which, true to Lady Juliana's word, had been washed and pressed and brought to her yesterday. It was hard to dress with only the burgeoning moon for light, but she managed it because she dared not light a candle.

She'd have to manage other things, too, she thought as she crept to the door. She'd have to find writing paper and a pen to write a note, for she couldn't leave Evan wondering where she'd gone, and she'd have to saddle a horse by herself. She'd have to manage all of that without rousing any of the servants. But she'd do it because she must.

Where should she go to look for David, though? Carmarthen? No, it had been more than three days since he'd left her and Evan on the road. By now, he would have heard that they weren't on the coach, and would have given up the pursuit to return to Llanddeusant.

That's where she would go. With any luck, by the time Evan found her note, she'd be halfway to Llanddeusant. Then even if he or the Vaughans came after her, she'd have time to reach David and coax him to give her the chalice before anyone showed up to ruin her plans.

She paused at the door to look at Evan. He turned toward the door, as if even in his sleep he sensed that she was leaving, and she gazed a long time at his handsome features. Never in her life had she wanted something so badly. Yesterday had been merely a taste of what living with Evan might be like, and it had thoroughly whetted her appetite for more.

Well, this time the curse wouldn't keep her from having what she wanted. This time she would triumph over it, even if it meant hitting that blasted David over the head again.

Because Evan had been absolutely right. There *were* other kinds of deaths, and a lifetime without him would be one of them.

The throbbing in his shoulder awakened Evan. To his surprise sunlight streamed through the window. He rubbed his eyes and pushed himself into a sitting position. Good God, it was late in the morning. It wasn't like him to sleep past dawn, but perhaps he was still weary from the blood he'd lost.

Then he remembered how he'd spent the day before and knew exactly why he'd slept so heavily. All that lovemaking with Catrin.

Where was she anyway? he wondered as he scanned the room. A smile split his face. No doubt she'd gone down to breakfast without him, afraid he might assault her under the table again.

When that particular memory made him hard, he groaned and got out of bed. Today would certainly not be like yesterday. Rhys and Juliana were returning, unfortunately. They would cast him and Catrin sly looks and refuse to give them a moment's peace. Catrin would spend the day trying to fool the Vaughans into thinking that he and she were perfectly respectable. He would spend the day wanting her. Always wanting her.

Was that to be his continual state? Did married people ever tire of desiring their partners? He certainly hoped it didn't continue to be this intense, or he'd be exhausted for the rest of his life. He wanted to make love to her night and day. He wanted to make love to her now.

But he'd have to find her first. He eyed his clothes, then cursed. The breeches he could manage, but not the shirt, not with his arm in a sling. He'd need help dressing, but Catrin would die of shame if he called for a servant to come to *her* room and help him dress.

Grumbling to himself, he pulled on his drawers, gathered up the rest of his clothing and scurried across the hall. Deuce take it, but he'd be glad when he didn't have to sneak about like this, when he could make love to her without having to worry about propriety.

Some time later, a servant responded to his summons and began helping him dress.

"Have the Vaughans returned?" Evan asked.

"No, sir, but we expect them any moment. They sent one of the footmen ahead to say they were on their way."

Evan stifled a groan. He supposed it had been too much to hope that they'd stay in Carmarthen a little longer and give him more time alone with Catrin.

Trying to sound nonchalant, he said, "I suppose Mrs. Price is already up and about."

"I don't believe so, sir. I believe she is still in her room."

No, she isn't, Evan nearly said aloud before he caught himself.

Then a frisson of fear rippled over him. Why did the man think Catrin was still in her room? Could the servant be mistaken? Was it possible she had risen and gone to the gardens or something without the staff realizing it?

He waited impatiently while the servant finished helping him dress. After the man left, Evan slipped across the hall and checked Catrin's room again, but she was clearly not there. The clothes that the maid had left for her the day before were gone, but that didn't mean anything, since she might have preferred to wear her own clothes today.

As he left the room, he tried to remember if she'd mentioned anything yesterday about her plans for today, but they'd both been so caught up in each other that they hadn't really spoken of the future, either immediate or distant. He'd been afraid to press her too much about marriage, confident that they would work it all out when he was fully recovered. Now he wished he hadn't been so hesitant.

Quickly, he descended the stairs, hoping to find someone who might have seen her. As he reached the landing, he heard voices in the foyer downstairs and recognized Rhys's.

So they'd returned already, had they?

Evan hurried down the steps. The squire was speaking with the butler. He was alone and looking very solemn.

"You're back earlier than I expected," Evan said. "Where are Juliana and the others?"

Rhys looked up, but his somber expression only altered a fraction. "Everyone else is eating breakfast in the dining room. We left in too much of a hurry to eat."

"Why?"

Rhys glanced toward the dining room and lowered his voice. "I had to come back and let you know of the latest disturbing development in this whole mess with that schoolmaster."

"You mean Morys?" Evan asked with a jolt of unease.

"Yes. His dead body was found in the forest outside of Carmarthen early this morning. Someone murdered him."

Shock kept Evan speechless. He stared blindly at Rhys. Morys had been murdered? But why? And who would do such a thing?

"Apparently, it happened a day or two after he left here," Rhys continued as he took Evan's arm and led him toward the drawing room. "When they found him, he'd clearly been dead for a while. They weren't sure who he was, but when I heard the description, I went to take a look and recognized him."

"You're sure it was him?" Evan asked.

"Yes. And after I identified him, the innkeeper at The White Oak confirmed it. Apparently, the last time anyone saw him, Morys was eating lunch at the inn. The innkeeper said Morys asked about a wounded man and a woman traveling on the coach."

They entered the drawing room together. Rhys closed the door behind them, then turned to Evan. "Everyone in Carmarthen has assumed he was killed by thieves." He fixed Evan with a worried gaze. "But I couldn't help noticing that he'd been stabbed repeatedly. Like your friend Lord Mansfield."

Evan shuddered. "Oh, my God."

"Yes. I was told that nothing of any value was found on the body . . . like a chalice, for example. And since Morys hadn't yet taken a room in Carmarthen, anything of value he might have had would have been with him."

Evan felt as if someone had pole-axed him. Morys had obviously been murdered for the chalice. Perhaps Justin had been, too. He remembered what Catrin had said about her uneasy feeling that she was being watched . . . apparently, her feeling hadn't simply been the result of her fearful nature. Someone *had* been watching her, maybe even waiting for her to gain the chalice, so they could take it from her. And when she'd eluded them, they'd perhaps assumed that Lord Mansfield had it and had assaulted him.

But who?

"Obviously," Rhys went on, "this chalice is dangerous to one's health. You saw it. Is it valuable enough to kill someone for?"

Evan shook his head. "Until now, I thought its only value lay in its ability to end the curse on Catrin's family."

"Ah, yes, the curse," Rhys remarked. "Juliana told me about that. You don't really believe in it, do you?"

"No. But Catrin does." Evan's eyes narrowed. "And perhaps someone else does, too, someone who knows about the curse and knows she can't marry without it."

"Is there anyone who would want to keep her from marrying?" Rhys asked.

"I can't think of anyone." Evan rubbed his stubbly chin as he tried to remember who'd been most vocal in their disapproval of Catrin. "Unless it was her father-in-law, Sir Huw Price. He blames her for his son's death. He might steal it just to thwart her. He's something of a nasty creature, but I'm not sure I could see him committing two murders this brutal."

"The innkeeper did mention that an older man spoke briefly with Morys at the inn. But Morys left alone, although the man did leave shortly afterward." Rhys frowned. "I suppose we'll have to talk to Catrin and see if she thinks her father-in-law would go to such lengths to hurt her. She could also tell us if Sir Huw was gone from Llanddeusant while she was on her trip. Where is she?"

"I don't know. When I woke up, she wasn't in the bed and—" Evan stopped short as he realized what he'd just said.

Rhys had already raised one eyebrow. "In the bed?"

For probably the first time in his life, Evan was at a loss for words. "Well, she . . . I mean, we . . . deuce take it, Rhys, isn't that what you expected?"

Rhys smiled. "*I* didn't expect anything, but Juliana seemed rather certain that she'd pulled off the match of the century."

"Yes, well, half of the match seems to have disappeared," Evan grumbled.

His smile fading, Rhys said, "What do you mean?"

"I mean, one of the servants told me she hadn't arisen yet. But as you obviously ascertained, I knew she *had* arisen. So where the deuce is she?"

Rhys went to the door and opened it. "Oh, she probably slipped out into the gardens early or something like that. I'm sure we'll find her."

They were met in the hall, however, by Juliana, who waved an envelope at them. "There you are, Evan. The butler said we received no letters yesterday, but as I was passing the writing table in the hall, I saw this on the salver. It's addressed to you."

With a sinking sensation in his stomach, Evan took the envelope from her and tore it open. As he scanned it, he groaned.

"What is it?" Rhys asked.

"Catrin. She's gone off to Llanddeusant to get the chalice from Morys. She says she knew I'd do something foolish to get it back, and she thought it would be easier for her to convince Morys to give it to her if I weren't around."

He crumpled the note with an oath, then turned to Rhys. "I'm afraid I'll have to borrow a horse from you again. Catrin says she took one, too, so that's two horses we'll need to return. I hope you can spare them."

With a dismissive gesture Rhys said, "I can always spare two horses. But what do you plan to do? You shouldn't be riding yet, not with your shoulder still on the mend."

"I'm not going to sit here wondering where she is and what kind of trouble she's getting into," Evan bit out. "I know Catrin. She may be timid sometimes, but not when something matters a great deal to her. Then she turns bloody stubborn. They won't have heard about Morys's murder in Carmarthen yet, so she won't know about it. When she discovers that Morys hasn't returned, she'll start looking for him, and God knows where she'll go. You know as well as I do it's not safe for her to be traveling the countryside alone." Evan's throat tightened. "She might even run afoul of that murderer. We don't know why he wanted the chalice or if it has anything to do with Catrin."

"Yes, I see your point." Rhys turned to Juliana. "I'm going with him. Can you manage without me for a few days?"

"Of course," Juliana murmured.

"There's no need for that—" Evan began.

"You're still recovering from a life-threatening wound, and you don't know what you'll come up against on the other end," Rhys said. "This whole thing has become damned risky, and I'm not letting you go without me."

"Look here, Rhys," Evan retorted, "I'm sure I'm worrying about this for nothing. I'll probably find her at Plas Niwl, waiting for Morys to return to town so she can convince him to give her the chalice."

"And if you don't?" When Evan shifted his uneasy gaze from Rhys, the squire added, "The man who took the chalice has committed two murders to get it. We don't know why, and that disturbs me as much as it disturbs you. What if it's Catrin he's after? Morys took the chalice to make sure Catrin married him. Perhaps this other man did, too."

In which case, Catrin is in danger, Evan added, knowing that was Rhys's thought as well. He hated to take Rhys away from his family, but he *was* worried. In truth, he could use the help. Although he felt as if he'd regained his strength, he wouldn't know for sure until he was forced to fight, and then any weakness on his part might result in Catrin's being harmed. He couldn't risk her, even if it meant putting himself under obligation to the Vaughans yet again.

"Very well, come with me," Evan said. "I do need you, I'm afraid." He flashed Juliana an apologetic glance. "I'm sorry, Juliana. I hate to take Rhys off like this."

She patted his hand. "Nonsense. I'm happy he can help." She cast him a searching glance. "I hope I didn't cause any of this with my meddling."

He shook his head. "No. You were right about Catrin. She is the woman for me. And that's why I have to find her."

Rhys was already calling for the horses to be saddled. As the butler hurried off to relay Rhys's commands to the grooms, Rhys turned to Evan and laid a reassuring hand on Evan's good shoulder. "Don't worry, my friend. She can't have been gone long. If we hurry, we might even catch up to her before she reaches Llanddeusant."

Evan nodded, unable to speak. The more he thought about those two brutal murders, the more fear gripped him. It was possible the murderer wanted only the chalice and that it really had nothing to do with Catrin at all.

But he feared that wasn't the case. For the first time in his life, he found himself praying to a God whom he'd always believed had abandoned him in his youth.

Let her be safe, God. Keep her safe. Because if something happens to her, you might as well take me, too.

Chapter Twenty-two

Before me all afright and fear,
Above me darkness dense and drear.
—Anonymous, "The Mist"

Night had already fallen by the time Catrin stood in David's empty study at the school, feeling completely lost and alone. Where was David? As soon as she'd reached Llanddeusant this evening, she'd gone straight to David's house, but not a soul had answered when she'd knocked on his door.

Then she'd come to the school, only to find it also deserted. It made no sense. David ought to be at one place or the other. He couldn't still be searching for her and Evan, could he? Surely after four days he'd given up *that* pursuit.

So why wasn't he here?

She heard the door to the cottage open, and she froze. Perhaps that was David now. Her hands grew clammy as she rehearsed the words she planned to say to him. But the man who came through the door to the study wasn't David. It was Sir Reynald Jenkins.

At first, he seemed as startled to see her as she was to see him, but then he broke into a broad smile. "Why, Mrs. Price, what a pleasant surprise. You have come back from your long journey, have you? The whole town has been talking about the dreadful Mr. Quinley and his ridiculous accusations. I do hope your presence here means that you're finished with all that?"

"Yes," she murmured, wondering why Sir Reynald had come to the school. He had never shown an interest in it before. Why did he have to show up just now? She must think of a way to be rid of him and his probable questions about her "journey."

He flashed her a sympathetic smile, although there was

something cold about it. "Did you escape that traitorous Mr. Newcome?" When she looked at him questioningly, he added, "Oh, Mrs. Llewelyn has told us all about how he whisked you away. It was appalling. Simply appalling."

She tried to put an end to his curiosity with an innocuous answer. "Mr. Newcome has decided he made a mistake and is now in Carmarthen."

"How interesting. How did you convince him to believe in you?" He cast her a knowing smile. "Then again, I do not need to ask that. I think I can guess."

Although a blush stole over her face, she met Sir Reynald's faintly chilly gaze with a cold one of her own. How dare he? And how much had he heard about her and Evan through the gossip mill anyway?

No, she didn't want to know that. "I'm not interested in discussing this further with you, Sir Reynald," she remarked as she moved toward the door, "so if you'll let me by, I'll be on my way."

Sir Reynald's smile abruptly faded. He closed the door to the study, then fixed her with a gaze that glittered dangerously in the light of the one candle she'd lit when she'd entered the school.

"I am afraid I cannot do that, Mrs. Price."

A warning rang in her mind. "Why not?"

He ignored her question. "I already know what happened between you and our foolish Mr. Morys on the road. Your presence here indicates that you survived that ordeal none the worse for wear. But I must confess to being curious about how Mr. Newcome fared. Morys seemed convinced he had dealt the man a fatal wound."

She was stunned, not only by what Sir Reynald had learned of her encounter with David, but also by the change in his bearing. Sir Reynald had always struck her as something of a fop, but there was nothing foppish now in his demeanor. He looked purposeful and bold and . . . and threatening.

She resisted the impulse to back away from him. "I see you've talked to David. You must have, if you already know what he did. Where is he?"

"It is not David you're interested in, is it?" Sir Reynald remarked in a lazy tone.

"What do you mean?"

"It is the chalice you want." Reaching up, he unknotted his cravat and drew it off.

The strange action, combined with his words, started the blood pounding in Catrin's breast. This time she did back away. "How do you know about the chalice?"

"From your ancestress's diary, of course. Morys brought it to me for authentication. And that is when I began watching you and waiting for you to find the chalice. You see, although I was as astonished as you to read about the curse, what interested me the most was the chalice." He trained his steely gray eyes on her, unnerving her completely. "I do not suppose you have any idea of the significance of what you have found, do you? I mean, aside from its role in your family curse."

Unable to breathe or move, she merely stared at him, trying to understand what he was saying. He'd been watching her? For the chalice? But why?

"The warrior, the snake-wrapped maiden, and the raven are emblems of a sect of druids that practiced during the early Middle Ages," he was saying, "long after the original druids vanished from the shores of Brittany. In fact, artifacts from their sect are sometimes confused for artifacts from the earlier druids."

When her eyes went round in surprise, he added, "You did not know I shared your interest in such matters, did you, my dear? Of course, you and I have different reasons for our interest in the druids. You are attracted to their oneness with nature, their belief in the spirits of the forest."

Reaching into his waistcoat, he withdrew a long, curved knife and held it up. "I, on the other hand, am intrigued by their darker beliefs. They understood something that religion today has lost sight of. There is power in blood . . . the blood of the innocent *and* the blood of the guilty, sacrificed for the greater good of society."

She stared at the knife, every muscle in her body growing rigid with fear. By heaven, what did he intend to do with that thing. And why was he babbling about blood and the druids?

"That's not true," she whispered. "There is little to no evidence supporting the belief that the original druids practiced human sacrifice. Some scholars claim that the Roman church created the tales of such rituals to discredit the pagan culture."

"I know those theories. But they are wrong. Any fool who studies the Mabinogion and the culture of the ancient Celts recognizes that the shedding of blood was central to their faith." He frowned. "But enough of this discussion. As I have always known, you are much too tenderhearted to agree with me."

He stepped toward Catrin and lifted the knife to her throat. "Turn around," he murmured.

She was too shocked to move. Why was he doing this? What did he want from her that he would use a knife to get it?

"If you do as I say, Catrin, I shall not hurt you. But you *must* do as I say. Now turn around and put your hands behind your back."

Trembling from head to toe, she complied. She didn't quite believe he wouldn't hurt her, but neither did she want to find out what he'd do if she didn't obey him.

"Why do you want to hurt me?" she whispered as he grabbed her hands and wrapped his cravat around them. He must have put the knife away in order to tie her, but it did her little good to know that now.

"I do not want to hurt you," he answered. As if to contradict his own words, he twisted the cravat into a painfully tight knot.

She groaned, wishing she hadn't been so hasty to leave Evan behind. And where in God's name was David? This was one time she would welcome his appearance.

Leaning forward, Sir Reynald drew the scarf from around her neck. As he paused to stare down the front of her gown, his breath whispered over the bared upper swells of her breasts. "It would have been a shame to waste such loveliness on either Morys or Newcome. But I assure you I recognize its worth and will treat it with the tender care it deserves."

She shuddered. What did he mean? What did he intend to do with her?

With a sinking heart she felt him kneel behind her and secure her ankles with the scarf. When he drew the scarf tight and knotted it, she swayed a little, unable to keep her balance.

He steadied her with his hand, then rose and slid his arm about her waist. His mouth was just an inch from her ear as he rasped, "I am sorry to truss you this way, but I do not think you will play your proper role in tomorrow morning's little drama unless I do."

"T-tomorrow morning's drama?" she managed to whisper.

"Yes. Fate has dumped you in my lap. I certainly didn't expect to find you here waiting for me when I came to search Morys's desk for any . . . er . . . notes he might have left lying around that pointed to his relationship with me. I had intended to look for you later, then bring you here so I could put my plan into action. But Fate has placed you in my path. Now I won't have to delay the ceremony until Samhain."

With a shudder she recognized the name of the Celtic festival that fell in October, during the time when cattle were slaughtered in preparation for winter.

"I can hold it at dawn tomorrow," he continued, "on the day of the summer solstice, which is more fitting. As the sun rises for its day of greatest power, we will be joined in a union that will eclipse all others. We will be married, Catrin, at the altar, and then we will drink of the chalice."

He had the chalice? He was planning to marry her, for heaven's sake? "Married?" she choked out, uncertain whether to be relieved or horrified by the prospect. He wasn't going to kill her. But what he planned sounded worse.

"Yes, married. Oh, I know that you would never willingly marry me, but I have planned for that. After we are wed by one of the other druids of our sect, a priest, I will take you to my estate where you will have a room of your own."

An involuntary shiver rippled over her. "You will keep me a prisoner?"

"At least until you have sired my child, of course, and have given me a true descendant of the druids to mold in my image, to imbue with all the knowledge of the ancients. What happens next is up to you. You have two choices. Remain married to me and experience the power of the druids as it was meant to be . . . as your ancestress Morgana meant it to be. Or die. Either way, I shall have what I want—our child and your property and the altar that stands on it."

The altar? Did he mean the dolmen? He must, which

meant he was one of those strange men who crept onto her estate late at night to sacrifice birds and animals.

An involuntary shudder racked her as she forced herself to respond to what he was saying. "If you kill me, you'll never get my property."

"I'll be your husband. It will all be mine legally. Of course, I shall have to explain that you married me in secret, then fell ill and died, but no one will question that. The Ladies of the Mists have done stranger things. And I will, after all, have a will and testament in your own hand to prove that I am the rightful owner of Plas Niwl."

"You'll never get that from me," she whispered.

"Oh, I will, Catrin, I will. Do you think you can resist any torture? I don't think so. You are not made of the same stuff as your doughty old grandmother, are you?"

Terror gripped her, so powerful it made her every muscle go weak. Torture? He would torture her for her compliance? The man was mad, thoroughly mad! All this about druids and true descendants and altars . . . why had she never guessed that Sir Reynald was mad?

Because he was also crafty. But his insane plan couldn't succeed, could it? Evan knew she was here in Llanddeusant. He would come after her. He would find her.

How? a tiny voice whispered. *He won't know where to look for you, and he doesn't even realize that Sir Reynald is so treacherous. You certainly didn't.*

Suddenly, she remembered what Sir Reynald had said about watching her and waiting for her to find the chalice, and a deadly chill sliced through her. "You were the one who murdered Lord Mansfield, weren't you? It wasn't thieves. You followed me to London and you murdered him."

Surprising her with his strength, he lifted her and set her on David's desk so that she faced him. She had to brace herself with her bound hands to keep from falling over backward, but he didn't seem to care. "Yes, I did that. When Morys told me why you were going to London, I thought I finally had my chance to get both you and the chalice. I followed you to that dreadful inn, and when I saw a nobleman enter with a large box under his arm, I settled down to wait until you came out with the box. But you did not emerge. He did, and he no longer had a box. I waited for you as I watched him stroll down the street, but still you did not appear."

His eyes narrowed menacingly. "So I accosted him and asked him where you were. Unfortunately, he was decidedly uncommunicative about whom he had met with and where she had gone, and when I persisted in asking him questions, he put his hand on his sword hilt."

He shrugged. "I do not like it when people threaten me. So I made sure he did not have the chance to draw his sword."

Catrin shuddered, remembering what Evan had said about Lord Mansfield's brutal death. Sir Reynald truly was beyond reason if he could murder with so little cause. And he almost seemed to revel in it. His eyes were lit with glee and his face wore the expression of a boy pleased at his own naughtiness.

"Afterwards," he continued in a boasting tone, "I searched him to be sure he had nothing on him that might link him to me or you, and I took the letter and the money." He gave a cruel laugh. "It was rather amusing to steal back the 100 pounds I paid you for that painting and make a profit on it besides."

With voice hardening, he added, "Of course, it did not compensate for the loss of the chalice. I had thought to catch up to you at your lodgings, but you left before I got there and you never appeared on the ship, so I had no choice but to wait until you returned here to find out what had become of the chalice."

"Then I suppose David told you everything I told him," she whispered.

"Yes, although if I'd realized you were lying to him, I would have dispensed with his services sooner."

She almost didn't have to ask, but she did anyway. "Dispensed with his services? Have you . . . have you murdered David, too?"

He smiled. "Of course. How do you think I got the chalice back? Do you think he would have given it to me willingly? No, I had to take it from him." He leaned close to her, his eyes so bright with pleasure that she recoiled instantly. "I left him in the forest outside Carmarthen. I sacrificed him for the common good. Just as I sacrificed Lord Mansfield. And will sacrifice you, if you choose not to follow my rules."

Withdrawing the knife, he held the flat side of the blade against her cheek, letting her feel the cool metal as he stroked it along her jawbone and down her neck. "Things can be . . . pleasant between us, Catrin, or painful. I'd prefer pleasant. Wouldn't you?"

It suddenly dawned on her why he'd confessed his crimes to her. He wanted to frighten her into submission. He wanted her to know exactly what he was capable of, so she wouldn't waste his time with her attempts to avoid what he considered to be the inevitable.

That knowledge horrified her more than anything. She'd never met a man with no conscience, for whom reciting his crimes was merely a means to an end. A man like that might do anything.

Anything at all.

"We shall make a potent child together, you and I," he murmured. "A potent child indeed."

She searched for something . . . anything . . . she could say to put him off this mad course. "What if I tell you that I am already pregnant? With Evan Newcome's child?"

His face darkened. "Considering that you only met him a week ago, I would find that hard to believe. Even if you had let him bed you, you would not yet know if you were with child." He hesitated, searching her face. "But I know you, Catrin. You are not the sort of woman to leap into a man's bed without benefit of marriage. If you had wanted to take a lover, you would have done so before now."

"And . . . and if I had?" she persisted, wondering if that would make him release her.

"If I thought for one moment that you were not a virgin, I would kill you." The words hung between them, stark, cold, and sure. "But I know you are, so this ploy of yours will not work."

She trembled at the thought that she'd almost told him the truth. She'd almost provoked him to kill her. Not that her temporary release gained her much. If he ever did get so far as to bed her, he'd find out she wasn't a virgin anyway.

He brought the knife down to her breasts and amused himself by running the tip over each swell, smiling to see how her breath quickened in fear, making her breasts shake beneath the blade. She leaned back, trying to put some distance between herself and the knife, but the movement nearly overset her.

As her bound hands scrabbled for purchase on the desktop, she felt something cold and metallic beneath her fingers. She ran her hands along it, then vaguely remembered once seeing a silver letter opener on David's desk. Closing her fingers around it, she wedged it up between her tight bonds, hoping she could keep it hidden from Sir Reynald long enough to have the chance to use it.

He brought the tip of his knife down between her breasts and ran it along the hollow in a horrific caress. "It does no good to fight me, Catrin. No one who fights me ever wins. So any attempt to escape your fate is foolish, you know. In fact, now that you see what is planned for you, my dear, you should feel honored to be offered the chance to bear a new race."

"You won't get away with this," she whispered. "Evan will come in search of me, and he'll find me."

"Really? I do not believe you. And even if you are speaking the truth, it will do no good. He will not make it here before we are married, and by the time that is done, I shall have you locked up tight and cozy at my estate." With a chilling smile he brought the tip of the knife up along the side of one breast. "And we will have already begun the business of creating my heir."

Abruptly, he withdrew the knife and slid it inside his waistcoat. He drew out two handkerchiefs, stuffing one in her mouth until she gagged, then wrapping the other around her head to hold the first one in place.

"But for now, my dear, I shall have to dream of what will be between us once we are married. There is no time to do more. I still have to search Morys's office. Then I have to remove you from this too public place so I can make preparations for tomorrow morning."

He left her side to rifle David's desk, and she thought about sawing at her bonds with the letter opener. But he was at her back where he'd notice any movement she made, and she dared not risk having her puny weapon taken from her.

Despite the reassuring shaft of cold metal between her fingers, panic seized her. She was being held by a madman. And she could do nothing about it, nothing at all! She could only hope Evan found her, and as Sir Reynald had made quite clear, that was a slim hope indeed. Even the letter opener would help her only a little, for she had already determined that its edge was not in the least bit sharp.

The desk shuddered beneath her as Sir Reynald slammed drawer after drawer. Then he stopped as abruptly as he'd begun. "That is done then. Now it is time to leave." After an ominous silence he added, "But I do not want to deal with your struggles in the meantime. Sorry, my dear, I am afraid this is going to hurt."

Hurt? she thought.

Then something hit the back of her head, and she fell into complete darkness.

Chapter Twenty-three

I scarcely know a scurril name,
But dearly thou deserv'st the same;
Thou exhalation from the deep
Unknown, where ugly spirits keep!
—Anonymous, "The Mist"

Evan had thought he'd known terror before in his life, but he'd never known a terror like this. He felt as if someone were clawing his heart out with a hook bit by bit. Catrin had disappeared, and no one knew where to find her.

He and Rhys had ridden into Llanddeusant near midnight. They'd gone to Morys's house and school, but no Catrin. And now they were at Plas Niwl and Bos was telling them that he hadn't seen his mistress since she'd left to go to London with Evan.

Barely restraining the urge to grab the noncommittal butler by the throat, Evan growled, "Yes, Bos, I understand what you're saying, but we know she is in this vicinity. She left only a few hours before us. Surely you have some idea where she might be."

Bos pursed his lips. "Begging your pardon, sir, but if she left you, then perhaps she doesn't want to be found."

Only Rhys's hand on his shoulder prevented him from launching himself at the rigid-faced butler. "Listen to me, Bos!" Evan spat. "She may be in danger! Grave danger! That chalice she went to London to buy was taken from her—from us—by David Morys, and his murdered body turned up outside Carmarthen yesterday!"

Rhys added in more even tones, "We think Mr. Morys was killed by someone who wants the chalice. Unfortunately, Mrs. Price doesn't know of his murder and came here to get the chalice back from Mr. Morys."

Growing more frustrated by the moment, Evan thrust out the note Catrin had left behind, and Bos took it. As the butler scanned the note, his expression altered.

"We don't know who wanted that chalice so badly," Rhys continued, "but whoever it is has killed twice for it, and may not like the idea of her returning to get it."

When Bos glanced up at them, he was pale. "Truly, gentlemen, I have not seen my mistress. But I would be more than happy to join you in a search for her."

Worry twisted Evan's insides into knots. "Fine! But we don't know where the devil to search! She's not at Morys's, and she's not here, so where in God's green earth is she?"

Rhys frowned. "What if we try that father-in-law of hers? You said he had good cause to want to hurt her."

"I believe that is an excellent suggestion," Bos interjected. "Sir Huw has certainly never hidden his unwarranted dislike for my mistress."

Evan nodded. "He *is* a likely suspect. We'll go there next. It's the only possibility we haven't explored." As Rhys and Bos headed toward the entrance, Evan said, "Wait a minute. Bos, do you know where Catrin kept that diary, the one that describes the curse?"

The butler nodded. "It is still in the hidden shelf where she kept the chalice. She left the shelf open when you and she departed on your trip to Carmarthen."

"Good. I know it's unlikely, but perhaps something in the diary can give us an idea of why someone would kill for that chalice . . . or where Catrin might have gone to look for it."

"I shall fetch it at once," Bos said and strode off down the hall.

He returned a few moments later with an ancient-looking book. Evan took it and, after giving it a cursory glance, stuffed it into his waistcoat.

"Will you not peruse its contents?" Bos asked.

"There's no time," Evan said as he turned toward the door. "We must get to Sir Huw's house."

The next hour tried Evan sorely. It took them much too long to reach Sir Huw's estate, for although the moon was still full enough to give them ample light, the roads were bad. As they struggled along the last mile, Evan tried not to think about what danger Catrin might be in.

But it was difficult. He kept seeing Justin lying in a pool of blood. If that were ever Catrin—

He squelched that thought at once. He would not let her

be hurt. Somehow he'd find her . . . and the chalice, too, if that was what it took to win her.

Once they reached Sir Huw's estate, it took several minutes to rouse anyone and several more to convince the servants to awaken Sir Huw. But when the baronet strode down the stairs, still wearing his nightcap and belting a robe about his waist, Evan felt alarm set in. If Sir Huw had taken Catrin, he certainly hadn't let her presence deter him from sleep, had he?

"What is the meaning of this!" Sir Huw growled as he reached the bottom of the stairs and leveled a withering glance on all three men. "To wrench a man from his bed at this hour! To disturb his sleep! This is an outrage, and I want you all out of my house! Now!"

To everyone's surprise it was Bos who spoke first. "Begging your pardon, Sir Huw, but we are looking for Mrs. Price. It is a matter of some importance."

"Why the bloody hell would she be here?" the older man grumbled. He peered at Evan, then scowled when he recognized him. "Besides, I thought she'd run off to London with you, Mr. Newcome. That's what I heard, at any rate."

Bos and Rhys looked to Evan for the explanation. With an effort he tamped down his dislike of Sir Huw. "I'm afraid that Catrin is in some trouble, sir, and we thought you might shed light on where she might be." Then in as few words as possible, he told Sir Huw the tale of the curse and what had happened with the chalice. He finished by asking Sir Huw if he knew anything about the chalice at all or where Catrin might be.

Sir Huw looked as if someone had just hit him over the head with a shovel. His mouth was agape and his eyes glittered hollowly. He staggered forward a step, and when it looked as though he might fall, Bos stepped forward to steady him.

"Sir?" the butler asked, as always the perfect servant. "Are you ill?"

Sir Huw shook his head. "Come into my study, all of you," he whispered in a hoarse voice. "I want to hear more of this."

Impatient to be on with the search, Evan nearly refused, but Rhys's hand on his bandaged arm cautioned patience. So he followed Sir Huw and Bos as they headed toward the study together.

As soon as they were in the massive room and Bos had ensconced Sir Huw in a chair, Evan snapped, "Well? Do you know where she is? Or who might want the chalice?"

Sir Huw shook his head. "I have no idea. I know you've come here because you think I might have . . . done this thing. But I am innocent." He lifted his gaze to Bos. "Mr. Bos, you know I wouldn't do such a thing . . . murder people . . . steal. . . ."

Bos leveled on him a cold stare. "You must admit, sir, that you are not fond of my mistress. You have maligned her publicly."

"Only because I truly believed she caused my son's death," he protested.

"How?" Evan exploded. "By witchery? By spells and enchantments? What kind of a man are you to use superstition to punish a woman for a tragedy that harmed her as much as it did you?"

Sir Huw's face crumbled. "'Tis not so strange that I would believe it, is it? There *was* a curse upon my poor Willie, after all, though I didn't understand until this night the nature of it."

"I don't believe in your bloody curse!" Evan said. "But Catrin does. Have you any idea of the guilt she has lived with because of your son's death? She blames herself because she didn't know about the curse. And she's in this mess because although she wants a life and a future, she's determined to make sure no one else dies!"

"Like Willie, you mean," Sir Huw persisted.

"Oh, for God's sake—" Evan growled. "This is getting us nowhere." It was becoming more and more clear to him that Sir Huw had known nothing of the curse and the chalice, which meant it was unlikely he'd had anything to do with Catrin's disappearance. "Come, Rhys, let's see if we can find another who might know where she is."

"Wait!" the baronet said, rising from his chair. "I admit I was wrong to blame her. From what you say, she didn't know of the curse. And she *has* suffered for it." His voice dropped to a whisper. "I know that."

"Your remorse is touching, Sir Huw," Evan bit out, "but it doesn't help us find her."

"Perhaps it is time to look at the diary, sir," Bos prodded. "Although I cannot imagine how it would be of any help, one never knows."

Evan nodded. He didn't know where else to look. Drawing forth the leatherbound book, he opened it and scanned the thin, fragile pages. When he noticed that the book seemed to fall naturally open at one spot, he found that place.

"This is it," he said as he read the words there. "This is the part about the curse."

He read it aloud for the others, but was frustrated to discover that nothing in it was very informative. It was a basic rendering of what sounded almost like a myth, yet it gave him shivers. There was something very powerful in the words, something that automatically evoked fear and caution in the reader. No wonder Catrin had read it and believed it. When he coupled the words with what he knew of her family history, he could almost believe it himself.

"The chalice sounds ancient," Rhys remarked. "Perhaps it has intrinsic value. Perhaps someone wanted it solely because of that."

Evan shook his head. "I don't think so. This book is more likely to be of value than the chalice. Believe me, if the thing were truly of great monetary value, Lady Mansfield would have discovered that years ago and sold it off herself for what it was worth. Besides, I've seen the thing. It's ugly, and though it does have some sort of symbols on it . . . druidic, I think . . . it—"

He broke off as something nagged at his memory. He read the tale of the curse again. " 'Ancient ways.' From the use of the word 'Saxon,' I'd guess this is chronicling a medieval event. But 'ancient ways' might refer to the druids, mightn't it? I suppose there could still have been a few druids during the Middle Ages."

"There's a dolmen on Catrin's land—" Sir Huw began.

"Yes, I know," Evan said, his heart pounding. "And there are practicing druids hereabouts. I found that out one day when I came upon Sir Reynald and Catrin's gamekeeper, who were discussing how to deal with the men who'd trespassed on Catrin's land to perform sacrifices at the dolmen."

"Sir Reynald?" said Sir Huw with a scowl. "Now there's another person who's been wanting Catrin's land. It adjoins his, you know. He's made her offer after offer, but she won't sell to him."

"I don't see how gaining the chalice would help him with that," Rhys said. "If she remarries, she'd be more likely to sell it to him than less, for she needs the property as long as she's unmarried."

Evan shook his head. He felt as if a cold hand had reached in to grab his insides. "We're missing the point. Sir Reynald didn't take the chalice because he wants her land. He took it for the same reason he wants the land—because it's druidic just as the altar on her land is druidic."

He clutched the diary. "That day when I saw them at the altar, they said it was Sir Reynald's bull that had been sacrificed. It was the *second* one of his bulls that had been sacrificed." He shrugged, remembering the bloody, mangled body of that bull. "Don't you find that odd? If someone were going to steal cattle to use for such dastardly purposes, don't you think they'd steal from different people? Sir Reynald was furious, but I'd wager it wasn't because the bull had been butchered, but because his companions, whoever they might be, hadn't cleaned up the mess they'd left behind from the ritual of the night before."

"Isn't that jumping to conclusions a bit?" Rhys asked.

"I don't know," Evan countered. "But I find it very suspicious that it was Sir Reynald's bull that was butchered and Sir Reynald that wants the land with the altar on it."

"I hate to interrupt this intriguing discussion," said Bos, "but all of this talk of druids has reminded me of something. Today is June 21st."

"The summer solstice," Evan whispered. "Oh, God, we must get to that altar! I'll wager that's where we'll find both Catrin and the chalice!"

Sir Huw rose as the three of them headed toward the door. "I'm coming with you. It sounds as if there may be more than one of these druid fellows, and you'll need help."

"Why do you care?" Evan ground out. "I thought you hated Catrin."

"If that chalice caused my son's death, then I wish to make sure it causes no one else's." He stared solemnly at the three men. "It's the least I can do when my daughter-in-law has risked her life to do the same. Besides, you'll need weapons. And I'm something of a hunter, so I can provide them."

A curt nod was Evan's only answer, but in truth, he was glad to have yet another man on this mission, as well as the weapons. He had no idea what they would be facing—a single madman or several. And given what little he knew of druids and their sometimes bloody practices . . .

As Sir Huw hurried to gather his hunting weapons, Evan shuddered, trying not to think of Catrin lying atop that awful pagan altar. If anything happened to her, what would he do? How would he live the rest of his life without her, burdened by the knowledge that he had somehow failed her . . . that he had come too late?

Sir Huw brought out an impressive array of flintlock rifles and hunting knives, and Evan stared at them, then made a decision. Slowly, he drew off his shirt and coat, then unwrapped the sling that had held his arm in place for the past few days.

"What are you doing?" Rhys hissed. "You need that sling."

"I need the arm more right now," Evan retorted. "I can't fight with my arm in a sling." He flexed the muscle, wincing when he felt it pull on his shoulder. But he knew he had no choice. He wouldn't be much good to them with one arm tied up.

Ignoring Rhys's scowl, he donned his shirt and coat again, then chose two rifles and a sword for good measure. He could endure a little pain if he had to. But he could never endure the possibility of losing Catrin because he was hampered by his bandages.

He had one thing in his favor. He'd spent most of his early life dealing with physical pain. If he had to, he could go through the fires of hell and endure it, especially if it meant saving Catrin.

And he greatly feared he might have to do so before tonight was over.

When Catrin came to, she was still bound and gagged. She was sitting outdoors, propped against something cold. It was dark yet, but she could already sense the changes that came just before dawn . . . a far-off rooster crowing . . . birds chirping . . . the dimming of the stars.

Or were the stars dim because the night was overcast? She couldn't quite tell. There was a fire lit on the ground, but it was small and gave only the faintest light. For a second she wondered where she was and why she was bound. Then Sir Reynald stepped in front of her, and everything came back to her.

"I see that my druid princess is awake," he murmured. He had changed his clothing and now wore a long, belted white robe with ancient symbols embroidered on its hem. A crown of some sort of greenery, probably mistletoe, ringed his balding head, making him look like a ludicrous impersonation of Caesar.

But there was nothing ludicrous about the knife tucked into his woven belt, nor the evil smile that crossed his face as he gazed at her. "You know where you are, don't you, my dear? You should. It's on your land."

The dolmen, she thought, remembering what he'd said before about the altar. She peered around the dimly lit clearing and was just able to make out the towering shapes of trees.

The damp, cold air drove a chill into her bones. The fire was much too small and far away to provide her any heat. They'd probably lit it only to give a little light, and once dawn came, it wouldn't even be necessary.

But she would have liked to warm her hands at it. They seemed numb from both cold and all the hours of being bound. She flexed her fingers, and that's when she felt the metal shaft still wedged between her bound hands.

The letter opener. Thank heaven it was still there. It gave her a small measure of comfort. At least she had a weapon, even if it was a rather meager one.

She tried moving the shaft up and down against her bonds, and discovered, to her relief, that she could indeed do so. Although the letter opener was dull, at least it had an edge. Maybe if she sawed at the cravat long enough, she could free herself.

Suddenly, Sir Reynald startled her by clapping his hands. For a moment she feared he'd realized what she was doing. But she knew he hadn't when he called out, "Ifor! Where are you?"

A man materialized out of the darkness. He was dressed much as Sir Reynald was, except that he lacked the circlet of mistletoe. She'd seen him before. He was a laborer on Sir Reynald's land, which would explain why he was here.

"Have you posted a man at the road?"

"Yes," the man said. "And we've got someone at each corner of the clearing."

"Good." Sir Reynald scanned the clearing. "I don't expect encroachers, but we mustn't take any chances. The others will be arriving any minute." He paused. "I don't see the bull for the sacrifice."

"Dafydd is bringing it," the man called Ifor said. "'Tis difficult since he cannot follow the road."

"I don't care how difficult it is," Sir Reynald spat. "The bull must be here in time for the ceremony."

Catrin silently prayed that the bull would run off. But she knew that wasn't likely.

Thunder rumbled in the distance, and Ifor scowled. "There's a storm brewing. 'Tis a bad omen to have a storm on the morning of the solstice, the day of the sun. Perhaps we should wait—"

"No!" With a glance at her Sir Reynald added, "The Fates have already given her to me. That's a good omen. Besides, the storm is a symbol of power. I welcome the thunder and the lightning, for someday my descendants will rule them both."

She shivered at the thought of a race of Sir Reynalds. She'd kill herself before she let him make her part of that.

But she didn't intend to die yet, she told herself as she worked the letter opener up and down in the same spot. It didn't seem to be doing much, but she couldn't simply sit here like a trussed-up sheep and do nothing.

The clearing began to fill with men, and her heart sank when a flash of lightning revealed twenty in all. *Twenty men.* Even if she did saw through her bonds, how on earth would she escape twenty men? Especially when she was the main attraction at this absurd ritual.

She studied the faces, wondering who her oppressors were to be, but was surprised to find she didn't recognize most of them. There were a few farmers and a tradesman or two from Llanddeusant, but the others were all strangers.

This is probably the only druid ritual for miles, she thought acidly. *They had to make a special trip to participate in this.*

Then one man separated from the others, moving close to Sir Reynald, and she recognized the priest from a neighboring parish. It startled her to see a man of the cloth among such scoundrels, but if Jesus could have his Judas, she supposed the Anglican church could have its druid priest.

Everyone's eyes were on her now, and she shrank back involuntarily against the stone. Although she was fully dressed, except for her scarf, she felt naked before the assessing eyes of this throng. Briefly, she wondered what Sir Reynald would do with her once he discovered she wasn't a virgin. Would he bring her here again, only this time to sacrifice her? He and his companions practiced ghastly animal sacrifices, but did they ever sacrifice humans? Were they such monsters?

The wind was howling through the trees now, the otherworldly sound fueling her fear. She lifted her face to the wind, trying not to think of what was to come, of what Sir Reynald planned for her. It would only make her weak, and she must be strong now.

Sir Reynald gave a signal, and two men stepped forward. One of them bent to untie her ankles, while the other removed her gag. Then they caught her under the arms and jerked her up. As they did so, her wrists strained against the cravat, and she felt the cloth give a fraction.

As soon as she was on her feet, they released her, but her legs had long ago lost all feeling, thanks to her bonds, and she fell to her knees. This time it was Sir Reynald who came to her side and lifted her, holding her against him with one iron arm.

Her feet were on fire now as they came awake, and she had to bite her tongue to keep from crying out. She wasn't sure she could cry out anyway, for her mouth felt as dry as dust after having been stuffed with the handkerchief. Running her tongue over her lips, she wondered how they expected to force her to voice marriage vows. Or did they even care if she spoke any agreement?

Lightning streaked across the predawn sky as Sir Reynald began to speak of the wedding that the gods had sanctioned and the future that was to come of their holy union. As he droned on and on, she moved her wrists a fraction and discovered that between the sawing she'd done and the pressure the men had put on her bonds, she'd torn the cravat just enough to loosen it.

She thought she could wriggle out of it. But not yet, she told herself. She'd have to wait for the right moment. Still, at least she had her hands now. And that was something.

Chapter Twenty-four

The black night shall not toss
Nor for long the storm rage,
No man to carry the cross
Is dealt too long an age;
Delightful is yon rising dawn
Promising soon a glorious morn.
—William Williams Pantycelyn, "Fair Weather"

Evan and his companions crouched in the woods around the dolmen. Lightning crackled overhead, and Evan groaned as it lit up the clearing before them. They had Catrin. Even without the lightning, he could see her leaning against the dolmen. In the storm-dulled light of dawn, her pink gown stood in marked contrast to the white-robed men surrounding her.

She appeared to be unharmed, but it was hard to tell, for the wind whipped her beautiful hair about her face and her gown about her slender form. Her legs did seem too weak to hold her up, however, and he noticed that her hands were bound behind her back.

Rage surged through him, especially when Sir Reynald drew her close and planted a kiss on her lips. Evan leapt to his feet, but Rhys jerked him down again.

"Don't be a fool, man!" Rhys growled. "You won't save her that way." He scanned the clearing, then added, "There's near to twenty of them, and a nasty-looking lot, too."

Evan ground his teeth together. At the moment he felt capable of tearing every one of them limb from limb.

"What in God's name is the bloody bastard planning to do with her?" Sir Huw hissed. "I see he's got a bull out there. Surely he isn't planning to sacrifice her if he's got an animal to sacrifice. Wait! Look, he's pulling out that chalice you were telling me about! He's holding it up and saying something."

Sir Reynald did indeed have the chalice, and now he had

stepped away from Catrin to fill it with what looked like red wine. In any case, Evan hoped it was red wine and not something more gruesome.

Evan surveyed the clearing, a sense of urgency making his heart pound. "It looks like they've got men posted along the circumference of the clearing. One . . . two . . . I think there's four."

"One for each of us," Rhys said grimly. "Perhaps we should take them first, while everyone is engrossed in whatever bizarre ritual this is." He glanced at Bos. "Do you think you could manage that, Mr. Bos?"

Bos scowled. "I assure you, sir, I am perfectly capable of doing whatever it takes to defend my mistress from skullduggery of this sort."

"Good, we need every man we can get." Evan assessed the scene, then turned to Rhys. "The only way we'll get through this, I'm afraid, is by trickery. They outnumber us four to one. But we have the element of surprise . . . and we have rifles. Nothing alarms a man so quickly as the roar of a flintlock."

"How do you intend to keep Sir Reynald from harming my mistress?" Bos asked.

"Leave Sir Reynald to me," Evan retorted. He had a few ideas about how to manage this rescue, but he was afraid they had little chance of succeeding. Still, they must try. "Now here's what I think we should do. . . ."

Relief surged through Catrin when Sir Reynald insisted that they two stand on one side of the dolmen altar while the priest stood on the other side for the ceremony. Thanks to Sir Reynald's belief in his own self-importance, the crowd of men stood behind the priest so that Catrin and Sir Reynald were alone on the side of the dolmen closest to the trees.

That meant her hands were hidden from everyone. Thank heavens. If she could somehow distract the men long enough to run into the forest behind her and Sir Reynald, she might lose all of them, especially if the storm broke. It was a slim possibility at best, but somehow she knew that this would be her only chance to escape Sir Reynald. Once he had her on his estate, there'd be no escape. She felt sure of that.

But how to distract them? She wriggled the cravat off her

hands, then clenched the letter opener tightly between her fingers. There was one way. If she focused their concern on their leader, she might slip away in the confusion. It was worth the attempt.

She heard a faint rustle in the woods behind her and thought briefly of the snakes and boars that still roamed this area. But she refused to dwell on that horrible thought. At the moment she'd prefer the honest and predictable anger of a boar to the madness of the man at her side.

Her hands grew clammy on the letter opener. The priest was already intoning the words of the wedding mass. Thunder cracked overhead, making everyone jump. But the priest went on after only a short pause.

She must seize the moment now . . . or face a future too grisly to consider. Although the thought of what she was about to do nauseated her, she had no choice. None at all.

Before anyone could even notice what she was doing, she stepped back and lifted the letter opener in her right hand, bringing it down toward the center of Sir Reynald's back in what might have been a deadly stroke if he hadn't turned just as she brought her arm down with all her strength.

Instead, the letter opener drove into his shoulder. He let out a ear-splitting scream. For a moment she stood there in shock, watching the blood course down the pristine white sleeve of his robe. Then she turned to run.

At first, she was so intent on escaping that she didn't hear the sound of guns firing behind her. But when pandemonium ensued, and she spotted Evan running toward her from the trees, she realized that something more than her attack on their leader had occurred. There was a pause, then another volley of shots went off, sending the men in the clearing scattering into the woods around her.

"Evan!" she sobbed as he reached her and caught her up in his arms. "Evan, you're here!"

"We've got to get you away from this," he muttered as he hooked his good arm about her waist and pulled her with him toward the shelter of the trees behind them. "I told them to aim just above their heads, but a stray shot might still hit us."

As if to confirm his words, some shots whistled past them, but they were not at all high. Evan dropped to the ground, taking her with him. He glanced around and Catrin followed his gaze, alarmed to see two of Sir Reynald's men shoot at whomever fired at them from the woods. Sir Reynald himself leaned over the dolmen. As he shouted to his men, "Murder every one of the bastards," he wrenched the letter opener from his arm.

"Deuce take it, some of them are armed," Evan growled. "Someone should have told these bastards that druids don't carry pistols."

A brief silence hit the clearing, punctuated only by the whine of the wind and a nearby roll of thunder. "We'll have to take our chances," Evan muttered as he scanned the now empty clearing.

He sprang to a crouch and tugged on her arm. But as they turned toward the woods again, Catrin groaned, for five men were blocking their path.

Evan pushed her behind him and drew his sword, but Catrin could see at once that he would never win this fight. And when someone grabbed her from behind, put a knife to her neck, and called out to Evan, "Drop the sword!" she was almost relieved. She didn't want Evan to die in her defense.

With a cry of utter anguish Evan turned to see her with a knife at her throat. He dropped the sword at once, his face ash white as his gaze riveted on the knife. The five men rushed up behind him at once to restrain him. Only then did the man holding her take the knife from her throat.

Then other men filtered into the clearing, pushing three men ahead of them. Despair hit her as she realized who they were—Bos, Sir Huw, and Rhys Vaughan. They had all come to her rescue, and they would all die.

"You fools!" shouted a voice to the right of them, and everyone turned to see Sir Reynald standing atop the dolmen.

As Catrin caught sight of his bloody sleeve, she wondered how he'd managed to crawl atop the dolmen. But then, he didn't seem human anymore. Gone was any hint of age in his demeanor. His eyes were alight with fury, and in his white robe he looked like some invincible god.

Fear washed over her in waves. This was the man who intended to make her the mother of his child . . . who would torture her if she didn't comply. And if she'd had any doubt before that he could and would do it, she had none now.

Rain started to fall in fat drops, but Sir Reynald seemed

oblivious to it, for he withdrew the dagger from his belt and pointed it at Evan.

"You, sir, have made a grave mistake. You shall be our sacrifice for this evening instead of that bull there." He smiled, but to Catrin it looked more like a grimace than a smile. "But first you will watch me wed your love. And then take her here, on this very altar. I had planned something more private, but this is much better, is it not?"

Evan roared, straining against the men that held him. "You can't kill us all, Sir Reynald! How will you hide the murders of a baronet, a prominent squire, and a respected scholar? They'll find you! They'll hunt you down like the dog that you are and they'll hang you!"

Sir Reynald laughed. "You don't understand, you fool. *I* have power beyond what you ever dreamed. I have spent years studying the ways of the ancients, and when I couple my knowledge with the power of the chalice, no one will ever cross me. Never!" He held the chalice high. "As the legend of the chalice says, marriage to a descendant of Morgana's will make the husband as strong and powerful as the warrior! When Catrin and I say our vows and drink from the chalice, we will both be as gods, I tell you! Gods!"

Catrin's eyes went wide as she stared at the chalice, for it had begun to glow, as if to confirm what Sir Reynald said about the power imbued in it. An orange light shimmered over the bronze, growing more intense as she stared at it. It was like nothing she'd ever seen. The druids were murmuring and pointing, and for a moment absolute terror gripped her. How could she fight such power from the beyond? She and Evan and the rest of them were nothing but puny ants in the face of the ancient legend of the chalice.

But as Sir Reynald held the glowing vessel high, his face contorted with his greed for power, a clap of thunder sounded, so loud that she and the man who held her staggered back. And the sight before her struck her dumb.

Lightning had struck the chalice and now consumed Sir Reynald, pummeling him with a force beyond anything Catrin had ever witnessed. She couldn't turn her face away, couldn't move, couldn't utter a sound. Indeed, the only sound in the clearing was the crackling of nature's wrath at the center of the dolmen.

Then as suddenly as it had come, the lightning released

Sir Reynald, and he crumpled over, tumbling off the dolmen and to the ground like a marionette tossed aside by its maker.

Catrin averted her face from the sight of Sir Reynald's blackened body, but she couldn't keep out the smell of burned flesh. The man who'd been holding her cried, "It's an omen, a bad omen!" and fled, as did the other druids in the clearing, all shouting much the same thing.

In seconds the only ones left in the circle of trees were she and Evan and his companions. Evan rushed to her side, gathering her up in his arms with a cry.

She buried her face in his chest, her heart racing as the tears began to flow. "Oh, Evan . . . oh, my God, Evan . . ."

"Are you all right?" he whispered as he clutched her tightly to his chest. "Did that monster hurt you or touch you or—"

"No . . . No . . . although he was planning to marry me and keep me his prisoner . . . but you heard what he—" She broke off in a flurry of fresh sobs.

He stroked her back, whispering comforting words and endearments. "You're safe now, love. You're safe with me. He cannot hurt you anymore."

She went very still. "Is he dead?" she asked, though she knew he must be. No one survived a bolt of lightning like that.

"I'm sure he is." He buried his face in her hair. "Did you see the chalice, Catrin, before the lightning struck?"

"I saw." She lifted her face to his, knowing that her expression must hold the same look of shock that his now held. "What made it glow, Evan?"

He shook his head with a dazed look in his eyes. "I don't know, love. I don't know."

"Holy God in heaven!" exclaimed a voice behind them, and Catrin turned to see Sir Huw standing over the dolmen. "Would you look at this? The stone is split in two!"

Catrin shuddered from head to toe as she hid her face in Evan's shirt once more, unable even to bear the sight of the cracked dolmen. She would never forget the expression on Sir Reynald's face as the lightning hit him . . . a mixture of horror and disbelief and shock. No one deserved such a death, not even a villain like him.

And yet . . . and yet there was something fitting in it. He

had wanted power . . . and he'd gotten it, more power than a human could withstand. Perhaps there were things humans were not meant to have . . . or see or be.

"What about the chalice?" Evan called out to Sir Huw. "What happened to it?"

Catrin tensed. The chalice. Yes, what *had* happened to the chalice?

It was Rhys who answered, his voice low and full of awe. "Come see. You won't believe this."

Evan started to leave her side, but she shook her head and went with him. All of this had happened because of her strange heirloom from the past, and she wanted to see what had become of it. They were both careful to skirt the side of the dolmen where Bos was kneeling beside Sir Reynald's body, examining it for any signs of life.

As they went to Rhys's side, Catrin tried not to look at the dolmen and the black crack in the midst of it. But when she caught sight of the chalice—or what was left of it—lying on the edge of the dolmen, she gasped.

The lightning had melted the metal down to a misshapen lump. Where the image of the raven had been was only a swirled surface of blackened bronze.

But on the other side of the lump the image of the maiden and the warrior were perfectly intact.

Almost in a trance, Catrin reached out to touch it, but Evan grabbed her hand. "Don't. It's still hot, and you'll burn yourself."

She stared at the twisted metal, then whispered, "I don't suppose anyone will be drinking out of it now."

"No, love, I don't think so," Evan murmured.

"I'm thinking that someone needs to send for the constable in Carmarthen," Sir Huw said. "I'll see to that." He turned and walked from the clearing.

Rhys murmured, "I'll make sure none of those bastards is lurking in the forest, though I'd be surprised. I think they were all frightened out of their wits. I know I was." Then he headed off toward the woods skirting the clearing.

"With your permission, madam," Bos said, "I shall return to the house and inform the staff of what has occurred. They are all no doubt beside themselves with worry."

Catrin nodded, then watched as Bos, too, left, so that only she and Evan remained.

Clasping her about the waist, Evan led her away from the dolmen and through the clearing. The storm seemed miraculously to have disappeared. It was if Sir Reynald had created a disturbance in the very elements that subsided the moment his presence was removed.

Now the first light of dawn was breaking over the tops of the trees, limning the ancient oaks with golds and reds and lavenders . . . a veritable celebration of color.

Catrin paused in the center of the clearing and glanced up at the sky, thinking of all that had occurred, all the damage Sir Reynald had wrought. Yet Nature passed over it as if it were only a ripple in the surface of eternity.

"I think you should know," she told Evan. "It was Sir Reynald who killed your friend Justin. He . . . he learned about the chalice through David, and he has been waiting ever since to take it . . . and to take me."

"Yes, I know," Evan murmured, tightening his arm about her waist. "He also murdered David Morys."

A shiver passed over her. "Sir Reynald said as much to me." A tear slipped down her cheek. "So many men have died because of Morgana's wretched chalice. The men in my family. Willie. Your friend. And now David, poor man. I wonder if Morgana dreamed of the legacy of pain she would create in her petulance over her daughter's marriage."

Evan drew in a ragged breath. "You know, Catrin, I have never believed in . . . in magic or druids or such. But then, I have never seen anything like what I saw today. Never in my life."

Her pulse racing, she left his side to stand alone, looking at the clouds that had gone from black and thundering to white and floating in a matter of moments. "So what do we do now? What is to happen to us?"

He came up behind her and slipped his arm about her waist. "We marry and we have children and we love each other for the rest of our lives. That's what we do."

"But what about the curse?" she whispered in an aching voice.

"Don't you see, Catrin? The chalice has been destroyed. You can't be expected to drink from a chalice that no longer exists."

"Yes, but perhaps it was destroyed because I am meant to be cursed forever."

He nuzzled her hair. "I don't believe that. In fact, I think it's the opposite entirely. I think that when Sir Reynald tried to wrest the power of the chalice for evil purposes, Morgana put an end to it for all time. That's why the raven, a Celtic symbol of death, has been obliterated from what's left of the chalice, leaving only the image of the warrior and the maiden." He kissed her ear. "Us, my love. Us. I may not be much of a rescuer, and you may not have hair that twines down to your toes, but we are the warrior and the maiden all the same. And Morgana is giving us her blessing."

It made sense. Still, she'd lived so long in fear of the curse that it made her uneasy to think of marrying without the chalice, of risking Evan. "But what if—"

"Catrin," he murmured, turning her to face him. "I love you. I want to marry you. And you want to marry me. For once in your life, risk everything. Take hold of happiness with both hands and say, 'To hell with the curse and fear and death. I want to live. And I want to live with Evan.' "

He ventured a smile as he lifted her chin with the tip of his finger. "Because if you don't say it, love, I swear I will hound you until the day you die all alone and pining after me in your great mansion. And then I shall lay down beside you and die, too, for life without you is no life at all."

She stared up at the face of the man she loved more than breath, the only man she'd ever wanted to risk anything for. The thought of losing him to some nameless force beyond her understanding terrified her still, but what terrified her more was the thought of losing him to her own fear.

He was right. Even three years with the one she loved would be better than none. And no years with him would be like dying, so what would be the point?

"Will you risk it, my love?" he whispered. "Will you take the chance and be my wife?"

There really was no choice at all, was there? she thought. She twined her arms about his neck and smiled at him with all the love that warmed her soul. "Yes, my love. Oh, yes. Forever and ever and ever."

And the sweet, searing kiss that he then gave her was the best foretaste of forever that she could want. The very best.

Epilogue

While the waters murmur deep,
While the shepherd charms his sheep,
While the birds unbounded fly
And with music fill the sky—
Now, even now, my joys run high.
—John Dyer, "Grongar Hill"

Catrin awakened in the dark, predawn hours on the day after the third anniversary of her and Evan's wedding. She lay there a moment, thinking of the lovely celebration they'd had the night before—both the sedate one they'd had in the dining room and the scandalous one they'd had later in the bedroom.

With a contented smile she rolled over to face Evan, but the bed was empty, and her breathing stopped.

Three years. It had been three years and a day.

As she slipped out of bed and searched for her wrapper, she told herself she was being foolish to worry so. Evan was almost never in bed when she arose, for he favored mornings. He liked to watch the sun rise over the Carmarthenshire Fans to the east before he began the work of the day—helping her run Plas Niwl and writing his books.

Nonetheless, she dressed hurriedly and rushed out of the bedchamber that they shared at Plas Niwl. She wouldn't feel secure until she'd seen him.

She padded down the hall past the open door to the nursery, then stopped when she heard a deep male voice coming from inside the room.

A rush of relief hit her as she entered the nursery to find Evan sitting in a chair by the window. Two-year-old Justine was curled up in his lap with her thumb stuck in her mouth, and both father and daughter stared out the east-facing window, awaiting the dawn that trembled on the edge of the horizon.

Catrin smiled, a lump forming in her throat as she

watched them. Although Justine had Catrin's coloring and features, it was Evan that the little girl most emulated. She, too, could never sleep past dawn, and she was far braver than Catrin had ever been, getting into more scrapes than any young girl should. And already she was bilingual, speaking both Welsh and English words in her childish sentences.

But it was Welsh that she spoke now. "Papa," she said in her lilting voice, "sing me about the maid in the garden."

"Yes, my sweet," he murmured. Then in a low, rumbling voice he began to sing the first verse of an old Irish folk song that Justine had fallen in love with the first time she'd heard it:

> There was a maid in her father's garden
> A gentleman then passing by
> He stood a while and he gazed upon her
> Saying "Fair young lady, will you marry me?"

Catrin stood motionless as he continued singing about the maid whose long-lost love returns to claim her after seven years at sea. His hand stroked Justine's tousled curls, and Justine watched him with the trusting expression children reserve only for their parents.

The lump in Catrin's throat tightened into an almost painful knot. It was hard to believe that Evan had ever worried about being a father, that he'd once feared he might do violence to any child of theirs. He was so good to Justine, so kind and patient.

Sometimes he was *too* kind and patient, Catrin thought with a wry smile, for Justine wrapped him about her little finger with ease.

But Catrin could never deny him the pleasure of spoiling his daughter. She knew what it meant to him to see Justine's face light up at his words of praise.

Catrin placed her hand on the faint swell of her stomach. And she would let him spoil the next child and the next and the next, so long as he loved them all.

He finished the song and glanced up, then caught sight of her standing there.

A smile instantly broke over his face. "You're up early

this morning, my love. Have you come to watch the sunrise with us for a change?"

His words abruptly reminded her of why she'd been searching for him, but now her fears seemed utterly foolish. He probably didn't even realize what day it was. After all, neither of them had spoken of the curse since that morning in the clearing when she'd agreed to marry him.

"I . . . I woke up . . . and you weren't there and . . ." She trailed off, uncertain whether to even mention what had made her hurry from her bed in such an uncharacteristic manner.

But as she moved to his side, he took her hand and squeezed it. His eyes were solemn as he stared up at her. "I'm here, my love. I'm alive and well and plan to remain so for the rest of our lives."

So he *did* remember, she thought as he drew her to stand next to the chair. And he understood.

As always, he didn't belittle or chastise her for her fears. He simply showed them for what they were—shadows—mists and shapes that could not bear up under the light of day . . . the light of their all-consuming love.

She hadn't realized until now how much this particular fear had permeated her life . . . how much she'd been terrified of waking up to find at the end of three years that she was still accursed, doomed to lose the only man she'd ever loved.

"Life is good, isn't it, my love?" Evan said as he lifted his face to hers.

She smiled and bent to kiss his lips. "Life is indeed good," she murmured. "Very, very good."

And as the sun broke over the mountains in a shower of pink and orange and lavender, dusting the greening hills with a shimmer of golden light, the last vestiges of worry and despair melted away from her like so much dew beneath the heat of the morning sun.

WE NEED YOUR HELP

To continue to bring you quality romance
that meets your personal expectations,
we at TOPAZ books want to hear from you.
Help us by filling out this questionnaire, and in exchange
we will give you a **free gift** as a token of our gratitude.

- Is this the first TOPAZ book you've purchased? (circle one)

  YES NO

  The title and author of this book is: ____________________

- If this was not the first TOPAZ book you've purchased, how many have you bought in the past year?

  a: 0 - 5 b 6 - 10 c: more than 10 d: more than 20

- How many romances in total did you buy in the past year?

  a: 0 - 5 b: 6 - 10 c: more than 10 d: more than 20 ____

- How would you rate your overall satisfaction with this book?

  a: Excellent b: Good c: Fair d: Poor

- What was the main reason you bought this book?

  a: It is a TOPAZ novel, and I know that TOPAZ stands for quality romance fiction
  b: I liked the cover
  c: The story-line intrigued me
  d: I love this author
  e: I really liked the setting
  f: I love the cover models
  g: Other: ____________________

- Where did you buy this TOPAZ novel?

  a: Bookstore b: Airport c: Warehouse Club
  d: Department Store e: Supermarket f: Drugstore
  g: Other: ____________________

- Did you pay the full cover price for this TOPAZ novel? (circle one)

  YES NO

  If you did not, what price did you pay? ____________________

- Who are your favorite TOPAZ authors? (Please list)

- How did you first hear about TOPAZ books?

  a: I saw the books in a bookstore
  b: I saw the TOPAZ Man on TV or at a signing
  c: A friend told me about TOPAZ
  d: I saw an advertisement in ____________________ magazine
  e: Other: ____________________

- What type of romance do you generally prefer?

  a: Historical b: Contemporary
  c: Romantic Suspense d: Paranormal (time travel, futuristic, vampires, ghosts, warlocks, etc.)
  d: Regency e: Other: ____________________

- What historical settings do you prefer?

  a: England b: Regency England c: Scotland
  e: Ireland f: America g: Western Americana
  h: American Indian i: Other: ____________________

- What type of story do you prefer?
  - a: Very sexy
  - b: Sweet, less explicit
  - c: Light and humorous
  - d: More emotionally intense
  - e: Dealing with darker issues
  - f: Other

- What kind of covers do you prefer?
  - a: Illustrating both hero and heroine
  - b: Hero alone
  - c: No people (art only)
  - d: Other__________

- What other genres do you like to read (circle all that apply)

  Mystery, Medical Thrillers, Science Fiction, Suspense, Fantasy, Self-help, Classics, General Fiction, Legal Thrillers, Historical Fiction

- Who is your favorite author, and why?____________________

  ____

- What magazines do you like to read? (circle all that apply)
  - a: *People*
  - b: *Time/Newsweek*
  - c: *Entertainment Weekly*
  - d: *Romantic Times*
  - e: *Star*
  - f: *National Enquirer*
  - g: *Cosmopolitan*
  - h: *Woman's Day*
  - i: *Ladies' Home Journal*
  - j: *Redbook*
  - k: Other:______________________________

- In which region of the United States do you reside?
  - a: Northeast
  - b: Midatlantic
  - c: South
  - d: Midwest
  - e: Mountain
  - f: Southwest
  - g: Pacific Coast

- What is your age group/sex? a: Female b: Male
  - a: under 18
  - b: 19-25
  - c: 26-30
  - d: 31-35
  - e: 56-60
  - f: 41-45
  - g: 46-50
  - h: 51-55
  - i: 56-60
  - j: Over 60

- What is your marital status?
  - a: Married
  - b: Single
  - c: No longer married

- What is your current level of education?
  - a: High school
  - b: College Degree
  - c: Graduate Degree
  - d: Other: ____________________

- Do you receive the TOPAZ *Romantic Liaisons* newsletter, a quarterly newsletter with the latest information on Topaz books and authors?

  YES NO

  If not, would you like to? YES NO

  Fill in the address where you would like your free gift to be sent:

  Name: ____

  Address: ____

  City:______________________________Zip Code: __________

  You should receive your free gift in 6 to 8 weeks.
  Please send the completed survey to:

Penguin USA•Mass Market
Dept. TS
375 Hudson St.
New York, NY 10014